OF FLESH

"*Of Flesh and Blood* transported me to the humid swamps of Louisiana and made me double-check my doors and windows. Genuinely scary and stuffed with surprises, I only hope that the inevitable film is half as good as the novel."

Richard Chizmar, *New York Times* bestselling author of *Memorial* and *Chasing the Boogeyman*

"A meticulously detailed story of the Cajun Cannibal that will have true crime junkies salivating. A novel so true-crimey I'm still wondering if it really happened!"

J. H. Markert, author of *Sleep Tight*

"A delightfully chilling debut steeped in southern gothic, with a villain you won't soon forget, *Of Flesh and Blood* is a page-turning success. Beautifully rendered atmosphere and a haunting structure pull you in fast and hold you tight."

Scott Carson, *New York Times* bestselling author of *Lost Man's Lane* and *The Chill*

"Like the legendary bayou beast, the rougarou, *Of Flesh and Blood* digs its claws into you within the first few pages and refuses to let go. Rich in setting and characters, this compelling tale has more twists and turns than a rollercoaster. Each time you think you've got a handle on what's happening, the story loop-de-loops, or plunges around another hair-raising bend… I guarantee you'll stagger away, breathless and reeling."

Mark Morris, author of the Obsidian Heart trilogy

"A dry-mouthed read that burns slow and steady. True crime lovers will eat this assured psychological debut right up."

Gemma Amor, Bram Stoker and British Fantasy Award nominated author of *Dear Laura*, *Full Immersion* and *Itch!*

"Gritty, twisty, obsessive 'true crime' fiction wrapped around tantalising Louisiana folklore, *Of Flesh and Blood* will appeal to fans of Matt Wesolowski's *Six Stories* and John Darnielle's *Devil House*. A confident and deftly-handed debut."

Ally Wilkes, author of *Where the Dead Wait*

N.L. LAVIN & HUNTER BURKE

OF FLESH AND BLOOD

THE UNTOLD STORY OF THE CAJUN CANNIBAL

TITAN BOOKS

Of Flesh and Blood: The Untold Story of the Cajun Cannibal
Print edition ISBN: 9781835413951
E-book edition ISBN: 9781835413968

Published by Titan Books
A division of Titan Publishing Group Ltd
144 Southwark Street, London SE1 0UP
www.titanbooks.com

First edition: June 2025
10 9 8 7 6 5 4 3 2 1

This is a work of fiction. All of the characters, organizations, and events portrayed in this novel are either products of the author's imagination or are used fictitiously. Any resemblance to actual persons, living or dead (except for satirical purposes), is entirely coincidental.

Copyright © 2025 N. L. Lavin & Hunter Burke.

N. L. Lavin & Hunter Burke assert the moral right to be identified as the authors of this work.

No part of this publication may be reproduced, stored in a retrieval system, or transmitted, in any form or by any means without the prior written permission of the publisher, nor be otherwise circulated in any form of binding or cover other than that in which it is published and without a similar condition being imposed on the subsequent purchaser.

A CIP catalogue record for this title is available from the British Library.

EU RP (for authorities only)
eucomply OÜ, Pärnu mnt. 139b-14, 11317 Tallinn, Estonia
hello@eucompliancepartner.com, +3375690241

Typeset in Arno Pro 11/15pt by Richard Mason.

Printed and bound by CPI (UK) Ltd, Croydon, CR0 4YY.

N. L. Lavin

*For Meg, Jack, Marion, and Tom Tom.
Endless thanks for putting up with me.*

≈

Hunter Burke

For Donna and Neal. I guess Darci, too.

INTRODUCTION

I WAS BORN in a bathtub on September 16, 1984, in the sleepy Louisiana town of St. Martinville. It was a clawfoot tub, which I suppose adds a touch of elegance to the proceedings, but a water birth wasn't the plan. My parents had driven out to St. Martinville to watch the Saints game with my grandmother. When the contractions clutched my mother's womb a week early, her older (and soon-to-be estranged) brother, Mitch, convinced her she'd never make it all the way back into Lafayette on time. "The goddamn traffic in that city," he scoffed. The Saints were up three points over their then-division-rival 49ers[1] heading into the fourth quarter, and so my dad agreed that yes, they probably should stay. Mitch hacked the umbilical cord with a buck knife and cauterized my end with a branding iron. For most of my childhood, I blamed that branding iron for the rift between him and my mother. Everyone made it through the ordeal okay, but my parents probably should've just gone to the hospital. My

---

1 Somehow, the San Francisco 49ers, Los Angeles Rams, New Orleans Saints, and Atlanta Falcons all belonged to the NFC West before realignment in 2002.

mother pushed for nearly an hour, and the Saints lost by ten.

My father's company relocated us to Fort Wayne, Indiana, a few years later. Thereafter, we visited Louisiana every summer and Christmas. I'd follow my cousins around, rolling three-wheelers off levees and swimming in the Vermilion River, the murky green bayou that snakes through the Cajun heartlands like a varicose vein. We'd emerge, inevitably a few shades darker with a patina of muck, and pitch camp in the "devil worshipper" woods along the bank. We once spotted a raccoon skull lying atop a bundle of twigs and took this, as any self-respecting and terrified Catholic would, for an obvious message from Satan himself. But for all my tagalong misadventures, I was no longer one of them. I knew it, and so did they. By the time I was fourteen, we'd stopped making the yearly trips.

After finishing medical school at Indiana University in May of 2012, I felt sure of nothing but my fascination with the brain, that mysterious, wet, spongy bundle of circuits, and all the things that could go wrong in there. I had my reasons. I was also at what would soon become the end of a two-year relationship. Either oblivious to or in denial of our relationship's death throes, my girlfriend and I decided to enter the "couple's match," where fate and the great gods of medical education would determine our residency programs and ensure that they were in the same city. I wanted psychiatry at BU in Boston; she wanted dermatology at LSU in New Orleans. We sat in the auditorium with our entire class and all our families in attendance. My mom had bought one New England Patriots hat and one for the New Orleans Saints. As I walked onto the stage, the dean of students announced, "Dr. Vincent Blackburn... Tulane University School of Medicine in New Orleans for a residency and fellowship in forensic psychiatry." After twenty-four years away, under the influence of a fledgling relationship, I was a Louisianan again.

In July of 2012, I packed my things and moved to the Big Easy to begin my residency program. My girlfriend and I were broken up by September.

Four exhausting years of residency passed. And all the while I rarely thought of my family down the road in Cajun country.

That all changed in September of 2016, when, in the beginning of my forensics fellowship, I rotated through the stifling corridors of Angola State Penitentiary's death row.

I took my seat across the collapsible plastic table from my first patient and steadied my bouncing knee. He had a vacant, slack-jawed stare. A bit of tacky saliva had coagulated in the corner of his chapped lips and hung there, threatening to spring out at me should he pounce too forcefully on a *P*.

I scanned his chart. Born and raised in South Louisiana. History of paranoid delusions. Auditory and visual hallucinations in his late teens, and again after imprisonment. This was his fifteenth year on death row. I hadn't read his criminal record; I avoided such information back then, afraid it might hinder my ability to treat my patients with beneficence. I know better now. Sure, if you dig a little, what you find is usually appalling. But if you dig a little deeper, what you find is almost always tragic. And eventually, nearly all of it makes sense.

Before I could even introduce myself, his eyes locked onto mine with a strange sense of recognition. A wild, furious stare. "No," he mumbled. In an instant, he started slamming his hands on the table, shouting, "No! *No no no no!*" He shoved the table into my stomach, pinning me in my chair. Then I noticed that the look in his eye wasn't one of rage. It was terror. "Get me outta here!" he screamed. "It's him! The Cajun Cannibal! Cajun Cannibal!" When the guards rushed in, he bolted for the door and clung to their arms, hollering incoherently.

I sat there, heart pounding, mouth dry, room tilting and spinning, and glanced down at my pants to make sure I hadn't wet them.

≈

"First day's always a little overwhelming. But you, my man, might have set a record." My attending chuckled at me from across his desk. I sipped from a paper cup of water, still trying to reclaim some moisture for my mouth. "The old Cajun Cannibal. You know, you do kind of look like him." He grinned and squinted, as if studying my features. "Maybe you really are him, Henri Elton Judice himself, come back after all these years . . ." He chuckled again. I didn't.

Henri Elton Judice, the infamous game warden, had been a source of local panic nine years prior in South Louisiana. The "Cajun Cannibal" had brutally murdered eight people, per the official record. Unofficially, some say more. Five of his alleged victims were dismembered and, presumably, eaten by Judice. He was never apprehended. On the night of February 9, 2009, just as the authorities were closing in on him, multiple eyewitnesses reported watching Henri Elton Judice take his own life before he could ever see the inside of a jail cell.

"Boy. Henri Elton Judice . . ." My attending luxuriated in the name, like the killer was an old drinking buddy from high school. "You were probably still up in—what was it? Indiana?—during that whole hullabaloo. Did y'all ever hear about it? Do you know the story?"

I could still picture the iconic photo of Judice in his hunter-green game warden rain slicker. It had graced the front page of half a dozen tabloids back in 2009. The vacant eyes. The wide smile. The name echoed and reverberated inside my skull, feeding back on itself into a throbbing drone of nonsense. I took another sip and kept my eyes on the cup.

"Yeah," I finally muttered. "He's my cousin."

≈

My mom is a Judice, one of nine kids. I've done my best over the years to keep up with my thirty-seven cousins back home and the names of their spouses and children. But until my parents called with news of the murders during my first year of medical school, I had never once heard of a relative named Henri. My mom's eldest brother, Elton, had been more or less excommunicated from the family before I was born. Drugs, alcohol—it was never clear what unforgivable sins Elton had perpetuated, but he was rarely mentioned. He'd fallen in with a girl no one liked. "From bad stock," they said, just as her family probably said of his. Elton died a few months after I was born, and no one ever indicated that there might be any progeny to speak of in his unspeakable line.

After learning about the accusations against Henri early in my medical school training, I briefly tried to leverage my cousin's infamy for free drinks. I'd invent childhood stories about the cousin I'd never actually met, expound upon the signs we "always knew" were there. The bartenders grew weary of the stories, and the girls were decidedly unimpressed. Being the cousin of a serial killer doesn't get you many invites back to the house, it turns out. Once his legend was of no use to me, I forgot Henri in much the same way my family had done with his father, quietly sequestering him away to an unlit corner of my mind. But there in Angola, a place as close to hell on Earth as I've ever been, Henri's ghost had become impossible to ignore.

A month after my rotation at Angola, in October of 2016, my attending sent me an email. It was an invitation from the *International Journal of Forensic Medicine* to produce a long-form case study on sociopathic behavior in serial killers. Well, one serial killer in particular. Such a high-profile assignment was rarely offered to a first-year fellow, but my attending, who was old friends with a few of the editors, had apparently mentioned my personal connection to the case. I was a spectacle by blood. Freak-show adjacent. And I leapt at the chance. Forget the bored bartenders and the uninterested women back in Indiana. For the low price of my family's secrecy and shame, I could become a published author and a leader in the field of sociopathy. I quickly got to work exhuming our skeletons and dissecting the Cajun Cannibal.

In April of 2017, I published my case study on Henri Elton Judice and his supposed diagnosis of sociopathy, also known as antisocial personality disorder. As defined in the *DSM*, antisocial personality disorder reflects "a pervasive disregard and violation of the rights of others." A pathological lack of empathy and remorse. Only a little over half of what I submitted was actually printed; the editors had been unimpressed by my rambling fascination with the minutiae of the case, the people on the periphery, and the pain they'd endured.

I've reread the introduction of that case study a hundred times. Analyzed Henri's words, the very words that opened my case study, the words he recorded himself just minutes before his death. And each time, the picture of my cousin becomes cloudier.

> "I used to think I knew what I was. What was wrong with me. But I'm not really sure anymore. Is evil even real? Or is that just an easy word for something harder? I wonder that now. I've killed. I'm a hunter. A killer. Am I a monster? Are those things real? Do they all just get passed along? Inherited, maybe. I know what I see. It's obvious after a while, and you forget how you could've been so stupid and not seen it there all along. I know what I see, when I look in the mirror sometimes. Maybe it's something else. Why won't anyone ...
>
> "There's this thing inside me. A compulsion. I have to put an end to it. All of it. This curse. This rot. This infection. This ... this won't be over 'til whatever it is dies. If it has to take me with it, well, what does it matter anyway? How else are you supposed to get rid of a killer?"

There's something compelling about a case without a verdict, one that forces us to find our own resolutions. Our own truths. My research, and the personal obsession it spawned, led me into a niche world of online investigators and half-baked conspiracy theorists. The Reddit message boards could keep you occupied for months. Some claim Henri only committed some of the murders. Very few are delusional enough to label him innocent of all charges. More than a few believe he was a real-life, hand-to-God monster, a boogeyman embodiment who stalked through the swamps of Louisiana with the moonlight glinting off his fangs. Some claim that the true killer is still out there, biding his time. Others contend that Judice didn't die out there in the woods that fateful night, that the St. Landry Parish sheriff covered up his escape to save her own ass, and that he's still at large.

Those of us who find ourselves drawn into the gravity of this case seem seduced by all the loose ends. The whole puzzle, as it's conventionally accepted, doesn't quite fit. There are too many missing pieces. The ones we do have feel chewed off at the corners and hammered in. This case is a popcorn kernel in the back molar of an entire subculture, and with all the bizarre, misaligned details, some people can't help but pick their tongues raw. The more I picked, the more material I found there waiting underneath, all of it obscuring still more.

Several of the chapters in this recounting pull directly from my case study—the unabridged, unpublished version. The bulk of the information was painstakingly compiled in the years following, when I sat to interview witnesses, exchanged emails, pored over medical histories, combed through personal journals, shared afternoon coffees with the family and friends of the people mentioned in this book. When, the more I studied Henri's words, listened to his copious field recordings, and read his statements to police, the less I felt I knew him. When I began to appreciate the transmissible nature of evil—if there is such a thing.

When the killings started again. When he felt more and more real. When I started to question if he was still out there somewhere, alive.

When my own world became irrevocably entangled with the Cajun Cannibal's.

PART I

IN ANOTHER LIFETIME . . .

THE ROAD WAS FULL OF MUD

(Excerpts originally published in the
International Journal of Forensic Medicine)

August 4, 2008

THE FIRST THING Liu Wen noticed was the dirt under his fingernails. Or was it grease? His knuckles were cracked and dry. Rubbed raw. The dirt had also found its way into the dozen little cuts peppering his hands, tattooing crisscrosses along his calloused fingers.

Why won't his hands stop shaking? she wondered to herself from the driver's seat of the Toyota Camry.

The passenger in question was a stranger. They had only met about twenty, thirty minutes ago. His silence had initially been a welcome comfort, almost a piece of home. Now, it was beginning to make her skin crawl for some reason she couldn't quite pin down.

Wen had been in Louisiana for almost a year, attending the University of Louisiana at Lafayette through a student exchange. She'd found the local Cajuns to be a friendly group, at times aggressively so, with their bear hugs and pet names and roaring laughs. In the past year, she hadn't met anyone as quiet and withdrawn as the stranger sitting beside her now.

She swerved the Camry to avoid a pothole. The tires hiccupped as if surprised and then caught traction again.

She should have been home, in Changzhi. Surrounded by her family and her cats and her mother's food on the stove, simmering especially for her. But she was here, stuck at the tail end of a two-month lab assistant job she had reluctantly taken on for a little extra money. As the summer had worn on, she'd grown more and more homesick and regretful of that decision. Tired. Permeated each evening with the sickly sweet smell of Pseudomonas and Petri dishes. Waiting. Crossing the squares off on her calendar every day until finally making it to August 1st, just two days before her departure. Her bags had been packed for a week. But the warm waters of the Gulf had brewed up other plans.

Not quite a hurricane, but as close as you can get without being one, the tropical storm would delay all flights, postponing her departure by two days. Upon learning of the delay, Wen had broken down, biking furiously across ULL's campus and collecting whatever ingredients she could find that might approximate her mother's vinegar-stewed carp. The one her mother always made when Wen was sick, though now it was a different kind of sickness that consumed her. Never mind that she didn't have any pots in her dorm. Or a stove. Or a kitchen for that matter. She would figure it out.

A divot in the road jostled the Camry now, the tires spinning out in a fishtail toward the steep ditch to their left. The stranger didn't seem to notice. Wen clutched the wheel even tighter and regained control of the car. This storm and its aftermath reminded her of the monsoon season in her hometown. Everything reminded her of Changzhi these days, but especially this. The dull darkness at noon. The heavy, humid air. The deserted streets.

As luck would have it, she had run into her TA, Johnny, at the grocery store, her arms loaded down with fish and vinegar. He'd insisted that she ride out the storm in his two-bedroom rental home, about thirty miles northeast of campus along the rural backroads of Arnaudville. "Better than the dorms," he said. Johnny and his boyfriend had made plans to evacuate north to stay with family. "Feel free to use the car too," Johnny had offered, to which she'd shaken her head politely. Not without a license. No way. Still, at least now she'd have a kitchen to cook in.

The stew she'd prepared in Johnny's house was weak, the fish mushy, the vinegar a sad replacement for the local treasure back home. And still, it had brought tears to her eyes.

By the morning of August 3rd, Tropical Storm Edouard had made landfall and knocked down the power line supplying Johnny's house with electricity. As the hours crawled by and the temperature inside climbed, Wen had grown more and more sure she could smell the stew spoiling in the fridge, that little taste of home disappearing. Who knew how long it would be before the power returned. The stories from Hurricane Katrina in 2005 were still fresh on everyone's lips in South Louisiana. And the devastating flooding of the Jiangsu Province had only happened five years ago.

The next morning, she woke to find the house still without power. By four PM, after hours of consternation, she'd finally given in and made the decision to head out for ice. Just a quick drive.

The anxiety dug its claws into her shoulders and her neck a

little more tightly with each empty store she passed, boarded up and shut down for the storm. She was ready to turn back, when T-Cups Bar materialized like an oasis. A narrow parking lot, graveled over in patches with broken shells and sea rubble. Two cars, one motorcycle. Busted sign outside. But the bar's state of disrepair had obviously existed before the storm. These wounds weren't fresh.

The bartender inside couldn't run her card on account of the system being down. Without any cash and eager to return home, Wen had nearly given up hope of procuring any ice when a stranger slapped three bills and a handful of coins on the bar top and said, "Two bags." Having gone there with money for cigarettes, but finding the bar regrettably out, he'd noticed Wen's predicament, paid for her ice with his cigarette money, and left with barely a word.

On her way back to Johnny's, Wen had spotted the benevolent stranger walking down the highway alone. What else could she do but offer him a ride?

"Thank you again for the ice," she said in her effortful but accomplished English, accent thick and sticking to her words like peanut butter.

"Welcome," he answered, almost managing to compact it into a single syllable. His eyes never left the ditch running along the road. His gray shirt smelled of sweat and stale cigarette smoke. And those hands. She should have been home. Not here, not smelling this guy's sour sweat and listening to his teeth click together with each edge of nail he chewed off his dirty fingers.

An occasional branch or slick of mud across the old, busted sugarcane road known as LA 31 had Wen trolling along and zigzagging down the highway, doing twenty-five in a fifty-five.

The stranger's knee hadn't stopped since he'd climbed in the passenger seat.

"Do you often walk?" she asked now.

"Truck's busted," he mumbled, teeth clamped firmly onto a thumbnail. *Click.*

"Oh."

No one spoke for another mile. Wen imagined how many steps had passed. How far would some men walk for a pack of cigarettes?

She watched his left hand clench into a fist and release. Clench and release.

She felt the thump of her own pulse in her neck. The speedometer said thirty-five now.

"Is your home not far?"

"Not far."

She nodded, fully aware that he didn't see the gesture. He hadn't turned her way once.

"You can drop me at the corner up ahead, though, if it's easier," he said.

"No. I do not mind," she said, and immediately regretted it. Her incessant politeness would be the death of her one day, she thought.

A gust of wind leaned into the car. She felt as though it had nudged him closer somehow.

Johnny's house was a left two turns back. She tried to picture a map in her head, plotting the way back like a GPS recalculating the route with each wrong turn.

"Hang a right up ahead." He pointed to a four-way stop about a hundred meters down. *That will be a left on the way back,* she thought. The thick woods cornered against the intersection on all sides. "And keep your eyes peeled. There was a dead deer on the side of the road earlier. Or at least what was left of him."

There was a coldness in the way he spoke of death. A nonchalance that she couldn't fathom. She had never understood the way people could slaughter and dismember such innocent creatures.

She eased the car around the corner, preparing her pescatarian stomach for a glimpse of the carcass.

Instead, she found a black truck parked two wheels on the road, two in the ditch. Flashing police lights atop the cab.

"Bèn dàn," she cursed under her breath. She should've been home, not driving without a license. But she hadn't been caught yet. Just act cool. She started to press down on the gas when she noticed the stranger's bouncing knee quicken its tempo. He seemed even more anxious about the flashing lights than she did.

Something instinctive forced her foot onto the brake. Hard. The stranger braced himself against the dash as the Camry slid to a stop on the wet, leafy road.

"You alright?" he asked.

"Yes," she said, squinting through the rainy window to better study the writing on the truck. "Wildlife Agent?" she read aloud.

The stranger squirmed. "Looks like nobody's here." He cleared his throat. "It's just a little farther up the road."

She turned and studied him, his dark brown eyes looking at her for maybe the first time, urging her along from under his shock of wild orange hair.

"C'mon," he said. "I got an ice chest I could give you. For the ice."

She thought about running, about how silly she would look, about what this guy would think of her as she slipped and slid down the road for probably no reason. Probably nothing at all.

A bang on the driver side window jolted her, a small shriek escaping her lips. She turned to find a dark silhouette standing at her door. She rolled down the window, allowing the misty remnants of the storm to pepper her face. A man stood there in his dark green rain slicker; yellow letters on the right breast read "WARDEN."

"Officer!" she nearly shouted, surprising herself.

"Ma'am?" He squinted.

"Is everything okay, Officer?" she asked.

"Um." He studied her. "Yes, ma'am. Everything's fine. Just cleaning up."

She smiled and nodded, and she felt tears beginning to sting her eyes.

He stole a quick glance at the stranger in the passenger seat. "Is everything okay with *you*, ma'am?"

"With me?" she said. "Oh. Yes. I am just giving my friend . . ." She looked at the stranger.

The orange-headed man cleared his throat. "Anders."

"Anders. Just giving Anders a ride home."

"Okay . . ." the warden said.

Before he could back away from the window, Wen forced a chuckle. "But, Officer, I am running a little late for . . . something. Would you please be able to help?"

"Help?" The warden peered into her eyes.

"Yes." She nodded. *"Help."*

"I really don't mind walking," Anders whispered to her.

"Don't be silly." She turned to him. "I would not just leave you to walk."

"Right," he said, studying the warden.

The warden studied him right back with bleary, bloodshot eyes. "Well," he said, licking his chapped lips, "I'm just about finished here. I'd be happy to help."

"Oh, thank you," Wen blurted before Anders could protest.

"Well, okay..." Anders said. "Thanks, I guess, for the lift."

He climbed out into the drizzle and shut the door. Wen immediately released a shaky exhale and pounded her finger onto the automatic lock button. He seemed to hear the click, so she flashed an extra smile to remind him how polite she was. Then she threw the Camry in reverse and backed into the intersection.

As she watched Anders and the warden there in the middle of the road, now a comfortable and miniaturizing distance between her and them, she couldn't shake the feeling that she had just narrowly avoided some terrible fate. But whatever that was, it was over now.

She turned back in the direction of Johnny's house. Straight through the next intersection, and then a right. She could almost taste the stew. In two days, she would be on her way back home. Far from here.

≈

It seems Anders Barrilleaux never got in the warden's truck. His history reveals a long and often healthy distrust of law enforcement, dating back to a stint in juvenile detention and five involuntary admissions to a series of behavioral hospitals across Louisiana before the age of eighteen. His mom had called the police on him at least ten times. "That woman's a heat-seeking missile for misunderstandings," he'd once told a court-mandated therapist. Flashing red lights had frequently painted the Barrilleaux house, adding to the soundtrack of hollering voices and slamming doors. Twice, he had said the wrong thing to a cop in his living room and ended up on the inpatient unit at Vermilion Behavioral Hospital, where he'd sworn he would never speak to another officer again.

So Anders likely wasn't interested in hanging around with some game warden staring him down, wondering what he'd done to scare that sweet, innocent girl. Just another misunderstanding.

His house was a fifteen-minute walk from the intersection, down the road as it dog-legged right. Something must have told Anders—either his previous interactions or the warden's current demeanor—that he didn't have fifteen minutes. Despite the fallen foliage and the muddy terrain, he took a shortcut through the woods, aiming for a more direct route home.

About seventy yards in, the forest grew thick, branches blocking nearly every clear path. It might have been quicker to turn right, deeper into the woods for just a bit. He could cross the coulee, come out on the Singleton property, and get a clear sprint down the levee. But Anders didn't know Singleton, and the last thing he probably wanted was some upstanding asshole farmer turning him over to the warden for trespassing. Or worse. So instead, Anders stuck to the woods, climbing over, crawling under, crashing through every impediment, inching closer and closer to the clearing on the other side. And his house.

Just ahead.

Something made him take out his phone and call his mom, an uncharacteristic move to say the least. Turns out the number was disconnected—had been for two years.

Through the tangled branches and limbs ahead, he would've just barely been able to make out his carport light illuminating swarms of June bugs.

The place was a shithole. But it was his shithole. He'd left home the day he turned eighteen and started pulling work in the oil field. But the whole industry was in the tank in 2008, and a recent round of layoffs had hit him first, accounting for the shithole. And the broke-down truck. And the two-hour walk for a pack of cigarettes he never even got. And the ride he never even asked for. And the asshole warden staring him down just like every other asshole cop he'd ever met. And his muddy shoes. And his racing heart. And the sweat stinging his eyes.

Something heavy slammed into his back, cracking two of his ribs and sending him face-first into the mud. His phone tumbled out of his hand and would later be found about a meter away.

Surely, by this point, Anders knew the drill. Loosen your shoulders. Don't twist or fight it. Otherwise, you'll get a dislocation while they throw the cuffs on you.

But the cuffs never came.

What came instead was a searing tear ripping across his back. Blood and tissue splattered all the way to his phone screen.

His empty house, just through the clearing, was so close. No one besides the warden was around to hear his screams.

Something grabbed the back of his scalp and slammed his face down into the muck, fracturing his orbital bone. Ripped a chunk of hair from his head and left it behind.

The next tear down his back wouldn't have been as excruciating as the first. It would have been dull. Vague.

He'd spilled nearly a liter of blood into the mud around him. With the loss, his fingers would grow cold, and his stomach would start to hurt. For a moment, he'd feel sick, but nothing would come up.

Soon, he would forget where he was.

He would hardly feel the strips of muscle being ripped and gnawed out of his back.

Then, he would close his eyes.

DUCK BLIND

(Excerpts originally published in the
International Journal of Forensic Medicine)

August 7, 2008

JUDE SINGLETON RECEIVED a strange call from his neighbor, "High Pocket" Breaux, who lived about a half mile down the two-lane highway.

Jude had been out filling up his truck before going to bed. He had a long drive ahead of him to see about farming up in Oklahoma, and if filling up now meant an extra ten minutes of sipping his coffee in the morning, by God, he'd take it. Jude was the kind of man practiced at postponing gratification. He'd toiled through his twenties so he could buy a farm in his thirties so he could retire in his sixties and enjoy his seventies if his back managed to hold out that long. He attended mass every Sunday. He drank sparingly, shunned most vices, hoping paradise would await as repayment for his sacrifice. Jude backed into any parking spot he ever took.

He had been working soybean farms in Arnaudville since he was twelve, and at forty-three, had built up a respectable spread of his own, but High Pocket's thriving sugarcane fields were threatening to overtake Jude's property. With High Pocket's offer on the table—a decent sum, all told—Jude couldn't reasonably turn down the hefty payout. So he thought he'd take his skills and his new small fortune to the prairies, where cane wasn't king.

He was on his way home, bouncing along his gravel drive, with an uncomfortably full bladder, the relief of which his swelling prostate would certainly thwart, when he saw High Pocket pop up on the caller ID. High Pocket never called past suppertime.

Arnaudville was one of the few remaining places in the country that allowed its residents to use nicknames in the official listings of the phone book. Jude didn't even know High Pocket's Christian name. No one did. Per one former classmate, "He was the tallest guy in school. So his pockets were higher than everyone else's. That's it. High Pocket."

High Pocket apologized for the late hour but said he thought Jude might want to know that he'd spotted something stalking along the back edge of the property, first toward and then away from Jude's land. "Prolly a bear, I'm guessing," High Pocket said. He'd first seen the culprit a few evenings before, not long after noticing a black Wildlife and Fisheries pickup trolling around in the area. And then he'd spotted the "animal" again tonight, trekking down the same stretch of land, toward the Singleton farm and back. High Pocket had fired a couple shots in the air to scare the thing off. He just wanted to let Jude know to be careful out there.

Along the back edge was where Jude kept his dugout duck blind, the homemade four-by-four-by-twelve-foot metal box where he did most of his hunting. It was a magnet for rodents and other critters that would occasionally scurry under the rusty lid during the offseason and find themselves stuck four feet below ground level with no way out. He thought maybe a black bear had caught wind of a subterranean snack and found his way in. Black bears will eat just about anything. Jude decided he'd go have a look in the morning. Maybe he could spray some bear deterrent and hopefully nudge the thing along.

But when he got home, something about the whole thing felt off. Mulling over his rodent hypothesis, he felt the strange sensation that he was forcing a flimsy explanation onto the situation. The barn behind the house was lousy with rodents, a problem Jude would be glad to rid himself of if he did in fact move. Any bear with a working snout would've smelled those fat bastards well before it caught the scent of whatever tiny things could've squeezed into the blind. A bear problem would've been a barn problem, Jude reckoned.

Maybe the bear was just passing through in search of new territory, which is known to happen, especially after a big storm like the one they'd suffered a couple days before. But High Pocket's description of the thing wandering onto the property and then doubling back felt uncharacteristic. It felt intentional.

Jude recalled hearing a bit of faint hollering coming from the back of his property a couple days prior, right after the storm. He hadn't thought much of it at the time, but now he wondered if some campers might have been messing around back there. Maybe they'd left a cache of food and garbage. If so, the bear would probably keep returning in the hopes of finding more.

He felt an instinctive urge to talk the situation over with someone, but the Singleton house was empty. His wife, Denise,[2]

---

2 A pseudonym.

had fled the farm three years earlier, leaving Jude to raise both the soybean crop and their teenage son alone. He hadn't heard from Denise in over a year; she might be in Galveston now, but he wasn't sure.

The wound of her absence had for the most part scarred over. That of his son's was still tender. Kipp had moved to Baton Rouge just yesterday to study agricultural business at LSU. Jude had pushed college on the boy, saying of his own livelihood, "This farming life is hard work. And not the good kind of hard work that builds character. This just tears you down. You ache all the time, and you never know what the next year's gonna be like. I don't want my boy's whole future decided by floods and droughts and pestilence and a million other things that can wreck a harvest."

Jude dropped his keys in the ceramic bowl (one of Kipp's kindergarten arts and crafts projects) and studied his small kitchen. The surroundings used to feel so familiar but now were nearly unrecognizable in their emptiness. Four years ago—hell, four months ago—leaving Louisiana would have been unthinkable. Not anymore.

A simple chandelier above the tiny breakfast table was the home's only illumination at the moment. No lights or televisions or any other distractions were on outside the kitchen. He'd yet to develop the habit of keeping a few things running around the house to instill in himself the comforting impression that his was not the only room being used at any given time. That trick of self-delusion would come later. The darkness of the adjacent living room and the hallway beyond felt cavernous and eerie all of a sudden, ready to swallow him whole.

He stood there, contemplating all these recent changes, withering in the face of his shifting world and grappling with the sudden amorphous dread of isolation. Then he thought about the bear and felt fortified by the concreteness of this newfound conflict laid in his lap.

The simplicity and the understandability of man versus nature.

He hopped into his Mule 4x4 and sped out toward the duck blind with a loaded rifle.

The headlights of the Mule shone down the small levee that marked the edge of his soybean field. The duck blind sat about fifty yards out, growing closer every second but approaching more slowly than he'd expected. He realized he'd subconsciously eased off the throttle.

The headlights caught a glint of something. Up ahead, in the grass, lay the discarded sheet metal lid to his duck blind.

The 4×4 had stopped moving. Jude clutched his rifle and flashed the Q-Beam a full 360 degrees around.

Nothing.

He climbed down from the Mule. The twenty-foot walk to the duck blind stretched out before him. Eventually, he arrived at the big metal hole in the ground.

As his beam of light angled down into the pit, it landed on what Jude thought was a pile of old gray tarping. Probably had blown in after the storm, he figured. He climbed down the four-foot drop into the blind to retrieve it.

But as his foot landed on the floor of the blind, he realized that the gray mass before him was no tarp. There in the corner, his light illuminated a heap of pale, bloody nakedness. Curled up like a pile of discarded flesh.

A man.

A shock of curly orange hair atop his head.

Face down in a puddle of what Jude hoped was muddy water.

But the thick, metallic stench was too familiar for the experienced hunter to ignore.

Blood. Pooling there in the bottom of his blind, soaking into the suede of his hiking boots.

The man's back was flayed in spots. Craters peppered his flank where chunks of flesh had been gouged out like driving range divots.

The metal walls around him had been clawed at. Blood and chunks of fingernail stuck in the vertical scrapes.

Jude stood and stared for he wasn't sure how long. Finally, he came to his senses and called 911 on his cell to inform them of the dead body. "A bear attack, I think," he told the operator. But as he leaned in to confirm his assessment, the mass of flesh trembled.

Just the tiniest jerk of his neck muscle. Jude craned his own neck forward and heard the faint whispers of quick, sharp breaths echoing inside the chamber. "Then I noticed his belly was, like, twitching with this sort of panting," Jude recounted later. "Almost like an old dog's does when he's out in the sun too long."

Jude felt a flash of warmth on the front of his jeans. There were some reactions even his prostate couldn't hold back. He put the phone back up to his ear and informed the operator that he had *not*, in fact, found a dead body.

≈

Anders Barrilleaux's ICU room was a quiet, sterile symphony of beeps and ventilations. No one came or went besides the hospital staff. There were no visitors to speak of.

The EMS first responders had done their best, racing against time through the muddy field to retrieve Barrilleaux and rush him to the nearest hospital. In the process, they had trampled what would later, in hindsight, be ruled an active crime scene.

The St. Landry Parish sheriff had made a quick scan of the area, finding Barrilleaux's clothes discarded in a heap about twenty yards from the duck blind. Authorities may have never identified him if not for the wallet in his jeans.

At the hospital, the medical team scrambled to identify a source of the infection that Barrilleaux's unstable condition insisted must be present. His lungs panted, his heart raced, his temperature climbed... and still nothing.

Mr. Barrilleaux had lost an estimated ten pounds of flesh and three liters of blood before being discovered in Jude Singleton's duck blind. Some of the wounds were fresh, only hours old and still bleeding. Others appeared older, inflamed and angry where the fiery pink skin met open tissue.

Dr. Edward Harper's progress notes on Mr. Barrilleaux would later be collected for evidence. The first reads as follows:

PATIENT PROGRESS NOTE

Subjective: Patient is a 23 yo White M, brought in by ambulance and admitted on 8/7/08 for severe blood loss following multiple lacerations to back and lower extremities. Pt still unable to answer any questions as of the time of rounds this morning.

Objective:
Temp: 102.5° F
BP: 165/102

Pulse: 160 bpm
Respirations: 44 [breaths per minute]

General appearance: Pt. appears to be hyperventilating/panting, diaphoretic/clammy. Eyes are open, occasionally tracking movement, but otherwise unresponsive to stimuli.

Head/neck: Both pupils fully dilated to 9 mm, almost no iris visible; significant conjunctival injection—eye sclera are bloodshot red around black pupils. Slight bleeding from gums—no identifiable cause. Poor dentition.

Chest/lungs: Clear breath sounds. No evidence of respiratory infection.

Abdomen: Non-distended. Hyperactive bowel sounds.

Skin: Extremely pale, nearly to the point of translucency at rib cage, wrists, popliteal fossa, etc. Vessels clearly visible beneath surface. No significant telangiectasia. Posterior lacerations bandaged per wound care. Laceration on neck is surrounded by bright red tissue, highly inflamed. Black along the lacerated edges.

Labs reviewed—White blood cell count below normal range. Low iron, low zinc, elevated TIBC. Elevated bilirubin, low LDH. Extreme elevation of porphyrins in blood and urine samples (see attached values).[3]

---

[3] There are several perplexing items in this lab report. First, the low WBC in a case with a high risk of infection is unusual, to say the least. Second, the report of low iron, low zinc, elevated TIBC, and elevated porphyrins seems to indicate a mixture of several separate irregularities: nutrient deficient anemia, some rare form of red blood cell destruction, and porphyria. The

Assessment: 23 yo M with confounding presentation: multiple lacerations with altered mental status and hyperactive autonomic nervous system functions, yet no lab evidence of offending agent infectious process.

Plan:
- Cont. current regimen of IV fluids and antibiotic prophylaxis for *staph*, *strep*, *leptospira*, and other potential organisms typically involved in bite wounds.
- Immunization for tetanus and rabies administered.
- Cont. vital checks every 4 hours.
- [Infectious disease] and plastics following. Appreciate their recs.
- Awaiting neurology consult for possible head trauma/concussion. Likely to see pt this a.m.
- Rule out delirium vs. unspecified psychosis. Will consult psychiatry.

Dr. Edward Harper
Internal Medicine, St. Martin Hospital, Lafayette General
St. Landry Parish Coroner
08/08/2008

Reading between the lines of the following progress notes, it appears psychiatry never evaluated the patient, despite Dr. Harper's consult. They likely cited his unresponsiveness as

---

cause of these lab values was never accounted for, and Dr. Harper never gave any specific reason for checking the patient's porphyrin levels. In the absence of known genetic predispositions, this precaution would be highly unexpected in a routine workup for infectious disease.

an impenetrable obstacle, and furthermore they undoubtedly caught a whiff of the usual stink that accompanies a psychiatry consult, that nebulous request that pleads with hands in the air, *"What the fuck is going on here? I'm not even sure what I'm asking, but can you shrinks just come sort it out?"* Nevertheless, Dr. Harper continued to write for the consult, and psychiatry continued to ignore it, in an all-too-common pissing contest between departments.

One in desperation, demanding answers.

The other in defiance, demanding an actual question.

ONE CUP OF COFFEE

August 21, 1791

ON A BALMY Sunday night in 1791, a vicious tropical storm struck the French colony of Haiti. Catastrophic winds and cacophonous thunder would crash down on a vodou ceremony in Saint Domingue, where thousands of enslaved Africans had gathered in secret. Those men and women took Mother Nature's wrath as an omen, a rallying cry to revolution. They rose up, dragging their enslavers from the soft tranquility of their beds and into the furious night. They murdered their owners and paraded the heads of their children on stakes. The storm and the revolt it incited plunged the entire colony into civil war.

The Haitian Revolution would eventually birth the first Black republic in the Western Hemisphere. Over the ensuing two decades, a great many Haitians of African descent, those self-emancipated people made free by the revolution, would migrate across the Gulf of Mexico, finding a new home in the fertile lands of South Louisiana.

August 9, 2008

Sheriff Yvette Lemonia Fuselier woke up to the sound of a ringing telephone—never a good sign. She'd probably snuck in three hours of sleep.

The past week had been a hectic one for the sheriff. Tropical Storm Edouard had ravaged her parish, leaving Yvette and her department scrambling to pick up the pieces. It was a familiar ritual and one she'd been anticipating. Even before Edouard's landfall, before the meteorologist's giddy warnings and the long lines at the pump, she knew that damn storm was coming. She'd always had that sensitivity about her, something in her marrow that seemed to connect her to those subtle barometric shifts. She'd feel a change in the angle of the wind and suddenly find herself mumbling the old Haitian folk song her grandmother used to sing:

> "Fèy yo gade mwen nan branch mwem,
> yon move tan pase li voye'm jete.
> Jou ou wè'm tonbe a, se pa jou a m'mouri,
> Men jou ou wè'm tonbe a, se pa jou a m'mouri."

I'm a leaf. Look at me on my branch, she'd think to herself, translating without even realizing it.

A terrible storm came along and knocked me off.

But the day you see me fall is not the day I die.

And she'd think of those enslaved ancestors who, two centuries ago, had coupled themselves to the power of nature and won their freedom.

The day you see me fall is not the day I die.

But Yvette, of all people, knew that Mother Nature's allegiances were fickle. Hurricanes and the like only brought devastation and change. What might mean salvation for some would surely mean suffering for others, and the floodwaters didn't care. Noah's Ark was just a story told by the survivors, who convinced themselves they had been chosen. She'd seen her share of storms, had stood out there and felt the brutality, and it all somehow seemed a part of her. The tragedy and violence and anger and power that echoed through her DNA seemed to manifest itself each year in the seasonal barrage, in the cracked limbs and the wet blankets of leaves ripped from their branches and strewn on the ground. The turbulence was all too common around here.

And yet she stayed.

Those who've lived long enough on the Gulf Coast know that volatility. They know the howl of the wind. The flicker of the lights. That eerie and familiar feeling of sifting through all that fallen greenery, none of it autumnal or crisp or appropriately dead and crackly dry. All of it was supposed to be alive somewhere else.

And now it was in a hundred thousand wet garbage bags.

She wearily answered the phone. It was Deputy Nick Roger with news from St. Martin Hospital.

Anders Barrilleaux, the poor soul pulled out of that Arnaudville duck blind, was dead.

Sheriff Fuselier untied her hair wrap, releasing her short, natural curls. The new silk scarf had recently been gifted by her daughter-in-law, Celeste. The fit of it would take some getting used to. The fabric often loosened up in the middle of the night, forcing her to overcompensate by securing it too tight and waking with a headache. She preferred her old wrap, but even she had to admit it had seen better days. She could relate—sixty-two felt more like seventy-two lately.

She pulled on a pair of gator-skin cowboy boots. They added an extra couple of inches to her five-and-a-half-foot frame, putting her solidly above most of the women in the community, and still a few inches shy of most men. Her bloodshot and bleary eyes (they were always so bloodshot these days) scanned the nightstand for her watch. It was hard to see in the dim lamplight. She spotted the new readers lying there, the ones her son had finally convinced her to get. She considered putting them on, knowing they would aid her search. With a scoff, she pushed them aside and found the goddamn watch with her hands. *They* hadn't stopped working yet.

She grabbed her badge and rushed out into the navy-blue predawn. It was Saturday, not that it mattered. She couldn't remember the last weekend that had gone by when she hadn't put her badge on. She craved a cup of coffee but couldn't justify standing in her kitchen, twiddling her thumbs for five extra minutes, waiting for the pot to brew. A man had just died. An entire team of medical professionals had watched him slip away during the night shift. She couldn't let them see her walk in with a thermos full of homemade brew. They'd know.

Fuselier was used to making these kinds of decisions, instantaneously weighing small conveniences and miniscule personal gains against appearances and public perceptions. Female elected officials were rare in her corner of the world. A Black woman in office was flat unheard of. She bore the weight of being a woman, a widow, a mother, a person of color, an officer of the law, a figurehead of the department, a punching bag for the governor, and a scapegoat for the public.

Sheriff Fuselier arrived at the hospital, ready to make the

rounds: a debriefing from her deputy sheriff; a word with the doctor; and typically, a shoulder for the sorrowful family to cry on. Yvette, by rote, walked into the lobby, expecting a wailing mother. But no one was there. No family. No friends.

She took a moment with the body. All of this was in a fairly unofficial capacity; her presence at the hospital was more a symbol of support than anything investigative. At this point, no one was convinced that this was a homicide.

Jude Singleton's comment during his 911 call about a bear attack seemed to carry over into the official report. A handful of probable bear sightings in the area lately supported the theory, and the gashes across Barrilleaux's shredded back obviously did little to change anyone's mind. Sheriff Fuselier had gone out to the duck blind the night of Barrilleaux's discovery, after EMS had trampled through. She had gone out there alone, and she had determined on her own that the scene wasn't worth an official report. Barrilleaux's nakedness had never been explained, but he had his own checkered history with mental health and substance abuse issues, a history that would be called on to account for his odd state of dress as well as the lack of mourners at his bedside.

The scene at the Singleton property looked pretty consistent with a bear attack. There were no witnesses to attest otherwise.[4] Whether Anders Barrilleaux had been dragged to the duck blind or had crawled there in an attempt to escape his attacker was undetermined.

Fuselier left the hospital around seven AM. By eight, she was in her office, staring at a pile of paper she'd rather not touch, and

---

[4] Liu Wen, having flown back to Changzhi on August 7, wouldn't learn of the "bear attack" until several months later.

praying for some emergency that might steal her away. When a call came in about a house fire in Port Barre, she hopped out of her chair eagerly before realizing she knew the old man who lived there. She hurried out the door, and before she could even nab a sip from her Styrofoam cup of coffee, she was racing east along Highway 190.

Firefighters were snuffing out the blaze by the time she arrived. The house was a total loss, but the homeowner had already been accounted for elsewhere, to Fuselier's relief. Still, she wondered how he'd rebuild his life so late in the game and with so little left.

In her head, she was already strategizing and organizing the community fundraiser.

She had lunch at Myran's Maison De Manger with her daughter-in-law Celeste. Her son Dane usually joined them for these lunches but was absent today.

Yvette sat down beside the empty seat that would otherwise belong to her game warden son and remarked, "So what? Mr. Big Shot got better things to do than eat with us?" Celeste shrugged and muttered something about Dane being "real busy since the storm, I guess," and Yvette could tell from the terse reply that the issue should be left alone. She'd dealt with her own share of marital discord in her time, before Kenny's passing. The last thing she had ever wanted was a nosy mother-in-law asking if she was keeping her husband happy.

Still, she wondered where Dane was, and made a note to call her other son, Henri, later to ask if he'd seen him.

Yvette declined her post-meal cup of coffee, still feeling invigorated by the fire and a little anxious to wrap up the uncomfortable rendezvous. She spent the rest of her day in the office, forcing herself to sift through the paperwork—mostly invoices and bills for the department. A few small favors requested from local leaders, squeaky wheels in need of a little grease. She signed a contract for Steve Huval's Coteaux Bakery to become the sole bread provider for the St. Landry Parish Jail's kitchen. Steve's brother-in-law, Mayor Stipes (also a Steve) of Arnaudville, had promised to back Yvette in her upcoming bid for reelection. Not that his support had anything to do with the contract. The inmates needed bread, that's all. Steve Number One was happy to help the inmates, Yvette was happy to help Steve Number One, and Steve Number Two was happy to help Yvette. Win, win, win.

She never did call Henri.

By the time six PM rolled around, she was dragging again and considered brewing that elusive cup of caffeine for the last leg of her clerical marathon, but she decided against it, hoping she'd wrap up soon and get to bed early tonight.

She was home by eight thirty and in bed by nine, having bypassed dinner for the embrace of her pillow. One last time, she would try out her daughter-in-law's gift. She cinched the silk up against her scalp and admired the design in the mirror. It did look nice.

Not that anyone was there to notice.

She closed her eyes and unleashed a sigh of relief that the day was finally done.

And then, serving as a cruel and foreboding bookend to her day, her cell phone rang.

~

Often referred to as game wardens; conservation officers; or, depending on your circle, "good-for-nothing fish pig water

Nazis," Louisiana Wildlife and Fisheries agents are responsible for enforcing all wild game laws, in the name of conservation. The work brings them to rough, remote, and isolated terrain, often in inclement and unforgiving weather.

To the casual observer, a game warden operates much like a police officer might (but don't tell that to either). Like an officer, he makes arrests, doles out citations, engages with the community, and hopefully strives to keep the peace. Like an officer, he might be proficient, incompetent, or somewhere in between. Like an officer, he might have gone into the profession with a passion for community and justice. Or, as is sometimes the case, he might have coveted the status of the position and the exceptionality bestowed by the badge, the knowledge of an area's underbelly, of its inhabitants' weaknesses.

When Henri and Dane decided to go into training with Wildlife and Fisheries, many assumed that Yvette was filled with pride that her boys should follow her down a noble path of law enforcement. A couple of chips off the old block.

What they didn't fully sense, what Yvette buried deep under a practiced, stone-faced military exterior, was a bitter mix of disappointment and dread. Especially for her biological son, Dane.

At nearly six-and-a-half-feet tall, Dane stood out in a crowd, and he had what his mother lovingly called "skin as beautiful and dark as a two-hour roux." (The Caucasian complexion of her adopted son, Henri, she teased, had only been on the stove a few minutes.) A Black man with a badge faces an uphill battle in these small rural towns. His own community clung to their hard-earned and deserved distrust of law enforcement, even if Dane was just a "nature cop." Among their open arms and broad smiles, he could feel their wariness toward him, the way their tall tales and shit shooting always fizzled out one or two details short of the full picture, like the teller had just remembered that a Johnny Law was in their midst. Outside of his community, things were even worse. Most of his time on the job had him running down good ol' boys with second amendment rights and Confederate flag bumper stickers. They snatched their citations and spat back a slew of epithets and adjectives, none more telling than their consensus second favorite: "uppity." You can probably guess their number one.

Yvette damn well knew the difference between the police department and the game wardens. She knew that the next time she saw a pissed-off good ol' boy with a gun, she would shield herself behind her squad car door. She'd call in backup. She'd command him to put his hands behind his head and back slowly toward her. She'd distance him from his weapon and methodically de-escalate the situation.

And Yvette knew that every single person Dane encountered in the field would have a loaded weapon and a practiced aim. She knew he couldn't hide or holler or radio in for backup with every stop. She knew he'd have to smile and stroll over and put the hunter's trigger finger at ease with a casual conversation: *"Hey, friend. Any luck today?"*

~

Her cell phone rang again. Finally, she answered. "Better be good."

On the other line, a familiar voice. Her adopted son. "Hey, Ma. Um . . . you should come down to Dupre Road. Off LA 105."

She sat up at the cold, robotic tone of his voice.

"Henri. What's wrong, baby?"

And he said the two words she'd been secretly dreading for

over a decade, the ones that popped up sometimes in her nightmares, the ones she tried to shake from her consciousness in the middle of a sleepless night:

"It's Dane."

"I'm on my way."

The I-49 streetlights raced by her windshield, steadily strobing across her stone-faced countenance. She turned off the interstate, sucked into the darkness of the rural highway. Her mind became a machine of stripped-down pragmatic operations, back to factory settings: breathe, blink, brake, clutch, downshift, turn, breathe, gas, clutch, upshift, gas, blink, breathe.

The highway was gone before she even realized she'd made her turn down Dupre Road.

Four patrol cars waited in a muddy field encircling an old mobile home. Their lights painted the surrounding tree line. A strange scene of red and blue, day for night.

Deeper, beyond the first few rows of chromatically illuminated trees, the night loomed, pitch black and unfazed. Knobby, twisted cypress knees reached up from the damp earth, grasping at the dense fog like fingers, beckoning her into the night beyond.

Fallen branches and debris littered the ground, disarray left over from the storm. Dane's truck was there, still running. Tailpipe pumping smoke into the atmosphere. The left blinker flashed on and off, on and off. An officer whose name Yvette knew but couldn't remember unrolled a strip of police tape across the home's open doorway. He left enough room for investigators to duck under.

She found herself at the bottom step to the mobile home. She didn't remember getting out of her car. Henri stood there next to her, ready to follow her inside. She turned to him. "You found him?" He nodded, not saying anything. Not looking her in the eye. He placed crime scene booties over the thick Louisiana blackjack caked to the bottom of her jogging shoes. She hadn't thought to grab her boots. They were right by the kitchen door.

She ducked under the tape and stopped on the other side. There on the floor, she spotted it. The familiar forest green of a game warden uniform. Tattered. Filthy. She swallowed a thick lump of saliva. Staring down at the gunshot-riddled body of her son.

"We're—" Her voice unrecognizably thin. She cleared her throat and turned to the men outside. "We're gonna need the coroner out here now. Get detectives checking the area for boot impressions, tire tracks. Anything." She looked straight into Henri's eyes. "Where's the son of a bitch who did this?"

Still, he didn't look at her. Didn't say anything.

~

From *The Daily Advertiser*:

GAME WARDEN GUNNED DOWN ON DUTY

August 10, 2008

ARNAUDVILLE—Wildlife and Fisheries Senior Agent Dane Fuselier was found dead Saturday by his partner and brother, Senior Agent Henri Judice. Agent Fuselier's body was discovered in the home of Troy Langlinais, a local fisherman and lifelong St. Landry Parish resident, at approximately 9 p.m. on August 9. Early reports from the St. Landry Parish Police Department indicate multiple gunshot wounds as the cause of death. There have been no updates to the whereabouts of Troy Langlinais as of press time.

HENRI ELTON JUDICE

(Excerpts originally published in the
International Journal of Forensic Medicine)

IN AUGUST OF 2008, Henri Elton Judice was thirty-five years old and recently divorced from his wife of five years, Brittany. His solid five-foot eleven-inch frame put him at slightly above average height for the notoriously short-statured Cajuns, but Henri didn't give off an imposing presence, mostly due to his congenial tone of voice. His cool blue eyes seemed to hold a constant light, even in the deep recesses of their sockets, engaging you, inviting you in. Making you feel at home. His hairline of curly caramel locks was retreating faster than a battle line of troops in the last gasps of an unwinnable war.

His marriage to Brittany Alleman Judice had started as one pulled from a cozy Lifetime movie. Former beauty queen meets rugged outdoorsman. After a courtship that some said lasted too long (six years), they wed on Christmas Day in a private ceremony, surrounded by close family and friends on a plot of land beside the Bayou Teche, under a canopy of thousand-year-old oak trees.

Not long after the wedding, Yvette confided in a family friend that, although she loved Brittany, she didn't think that the two were ultimately good for each other. Her instincts proved right, as they were divorced five years later.

Henri was well liked within the community, if not exactly popular. "Charming" was maybe a better way to classify him. Game wardens tend to be pariahs in areas so invested in hunting and fishing, but Henri seemed immune to this curse. He always bought the first round and always finished the last. He had a good story for every topic of conversation, but he never began it without a prompt. Someone would shout across the bar to anyone listening, "Shit, speakin' of catchin' fish, Henri, you 'member that time in the Basin? The carp were jumping four fuckin' feet outta the water. This son of a bitch gunned the boat engine and started snatchin' 'em right outta the air!" And Henri would flash a beguiling grin and slip a little more heavily into his Cajun accent to tell the tale. Almost as if he'd been rehearsing the performance all day.

He was a man of the outdoors in an area that placed a premium on such social currency. He drank well. He laughed hard. He fished. He hunted.

No one suspected the kind of prey he had in mind.

The Fuselier family had become Henri's own over the years. At eleven years of age, after tragedy struck the young Judice's life, he transitioned from Dane's best friend into his brother. Yvette took him into her home, legally adopting him (while allowing him to retain his last name). After what had happened to the poor boy, she felt she had little choice. It was either that or allow him to end up with his good-for-nothing burnout of an uncle, Mitch. So, she did the right thing. The Christian thing.

Late at night in those first few years, when he longed for his old home despite all its terror and neglect, she would sing him a gentle tune in a language he couldn't understand. But he understood the feeling. A leaf blown off a branch. Falling to the ground, but not dead.

≈

FROM DCFS REPORT DATED MARCH 6, 1984

Department of Children & Family Services was notified by authorities of a case of severe child neglect. The referred children were Cedric Judice (age 8, deceased) and Henri Judice (age 11). The case came to the attention of St. Landry Parish Police Department on the morning of March 1, 1984, when officers were called to the scene of an unresponsive child by the child's parents Elton Judice and Nan Begneaux. On arriving, they discovered Cedric Judice, who has a medical history of epileptic seizures, unconscious in his bed and lacking vital signs. Parents were malodorous and disheveled on initial inspection.

[Detailed description of the condition of the deceased redacted by this author.]

Both parents tested positive for methamphetamines, cocaine, and marijuana on urine drug screens. Paraphernalia was found in several locations around the home, including but not limited to a glass pipe found on the dresser in the children's bedroom and an unsecured bag of cocaine in the shared family bathroom. (Toxicology screens on both children were negative.)

The pantry was empty beyond a bag of hotdog buns and some stale potato chips. The refrigerator contained a half case of beer, a liter of soda, a jar of grape jelly, a carton of spoiled milk, and a Tupperware container of spaghetti, which the older child claimed to have cooked for his younger brother three days prior.

There were no smoke detectors in the home. Full access to pesticides, bleach, and other household cleaners was readily available, with no evidence of child-safety measures. A loaded 12-gauge shotgun was found on the floor of the parents' closet.

Henri Judice was interviewed by a clinical social worker on March 2. He stated that he was sleeping over at a friend's house the evening in question. When asked if his parents knew where he was that night, the child shrugged.

The surviving child (Henri) will be removed from the home and placed in DCFS custody until a suitable living environment can be secured.

"HAPPIEST CITY IN AMERICA"

Mardi Gras, jazz, creole gumbo. Alligators and mosquitoes. Haunted swamps and voodoo dolls.

Louisiana conjures up a smattering of buzzwords and clichés, most of them dominated by the stereotypes churned out by the New Orleans tourism factory. But just a couple hours west of the Big Easy lies a region of Louisiana as eclectic and romantic as its more famous neighbor, but much harder to distill into a souvenir T-shirt.

This vaguely delineated region is called Acadiana.

The land was occupied by several Indigenous tribes before Europeans did them all the honor of "settling" the region in the seventeenth century. Soon, the Acadians (a term that morphed over time into "Cajuns") would arrive, following their expulsion from Nova Scotia.

Before long, Cajun culture would become synonymous with the region. But those evicted Francophones were far from the only wanderers who stopped in the sweaty swamps. There are still a good many descendants of those aforementioned Indigenous bloodlines (Chitimacha, Atakapa, Choctaw, to name a few). You'll find plenty of Spanish Viators and Romeros roaming around. Over time, the cultural gumbo was peppered with Anglo, Irish, German, and Lebanese immigrants; free people of color; enslaved Africans (primarily from Senegambia, West-Central Africa, and the Bay of Benin); and Afro-Haitians. These days, a visitor with a map will be hard pressed to properly pronounce half the streets and waterways in South Louisiana, so varied are the etymologies.

The sociopolitical landscape in this melting pot is in constant friction. American nationalism is strong among the conservative core, but you'll find French on everything from the street signs to the morning news on your FM dial, as if you're suddenly driving through a ninety-five-degree version of Quebec. Faith and love permeate the community while the stench of segregation still lingers.

The music is good. The food is better. Visitors invariably find themselves welcomed with open arms, exaggerated stories, and heaping plates. Lafayette, Acadiana's unofficial center, was named the "Happiest City in America" by *The Wall Street Journal* in 2007. The honor was the talk of the town for months—they aren't just happy; they take pride in their happiness, cherishing it for the lost art that it is.

But just one year after Acadiana claimed that beloved title, a killing spree would cut down at least eight souls and shake the area back into the stark reality that their blissfulness was not immune to what had seemed like a plague only suffered by the world around them.

Their happiness had a limit.

AFTER THE STORM

(Excerpts originally published in the
International Journal of Forensic Medicine)

August 10, 2008

DEEP AMONG LOUISIANA'S palmettos and mossy oaks, morning often takes you by surprise. You look up, and the starry heavens have given birth to a deep indigo sky. In defiance of the shift, the canopy of limbs just above holds onto its blackness, silhouetting itself against the dawn, retaining the last vestiges of night. Inside that cage of black bramble, it feels as though the daylight might never reach you.

Henri Elton Judice hung around Langlinais's mobile home for several hours, defying instructions from multiple law enforcement agents to head home and get some rest. Some officers' accounts had him trampling through the scene multiple times, murmuring notes into a tape recorder and giving his two cents to investigators about possible leads. Others' had him hovering along the perimeter, keeping a prying eye on the proceedings as the night dragged on.

Per his official statement to police: "I made it out here around, I don't know, nine-ish o'clock. Senior Agent Fuselier's wife, Celeste, had asked me to check in on him. That's why I came. We hadn't heard from him in a minute, and I was worried he might be out here."

The interviewing officer apparently asked Judice why he had reason to believe Agent Fuselier would be at the home of Troy Langlinais.

Judice explained: "I mean it seemed like he was going through hard times. See, I've heard rumors about this Langlinais guy. I'm sure you have too. I started worrying that Dane might come out here to buy something off him. Something to help him get through whatever. We all slip up sometimes. So I came and saw his truck running, like that. And the door to the camper was wide open. I looked in his truck first. Saw his belt in there, with his gun and badge. So I went to check the camper. I noticed a fresh boot print heading away from the house right there. Then I found the Ruger on the ground outside. Picked it up and checked to see if it was loaded. Wait—no. I didn't notice the boot print until after. But before that I went inside and found him lying right there. That's when I called Sheriff Fuselier."

The case seemed fairly cut-and-dried at the time. Dead body in a drug dealer's home, shot down with the dealer's own handgun. Only prints on the gun were from its owner and from the affable game warden who found it. With the lowlife dealer on the run, they had their prime and only suspect . . . if they could find him.

Troy Langlinais's '96 Chevy Corsica had been left behind, sitting in the tall grass behind the trailer with a busted alternator that he hadn't gotten around to fixing. It seemed he hadn't even tried to start it before he took off into the woods. His cell phone was found a stone's throw from the trailer, no service. No incoming or outgoing calls. No leads.

Astoundingly, it would be over five months before anyone would even think to check Troy Langlinais's landline phone records from that night. Most mobile home owners depend on cellular service, but Langlinais had wired his trailer to a nearby pole the year before.

When they finally did look into the records from August 9, they would discover that at 8:32 PM, minutes before Dane Fuselier was killed, the presumed guilty drug dealer had placed a call to the cell phone of Senior Agent Henri Elton Judice.

~

Parish Coroner Edward Harper Jr. watched a med tech zip the black bag over Senior Agent Dane Fuselier's face. He made sure to stay until they had him loaded up, mosquitoes be damned. Rounds at the hospital could wait.

He flipped through the notes he'd scribbled after a brief conversation with "Henry Judice." Edward stared at the word he'd jotted down under the misspelled name. "Likeable." He couldn't shake the oddity of it. Why had he even written it down?

He turned to watch two men heave the cumbersome weight of Fuselier's corpse into the truck.

Born into the humid August air of 1962 in Bessemer, Alabama, to Edward Sr. and Mary Harper, Edward had moved with his parents to Baltimore, at age four, as part of the Second Great Migration, his family seeking better job prospects and an escape from Jim Crow. Standing at five foot ten, Edward Harper had been a pretty decent point guard back at Paul Laurence

Dunbar High School, but he rode the bench (with considerable embarrassment) behind a five-foot-three sophomore. That the sophomore was future NBA great Muggsy Bogues would only alleviate his embarrassment in hindsight.

Clad in a fitted button-down with a patterned tie, Edward had an elegant "small-town movie-star" air about him. His attire was restrained and practical, but he was conscientious of his inseam. With a standing appointment at Simm's Barbershop in Breaux Bridge every two weeks, he kept his hair short on top, with a slight fade at the sides and a little more salt peppered in after each trim.

He stopped for coffee on his way to the hospital. The night on the scene probably hadn't robbed him of all that much rest. His sleep had been shallow and fitful ever since Anders Barrilleaux had been brought into the ER just a few days earlier. Edward was unaccustomed to losing patients, especially under such gruesome, mysterious circumstances. Barrilleaux's wide-open pupils, the black maws that seemed to swallow his irises and plunge into the pool of bloodred surrounding them, haunted Edward's waking moments and crept into his dreams. That pale translucent skin like tissue paper, revealing the serpentine veins beneath. The brutality of the wounds that hinted at a hyperviolent encounter, the likes of which he'd never seen before and hoped he never would again. Barrilleaux's ghost weighed on his mind, and now he had another death to sort out.

At least Fuselier's would add up, he told himself. Makes decent sense that a body with five extra holes in it should be dead. A man typically only needs the usual nine.

From breakfast onward, his day was an utter bore. Sore throats, dry coughs, unspecified rashes. A fisherman from

St. Martinville had a red patch on his back that itched sometimes when he drank beer and also sometimes when he didn't.

He called home to let his mother-in-law, Mama T (real name Amelie) know she'd be on babysitting duty a little later than usual.

Edward's late wife, Simone Harper, had inherited a rare but severe case of myotonic dystrophy from Mama T. At times, against his better instincts and the mournful love his heart still possessed for her, he found himself resenting Simone, who hadn't mentioned the possibility of the disorder to him until after she'd become pregnant. She refused to have her DNA tested, even after Mama T began showing signs of the disease in her early fifties. "Ignorance is bliss" had been her preferred platitude.

Myotonic dystrophy is a disorder of anticipation; each successive afflicted generation displays the symptoms earlier (and often more severely) than the previous. The child of an affected individual has a fifty percent chance of inheriting it.

So when Mama T began to suffer from the characteristic muscle fatigue and poor vision, Simone knew her own fate would be that of a coin toss and that multiplying those odds to any child she ever bore would now give the baby a one in four chance of acquiring the curse.

When she unexpectedly became pregnant, she would confess to Edward her weakening calves, her smile's ferocity dimming as she struggled to maintain a positive outlook. And Edward could feel their little cherub's chances double from a quarter to a half as Simone's own odds grew from a toss-up to a certainty.

Simone died less than a year after giving birth to a beautiful baby girl named Nicole.

The strain of the pregnancy had proven to be too much. Edward showed none of Simone's hesitation when it came to testing his daughter's genes; he had no compulsions toward blissful ignorance. He was prepared for the agony of knowledge.

Or so he'd thought. Then the results had come back. The family curse would continue in Nicole's DNA.

At one point, he considered moving away from Simone's hometown of Breaux Bridge and back to Baltimore, but he couldn't bring himself to pull his now five-year-old daughter away from her mother's world, especially knowing the hard road ahead. It may take a village to raise a child, but it took a dedicated grandmother like Mama T to care for a motherless baby with a congenital affliction and an overworked physician for a father.

Mama T said she would put his dinner in the fridge, and Edward promised he'd be home in time to sing Nicole to bed, which really meant he'd be lying beside her while she sang an approximation of the lyrics to whatever song had most recently caught her obsession.

Lately, she'd been stuck on a melodramatic rendition of "No One" by Alicia Keys.

The window unit cranked to life as he entered the lab. He recognized the 1985 Sears Kenmore's usual howl, but noted a new, plastic "click" buried in the background. The sound was barely audible, but to the son of an electronics repairman, it might as well have been a bullhorn.

He pulled the face off the ancient wood-grain machine and placed his ear up to it. By the sound of it, the fan blades were misaligned. The condenser coils would probably need a cleanup too. He'd visit the junkyard in the morning to see if he could find the supplies needed. It was a point of pride that the '85 model had survived so long under Edward's care. He'd miss it when it inevitably limped beyond the limits of his expertise.

He washed up, donned his gown and gloves, turned on his digital recorder, and studied Dane Fuselier's naked body on the table.

≈

Excerpt of Dr. Edward Harper's Autopsy Report on Senior Agent Dane Fuselier:

EXTERNAL EXAMINATION

The autopsy is started at 1800, August 10, 2008. The body was delivered in a black bag. Clothing: one hunter-green polo shirt with Wildlife and Fisheries patch, size XL. One pair of gray cargo pants, size 38/40, with black belt. One pair of black combat boots, size 12.

The victim is a black male, weighing 198 lbs, measuring 77 inches in height, appearing consistent with reported age of 36 years. The body is cold and unembalmed. Fixed lividity in distal limbs.

Two close-range gunshot wounds noted in chest, both bearing stippling and residue: wound A, 2 cm below right clavicular bone; wound B, 1 cm medial to left nipple, piercing the heart, the immediate cause of death.

One medium-close-range gunshot wound (C) to the abdomen, piercing the victim's liver.

One medium-close-range gunshot wound (D) to the left bicep.

One medium-close-range gunshot wound (E) to right leg, 4 cm above knee.

Projectiles from wounds B, C, and E were still in the body. Upon extraction, these appear to be 9 mm rounds, consistent with the Ruger handgun found at the scene.

There is dirt and debris under the fingernails on both hands. Possibly some human tissue present, perhaps defensive in nature on the part of the victim. Will send off tissue sample for testing.

Of note, the tissue found beneath Fuselier's nails would reveal DNA matches to his wife Celeste, Troy Langlinais, and at least one other unknown individual. Curiously, the sample would never be checked against Judice's DNA for identification as the unknown individual. The report continues:

There is an unhealed laceration on the right shoulder, approximately 3–4 weeks old. Appears consistent with a deep scratch/gash to the level of muscle tissue. This cut was not sutured or stapled (though it certainly warranted as much) and appears not to have been thoroughly cleaned. Notable for odd discoloration of surrounding skin—particularly the black scab tissue bordered by deep red inflammation. Does not appear to be pertinent to the immediate cause of death.

Labs resulted on 8/11/2008: WBC is within normal limits. Low zinc, low iron, elevated TIBC, significant elevation of porphyrins in blood sample.

Toxicology screen significant for trace levels of propofol in victim's system.

The propofol in Fuselier's system would be explained clumsily as the result of a "relapse." Investigators cited his brief history of painkiller use after an injury in high school, though he had been sober for at least fifteen years and had never, to anyone's knowledge, used a sedative/anesthetic like propofol. Months later, an old acquaintance of Henri Judice's would come forward, giving a statement to police that he and Judice had both purchased propofol from Troy Langlinais as recently as 2006. A search of Judice's home after his death would turn up a half-empty bottle of the drug and a collection of as yet unused syringes. How the medication ended up in Dane Fuselier's system before his death is still up for debate.

> I spoke with Senior Agent Henry [sic] Judice, the Wildlife and Fisheries agent who found the body at the scene of the crime. He reports finding the body sometime around 9:00 p.m. on 08/09/2008, at least 30 minutes after the approximate time of death.

> The victim was likely shot with a 9 mm handgun, given the caliber extracted and the firearm found on-site.

> **Opinion:**

> (1) Time of death: Body temperature, livor and rigor mortis, and stomach contents approximate time of death between 5:00 p.m. and 8:30 p.m. on 08/09/2008.

(2) Immediate cause of death: Gunshot wounds to left chest.
(3) Manner of death: Homicide.

Dr. Edward Harper
Internal Medicine, St. Martin Hospital, Lafayette General
St. Landry Parish Coroner
08/11/08

BURNING CANE

(Excerpts originally published in the
International Journal of Forensic Medicine)

October 10, 2008

Yvette Fuselier drank all the coffee she could stomach now.

Over the past two months, she'd done whatever she could to keep her mind functional. Sleep eluded her almost entirely. Her eyes burned and her guts writhed into knots most days. Whether that was from the deluge of caffeine, the insomnia, or the visceral agony of grief, she wasn't sure. She'd spent the majority of her time running the case over in her head. Rereading the notes. Staring at the pictures. All of them. Even the ones she'd never need to see again, the ones she wouldn't forget for the rest of her life, every shadow and contour carved into her brain.

She took a sip and stared out from her back porch into the horizon's strip of golden daybreak.

Fall isn't really a season in Louisiana so much as a series of momentary reprieves from the heat, a daily fluctuation of a few degrees and a percentage point or two of humidity in the air. Maybe you walk through the right patch of shade in late September, and you remember what it was like to wear a sweater so many months ago. And tomorrow, you're drenched again in sweat, waiting for another "cool front." Those first gasps of autumnal crispness came in early October that year, but they'd surely vacillate back into summer a few more times before sticking the landing sometime in late November.

She remembered wearing a windbreaker for Labor Day once, but that felt like a long time ago.

Her coffee was cold, but she didn't care. It was three hours old; no point microwaving it again.

They still hadn't found Troy Langlinais, the man she was certain had murdered her son.

From her back porch, she watched a million glowing embers floating overhead. The farm that abutted her property was on fire. Dave Legé was burning his sugarcane fields, scorching the crop's outer leaves in preparation for harvest and the roulaison, or "grinding season."

For a moment, her thoughts drifted away from her boy. She thought about old Legé and what a bastard he'd been after last year's disappointing harvest. She thought about how the slump had nearly wrecked him and a dozen other farmers in the area, how much they all depended on something so fickle. She thought about the cane and the men who work it now and the very different men who used to work it not so very long ago, enslaved people whose hands bled as they cut it down, loaded the rough stalks into carts, and hauled the cache to the sugar mills. She thought of all the money that jumped from hand to hand for a little sugar. She thought of the men who had died in the name of cane.

She thought about their mothers.

She was sick of thinking. She knew too much about too many things and not enough about this one, the answer to this most important question:

Where is he?

She should have arrested that piece of shit five months ago. Henri had always dabbled in recreational drugs—she knew that. Maybe a little too much of his genetics to overcome. She tried to keep a level head and steer him back on course any time he strayed. But after his wife, Brittany, left, Henri had veered a little too far and stopped showing up to work. She and Dane had found him in his new "bachelor pad," stoned into oblivion, a puddle of vomit on the floor beside him. After they'd managed to wake him, he finally admitted that he'd been buying from Langlinais. She'd let the offense slide, as she so often did with her wayward boy, and she quietly sent him to a rehab facility in Arizona. Never brought a charge on Langlinais. Never even knocked on his door.

But why had *Dane* been at Langlinais's?

At around nine o'clock the morning after Dane's murder, Yvette had shown up to the Carencro branch of St. Landry Bank to break the news to his wife, Celeste. Yvette found her daughter-in-law packing her office into a cardboard box. In 2008, layoffs were at an all-time high, and Celeste had been given her walking papers that morning.

Celeste looked up, saw Yvette there, and knew by just the way she stood that it was something even more terrible than getting fired.

"Goddamn it, Celeste," Yvette choked out, tears erupting in her eyes.

Back home, the two women held each other and cried. Once

the tears had run dry, Yvette, bound by her civic duty, had questioned her daughter-in-law about Dane's behavior. Celeste was short on useful details, reluctant to paint anything but a glowing picture for Yvette about her son.

The days dragged on. The funeral was hard. And life somehow kept going. The two women became entwined in each other's lives for a time, two pillars nearing collapse but able to remain upright so long as they leaned into each other. Celeste would spend her days searching for a job, Yvette for Dane's killer. Their daily routine would typically see Yvette winding the evening down in Celeste's kitchen with a bottle of wine, sometimes sleeping in the guest bedroom.

Two weeks after the funeral, over a box of red, Celeste gradually disclosed to Yvette how her marriage to Dane had turned sour, their hopes of having a child gone by the wayside. Her husband used to rush home at the end of his shifts. But not lately. Rarely had he shown his face before nine or ten PM anymore. And when he would, his mind was distant, somewhere else, maybe with someone else. Sometimes he smelled like her. Sometimes he wanted things different in bed, and Celeste suspected where he'd learned it. After Tropical Storm Edouard had rolled in, game warden Dane had rolled out, as is customary. And for some reason it had felt to Celeste like it might be for good this time. Celeste's admission that he had been out on duty for five days straight without returning home was not the reassurance Yvette had been looking for. And the propofol found in Dane's system had only added to the growing unease that Yvette had never truly known her son.

She should have buried that clown Langlinais under the goddamned jail five months ago.

She stood up from her old plaid lawn chair and tossed the dregs of her coffee into the backyard. She zipped her sheriff's bomber jacket and took one last look at the smoldering cane in the distance, taking in that familiar, acrid smell.

Annihilation and rebirth.

She marched through the house and out front toward her new truck—her new *old* truck. More than a few eyebrows had lifted in town when she'd started driving her dead son's vehicle. People had wondered if she should maybe mourn a little differently, a little more privately. They'd wondered this without a modicum of irony as they peeked through their blinds and muttered into their telephones, "Have you seen Yvette's new ride?"

The muted green 1975 Chevy Blazer was still in good condition. Dane had driven it mostly on his weekends off duty. When Celeste brought up selling the Blazer, Yvette had insisted she be the one to take it off her hands. She knew the money would help, and she certainly didn't want the Blazer being sold off to some stranger in town. She could just imagine herself at a stoplight one day, looking up to see his truck heading in the opposite direction. And for a split second, she'd think it was him. And then she'd have to remember everything all over again. She'd rather drive it into that motherfucker Legé's field and burn it.

She'd given Celeste the asking price plus a thousand, but in the end, it hadn't been enough to keep her daughter-in-law by her side.

In late September, over a month after Dane's death, Celeste moved to Arizona, where a cousin had pulled some strings and gotten her a job at a small local bank. As Yvette watched her daughter-in-law, this vestige of her son, pack all her belongings into a U-Haul and drive off, she wondered to herself if it was that simple. Could you really just start over? Find a new life?

Become a new person?

It wasn't that simple for her. She had too much here. The case. The reelection. And Henri, the only family she had left.

Over the years Yvette had occasionally wondered if taking in such a wounded soul might be too much for her family, if he might somehow contaminate her home. If the sins of his parents had seeped into him and whether that malice could touch her own flock. It was in the tiny tilts of his head or the subtle eye twitches when he was tired, those little tics that reminded her of his good-for-nothing father. The complaints from her neighbors certainly didn't help, nor did his run-ins with Langlinais over the years. But there was always something, some unknowable, mysterious pull, that allowed him to convince her otherwise.

They'd barely spoken in the two months since the funeral, but today she would put an end to the silence.

She cranked the engine in the old Blazer and headed out to meet her adopted boy at McGee's Landing.

≈

From a 1985 St. Landry Parish Police Report:

Case number: LA4/1/21/17775
Incident: Animal cruelty
Reporting Officer: Toby Delahoussaye
Date of Report: 06/07/85

At approximately 9:30 a.m. on June 7, 1985, a Mrs. Reba Chase[5] contacted dispatch regarding an incident with her

---

5 Pseudonym.

pet terrier. I arrived at [address redacted], Mrs. Chase's domicile, to find her on the front step waiting. She gave the following statement:

"It was him. That little monster next door. I know it was him. I know his mama's a cop, and so y'all ain't gonna do nothing, but it was him." She clarified that "him" referred to Henri Judice, the adopted son of her neighbor across the street, Officer Yvette Fuselier. "I see him out there all the time. Trapping squirrels in his little cage. Shooting them out of trees with his pellet gun or whatever. Look right there, you can see it from here. He's got a whole wall with them things nailed to it."

Mrs. Chase pointed out a four-by-five-foot plywood board in Fuselier's carport with six squirrel pelts stretched and salted for drying. Upon closer inspection later, it was also observed to be holding three severed rabbit's feet and a crow's foot, also salted and drying.

She continued: "He slingshotted a blue jay right in the head yesterday. Dropped him dead right off my mailbox. I saw him plucking the thing later on and digging into it with a pocketknife. That boy shouldn't be let anywhere near a knife, you ask me."

Regarding the incident in question, Mrs. Chase stated: "I got home from the Piggly Wiggly around nine. I called out for Charlie cause he's usually nipping at my heels when I pull up, but he wasn't there, and I thought it odd. So I call and call, and nothing. I start carrying my groceries inside, and when I go to unlock the door, I notice something in the flower bed. I look down and it was Charlie down there. Filthy."

Mrs. Chase had difficulty providing any more of a statement. She led me to the flower bed that runs along the front of the house. A small terrier mix was found lying on the dirt. Its neck was severely indented, appearing to have been crushed by some blunt object. There were no signs of a weapon around.

I interviewed Officer Fuselier and was permitted to speak with her son. The boy claimed no responsibility for Mrs. Chase's dog but did admit to the incident with the blue jay. He also volunteered that he had found a dead cat in the ditch outside a week prior, but said he did not know how it had died or who it belonged to. Officer Fuselier stated that Mrs. Chase's dog often ran out into the street when cars or bike riders passed.

With no further evidence to support any foul play, I left and encouraged Mrs. Chase to call with any other concerns.

HIS OWN WORDS

(Excerpts originally published in the
International Journal of Forensic Medicine)

October 10, 2008

From early on in his career as a Wildlife and Fisheries agent, Judice had documented his own field notes with a portable tape recorder.

Between August and October of 2008, he produced over thirty hours of these recordings. The material ranged from work reports to his musings on the migrating habits of wood ducks to his take on the best Saint ever (for his money, Joe Horn). But all, in some vague, circuitous way at least wound up on the topic of Dane Fuselier's murder. Whether that was a product of obsession, grief, or guilt is difficult to say.

"It's quiet out here today. The quieter it is the louder it gets inside. I swear I could almost hear him. Following me. Footsteps in the leaves. Like he was about to reach out and grab my shoulder and... But nothing was there. Nothing's ever there... You could just die out here and disappear forever."

≈

McGee's Landing in Henderson, Louisiana, used to hover over the edge of the Atchafalaya Basin on its wooden pilon stilts, like a final outpost on the brink of the frontier. For decades, it served as a boat launch for fishermen on their way out and a bar and grill for those on their way back in, a reliable stop for a quick, quiet bite, hidden on the other side of the levee from the prying eyes of society.

From McGee's back steps, the muddy brown Basin lay at your feet. Towering cypresses loomed, clad in scraggly Spanish moss. Their skeletal reflections stretched out to you across the placid harbor, like the corpses of ancient giants sunken underneath.

Yvette had always appreciated the mysterious serenity of this place, far from any towns, farther from her own jurisdiction. She had a respect for all secrets someone could hide in a place like the Basin.

The following is a transcript from one of Henri Judice's tapes, dated October 10, 2008, in which Sheriff Yvette Fusilier met her son Henri Elton Judice at McGee's Landing.

The recording starts with a click, followed by Judice's mumbling voice:

Henri Judice: "Okay, so . . . Remains of the deer carcass were left about two miles south-southwest of Two O'Clock Bayou. Location is marked on the map. I guess black bears have been known to attack deer, so maybe that could be something. But I don't know if it's convincing enough to—"

[Judice stops abruptly. Yvette Fuselier's voice can be heard faintly, but the most distinguishable sound is the rustling of Judice's map being folded, followed by a loud thump and slide against the recorder, as presumably he quickly made to hide the listening device with his map.] Good to see you, Sheriff.

Yvette Fuselier: Boy, look around. Ain't nobody here.
HJ: Right. Okay, Ma.

[The chairs shuffle as they take their seats.]

YF: That little waitress Angelle's still cute.
HJ: Stop.
YF: Hey, just here to help. Figured you could use a little backup. 'Specially around all these characters. You ain't handin' out tickets to anyone yet, are you?
HJ: Prolly shoulda left my uniform at home.
YF: Game wardens ... Umpires in a town of ballplayers. That's what I told Dane when y'all hitched up with Wildlife and Fisheries.

[There's a brief but noticeable pause between them.]

YF: So, how you doin'?
HJ: Good. Good. You?
YF: Yeah. Good.
HJ: Anything new on the case?
YF: Henri. We don't have to ... we can talk about other things.

HJ: I know.

[Another pause. Then the sheriff lowers her voice.]

YF: Well, they found drugs in his system.

HJ: Oh.

YF: And there was DNA under his fingernails. You knew that?

HJ: Whose?

YF: Celeste, Langlinais. And there was at least one person they didn't identify.

HJ: Oh.

YF: Celeste heard about the other set. She thinks he was messing around.

HJ: She's stressed.

YF: Maybe... I keep wondering why he left his gun in the truck. My boy wasn't that stupid.

HJ: Prolly figured he could handle himself against Langlinais.

YF: I wonder if he left it because he thought he could trust him. Or whoever was inside.

HJ: You think there was somebody else?

YF: No. Maybe. I don't know. I doubt it.

[Another brief pause.]

YF: Henri... baby, what were you doing out there that night?

HJ: I told you. I was worried about him.

YF: Baby. I know. I'm not trying to... Henri. I know you've had a rough road. And we both know that son of a bitch Troy Langlinais is a part of that road.

	I just want to be . . . Henri, you weren't using again, were you?
HJ:	Oh, fuck this.
YF:	I know, I know. I'm not trying to . . . I just want to make sure you're okay.
HJ:	I'm not using, alright? You wanna piss test me right here? Go ahead.
YF:	I'm sorry, baby. I'm not trying to accuse you. Just, how did you know Dane would be out there?
HJ:	I didn't. I mean, I guess Dane had asked me about pills or something to help him sleep.
YF:	He did *what*?
HJ:	I know. It sounds . . . crazy. But it's the truth. I swear. A few days before. A week before, I think. That's probably why they found the propofol in his system.

Sheriff Fuselier apparently overlooked it in the moment, but it's worth noting that she hadn't mentioned to Judice which drug had been found in Dane's system.

HJ:	So, eventually I decided I should go check and see. Look, don't you think if I'd known he was there, I would've gotten there sooner? I could've stopped this if only . . .
YF:	I know, baby. I know. It's not your fault. That's not—
HJ:	And now fuckin' Joey Darden going after you in the ads. I saw his commercial the other—

[A new voice interrupts them as the waitress, Angelle Reed, approaches the table.]

Angelle Reed: Hey hey, Sheriff.

YF: Hey, sweetheart.

AR: Getcha anything?

YF: I'm all good, thanks.

AR: How 'bout you, Slick? 'Nother round of coffee.

HJ: All set.

AR: Alrighty. I'll be round there if y'all need. Just holler.

[Her footsteps descend out of earshot.]

YF: *Slick?*

HJ: Okay.

YF: Nothing. Nothing. Just my boy's *slick*, that's all.

HJ: Okay...

YF: She's cute. Can't believe little Skunk is all grown up.

HJ: Nobody calls her Skunk anymore.

YF: No, I bet not. I bet all those little assholes always makin' fun of that white streak of hair are bangin' down her door now.

HJ: Mm-hmm.

YF: You bangin' down that door too, Ree?

HJ: You done?

YF: All finished. Thanks. I needed that.

[Silence as her chuckles fade out.]

YF: Henri, you're okay, right?

HJ: I'm fine, Ma.

YF: I gotta run. You coming to the fundraiser tomorrow?

HJ: I'll try to swing by.

YF: Henri. I know you been putting in time out there.

> Trying to find answers. Just take a break, okay? Get yourself outta all this. For me.

HJ: Yes ma'am.

YF: C'mon, gimme some love. I'm going.

[They stand. Fuselier whispers something indecipherable.]

YF: I love you, Ree.

HJ: Love you too, Ma.

[Footsteps leading away. The map rustles against the recorder's microphone as Judice removes it. Then a click.]

Later, after Judice's suicide, investigators would ask Sheriff Fuselier about the purpose of this meeting. She would claim that she simply needed to lay eyes on him. He had been a ghost since August, and she couldn't make sense of his sudden distance.

Sheriff Fuselier would explicitly deny that they'd spent any of the conversation discussing the case. They exchanged pleasantries, she said. That's it.

At the time of her statement, no one knew that Judice had recorded the encounter. His tapes wouldn't be discovered for another week.

Did they discuss any details of the murder investigation? "No. I was so fed up with the details by that point. That was the last thing I wanted to go on talking about," she claimed.

Did Henri say what he'd been doing for the last two months? "No, but he seemed okay. A little too okay now that I think back on it. At the time I figured he'd just been keeping busy with hunting season kicking up. But now I know."

Did Henri mention why he'd gone to Langlinais's mobile

home in the first place? "Just said he thought Dane might be there," she answered. "That's all."

Did he mention anything else about Langlinais? "No."

Was Yvette aware that Henri knew Langlinais? "No."

OCTOBER 11, 2008

10:11 AM

EVERYWHERE SHE WENT in those days, Yvette saw her own face smiling back. But it was some other version of her, one only a few months younger but one who seemed to exist a lifetime ago. "Reelect Yvette Fuselier for St. Landry Parish Sheriff!"

It was an election year for a number of positions, including hers. In 2008, most of the rhetoric around town revolved around the national campaigns and what was less likely: a Black president or a female vice president. Yvette's own ticket checked both underrepresented boxes, which made her incumbency all the more surprising and fundraising all the more critical. This morning, it was a boucherie organized by a few of her donors and supporters: local union presidents, school board members, one or two "government men" from down the I-10 corridor in Baton Rouge.

Her opponent was Joey Darden, a sixty-year-old ex-pat of sorts, if you can be considered an ex-pat on the same soil your ancestors called home, when your location hadn't changed but the world around your people had.

He was from a long line of tribal chiefs and chairmen of the Chitimacha tribe in Charenton, Louisiana. It would be a tough race, Yvette knew. For all the slaughtering and treachery and indecency their ancestors had inflicted upon Indigenous peoples, folks around here seemed to have a soft spot for their native neighbors. She often wondered if those sympathies had gotten lost in the mail when it came to her own historically mistreated people.

The tires of her Blazer dug into a soggy rice field and spun toward a makeshift parking lot. She pulled headfirst into a spot at the end of a row of trucks.

She used to back in every time, but not anymore. Why bother?

She dragged herself out of the Blazer and trekked across the field, her boots lapping up the morning dew. The various boucherie chefs prepped their stations, readying themselves for the hog that would soon be slaughtered and divvied up among them. A squeal echoed across the fairground, from the rusty metal cage on the other end, letting Yvette know that the hog was already there. Today, the piercing yelps felt especially desperate. The chefs sipped coffee (or at least whatever they were smuggling in their mugs), sharpened knives, and unsheathed their cleavers. A handful of early birds with nothing to do danced as a Cajun trio that never seemed to maintain a consistent lineup (it sometimes seems everyone in South Louisiana plays an instrument) warmed up. There was a small stage set off to one side, a cheap lectern erected in the center with a campaign sign for Yvette. She switched into gear and began to work the "room." Her Cajun French was decent, the language bearing a strong resemblance to the ancestral Creole from her own childhood household, and she enjoyed the strategic kinship of conversing with the old guard in their native tongue. "Comment ça va?" She glad-handed. Backslapped. Shit-shot.

But for all the congenial formalities exchanged, the weight of that one question nearly crushed her. Where was her son's killer? They all wanted to know—and they all judged her for not having the answer, when no one wanted to know more desperately, no one judged her more mercilessly, than she herself.

Soon, a sizable crowd had gathered. Mr. Wilson Melancon, the portly owner of this property, beckoned her to the stage area. "I don't like the spotlight," he said to the crowd, "so I'ma keep it quick. Y'all all know who she is anyway. For Christ's sake it's why you're here. Sheriff Yvette Fuselier!" They applauded as she took her place behind the lectern.

There was no microphone, so she raised her voice to greet the crowd. She'd planned on there being a microphone. She started her speech, well-rehearsed and rhythmic. "It is with great pride that I seek reelection to represent this great parish and its citizens. Serving y'all has been without a doubt one of the greatest achievements of my life."

Mr. Melancon hollered behind her, "And that's coming from the woman who outshot every recruit, man or woman, at Fort McClellan on a bet. Am I right, Sheriff?"

Yvette forced a smile. "You got that right, Wilson. They didn't know they were dealing with a Louisiana girl!" She hated this bit of pandering, never mind that the story's legend had outgrown the edges of its truth long ago. She maintained a morally complicated relationship with her past military service. At age eighteen and in the thick of the Jim Crow South, Yvette had sought escape, as her father had, in the armed services. Joining the Women's

Army Coalition with the intent of becoming a nurse, Yvette had soon gravitated toward a concentration in intelligence. After serving out her contract and nearing the end of the Vietnam War, she elected not to pursue another tour and was honorably discharged. But the legendary "bet" in question never failed to rally the base, especially the conservatives she so desperately needed to win over. It was a cheap card, but she needed to play it in preparation for what she knew would eventually come.

And it did, earlier in the speech than she expected.

A twenty-something-year-old blonde two rows back from the front, reporting for KATC, the local ABC affiliate, raised a hand. "Sheriff Fuselier, have there been any new leads as to the whereabouts of Troy Langlinais?"

"Helen, I'll gladly answer any questions related to the election; however, I am unable to comment on that as it is an ongoing and active investigation."

Just like she'd practiced so many times before.

The reporter continued, "In that case, what do you say to your opponent, Joey Darden's statement, that perhaps you are 'unfit to lead an investigation into your own son's murder case'?"

That was a new one for Yvette.

She cursed Darden under her breath and cursed Melancon for being too cheap to rig up a microphone. Unamplified and on the defensive, she could easily be seen as shouting if she wasn't careful. Shouting would be played up as hollering and hollering would be interpreted as screaming, and like that, she'd be *hysterical*. She measured her tone and volume carefully.

"Well, I'd tell him he should spend less time worrying about my ability to do my job and be more concerned with the fact that the polls say I'm gonna be keeping it."

The crowd clapped and chuckled. Not a perfect spin, but she'd take it.

Somewhere close by, the pig squealed again in its cage. She tried to ignore it as she wrapped up her speech to a solid round of applause. She waved and dismounted the stage when Mr. Duhon sidled up with a revolver.

"Want to do the honors, Sheriff?"

She really didn't. She always showed up late to boucheries to avoid this part.

She looked into the crowd and could almost hear their thoughts.

"Is she too soft to do it?"

"If she can't find her son's killer and she can't kill a pig, how is she supposed to serve and protect our community?"

She'd had enough. Enough of the speeches, the politicking, the mourning, the sleeplessness, the ache in her stomach, all of it.

She grabbed the revolver from Duhon, ran it through a quick inspection, popping out the rotating cylinder, checking the barrel for any blockage.

Dane's bullet-riddled corpse flashed in her mind.

She shook the image out.

Six live rounds.

She clicked the cylinder back in and raised the revolver. Five feet from the pig.

She could picture the gun residue, the stippling on Dane's dead body. The barrel had been so close to him.

She took a step back. And then another. Putting distance between her and the pig's panicking eyes.

With each backward step, the crowd cheered louder.

She stopped at about twenty feet away. Out of sight of those eyes.

The crowd went wild.

She inhaled.

Langlinais's face.

BOOM.

She caught the pig square between the eyes. It collapsed. A few spasms, then nothing.

Annie fuckin' Oakley. The crowd ate it up. She handed the gun back to Duhon.

That shot would get her more votes than any amount of community engagement or criminal justice reform could ever do.

It made her sick.

≈

2:35 PM

Dr. Edward Harper hadn't even intended to leave the house that day, his day off. He preferred to spend the rare weekends without a call shift busying himself at home, toiling away on whatever project required his attention. He was a tinkerer. A problem solver. Once, in an effort to fix Nicole's Tickle Me Elmo's busted voice box, Edward had inadvertently pitched the thing down a couple of octaves, until it sounded more like Jack Nicholson's Joker after his fall from the bell tower.

Today, Mama T had to physically pull him away from the autopsy reports and drag him out the door. He offered his usual protestations, but she wasn't having any of it. "Go, go. And find you a life or something like one while y'at it!" she cackled. There would be women there, she pressed, and he felt his stomach curl itself into a knot.

His queasiness wasn't because of any puritanical shyness. It was the same discomfort that bubbled up any time he had to listen to Mama T—the woman who had raised his late wife—speak of him, her daughter's widower, as a sexual being in need of another. He kept waiting for her to spring the trap, to turn on her heel and ask if he'd forgotten about her baby girl, the love of his life, the mother of his only child. But she never did.

Mama T knew Edward needed to get out. Not right for a man his age to be solo. And as good-looking as he was. "Damn shame," she'd often mutter to a chorus of head nods and affirmative hums from her Bible study group, Edward usually in earshot. So she pushed Edward out the door at around noon, assuring him that she and Nicole would have a perfectly fine afternoon without his sorry ass.

The event Mama T had in mind for Edward was a Zydeco Trail Ride, a Black Creole tradition derived from enslaved African cowboys, or "vacheres," of the South Louisiana prairies and valleys. Over the years, the Creole Cowboy customs evolved into a trail ride on horseback (or ATVs and 4x4 trucks) set to the steady R&B beat of a zydeco soundtrack, with the ride eventually concluding in an open field full of food, drink, and dance.

By the time Edward finally arrived, the sun was low, and the attendees had been two-stepping through the mud for hours, already several beers in. His barber from Simm's slapped a Crown and Coke in his hand and corralled him into a group of bullshitting cowboys. Most of the time, Edward had no idea what they were going on about. A Westinghouse generator hummed politely from the edge of the field, only audible in the silence between songs. It was a 12,000-watt model; Edward hadn't known they were even out yet. He had made some improvements to his 9500 last hurricane season—adding an AC ammeter, swapping out for platinum spark plugs, hooking up an automatic start, and so on. His was the envy of the neighborhood the last time the lights had gone out. Kept the AC running throughout a sweltering August night, even at the other end of the house where Nicole's room was. Not that it had mattered. As usual, the noise of the thing had forced her across the home and into his bed.

One of the cowboys was still talking to him about an enlarged testicle. Occupational hazard. Edward nodded agreeably and made a show of checking his phone, for an excuse to back away from the conversation.

He hoped for an update from Mama T, but there was nothing on the screen. They were getting along fine without him. As the light dimmed on the horizon, Keith Frank and the Soileau Zydeco Band took over the stage, and attendees began passing around bits of sweet-smelling BBQ. Edward, perched on the back of a tailgate, sipped from a water bottle (having caught enough of a buzz from the one Crown drink) and studied the dancing crowd, more as a small mass of humanity than a collection of individuals. They undulated on the dance floor as one. Unified. Coalesced. Separate entirely from him.

The thumping zydeco bass, which had been rattling his heart and lungs, seemed poised to wake the dead. He kept imagining that zombie TV show Mama T was always watching, the one with the southern sheriff she was so fond of looking at. "That boy knows how to sweat," she'd say, and cackle at Edward's ensuing cringe. Sitting there, he'd been imagining the Soileau Zydeco Band and their furious vibrations trembling the earth below, dislodging just enough dirt for a gray, decaying hand to claw its lifeless way through . . .

"Doctor Harper!" called a familiar voice, breaking him from his macabre spell. "Look at you! You been here the whole time?" Emerging from the crowd and wiping the sweat from her brow, Sheriff Yvette Fuselier, in plain clothes, sidled up from the dance floor.

"Not quite. Some party you throw, Sheriff," he yelled over the amplified accordion's bellowing reeds.

"Ahh, this is my nephew Herman's doing. Not often I get out here, but you know, elections are coming up, and hell, I been making the damn rounds all day." She flashed a weary smile.

Edward grinned back. He liked Yvette. She was easy to talk to. Introspective, disarming. And also, to put it bluntly, there was a reason her face was plastered so large on all those campaign signs. Sure, she had about ten years on him, but she wore every one of them well. "You look good out of the uniform, Sheriff. Not that you don't look good in the uniform. Just, it's nice to see you off duty is what I mean."

Yvette grinned at the flub of a compliment. She sat down next to him on the truck bed and watched the dancers. He tried to strike up some conversation, careful to refrain from the subject of work, both hers and his. But he found it especially difficult given his unresolved questions about Anders Barrilleaux, whom the sheriff had signed off on as a bear attack. He wanted to point out that the incomplete bite marks found on the victim were closer in size to a human's, that her assignment of the death was rushed and at the very least ill advised. But before he could get anything out, she pulled him onto the dance floor. He'd only danced to zydeco once at a wedding, and he found it easiest to just follow her lead.

For a moment, he lost himself in the good time. You'd almost peg him for a local. Keith Frank was cranking out his cover of LeVert's 1987 hit "Casanova." Edward even chanced a few twirls with his partner; she gaped playfully at his newfound command of the dance floor. And as if on cue, Keith and the band transitioned "Casanova" into their classic slow waltz, "Pieces to My Heart." Edward hesitated, but Yvette grabbed his arm. "No, no. You ain't done yet, Doc."

The two swayed under the Christmas lights strung over the field. They didn't speak a word. And when she seemed to stagger in her step and land just a few inches closer, he didn't back away.

It was the most alive he'd felt in years. For a second, he forgot about Mama T and Nicole back home. For a second, he forgot that he was a widower and that at some point he'd convinced himself that attraction should be a shameful thing.

And then he felt a phone vibrate against his thigh. He broke out in a cold sweat, his paranoid conscience convinced that Mama T had finally caught him, that she was finally ready to ask if he'd stopped loving her daughter, if he'd ever loved her at all. He reached for his phone, cringing, but it wasn't ringing.

Yvette pulled hers from her pocket. She tried to hear the other end of the line over Keith Frank's soaring vocals. She shouted, "Henri, baby, I can barely hear you!"

And Edward watched that protective, stoic veil fall back onto her face as she hollered, "You found a *what*?"

~

(Excerpts originally published in the
International Journal of Forensic Medicine)

5:25 PM

The woods around Troy Langlinais's mobile home had become a mud pit by then. Any unnoticed evidence that might have existed at one point had been trodden into a crater of muck and dead grass, mostly by Judice's own boots. His were the only tracks left by the time detectives finally made their way back to the scene days after the murder. Several reports have his truck parked out there at all hours of the day and night. Occasionally, an officer would accompany him to make sure he didn't tear up the area too much, but even a rotating shift of four couldn't keep up with his schedule.

If you find it odd that someone outside the police department, someone who had been the sole witness to a crime scene and who had a personal relationship with the deceased, was then allowed to retread that very crime scene for weeks on end with little more than a courtesy chaperone at his side, you're not alone. At least two separate detectives filed complaints, arguing that the game warden's zeal was hindering the investigation. But even then, his behavior was cited as misguided and bothersome at worst. No one actually suspected anything nefarious. Judice was never reprimanded. He was likable. Respected. And his mother was the sheriff.

Judice expanded his search area over the course of several weeks. He began gravitating south after a cashier at Mom 'n' Pop's Stop 'n' Shop called to report gunshots in the woods along Bayou Courtableau in the middle of the night. The cashier claimed to have seen a "suspicious-looking" olive-green Ford pickup—"the old boxy kind, before they got all pussied out and round and shit"—driving by about a half hour before the shots.

On October 11, Judice stalked through the woods along Bayou Courtableau, retreading the area that police had briefly (and unenthusiastically) checked out. Today, he was accompanied by Officer Brian Degeyter. After spotting the remains of a deer carcass in the ditch along the highway, the pair proceeded inward, toward the bayou. Once again, Judice mumbled his thoughts into his tape recorder.

> [Leaves crackle under footsteps. An occasional gust of wind muffles his words. He speaks quietly into the microphone, almost surreptitiously.]
>
> **Henri Judice:** Nothing here. No tire tracks. No boot prints. Nothing for anybody to go off of. It all looks pretty clear. Not that it matters, probably. I don't think any of these idiots could find a piece of evidence if it dangled out of a tree and slapped 'em in the dick.
>
> [Another more distant set of footsteps can be heard in the background. Judice raises his voice.]
>
> **HJ:** Hey, Degeyter, over here. You're gonna catch poison ivy in that shit.
>
> [The other footsteps stop momentarily, and Judice lowers his voice back down to nearly a whisper.]
>
> **HJ:** Got that fuckin' dipshit Degeyter today. Johnson, I don't mind. At least he makes himself useful. Tells a

good joke every now and then. But this Degeyter jackass—I don't even know if he can speak. All he does is just stare at me with that big, dumb, mouth-breathing face of his. I wonder if maybe he suspects ... [He shouts again.] Back this way, man! C'mon! Trust me. You're gonna be itching yourself bloody for days.

[Degeyter shouts in the distance.]

Brian Degeyter: What?

HJ: Come on! Get outta there. Gotta head back south again.

BD: *What?*

HJ: I said, come on! We gotta get outta here. I dropped my fuckin' knife somewhere back by the truck. I want to go find it.

BD: Alright. Hold your horses, Judice. This shit's thick out here.

HJ: You can do it, Degeyter. Just pump those little flat feet. [He lowers his voice back to a whisper.] I swear, Brit, if this is what passes for police around here, no wonder Ma's so tired all the time. I'm about ready to just ...

[Another shout from Degeyter, louder this time. More frantic.]

BD: Judice! Judice, get over here!

HJ: Fuck. [Then, more loudly] I told you to get outta ...

[There's a loud rustling sound. It's difficult to make out Degeyter's words under the noise.]

HJ: Calm down, Degeyter. Just take a breath.

BD: Shit. It's a ... shit ... it's a hand.

HJ: A what?

BD: I'm calling it in. Sue. Sue, you read me? It's Brian. I need ...

[Judice speaks into the microphone, drowning out the officer's call.]

HJ: Shit. Um. Okay, it's October 11th. Um, 5:25 PM. I'm out here about a quarter mile north of Bayou Courtableau. Here with Officer Brian Degeyter. We've come upon what looks like a human hand. Or part of a human hand. Looks to be Caucasian, probably male—

[He stops abruptly and shushes Degeyter, as if perhaps he heard something, or maybe he's thinking of what to do or say next. After almost seven long seconds of silence, he continues.]

HJ: Officer Degeyter found it. No other evidence in sight. Okay. I'm gonna call Ma.

[The recording ends.]

THE HAND THAT FEEDS

(Excerpts originally published in the
International Journal of Forensic Medicine)

October 14, 2008

FOUR PAGES INTO the Tuesday edition of *The Daily Advertiser*, political cartoonist and satirist Bart Habton provided his own take on the recent events in the woods:

Dr. Edward Harper's forensic report on the severed hand revealed very little. Much of the tissue had been gnawed away weeks before, leaving only one partially usable print, which produced no matches in the database. While the general consensus landed on coyotes as an explanation, Edward, in what may have been the first suggestion of cannibalism pertaining to this case on record, did note that "whatever *or whoever*" had attacked the victim had likely chewed away at the flesh at or near the time of the attack. This wording, while prescient, didn't seem to make many waves until over a month later, when subsequent discoveries would make the theory of a cannibal attacker impossible to ignore.

Useful forensic material was lacking. The tissue that did survive the supposed coyotes had been degraded by bacteria and decomposition—the nails had fallen out, the palm had hardened into a rust-brown hide, and the back of the hand (which was found lying face down) had already begun to liquify. The DNA samples taken were unusable given the putrescent state of the specimen. The precise nature of amputation also remained a mystery, but Edward did note a distinct lack of knife marks along the bones of the wrist. Instead, the few "tooth scrapings" that were visible indicated that the hand had been "chewed and ripped off rather than severed cleanly with a cutting instrument."

At the time, the discovery was treated by most as a punch line, another clue taunting an inept sheriff who was more focused on her candidacy than on crime. In fact, as had been the case with Anders Barrilleaux, most assumed this was a matter of animal attack rather than anything criminal. That theory would be impossible to maintain within just a few weeks.

LIGHTING THE FUSE

October 22, 2008

EDWARD KNOCKED ON the dilapidated door and waited. He scanned the road leading toward Henri Judice's mobile home. No streetlights. No pavement. Just a narrow gravel lane and a few trailers down the way. A black Wildlife and Fisheries truck sat parked in the tall grass out front, and an overcast sky blotted out the early afternoon sun. He knocked again.

Suddenly, a booming voice hollered, "Out back!"

Edward made his way around the trailer. Behind the home, he found a folding table with empty beer bottles and an overflowing ashtray, one of the darts still smoldering. A bolt-action rifle with something just shy of a telescope mounted to the stock lay on the table. There were two folding chairs, an ice chest, an old bench press with free weight plates on either side of it, a workbench with miscellaneous odds and ends, and a giant pile of moss and leaves—like something out of the Swamp Thing comics—slumped over the bench.

"Agent Judice?" Edward managed.

The pile came to life as Henri turned, his face smeared with green and brown paint. "Yeah? Oh. Doctor, um, Harper, right? What is this, a house call?" Edward marveled at Henri's getup, which later he would learn to call a ghillie suit.

"*Edward* Harper. And not exactly. I'm here off the clock."

"Too bad. Was gonna get you to write me some scripts for the good stuff." Henri dipped into the ice chest and grabbed two fresh beer bottles. He popped the tops off against the edge of the table and handed one to Edward. "Guess these'll have to do. Take a load off, Doc." He clinked beers with Edward. "So. Whatchu want?" He moved back to the workbench.

Edward scanned his eyes over the chaos and sipped his beer. To his left, two bulletproof vests hung on a clothesline, shreds of tattered fabric blown off by multiple rounds. "Jesus Christ, what happened there?" he blurted out.

Henri turned to match his gaze. "Oh that? That's just Spit Shot," he said, as if that answered anything. Registering the doctor's dumbfounded expression, he clarified. "You each put a vest on, you and ya padna. Take a swig of beer, hold it in ya mouth, and take turns shooting each other in the chest. First one to spit the beer out has to chug a wine cooler."

"You *shoot* each other? With guns?"

"Yeah. But don't use anything bigger than a .380 pistol. Shit, me and Dane tried it with a 9 mm once. That shit sucked." He cleared his throat, and his gaze trailed off into the woods at the mention of his brother. Finally, he looked back at Edward. "Why? You wanna play?"

"No, I'm all set."

Henri shrugged and turned back to his work.

"I do need your help with something. Do you have a minute?"

"Whatchu got?" Henri was adding different powders into a red Solo cup, concocting a grayish oatmeal-like putty.

Edward reached into his folder, pulled out a series of photographs, and dropped them onto the workbench next to Henri. Anders Barrilleaux's flayed back. The gash on the back of his skull, peeking up from the parted tangle of dirty orange hair. His bloodred eyes, the inky hole of a pupil staring back. The laceration on the side of his neck, black necrotic edges bordered against angry pink inflammation. "This is from a bear attack a couple months back. Anders Barrilleaux."

"Mm-hmm," was all the game warden said. He kept stirring the mixture.

Edward threw down another stack of pictures. A puffy, waterlogged leg. The skin was gray and mottled and peeling away in parts. And a puncture wound, roughly the size and shape of a hickey on the upper thigh. Like the one on Barrilleaux's neck, it revealed a rim of black on what had probably been pink skin before it had lost all color. "And this was from a boating accident back in July. Patient of mine. April Theriot. She was found out in the Basin after she'd gone missing for a week or so."

"Mm-hm." Henri poured more of a yellow mystery liquid into the cup, stirring.

Edward dropped another stack. This one with photos of gunshot wounds. Five in total. Dane's green, blood-soaked game warden's uniform. His bruised right shoulder, a deep cut tearing across the bruise. Again, black scabs and fiery pink flesh. Edward noticed that Henri only glanced at these.

Henri finally looked at Edward. "Is this a consult or something? 'Cause I bill by the minute."

Edward picked up the stacks of photos. "A bear attack. A

boating accident. And a homicide. All bearing similar wounds. All presenting with similar labs."

"I imagine dead people have a lot of things in common." Henri took a long sip from his beer. "So what're you doing here? This sounds like something for the police."

"I came here because you're a game warden." Edward held up Anders Barrilleaux's photos again. The ones of his shredded back. "Does this really look like a bear attack? Bears attack head-on, right? They make a show of it. Barrilleaux's ribs were cracked in an initial attack that came from behind. Black bears' jaws are also narrower, completely inconsistent with these partials."

"Grab that Ziploc and hold this cup. Follow me." Henri hoisted what appeared to be about a fifty-pound anvil off the work bench. He waddled out into an open field with the cumbersome weight, his beer bottle hanging out of his mouth. Edward grabbed the Ziploc full of black powder and the plastic cup. He followed Henri about a hundred feet into the field behind the trailer.

Edward finally caught up to Henri at another anvil, positioned upside down in the field. Henri dropped his anvil and beckoned for the bag of black powder and the cup. He poured the black powder into a small custom cutout compartment on the upside-down anvil. Content with the amount, Henri grabbed a long wick from his pocket and laid it in the compartment. He grabbed the new anvil and positioned it on top.

"Are you ... gonna blow this anvil up?" Edward said with morbid fascination, like a seven-year-old introduced to fireworks for the first time.

"Oh yeah. Straight up, Doc. I got about fifty feet high last time." Henri smeared the putty from the plastic cup on the sides of the two anvils, sealing them.

"You know," Edward started with some reluctance, "you'd get more height if you shored up your foundation under the support anvil."

Henri looked at Edward. "With what?"

"Offhand, maybe those bench press weight plates you got back there."

Henri's eyes lit up.

After laying the weight plates for support and lighting the long wick, the two took cover back by the trailer.

The wick sizzled toward the anvil combo, sparks flying. The two grown adults leaned forward in anticipation of a big bang.

Ssssssstt.

The flame fizzled out. "Shit," Henri lamented. "The wick fucked up." He started walking back out to the conjoined anvils. "It was those damn free weights. They snuffed it out or something. Pinched the line. See? You don't fix what ain't broke."

Edward shook his head. "The weights were a good idea."

Henri trudged forward and spat in the dirt. "Okay, what about a gator then? Those bite marks. That fella."

Edward, resolute in his theory, chased after Henri to plead his case.

"Come on. A gator's not jumping up and breaking Anders Barrilleaux's ribs. It's not dragging him into a duck blind and eating him bit by bit."

"So, what is?" Henri said over his shoulder.

"I think you know what I'm suggesting."

"Yeah," Henri said, closing in on the half-assed launch pad, about twenty feet away. He stopped suddenly and turned on Edward. "You're suggesting a person did this." The way he said it sounded like an accusation. A challenge.

Edward felt his determination waiver for some reason. "I don't know. But I—"

Tsssssss!

The wick flamed to life.

Henri's eyes widened. "Oh fu—"

BOOM!

A percussive sound wave blew them back on their heels.

The anvil rocketed up eighty feet and out of sight against the gunmetal sky. The two men gaped in awe, like a pair of smitten stargazers.

Henri came to his senses first. "Run!" he yelled and began sprinting back toward the trailer.

Edward started in the wrong direction, bumped into Henri, turned, and raced as fast as he could.

He was twenty feet from the trailer now, Henri just ahead, sneaking quick glances up at the sky.

Ten feet. Well out of the clearing.

Henri slowed to a stop and looked up, puzzled. "Huh. Should've come down by—"

CRASH!

Ten feet to their left, the anvil came plummeting down on a picnic table, splintering it into shrapnel.

The two men stood and stared.

Then they both burst out in uncontrollable hysterics.

"Hot damn, Doc!" Henri hollered, slapping him on the back. "That's the highest I've ever gotten it! Fuckin' free weights, huh?"

"The noble pursuit of science." Edward grinned.

Just then a piercing screech cut through the afternoon air.

A feral hog blasted through the underbrush seventy yards away, spooked by the explosion. With chilling swiftness and machine-like efficiency, Henri grabbed the rifle off the table, sighted up, exhaled, and squeezed the trigger. The blast rang in Edward's ear as he watched the hog nosedive into the mud. Dead. Henri looked at Edward. "They're invasive."

Edward nodded.

"Hungry?"

He stomped off toward his kill, sliding a buck knife from the sheath on his hip.

"Stay a while. I got a potato cannon I want you to take a look at too. Then you can show me more of that science."

≈

"And I did. I showed him everything I had," Edward would later confess to investigators during his deposition, less than a week after the crimes of Henri Judice had come to light.

"What exactly did you show him?" the lead investigator asked.

"Autopsy reports. Lab panels. Crime scene photos. Whatever police reports had been made available to me."

"And at no point did you even suspect that he might be the very person you were after? That you might be serving him the case on a platter? Helping him?"

"No. It seems stupid now, but no. I had no idea what kind of person I was talking to. What kind of monster I was inviting into my home. Into my life. Until it was too late."

TANGLED UP IN RED, WHITE, AND BLUE

November 4, 2008

YVETTE STOOD OFF to the side of the stage, a sweating beer in hand. She looked up and noticed the net above the podium, the red, white, and blue balloons suspended on the other side, eager to fall on the Knights of Columbus Hall in the event of her victory. Who was in charge of releasing them? How sure could she be that the responsible party wouldn't catch a happy trigger finger and open the net if Joey Darden won instead? Showering festive humiliation down upon her. She wasn't worried about the other two candidates, who hadn't made much of a showing. It was hers or Darden's race to win.

The race had turned more heated than she would have liked. Darden kept bringing up Dane's unsolved murder, and Yvette was left with a choice: Take the high road and stay silent, or lower herself to the bait.

The high road doesn't get you elected.

She bit back a little. Maybe not enough, but as much as she could stomach. She—or her campaign manager, rather—subtly referenced Darden's lack of experience and his comment last year about women being an "emotional Achilles heel" in law enforcement. But she was skeptical that it would have any effect. To be honest, the types of people who cared about such rhetoric weren't the ones she needed to win over.

It was rare in the world of Louisiana politics for a first-term sheriff to be challenged for reelection. Usually, you had some time to build your office, instill a culture of your own. But her bid saw a shift in this common etiquette, and she was well aware why. The girls had had their fun; now it was time for a man to come back in and right the ship. In the fraternity of Louisiana politics, women were given a short leash if they were allowed in the arena at all. If not for the vocal endorsement of the public leaders she'd befriended in her many years of service, she'd already be dead as a lame duck. She saw the two Steves—the baker and the mayor—circulating through the crowd. She thought of all the contracts she'd signed, favors she'd supplied. She hated the game but knew it had to be played, especially for someone as politically vulnerable in Louisiana as a woman. Public safety (or at least the perception of it) was on the table, and people around here didn't take the position lightly. As Harry Lee, the seven-time-elected sheriff of Jefferson Parish famously said of the power in his grip, "Why would I want to be governor when I can be king?"

This idea of power wasn't lost on her, of course. The very notion that she should lead an institution that buried its roots in a history of hunting, apprehending, and punishing runaway enslaved people was at the same time tragic and inspiring. Hell, not fifteen minutes down the road from her corner office was the site of the Opelousas Massacre of 1868. After a group of Black citizens in the area attempted to join a Democratic political party in the neighboring town of Washington, an armed militia, still sore over abolition, took twenty-nine Black men prisoner, executing all but two. Subsequent open attacks on the Black population left reportedly over two hundred dead in roughly three months. The police, unsurprisingly, are unaccounted for in the history of these events. Yvette's own friends often aired their disdain in clichés: "You can't put a fire out from inside the house," to which she would retort, "I'm just tryin' to stop the damn fire from getting lit all the time."

She checked her watch. The results should be in any minute. Out in the chattering crowd, she noticed a handsome head slightly taller than the rest, bobbing and weaving through traffic.

She hadn't seen Edward Harper since their dance at the trail ride almost three weeks ago.

Before she could make her way over to him, he angled for the side of the room and found Henri. The two started chatting, and for once this evening, it didn't seem to Yvette that Henri was conversing through gritted teeth. Her son had always been a man of the people. But these were not his people. He'd been huddling in the corner, taking sheepish sips of his beer, all night until Edward arrived. She checked her watch again.

Across the room, Mayor Prejean of Opelousas looked equally nervous. He liked Yvette. They saw eye to eye, and together they had hopes of changing the perception of St. Landry's capital city as a rundown den of crime. Joey Darden was an outsider with untested ideas and outsized ambition; no one within the system knew what he might bring to the table. For all they knew, he might throw the whole table out the window. She turned back to Henri and Edward. Still talking. They seemed almost friendly. When the hell had that started?

And how?

Suddenly, she felt herself walking over, unsure if the urge was out of concern, curiosity, or jealousy. It wasn't as if she had any intention of jumping the bones of an eligible bachelor a decade her junior. But she hadn't dismissed the idea entirely either. She did like talking to Edward. The smoothness of his voice, the calm focus of his eyes on hers while she spoke, reminded her of how her husband used to look at her. Kenny had been gone for over thirty years now, killed by an off-duty officer who thought he was trespassing on his own property, the snowball shop he'd bought from an older white couple a month before. Kenny was locking up for the night after a long evening of painting the interior walls. "Baby blue. It makes people happy," he'd said. But she knew he'd chosen the color for his baby boy at home, the little apple of his eye.

Dane had loved baby blue.

And then she was there, beside the two men who were not her husband or her dear baby boy, but maybe approximations enough of each. She just stood there a moment, too self-conscious even to interrupt a conversation at her own goddamn election party. Edward noticed her first.

"Yvette—Sheriff," he corrected himself, and glanced briefly at Henri. "You throw a mean party, Sheriff Fuselier."

"I can't take credit for an inch of it," she answered with a register of forced professionalism. "But thanks for coming by all the same, Dr. Harper."

Henri rolled his eyes and butted in, "Damn, y'all stuffy. Dr. Harper, Yvette. Sheriff Fuselier, Edward. Great. Now we're all friends."

"Pleasure's all mine, *Yvette*." Edward and Yvette shared an almost imperceptible grin and chose to leave their dance-floor encounter unspoken. "Y'know, I was just talking to Henri here."

The doctor was no longer mispronouncing Judice's name. "And I managed to twist his arm into having Thanksgiving dinner at my house in a few weeks."

"Thanksgiving," Yvette said, studying the two men, still trying to decode the source of their friendship.

Edward continued, "You're invited too, of course. Please come. We'd really love to have you there."

"Well," Yvette said, and she couldn't stop herself from smiling, "that sounds wonderful."

"Perfect." Edward beamed. The doctor continued, "It'll be great to have the whole family along."

"Whole family?" Yvette grinned dumbly.

"Well, I wouldn't dream of having Henri and his uncle over and not the woman who made him who he is today."

His uncle. Fucking Mitch Judice.

Henri shot her a shit-eating smirk. She'd just booked an evening with the Palmetto Playboy himself.

Someone in the crowd shouted, "Hey, turn that up!" The room's attention shifted to the CNN telecast, where the results of the 2008 presidential election were coming in. The anchor called it. A few elated screams rang out, smatterings of applause from different corners of the room. Some shook their heads in disbelief. Others in disappointment. Some eyes rolled. Some grew cloudy. And Yvette found herself just trying to picture the name Barack Obama in the district's future textbooks, one day alongside the Lincolns and Kennedys and Roosevelts of legend.

She felt her hand move to find Edward's. He would understand what this meant to her in a way that Henri never would or could. They clutched each other, hanging on while locking their eyes on the screen.

Henri ran off to get drinks, and most of the folks around her turned their attention to their own hugs and handshakes. Yvette and Edward, alone now in the sea of embraces, wrapped their arms around each other in kind. She planted a friendly, elated peck on his lips. A peck that lasted a half second longer than expected. But no one was looking. It was nice to have no one looking for a change. *So, this is civilian life,* she thought. She'd forgotten how nice anonymity could be. Unburdened of the responsibilities she had taken on for what seemed like two lifetimes. *Not too bad. Not too bad at all.*

Then her campaign manager waved her over; the results of her own race were coming in. She scrambled back to the stage and looked back up at the balloons. Primed and ready. Like a pack of salivating dogs on the other side of a gate.

The screen behind her lit up, ready to receive the projected results, and she thought to herself in that moment that either outcome would be okay. Win or lose, in two weeks, she'd be having a nice dinner at Edward's house, getting tipsy and ignoring Mitch's buffoonery, and the campaign and all the bullshit would be a memory. She caught herself wondering what his house smelled like.

And then the results came in. The balloons stayed where they were. She and Joey Darden would be in a runoff for another fucking month.

≈

At the Triple Crown Casinos' event center across town, they dropped the balloons. Joey Darden kissed his wife, Beverly, for the crowd and waved a thanks to his supporters. Here, a runoff meant a win. The buoyancy in the room was twofold: On a strategic level, with the other two male candidates out of the race and no longer splitting the vote of "red-blooded Americans" who couldn't fathom a woman in control of the law, he'd immediately gain an advantage. On a more personal front, the electrifying sense of hope was a reflection of just how unlikely his campaign had been from the start.

At age forty-five, Joseph "Joey" Darden was an academic, a sociology graduate from LSU with a master's and a doctorate in criminal justice. He, of all people, hadn't intended to challenge the incumbent sheriff, who, for his money, had at least been doing a better job than her predecessor. But after a friend approached him with the prospect of running, he did have to admit that, for all the exterior bells and whistles that set Yvette Fuselier apart from the fold, at her core, she was probably just another bureaucratic insider. Military background. A career spent climbing through the ranks, accumulating back-scratching friends along the way, playing fast and loose with the rules, justifying all the morally gray means with the slogan-friendly ends. Her performative tough-guy act at a recent fundraiser—gunning down a caged pig with a single skilled shot, which swept the "tough on crime" sycophants into a frenzy—had only served to eliminate any lingering reservations he might have still clung to.

The Chitimacha Tribe once inhabited the bulk of South Louisiana, from the Cajun heartlands to New Orleans and beyond; the banks of the Mississippi down to the shores of the Gulf. A rich, fertile territory. Home. Until a swarm of colonizers took turns passing the land around and paving it over. Now, the Chitimacha could only call a small sliver of territory in Charenton their own. Darden's father sat on the tribal council, and Joey had envisioned himself one day holding a seat as well, helping lead the affairs of the school and the tribal market and, most notably, the tribe's lucrative Cypress Bayou Casino and Hotel. But his brother had joined the old man's ranks instead, and Joey's road had taken him to LSU.

Joey Darden was no idiot. He knew that the "friend" who suggested his candidacy had other friends. Ones with lofty ambitions of expanding casino gaming operations in Opelousas. He knew that a sheriff with Chitimacha connections would certainly make it easier to bring in big-name contracts. Somewhere in the room, the owner of the Triple Crown pumped congratulatory handshakes.

But Darden could handle all the strong arms and deep pockets. He'd be no one's puppet if he won. He grabbed his cell phone. He knew he should reach out to Yvette and congratulate her on the runoff.

He'd felt lousy about his campaign manager's insistence on running those ads about her son's murder and the sheriff's fruitless search for the culprit. He couldn't imagine the agony of losing a child (he had two of his own) or the burden of policing in the face of that loss. He'd argued against the tactic, but his team had assured him that this was how it was done. What was that about being no one's puppet?

He should call her.

He began to dial the number he'd been given. But he hesitated, calculating the tone he would take. He had to admit, despite his regret about crawling into the mud and his urge to apologize, Sheriff Fuselier's judgment hadn't been impeccable. He couldn't necessarily blame her for Langlinais slipping off the grid, but he could certainly find fault in how carefully she coddled her adopted son.

In November of 2008, Joey Darden might have been the only person on the planet who suspected that Henri Judice was what would soon be known as the Cajun Cannibal. He didn't care how charming the guy was. He only saw the facts: Judice was among the last known to see Agent Dane Fuselier alive and the first to find him dead beside a murder weapon bearing Judice's prints. Any hint of a boot print had been erased by his constant tampering with the scene. And then he suddenly stumbled upon human remains just a few miles away? Something strange was going on. And the resident sheriff seemed to have little interest in sorting it out. Darden wondered if she would ever bring charges against her last remaining child, even if more damning evidence might yet come to light.

She almost certainly wouldn't, he feared. That's why he had to win. Before things got even further out of hand. He put his phone away and went back out into the crowd to shake hands and rally the troops for the victory they all needed so desperately.

LEMME
TELL YA . . .

November 6, 2008

THERE ARE PARTS of St. Landry Parish that are so old and untouched by modernity that even nature itself feels decrepit and rotting. The trees aren't so much individual entities as they are a collective thicket of strangulating vines and moss and shrubbery that looms in layers upon layers through which you can hardly see. The ground never actually dries under that tangle. The sun's honest path won't snake through enough to cancel out the moisture that has zigged and zagged and trickled down, seeping into the earth with each inch of rainfall. Grass is nowhere to be found here. Fungus and ferns and decomposing detritus dominate the terrain instead, thriving in the shadowy dampness.

It's here, intruding into this no man's land, that Mitch Judice has made his home for decades.

Before the oil-bust of the late 1980s in Lafayette, Louisiana, Mitch worked as an "entertainment liaison" for a big oil company in the I-10 corridor. His position had him flying clients to and from Las Vegas, arranging lavish hunting excursions everywhere from Texas to Africa, and procuring the right women and drugs to satiate Big Oil's big appetites. But after the crash, when, as he put it, "I lost my Mercedes and my house in Lafayette and my on-again/off-again fiancée in one failed swoop," Mitch's life was in shambles. Bouncing from odd job to odd job and battling an addiction to cocaine and a handful of other vices, Mitch fought an often losing battle with his own private demons.

After Henri went into the foster system in 1984, Mitch tried to obtain custodial rights but was deemed unfit, and Henri ended up with Yvette and Dane instead. Mitch bounced in and out of Henri's life and did the best he could, often taking him and Dane hunting or fishing. Mornings. Afternoons. Weekends, maybe. Any more responsibility than that and Mitch could feel the top beginning to wobble off its axis. By 2008, he was spending most of his time in a deer stand or a flat bottom boat and cashing a decent pension with some retirement. He hadn't had a sip in six years.

He didn't exactly settle down so much as he stopped rambling a little outside of a town that was a little outside of a slightly bigger town that most Louisianians have never heard of. Turn left off Nursing Home Drive and bounce down a road no one bothered to name, alongside a small slit of water that is still to this day called Negro Foot Bayou. The place was nice enough in the late '70s and early '80s: wood paneling, avocado-green kitchen appliances, linoleum floors that resisted the stains of whatever bleeding thing Mitch was dragging in on any given day. But over time, the panels began to crack and the linoleum peeled, and Mitch stopped noticing. He wasn't sure when it had happened, but at some point he quit referring to the place as his camp and started calling it home.

Henri climbed the front steps that were only still strong enough for weight-bearing because they were a solid block of concrete. There was a gap of about three inches between the top step and the camp's facade. The foundation of the home itself seemed to recoil from the stoop's cold gray stone, tilting and leaning away toward the trees behind, as if the structure's wooden frame were desperate to return to the forest whence it came.

Henri's tape recorder was already rolling when he knocked and waited at the door. When no one answered, he opened it for himself. Mitch was known to lock up only occasionally, when he went to bed or left town for a week.

Henri was already in the kitchen by the time the back door slid open and his uncle hollered out the opening lines of their usual call and response: "Mais, who the fuck is burglarizing mah residence?"

Henri's practiced reply: "It's the goddamn IRS comin' to collect!"

In strutted Mitch Judice, throwing his ever-growing gut around with authority. Built like a brick shithouse, this specimen was the culmination of so many converging ancestries: his blue McNulty eyes, his spongy Bourgeois nose, his sun-broiled Hernandez skin. He was a certain kind of American mutt, so many ingredients in the melting pot that he could only identify with one: Cajun.

Mitch slung a strap of four dead rabbits on the kitchen table with a wet smack, and Henri made a joke about maybe needing to call the Board of Health rather than the IRS.

They hugged and sat at the table, having coffee over the carcasses. Mitch had brewed a batch earlier that morning, which he reheated, whole pot, in the microwave. Aside from an awkward invitation to Thanksgiving dinner at some doctor's house, there wasn't much catching up to do; they visited like this on a weekly basis at least, more so since the divorce. The two men shot the shit for an appropriate stretch before Henri broached the subject of missing appendages and bear attacks.

Mitch had heard about the severed hand. And that poor Anders Barrilleaux bastard out on Jude Singleton's land.

Henri told Mitch that Singleton's neighbor High Pocket had called 911 a few days before the Barrilleaux kid was found. Reported a bear sighting out there. Naturally, Wildlife and Fisheries was alerted, and an agent was sent out.

Henri claimed that he was that agent, though there would be no official report to back up this claim.

Henri filed no paperwork or other documentation regarding any investigations he made into a bear attack in that area. Whatever he saw or did out there, he kept it uncharacteristically to himself.

Mitch asked Henri if he'd seen the bear. Henri shrugged and said that yeah, he thought that maybe he had.

"Maybe? Bear's a pretty damn hard thing to miss, don't ya think?" Mitch teased. Henri admitted that perhaps he'd seen something or someone out there and described it to Mitch with only a vague recollection. "About five or six feet tall, maybe. Not moving too fast, not too slow. Didn't really seem to be in much of a hurry..."

Mitch sipped his coffee and shared a long, meandering story about the night he went out drinking and a black bear stole his keys and drove his truck into a tree.

Eager to get back on point, Henri retrieved his phone and scrolled through some photos he had somehow obtained of

Anders Barrilleaux's remains, as well as the photos he'd taken of the severed hand and some mutilated deer carcasses he'd recently "happened upon." He asked his uncle if he, a man of the outdoors, would consider the evidence plausible for a bear attack. He seemed very concerned with how convincing it all looked.

Mitch started to comment, but Henri cut him off midsentence. "Wait," he said, and he pulled out his tape recorder to ensure a good recording. He set it on the table between them, beside a pool of rabbit blood.

Mitch Judice: The fuck is that thing? Whatchu think— you're the CIA now?

Henri Judice: Just ignore it. Now tell m—

MJ: Yes, um, this is Special Secret Agent Henri Judice. Reporting at double-oh-seven hundred hours . . .

HJ: I just want to make sure I get this recorded.

MJ: Why? What's the matter with your memory? You been drinkin' too much is your problem, hoss. Gonna get sclerosis before you know it. Take it from me.

HJ: Just say what you just said.

MJ: What? About my thigh cyst?

HJ: About the pictures. You looked at the body and said . . .

MJ: Do I talk into the little thing at the top here?

HJ: I told you. Ignore it.

MJ: Well shit, Henri, *you* put a fuckin' bug on my table, and then you tellin' me to ignore the thing.

HJ: Jesus Christ. You said, "That's a bear attack. Just like those twins." So you're saying you've seen a bear attack before. And you're convinced enough by . . . this is consistent with what you've seen?

MJ: Hey, you low. Want me to pour you some more?

HJ: Just . . . answer the question, Parrain.

MJ: Alright, alright. Well, when I was younger, much younger—it musta been '71—I was workin' on clearin' the land for them to build the Basin Bridge. Well, we was out there, day in and day out, sweatin' our asses off, choppin' down trees and wadin' through that swamp. Awful work. But I was in some good shape back then. Shoo, you shoulda seen me. You ever seen Brando in *Streetcar Named for Desire*? Puh, Donny Corleone *wishes*. So, I was crewed up with a boy from New Iberia and a coupla twins from Rayne. Odd ducks as I recall, even for twins.

We worked in pairs. Two men to a team. And one day, the twins don't clock out. We assume they hightailed it to the bar to get an early start. Well, next mornin', they both don't show. Prolly hung over, we figure. Anyway, their work has to be covered, so me and New Iberia go to the spot they been clearin'. And we get to workin' in some pretty dense brush. Well, all a the sudden, I hear my padna yellin' for me, I mean like bloody-murder yellin'. So I run over and we find one of the guys lookin' kinda like that fella in your picture there. All bloodied up. Missin' chunks outta his back. Just brutal. I flat lost my breakfast. And then, not too far down the way, we find the other fella, lookin' pretty much the same. I mean they twins so they always look pretty much the same, but you know what I mean. Just a mess. So we call the foreman over, and they get the cops, and they come pick up the bodies, and that's about the short and the long of it.

HJ: And it was a bear that killed those guys?

MJ: Well, we was clearin' out all that brush and swampland, got too close to a cub prolly, and then the mama made sure we wouldn't come around.

HJ: Okay.

MJ: And they did kill them a bear a few days later.

HJ: What do you mean *a* bear?

MJ: Well, I mean it's not like the bear can confess to eatin' them boys. But they found 'em a bear in the area. Black bear. And they shot it.

HJ: What'd they do with the cub?

MJ: I don't think he had any cubs with him.

HJ: Wait. *Him?*

MJ: Yeah.

HJ: You just said that it was a mother protecting her cubs.

MJ: I don't know, Henri. I'm not a damn bear attorney.

HJ: Jesus. Is any of this true?

MJ: I got a photogenic memory. This is how it went down, hoss. Mark it.

HJ: Is there anything else, anything useful you can tell me that would make you believe these photos are from a bear attack?

MJ: Nah, that's about it. I tore my rotator cuff not long after that and couldn't work no more. But I think Mama and Daddy were happy to see me get outta that swamp.

HJ: Why you say that?

MJ: Aw, you know how superstitious them old Cajuns are. They grew up with all that folklore and tales from the old country. "Behave or that Rougarou gonna get you!" Mama thought that old swamp monster was out prowlin' around. Pissed off 'bout the interstate comin' through. Figured him for more of a scenic route guy, I guess. She said her rosary every damn night after those old boys turned up like they did.

HJ: Rougarou, huh?

MJ: Neva know.

HJ: Oh, listen. I'm real sorry but I, um, I lost your buck knife the other day.

MJ: You did what?

HJ: I know. I was takin' a leak and—I don't know. I went back to search the spot and I couldn't find it. I'm gonna go out there later today and make another pass.

MJ: Henri, my ex-wife gave me that.

HJ: Ex-fiancée.

MJ: Still. She got my name engraved on it and everything.

HJ: She forgot the *T*.

MJ: The *T*'s silent, smartass.

HJ: I'll find it.

MJ: Lemme guess: You got spooked and dropped it when you saw that dude's hand. Betcha had Rougarous on the brain too.

HJ: Well, it's been a real blast, Parrain. But I gotta hit it. Thanks for the gourmet coffee.

[A chair scoots across the floor.]

MJ: Whatchu think this is—Starbucks? Jumped-up little shit, I'll take you down like Christmas lights in March. Oh, hol' up—before I forget, my clicker crapped out, and I need—

[The recording ends with a click.]

ROUGAROU

THE FIRST TIME I encountered a Rougarou was in 2018.

Early one February morning, somewhere in the backwoods of Mamou, Louisiana, my fiancée, Elsie, and I crept through the fog-blanketed forest. Our Subaru was parked about thirty yards back, tilting precipitously toward the ditch running alongside the road. "Are you sure this is it?" she asked. Her belly swelled with our child, due in just a few months. But nothing, not even "cankles" and morning sickness, could keep this woman away from an adventure.

"That's what they said on the phone. You wanna turn back?"

"Hell no." She grinned and straddled across a mud pit on the path.

Something howled nearby, and Elsie turned to me. "What was that?" she asked, stopping suddenly, her hands going to her stomach as if to protect our unborn baby.

~

We'd met during the fall of 2016, at a visual arts capstone for the BFA studio arts program at Loyola. "The Cuban Gaze in the Big Easy" by Elsie Armas was a collection of side-by-side photographs juxtaposing Cuban and New Orleanian architecture, cuisine, and people. It was breathtaking. And I fell hard. She was dating someone at the time, though, and paid me little more than a respectful amount of attention. I tried to forget about her afterward, losing myself in my Angola rotation by day and my burgeoning case study by night.

We would remeet months later at a crawfish boil hosted by a mutual friend. This time, she was single.

I proposed on Halloween night of 2017. Elsie has always been a huge horror movie fan, her favorite being *The Texas Chainsaw Massacre*. I got down on one knee, dressed as the blood-soaked heroine, Sally Hardesty; Elsie was Leatherface. I began my rehearsed speech, but before I could finish, she blurted, "I'm pregnant."

My eyes lit up. "Is that a yes?"

We kissed in the middle of Frenchman Street. She tossed her cardboard chainsaw over her shoulder like a bouquet.

She had fixed something in me that I couldn't admit was broken. And I swore I'd never let her get away again.

~

We heard something in the woods, off to our right.

Elsie froze. Gripped my hand.

The howling had stopped. Everything was silent.

Suddenly, a beastly figure charged out of the forest, knocked me down, grabbed my fiancée, and ran off into the brush with her cradled in his monstrous arms.

I followed her screams, trekking deeper into the woods, hollering after her.

When I finally caught up to the beast, he was posing in a

clearing, clutching a live chicken by the neck. Elsie was beaming, photographing him while the chicken flailed. We'd found what we were looking for: Mamou's traditional Courir de Mardi Gras. Forget the floats and beads and institutionalization of New Orleans. Mamou does Mardi Gras the old-school Medieval French way, with stampeding horses and hand-stitched costumes and chicken-chasing.

The costumed creature was festooned in furry strips of fabric and a headdress that was part bear and part wolf, with antlers twisting out the top. He flung the chicken into the air. The bird floated down in a flurry of panicked, flapping wings, where other "beasts" and "clowns" waited with open arms and drunken, cackling laughter.

After the chicken (and many others like it) had been transformed into a gumbo, we plopped down in bag chairs in the bed of a pickup, to eat. There, we made friends with the monster. His name was Louie, and he played fiddle in a local Cajun band. "I'm always the Rougarou," he boasted between bites.

Elsie stared, a bit puzzled.

"You don't know about the Rougarou, cher?" He guffawed, excited by the opportunity to regale us with his own legend. "Think Cajun werewolf: half man, half blood-hungry beast." The words poured from his smiling lips. "Prowlin' the swamps and the cane fields, lookin' to murder and pass along its terrible curse. Used to call it the Loup-Garou in France. Some 'round here still do." He shoveled another bite into his mouth. "Some ol' folks still talk 'bout all the Rougarous gettin' together once a year to dance at the Rougarou Ball. One minute, just normal folks like you and me. But then, that moon comes out, baby, and they turn straight on into something else."

Elsie was beaming. "Have you ever seen one?"

He took a sip from what was probably his twentieth beer of the day and grinned. "Look around you, cher."

All around the truck: judges and bankers and doctors and lawyers. Roughnecks and teachers and insurance salesmen. Fathers and sons. They howled and they danced and they chased livestock. They slaughtered chickens with their hands and flashed their genitals at anyone who would look. Through their masks, they poured beer and whiskey and vodka into their throats. And tomorrow, they would just be themselves again.

They might as well have been waltzing under the moon at the Rougarou Ball.

And for some reason I thought about Henri Judice.

DIFFERENTIAL DIAGNOSIS

My initial case study on the Cajun Cannibal for the *International Journal of Forensic Medicine* was published in April of 2017 and was met with little to no enthusiasm from my peers and senior advisors. It was focused on a sole pathology: antisocial personality disorder. I reasoned that for someone to have done the things Henri was accused of doing, he would have to be completely devoid of any compassion or sensitivity to human suffering. He would have to be an utter sociopath.

Case closed. Study published.

In 2018, just one year after the publication, the southern chapter of the American Academy of Psychiatry and the Law (AAPL) invited me to give a presentation on sociopathic behavior in serial killers at their conference in New Orleans. My résumé was thinner than the other presenters', but I had the distinct advantage of being a local (and not in need of hotel accommodations) as well as the Cajun Cannibal's cousin. This was my chance to redeem myself and erase the memory of my lackluster case presentation.

The Rougarou encounter in Mamou had given me pause. As I sat in my new home in Metairie, the light of dawn still an hour or so away, I couldn't help but think of those revelers in the field, of what they'd allowed themselves to become for just one day.

I reread my old notes, including Henri's conversation with Mitch. I realized I'd been careless with my case study and skipped a key step: the differential diagnosis, the list of other possible explanations for a patient's condition, no matter how far-fetched they might be. I started to suspect (and fear) that perhaps there was another potential explanation, that maybe my cousin *wasn't* a sociopath.

I had seen the photographs of Anders Barrilleaux's mutilated body. I'd seen the gash across Dane's shoulder. The chewed-up hand in the woods. And I'd seen the gruesome evidence from the five murders that followed. The crime scene photos. The autopsy reports. The witness accounts.

I returned to his final tape, the "suicide note" that had opened my original case presentation. "Am I evil? Am I a monster? Are those things real? Do they all just get passed along?" Henri mumbled. "I know what I see... when I look in the mirror sometimes... this curse. This rot. This infection." I no longer felt he was talking vaguely about the rot of humanity or the curse of his broken empathy. There was a different curse on his mind. Something more unbelievable.

Was it possible, I began to wonder, that Henri hadn't killed and eaten his victims because he'd lacked a bare minimum of empathy? Could his gregarious, charming persona have been a true display of decency rather than some Bundy-esque facade? Perhaps he did in fact feel regret and shame and disgust over what he'd done. Maybe, just maybe, he did it all because he was something else. Or, more precisely, because he *thought* he was something else.

A Rougarou.

I glanced out the window at the early morning darkness. A full moon hung on the horizon, staring at me.

And by the way, why all the superstitious fuss over full moons? There's been no evidence of any lunar effect on human behavior, despite terms like "lunatic" being common parlance, even clinical terminology at times in my own profession. The best anyone can figure is that the light afforded by a full moon gave history's poor bipolar souls in the throes of their manic all-nighters enough visibility to roam and terrorize their villages in pre-Edisonian days. But I don't know. I've seen mania up close, felt the panic and disarray pouring off my patients. And I know all too well the intensity, that inescapable feeling that your own veins are vibrating inside of you, the jolts of current surging through your brain as it shifts around in your skull. I've seen it too closely, felt its vibrations too deeply to believe that anyone afflicted would be very concerned with the amount of lumens available, that anyone would be slowed a single step by complete and total darkness.

So what of the moon?

I sat there in my study and stared at my notes with a shudder, and I began to suspect that Henri Elton Judice had believed he himself was the Rougarou. I set to work carving out a new addition to my case study.

~

I stood at the podium and set down my sweating glass of water. "Good after"—the echo of the PA system threw my rhythm—"noon." The Loews Hotel ballroom was more packed than I'd anticipated, much more so than the morning lecture on the metabolic impact of tricyclic antidepressants. It seems serial killers (and their cousins) draw a crowd.

"The title of my lecture today is 'Sociopathy and Culture-Bound Syndromes in Criminality: A Case Presentation on Henri Elton Judice, the Cajun Cannibal.' I'd like to talk about a slightly more obscure diagnosis as it may pertain to Judice."

Deep breath.

"Wendigo psychosis is not a condition found in the *Diagnostic and Statistical Manual of Mental Disorders*"—I could see the eyerolls among the first few rows of gray heads at the mere mention of wendigo—"though it could be classified under the section for 'culture-bound syndromes.' Features of wendigo psychosis include cannibalistic behavior in the context of other available food sources—in other, more evocative words, a taste for human flesh." A chuckle from the back. "The afflicted often cites a feeling of possession by or transformation into some other creature, helpless to intervene in his or her own actions, mirroring historical werewolf lore."

I clicked the overhead projector to begin my visuals, which highlighted the Rougarou legend and its relevancy even still in rural South Louisiana. The background photo was the one Elsie had taken of her abductor on Mardi Gras, clutching his prized chicken.

An unimpressed hand hovered above the sea of heads. I looked down to find Dr. Allen Schexnaildre, the department chair of my old training program and the president of the local AAPL chapter. I didn't even call on him before he started speaking in his usual bothered tone. "Dr. Blackburn. Question." That's when I knew the next sentence wouldn't be a question. "As I'm sure you're aware, wendigo psychosis, if it exists, is historically associated with northern Indigenous tribes, not any cultures associated with South Louisiana. It also bears little resemblance to cases of sociopathy, especially when gunshot wounds are involved, as is the case with Henri Elton Judice."

"True—" I admitted.

"True," the PA echoed before I could continue.

"Judice admitted to at least one of the shootings himself, correct? And one of his earlier victims, the game warden, had bullets in his chest. Not bite marks. Judice never publicly mentioned the Rougarou, and as far as I'm aware, he was never seen running around naked in the woods or howling at the moon or eating livestock or dancing in midnight balls."

He turned to the rest of the ballroom. "It's tempting in our profession to get swept up in the melodrama of these cases, to lose a sense of dispassionate objectivity. But when a patient is sitting across your desk, when a defendant is awaiting judgment based on your testimony, we must strive always for the appropriate balance of open-mindedness and skepticism."

He settled back into his chair and nodded for me to continue.

I clicked along through the PowerPoint presentation, skipping over any slides that mentioned wendigo. My hour-and-a-half lecture was over in just over thirty minutes.

The handshakes after came with cringes, my old colleagues shaking their heads and chuckling about my bad luck. *"Old Schexnaildre,"* their smirks said. *"Once a bastard, always a bastard."*

I skipped the rest of the conference, not out of embarrassment, but out of determination. Because I was right, and I knew it.

And the more I believed the unbelievable, the more terrified I became. My real trepidation lay not in his gruesome acts but in one simple ramification of his psychotic condition: genetics.

Psychosis typically carries a strong element of heritability, and I can't find any other evidence of thought disorders in our (considerably large Cajun) family. Sure, I've got a cousin who claims to have seen a ghost once. And yes, I have another cousin who doesn't believe in vaccines. But honestly, don't we all have a cousin who doesn't believe in vaccines? I myself have been on a mild antipsychotic regimen since my early thirties, but only for the purposes of mood stabilization and sleep maintenance, never for any signs of psychosis. The odds of overt psychosis for someone with an afflicted cousin are about three percent, triple that of the general population. At the last Judice family Christmas Eve soirée, we topped out at over one hundred attendees, nearly all of whom were directly related to Henri. Statistically speaking, three of us should have been psychotic. Three poor, vulnerable minds in that holly jolly room should have been lost, helplessly severed from the safe harbors of reality. Or at least on their merry way.

So where are we?

Where are the other schizophrenics? The deluded Judice minds unfit for the realities of the world? Was Henri an aberration? Or are we there, hiding in plain sight? Waiting.

Our daughter, Ivy, was born on July 4, 2018, a few months after that conference. Yet another twig in the overstuffed Judice family tree. I sat awake in the hospital room that first night, watching her sleep on my wife's chest, and thinking about the countless schizophrenics I'd treated in my years of practice. Their tortured minds. Their shell-shocked, haunted expressions. Their roles as outcasts, the new lepers in an intellectual society. And I thought about the thousands of genes I had passed along to that sleeping infant. How many did she share with the Cajun

Cannibal? Could something so perfect and angelic be at risk of such dreadful contamination? Was the threat already in there, lurking in her neurons? It was then that my obsession over Henri Judice's state of mind and the heritability of his condition became impossible to ignore.

If Henri Elton Judice had convinced himself that he was the Rougarou, if he had truly been that psychotic, was anyone else in my family doomed to a similar fate?

And was his delusion enough to explain what came next?

~

St. Martin Parish Sheriff's Office
400 St. Martin St., St. Martinville, LA 70582
November 16, 2008

MISSING PERSONS

The St. Martin Parish Sheriff's Office requests the public's assistance in locating the above pictured adults.

Angelle Reed (26), Tim Cormier (25), and Tim's younger brother Cole Cormier (17) were last seen around 2 p.m. on Friday, November 14, at McGee's Landing in Henderson, where Reed waitresses part-time. The trio left in Tim's black Toyota 4Runner for a camping trip to an unknown location. None checked in to work or school the following Monday. Family has been unable to contact any of the individuals in the week since.

Ms. Reed (around 5'5") has medium-length black hair with a distinctive white streak in the front. She was wearing a sky-blue toboggan hat and a white hoodie before leaving work that day.

Both Cormier boys are around 5'11", with short brown hair.

If you have any information on the whereabouts of the missing campers, please contact the St. Martin Parish Sheriff's Office.

PART II

PSYCHO KILLER

QU'EST-CE QUE C'EST?

November 27, 2008

THANKSGIVING MEANS GUMBO in Mama T's kitchen.

A gumbo starts with a roux, and a roux starts with flour and some type of fat, usually butter or oil. But Mama T does her fat one better. With every duck gumbo she completes, as the stew is simmering on the stove and aromatizing every cubic inch of the house with its perfection, Mama T skims the little layer of precious duck fat and gumbo grease that's risen to the top. Like most folks, she gets every last drop of the oil slick off the surface. But unlike most folks, Mama T doesn't throw it in the trash. She saves it, stowing it in a prized corner of her freezer. Forget vegetable oil or butter. Mama T's next gumbo starts with the rendered duck fat and gumbo grease from her last. Every batch you've had from her kitchen shares a bit of its DNA with the one before, and the one before that, and every other one she's made for the last twenty years. It all gets passed along.

Edward was happy to see her busying herself in his kitchen. Her myotonic dystrophy had begun to affect her gait lately. She'd been relying on her walker more than ever. Edward had offered to take over the gumbo prep this year, to which she scoffed, "You must be outta your mind! You'd probably put Old Bay in it, Baltimore Boy," and she shoved her walker aside in defiance. Edward's daughter, Nicole stood on a stool beside her, occasionally providing an approving taste test, watching each step of the process, concretizing it into her memory. One day, when Mama T was gone, Nicole might cook this very gumbo, and a piece of the old woman would be resurrected if only for an evening.

The doorbell rang and Edward perked up, recalling that moment on election night when everything seemed to be falling into place so perfectly, thinking about the way her hand fit into his.

He opened the door, but she wasn't there. Instead, he found Henri Judice and a stout Cajun standing on his porch. The Cajun held out a brown bag of cracklins, grease soaking the bottom into near translucency. "Doc!" he hollered. "Mitch Judice. Pleasure to meet your acquaintance!" Edward led them inside, and Mitch took in the foyer. "Wow, Doc. Quite the falatial abode you got here. That walnut?" He marched ahead for an inspection of the banister, and Edward thanked Henri for coming.

Once in the kitchen, Mitch started crunching away on cracklins and chatting up Mama T. Turns out she knew his cousin Clyde. Yes, Clyde was still living out in Duson. Yes, he was still raising emus. "Got eggs the size of footballs!" Mitch guffawed. "You know them bad boys gotta hurt comin' out."

Yvette arrived about ten minutes later. She was clad in jeans and a button-down blouse, but her weary smile was still dressed for work. Darden had recently doubled down, smelling blood in the water. His campaign was hinting at every chance that Henri might have had something to do with Dane's murder. Darden had called on Yvette to bring Henri in for questioning once again, but this time with a more impartial group of state police overseeing the interview. She'd refused, knowing it was all a dog and pony show to get a picture of Henri in cuffs. *"Sheriff's Son Brought in on Suspicion of Murder."* She could see it now. Besides, she had already talked to her boy. Looked him in the eye. He'd never lie to her. She was sure.

Maybe a part of her had hoped Henri would volunteer. Go in and clear the whole thing up. For his own good as well as hers. But she would never force him to. Her love was bigger than that.

Many in Yvette's own base had begun to turn their backs as well, unable to stomach her hesitancy to hold "Elton Judice's boy" accountable for the possible murder of Dane, her Black biological son.

Around eight fifteen, Yvette got a phone call and left abruptly, without much explanation other than "work." Mitch stood to leave not long after, wanting to get home in time to catch the end of *Who Wants to Be a Millionaire?* And when Henri told Mitch he wanted to finish his beer first, Edward offered to drive Henri home.

As if to confirm Yvette's election-night suspicions that the game warden and the doctor were growing increasingly and uncharacteristically friendly, Henri did stay behind. They sat and stoked the fire and watched the football game. And then the local news report cut into the game.

"I remember that part very clearly," Edward said of the breaking news. "That reporter was standing out there in front of that boy's 4Runner. The second it popped up, Henri was leaning forward. Ears perked up. Seemed he knew exactly what it meant."

The in-house anchor threw to reporter Nina Blankenship.

She stood before a black SUV parked alongside a small coulee, which ran beneath a low rectangular culvert in the distance. Two squad cars sat atop the culvert, flashing their lights on the scene. Blankenship began: "Scott, police here on the scene are still light on details at the moment. But what we do know is that St. Landry Parish police were called earlier this evening about an SUV that matched the description of missing camper Tim Cormier's black 4Runner. Cormier, his brother Cole, and friend Angelle Reed were reported missing last week, and authorities have had very few leads up to this point." The pictures of the three missing campers appeared on the screen. Angelle Reed beamed under a sky-blue toboggan hat. The Cormier boys were posing before the Roman colosseum in their picture, taken during their backpacking trip that August. "I've been given confirmation that the vehicle behind me is in fact Cormier's 4Runner, but there is still no word about whether there are any signs of the three missing campers in the area."

"Let's go," Henri said, and started for Edward's vehicle. But as Edward recalled and the news footage confirms, Nina Blankenship had not offered any details about the location of the scene. When pressed on this fact later, Judice would claim that he recognized the culvert on the screen as a spot off LA 31 that he frequented on his patrol. He said he knew it well.

≈

Yvette had been at the scene for only half an hour when she saw Edward's Audi SUV pull up. She sighed, knowing full well who was riding shotgun.

"Let him through," she muttered to the officer guarding the perimeter, before Henri even got out of the vehicle, because she didn't want the fight.

Henri stormed into the crime scene, Edward sheepishly dragging ass behind him. A few deputies kept a judgmental eye on the increasingly meddlesome game warden.

"Angelle. Is she here?" Henri demanded.

"No one's here," Yvette said. "Just the car."

Henri started scanning the ground around them, presumably looking for tracks or any evidence left behind.

Still Yvette didn't stop him or have him taken away from a dark, sprawling crime scene that was just begging to be compromised. She simply tried to ignore him and focus on her work. Edward could tell she was peeved at their presence. "Sorry," he offered. "He's ... um, he's persuasive, isn't he?"

She smiled weakly. "Yeah. Sorry about taking off."

"You should get a planner. So you don't double-book like this. It's just embarrassing." For the briefest of seconds, her smile turned genuine.

"Sheriff!" a deputy shouted from down the coulee. Yvette rushed over.

Between a pair of collecting tongs, the deputy held a three-foot stretch of nylon rope, pink on mint green and frayed only slightly at the ends. Yvette leaned in to examine it a little more closely. It was fairly clean, unfaded, still pliable. Hadn't been out there long. "That all?" Yvette asked.

"Yeah."

"Bag it. And keep looking." She drew a deep breath, readying herself for an attempt at getting Henri out of her hair and on his way home. But when she turned around, he and Edward were gone.

She spotted Edward's Audi turning onto LA 31 and taking off into the night.

PULLING THREADS

HENRI HARDLY SPOKE a word on the drive from the 4Runner to his house. Edward still wasn't even sure why they had left so abruptly.

The home was dark; Henri didn't bother turning on a light or even a lamp.

He strode straight into his bedroom, and began rifling through his dresser drawers, tossing notebooks and logbooks aside until he found what he was looking for.

The double bed barely fit in the cramped quarters. Laundry littered the floor. Edward could hardly find a place to stand. There were no pictures on the walls. No curtains over the blinds.

Henri opened a logbook dated 2005, flipping frantically through the pages.

"Henri? What the hell's going on?"

"Just a second!" the game warden barked back. "Here. Look at this." He shoved the book into Edward's hands.

Edward mumbled aloud whatever he could make of the chicken scratch. "Leonard Pinkley... citation... hunting deer out of season. Okay, so what?"

Henri took it back. "That asshole—Leonard Fucking

Pinkley—was one of the dumbest sons of bitches I ever stopped. And that's saying something. Caught him hunting deer in September. Bastard tried to talk his way out of it, saying I musta made a mistake. Meanwhile, he's got the damn thing tied to the hood of his car about twenty feet behind him."

"I'm not following."

Henri ignored the prompt and flipped to the next page, but he didn't seem to find anything useful. He dove back into the drawer, now digging through piles of cassette tapes. Finally, he found one from September 2005, inserted into a portable player on the dresser, and hit "Play."

It took a few tries of fast-forwarding and rewinding before he found the day in question. Then his voice crackled to life on the speaker:

...Leonard Pinkley of Krotz Springs. Address is...21 Kildee Lane. Seven other violations in the system, three for hunting ducks out of season, one for deer, three illegal perch traps without a commercial license. As for evidence, well, the genius had the deer tied up to his hood with a length of rope and a mess of loose, haphazard knots...if you can even call them that. I'm guessing he never even learned to tie his shoes. On that note, he *was* wearing shrimping boots, so I may be onto something there. And as for the rope he used...Nylon. About fifty to seventy-five feet. Pink and mint green..."

He clicked "Stop" and looked up at Edward.

"Shit," the doctor muttered.

"Exactly. Just like the rope they found out there tonight. Pink and mint-green nylon."

"Okay, but that could just be a coincidence."

"I thought so too at first, but then I remembered something. Something I'd completely forgotten until tonight. Typically, hunting out of season will get you nearly a grand in fines and even some jail time, especially with a record like his. But I remember I let Pinkley go with just a minimum fine of a hundred and fifty bucks."

"Why?"

Henri fast-forwarded a bit and pressed "Play."

...decided to send Pinkley home with a minimum fine. I spoke on the phone with his cousin, Troy Langlinais, who has assured me he will make sure Pinkley finds something better to do with his time than hunt deer.

Click. Henri gazed up at Edward.

"Troy Langlinais..." Edward repeated.

"That's right. I knew him from back in the day...high school." Henri's eyes looked away, back at the dresser. "Anyway, I let Pinkley go. But now..."

Edward finished his thought for him. "Pink and green nylon rope, connection to Langlinais..."

Henri stood. "I say we pay Mr. Pinkley a visit."

"Okay, I'll cancel my clinic. We can go first thing in the morning."

Henri's eyes gleamed. "We can go now."

EYEWITNESS

Henri steered his truck along the empty backroads and twisting bayou scenic routes, Edward peering ahead into the darkness from the passenger seat. The new moon proved stingy, withholding any light from their wide-open, starving pupils. But even in the dead of night, Henri seemed to know every twist and turn better than Edward knew his own subdivision.

In the thick fog, Henri's headlights stopped dead ten feet in front of them. After a minute or two, Edward spotted a buckshot-riddled street sign reading "Kildee Ln." Henri turned onto the narrow gravel lane that snaked alongside a ditch, winding through a thicket of dense woods. The trees hanging overhead made Edward feel like he was entering a tunnel to another realm.

Soon, a wooden sign appeared with "21" painted in white. There was a sideways bucket next to it, staked into the ground, which Edward took for a mailbox. Henri turned onto the dirt drive indicated.

"Shit!" Henri shouted and slammed on the brakes, just inches away from rear-ending a pickup truck blocking the way. It had an old, boxy body type and plenty of rust to accent what was left of its olive-green paint. The front bumper was wrapped around a tree.

Henri climbed out first, grabbing his gun and his badge. Edward followed with nothing but a flashlight.

The driver side door was ajar, the interior damp and covered in mildew. The vinyl bench seat was crisscrossed with strips of duct tape, patching up years of cracks in the upholstery. Most of it was tan, but the bulk of the passenger end was sticky and black with what appeared to be old coagulated blood. The window on that side was shattered. Glass shrapnel crunched under their feet on the ground outside the door. The window had been broken from the inside.

The registration in the glove box was made out to Leonard Pinkley.

"Pinkley's truck," Henri muttered. "Guess he upgraded from the sedan."

"Who the hell hits a tree in their own driveway?" Edward wondered aloud.

He pointed the flashlight down the drive, but the house was still invisible.

Behind them, they suddenly heard the grating sound of metal scraping along gravel. They froze. The sound disappeared for a moment, and they wondered if they'd both imagined it, when it returned. Louder.

Closer.

They ducked into the tree line beside the truck.

The scraping grew louder. And louder.

It was almost impossible to see anything in the near pitch-black darkness, but Edward thanked God that Henri's headlights were still on, bouncing at least a little ambience off the trees and into the fog. Finally, just when Edward thought the scraping sound was coming from inside his own skull, they spotted movement.

Just around the bend, a pit bull limped out of the fog, dragging a chain from his neck. A large metal spike dangled from the other end, scraping up gravel in its wake. In contrast to the beast's imposing frame, his emaciated belly and heaving ribs betrayed weeks of hunger. Gobs of foam dripped from his jowls.

The dog panted in slow, pained grunts and limped past them. Past the wildlife and fisheries truck and past Pinkley's wreck, down the drive, toward the house.

Edward turned, whispering, "Let's get the hell . . ."

But Henri was already following the dog down the drive.

Edward hesitated and then hurried after him.

It took a full minute of stalking after the panting sound before they could see the house. At first, Edward assumed they'd taken a wrong turn. He couldn't imagine anyone living in there at any point in this century. The wooden strips of paneling had peeled and rotted long ago, and the rust-brown roof sagged and buckled under a decade's worth of fallen leaves and pine needles.

They followed the dog's heavy wheezing around the back of the house. And then it stopped. In the stillness, Edward could just faintly make out the sound of running water nearby.

A wet, smacking sound drew his attention. Gnawing and grinding. Edward moved forward, despite himself.

He aimed the flashlight up. It landed on the dog's blue-gray hindquarters. The thing was bent over, oblivious to the light. Eating something.

Edward angled around slightly until he finally spotted the pit bull's meal: the carcass of another dog, a pit bull too, by the looks of it. What was left of its white body and pink face was still chained to the ground. This one hadn't managed to pull free.

The blue dog finally looked up and glared at Edward, who only responded by freezing on the spot. Bloody chunks of meat fell from the animal's jaws, and a thick wet tongue lapped up whatever was left around its muzzle.

It dove back into the carcass for some more.

Edward backed away, scanning the fog for signs of Henri. He was over along the side of the house, crouching in the overgrown grass. Edward ambled over to him. Henri was holding something. He aimed the flashlight to find a tangle of rope.

Pink and green nylon.

In Henri's other hand, a sky-blue toboggan hat, just like the one that Angelle Reed girl was wearing in the picture.

"What are you doing?!" Edward hissed.

"It's him. I fucking knew it."

"That's evidence. Put it down!"

Henri stood up. "Go back to the truck and call for help."

"I'm not going anywhere." He wasn't sure why he said it. Maybe it was loyalty to his new friend. Maybe it was the fact that his new friend had a gun on his hip, and he didn't. Maybe it was something else entirely. But Edward wasn't about to let Henri out of his sight.

A little click startled him, followed by a rattling hum. Something electrical running inside the house.

They snuck around to the front porch. No railing. Buckled posts for pillars. A single window there, but it was impossible to see inside for all the dust and film caked onto the outside and all the darkness within.

Henri stepped onto the porch. It bowed at least an inch

under his boots. Edward lowered the flashlight's beam. A black streak of blood smeared across the wooden planks, from the door down into the yard.

Edward glanced back down the drive, reconsidering Henri's instructions to go back, imagining the truck and thinking about how many steps it would take and how dark the night was and how, if anything happened to Henri, Edward didn't have a set of keys.

His racing mind was interrupted by the sound of a knock.

He turned to find Henri's hammering fist still hovering at the door.

Eeeeeekkkk.

The door creaked open.

Henri glanced back at Edward momentarily. "Guess it was open." The cavernous black inside the house felt as if it might inhale them both.

Henri cleared his throat and called into the house, "Wildlife and Fisheries! Anybody home?"

Silence.

He nudged the door open a bit more with his foot and stepped inside. "Wildlife and Fisheries! Is there anybody here?"

Edward followed Henri inside the house, greeted by the smell of sour sweat and mold. In one corner, all the furniture and miscellanea had been piled up, making space for a clearing in the middle of the living room. A solid black circle marked the center of the room, where the floor had been charred and burned from what must have been a fire.

"If anybody's in here," Henri hollered, "come the fuck out now!"

Edward scanned the walls. Shuffling closer, he saw torn

shreds of wallpaper. Even the wood paneling behind the torn paper had been scraped and clawed at.

"Something in here really wanted to get out."

Breaking from his trance, Edward turned to see Henri inching down the hallway toward a mystery door, his gun drawn and ready. "Doc," he whispered, "get that light ready."

Against all his instincts, Edward stepped out from behind Henri and positioned himself at his side, staring down the closed door. Henri wrapped his fingers around the doorknob. A deep breath. He turned the knob.

The rusty knob ground against the back plate. In the silence, it might as well have been a bag of pots and pans tumbling down stairs.

With a burst, Henri threw the door open and stormed into the room.

Edward's flashlight swept over the stillness inside.

An old, yellowing mattress lay on the floor, torn open down the middle, stuffing spilling out into a sort of makeshift nest. Dirt and leaves and hair were twisted and tangled into the stuffing.

The walls around them were adorned with a macabre collection of fantasized taxidermy. One stuffed creature had started out life as a squirrel, but in death had had a rabbit's head sewn onto its body. Another, a raccoon sprouting the black wings of a crow where its front limbs had once been. Its face had been contorted into an unnatural and unholy grimace to reveal its collection of sharp teeth, its muzzle wrinkled and gathered in a way no living thing could manage.

Henri maneuvered to the closed closet door, and Edward realized that if something were to spring out, he'd have no furniture in the room to hide behind. The game warden slid the door open, allowing the beam of the flashlight inside. Nothing but a pile of clothes.

They headed back into the main living quarters. Edward began to consider making the long trip back to Henri's truck to get his phone.

Henri, for his part, started rummaging through drawers and cupboards.

The window AC unit rattled and hummed, and Edward's mind couldn't help but contemplate what faulty parts might account for the racket.

The AC cut off.

Suddenly, Edward could hear a new sound. An electrical buzz coming from his left, just through the open door.

He poked his head inside.

A bathroom. Or some semblance of one. A bathtub remained, but the toilet and sink had been ripped out of the floor. In their place, a deep freezer. He moved into the room toward the bathtub. The closer he got, the farther away he wanted to be. Bloodstains caked the inside of the tub. And at the center, rope. A series of bowline knots, still tight in the lines, as if someone had either managed to squeeze out—which seemed unlikely— or had never gotten untied. The blood stains were shiny.

He turned to reach for the freezer but was stopped by the bang of the front door being thrown open. Heart hammering, Edward dropped into a crouch.

Henri's voice cut through. "What the fuck!"

BOOM. The blast of a rifle filled the house.

Followed by a dull thud.

Edward waited on the bathroom floor, face pressed into the filthy linoleum, for God knew how long. He finally mustered the courage to leave the bathroom. There on the living room floor, he saw Troy Langlinais's lifeless, naked body.

Langlinais's entire being was caked in mud and blood and filth. A gaping wound climbed from the top of his abdomen up to his chest. It was old and ragged and poorly healed, black and red around the edges. A hole in his head was emptying the stuff inside him out onto the floor, mixing in with whatever else was there.

A rifle lay beside him.

Henri was across the room, bracing himself against the wall and still holding onto his pistol, as if waiting for Jason Voorhees to spring back to life for one last jump scare. He turned to Edward, his face white as a ghost. "Jesus H. Christ."

EVIDENCE

(Excerpts originally published in the
International Journal of Forensic Medicine)

THE FREEZER WAS a white three-by-two-foot box standing just under a meter tall. A frayed extension cord connected it by way of a three-to-two prong adapter to the bathroom's only outlet. At least two detectives would later note the loud buzz emitted by the machine, loud enough even to be heard from just outside the bathroom when the window AC unit was running. Langlinais had bought it secondhand sometime in September from a friend of a friend who described the cash transaction as "unsettling."

It was a fairly unremarkable home appliance but for its curious placement in the bathroom. That and the contents inside.

After managing to settle his heart rate to an acceptable level of panic, Edward finally decided that someone should run back to the truck for a phone.

He studied Henri, who was sitting in the corner of the kitchen, staring at his hands. "Henri?"

The game warden didn't move.

"Henri," he repeated more sternly. Finally, Henri glanced up, but he didn't seem to be in any condition to do much of anything useful. Edward spoke calmly. "Don't touch anything until I get back, you understand?"

Henri nodded, his face still a blank slate. "Yeah. I got it."

Edward grabbed the keys from Henri and raced down the lane to the truck. The dawn was just beginning to hint at an entrance, and the path was at least a little more navigable than it had been on the way in.

Edward reached into Henri's truck and grabbed his phone from the passenger seat. He found a pair of work gloves in the back cab and ran back to the house.

When he got back, Henri was still in the kitchen where he'd left him. Edward donned the gloves and headed into the bathroom. Only once he was inside, staring at the freezer, did he notice Henri had followed him and was now hovering in the bathroom doorway.

Edward considered waiting, knew it would be best to leave this part to the police. But he couldn't help himself. He had to know what was inside. Henri seemed totally incurious. As if he already knew.

Edward grabbed the lid with a gloved hand and lifted. The door stuck at first, so Edward gripped it with both hands and lifted harder.

It opened, and Edward peered in.

Frost lined the sides and the lid in thick sheets. At first, all that seemed to be inside were some packs of raw ground beef, but then he noticed something poking up from between the packs. A blue finger with purple nail polish.

He nudged the packs aside and found the rest of the fingers and the hand they belonged to, all the way down to the wrist. The rest of the arm was buried deeper inside.

He closed the lid and called Yvette.

~

Investigators arrived about twenty minutes later. They taped off the room, collected samples, dusted for prints. As Edward photographed the body, detectives huddled around the freezer, cramped in the small confines of the bathroom. They gently lifted the lid and gazed inside.

Under the top layer of frost, they found four human arms, three human legs, one human heart, one human tongue, one hindquarter from a wild hog, three pounds of raw ground beef, and one squirrel, whole and unskinned. The squirrel was determined to have been placed in alive, judging by the tiny scratches and gnaw marks it imparted on the human remains that it had suddenly found sharing its frigid tomb.

Beneath all of this, they found the head of Leonard Pinkley, staring up at them through white, frost-coated eyes.

Yvette stormed in as the detectives were sorting through the frozen items, trying to match off pairs of limbs and get an idea of how many individuals were accounted for. She looked at Langlinais's naked corpse on the floor before her gaze found Henri in the corner. The officer beside him had already confiscated his gun and his knife.

The mother and son stared at each other silently, then Yvette finally looked at the officer and said, "Put him in my car."

She got a report from the lead detective, said nothing to Edward, and left.

Henri was already inside Yvette's Blazer when she got behind the wheel. She didn't even turn to look at him. Henri opened his mouth to speak, but he was cut off immediately as Yvette barked something, started the Blazer, and then drove off.

After the mess at Pinkley's, Joey Darden would successfully convince investigators with the Louisiana State Police Department to get involved. They brought Henri and Edward in to give official statements. Henri stayed behind for further questioning while Edward was let go after his initial conversation with State Detective Beals. The video transcript of Edward's questioning paints an interesting picture of someone drawn into Henri's web:

The room is small, a two-way mirror to Edward's back. State Detective Beals sits across from Edward. Shiny bald head. Mustache. Southern twang. He consults a file on the flimsy table between them.

Detective Beals: So how exactly did you and Agent Judice get to be so chummy in the first place?

Edward Harper: I went over to his house a few weeks ago. I wanted to talk through a theory I had at the time.

DB: What kind of theory?

EH: I just thought that there were some similarities between Dane Fuselier's autopsy and a recent patient of mine. Supposedly a bear attack.

DB: Similarities?

EH: Yeah. Nothing specific. Just a hunch. Trying to get to the bottom of things.

DB: And here you are. At the bottom of things.

EH: Yeah. Here I am.

DB: So, you guys hit it off, you give him all the info you have, and then y'all find yourselves at a fresh crime scene out by the culvert. *Then* he takes you to his trailer, reads all of these notes, and plays all of these tapes for you, right then and there?

EH: Yes, sir.

DB: Seems he really wanted to know about all the info you had. And he really, *really* wanted you to know all of the info he had on Pinkley.

EH: I'm not sure what you're getting at.

DB: I just mean, do you think it's at all possible that Agent Judice saw that rope out there, got nervous, thought maybe he'd slipped up and gotten sloppy? Maybe he wanted to make sure someone was around to help him . . . stumble upon new evidence. Evidence that might point away from him. To someone like Langlinais and Pinkley?

EH: That's not what happened.

DB: Don't worry. I'm not implying you're in on it or gullible or anything. I'm just wondering. Just thinking out loud.

~

Within two hours, detectives had gathered enough evidence to connect Langlinais to each of the killings: Fuselier, Pinkley, and the campers. [Barrilleaux's death was still considered nothing more than a bear attack at this point.]

First, there were Langlinais's fingerprints, which were all over the house and had also been found on at least four different spots on and in the campers' Toyota 4Runner. A bundle of the pink and mint-green rope was found under the kitchen sink, beside a pocketknife that was lousy with Langlinais's prints.

The rifle beside Langlinais's corpse had prints on it as well. Most of them belonged to Pinkley (the firearm was registered to him). But there was one print on the grip that was a match to Langlinais. The fact that it was a match to his left hand—Langlinais was right-handed—was never explained.

Limbs found in the freezer were matched and identified as belonging to two of the missing three campers, Angelle Reed and Tim Cormier. A sample of blood pulled from the bathtub belonged to the younger Cormier brother, Cole.

By late that evening, canines had sniffed out three burial sites around Pinkley's house. One of the sites contained a partially decomposed human torso, along with both femurs, which had been picked clean of flesh prior to burial. The torso's arms were severed but present; they each retained varying degrees of muscle tissue, most of which had been degraded into mush by the elements. The left arm had been relieved of its hand at the precise location that would match the missing hand found in the woods near Langlinais's camper. Forensics were later able to match the remains and the severed hand to the owner of the property, Leonard Pinkley. The other two sites had assorted human remains presumed (and later confirmed) to be those of Angelle Reed and Tim Cormier. Much of Angelle's torso was intact, with minimal decomposition, and it was determined that while no sexual penetration had likely occurred, her breasts had been eaten first. What was left of Angelle's head was found in the farthest site. Tim's was never unearthed. Aside from the blood and some hair samples gathered from the bathtub, police found no remains belonging to Cole Cormier at the scene. He was a large young man, an athlete, and there was some hope that he might have overpowered his abductor and escaped.

The dried blood on the passenger seat of Pinkley's truck would later be matched to the truck's owner as well. It was thought that Pinkley had taken Langlinais night hunting along Bayou Courtableau in the months since August. A truck matching its description had been seen rumbling along by Mom 'n' Pop's Stop 'n' Shop by at least one witness. Detectives determined that at some point Langlinais attacked Leonard Pinkley and left his severed hand behind, then drove him, bloody and dying, back to the house. In all the chaos, he must have wrecked his truck turning into the driveway and tried to finish the job there. Pinkley had made one last attempt at an escape, breaking through the passenger window. But the effort was too little, too late.

Henri's account of what happened was consistent enough with Edward's that he had been released from custody by early afternoon. The stories lined up perfectly, which, given the usual unreliability of eyewitness testimony, Joey Darden found just as suspicious as if the two accounts had been complete contradictions. But the state investigators reminded him that they couldn't hold a man in custody because his story was too consistent with other eyewitness testimony, and Judice was released for an official debriefing with Wildlife and Fisheries, usual procedure for an agent having to fire on an armed civilian in self-defense.

When Joey Darden asked the interviewer if Judice had seemed guilty throughout questioning, Detective Beals answered, "I'm not real sure."

"Okay..." Darden tried to restrain his frustration. "So how did he seem?"

The detective measured his words carefully. "He seemed... like he was pretty good at pretending to be okay. He seemed like he'd had a lot of practice at it."

MORE TO THE STORY

September—October 2019

THERE ARE MOMENTS in your life when you arrive at two diverging paths. Inevitably, whether by fate or choice or a combination of the two, you'll either become one version of yourself or another. I could have been up in Boston, cheering for the Red Sox, with some strange, beautiful wife, in some strange, beautiful house.

But as fate would have it, I returned home to Louisiana instead.

Another such junction was on its way in September 2019.

The phone buzzed on my desk, waking me from an accidental nap. The area code was for Durham, North Carolina, which almost certainly meant a headhunter. These calls came all the time. I was happy with my clinic in New Orleans and our home in the Metairie suburbs, and moreover, I was uninterested in thrusting any more upheaval into our lives. Since Ivy's birth in July, it seemed that our lives belonged to someone else, which was true in more ways than one. We'd been placed into the role of parents, like a new set of skin. And now, every decision revolved around this little stranger who depended on us. More change was the last thing I needed, and so I tapped the phone screen to hang up on the call. And I let my eyes close again.

But as fate would have it, I was a new father, which, by definition, meant that I was sleep deprived and stupid.

"Dr. Blackburn? Hello? Dr. Blackburn?" Her voice cut in thinly from the phone that I had, it turns out, not hung up.

Annoyed, I picked it up. "Sorry. I'm afraid I can't really talk now."

"Just calling to talk with you about an exciting position—"

"In my area. Yeah, I know."

"—in Breaux Bridge, Louisiana," she continued.

Breaux Bridge. Just a few miles south of St. Landry Parish, the site where all my focus for the last five years had been aimed. Ground zero for my obsession.

I kept listening.

I mentioned the job offer to Elsie a few days later, casually over dinner, as an interesting but still absurd notion.

"Then again," I continued after a few seconds of silence, "it might be a good opportunity to raise Ivy somewhere smaller. Quieter." I chewed on a bite of pork. We could get twice the house in Breaux Bridge. Even a proper dark room for Elsie's photography. Plus, the reduced hours would provide me more free time, which I would be able to devote to my family. I suddenly had lots of reasons as to why this absurd notion actually made sense. After a few weeks of vacillation, we accepted the job offer.

In October of 2019, we bought a four-bedroom house with a big backyard near Main Street, and within the month, we were Breaux Bridgers.

Weeks went by and we settled into our home nicely. I went to work during the day and decorated the house at night, always trying to sneak some of Elsie's portfolio into the halls of our homes, where I knew I'd pass them up close on a daily basis. My absolute favorites were the photographs she had taken while on a clandestine trip to her parents' home country of Cuba. The old men playing dominos in Old Havana. The vaca frita cooling on an afternoon window, its steam captured in a slant of sunlight.

She walked in while I was hanging the last photograph, a portrait of her hugging her grandparents, her back to the camera. As I studied her grandmother's hands, the knobby knuckles and liver-spotted skin, I caught Elsie's reflection in the glass, the author of her own past. And before she could say a word, it all came rushing out of me: the failure I felt every time I thought about the case study and the presentation. The story with no end. My story. My ongoing uncertainty about whether Henri Judice was just a run-of-the-mill sociopath or something else. Some other kind of killer. The proximity of it all taunting as I took my daily drives to work. Everything.

She listened. We shared a bottle of wine. And when I was done, I blurted, "I think it's a book." She smiled at me, settled into my lap, and said, "If you don't find yourself, someone else will do it for you." She took one last sip of wine and whispered, "Just make sure you don't get lost along the way, yeah?"

In late October, I resumed my search for answers.

I wound through old microfilm of local newspapers at the library. I perused the big box bookstores' local sections for pulpy "histories" on my cousin like *Carnival of the Cajun Cannibal* and *The Warden's Game*. I read both in one all-nighter. Music no longer accompanied me on my drives; my car radio was devoted to true-crime podcasts. Even when my daughter rode in the car seat behind me, her infantile ears were subjected to homicide reconstructions and autopsy details. I replayed Henri's old field notes, documenting anything that could be considered noteworthy. I have to admit that hearing his voice on those old recordings sent a shiver down my spine sometimes late at night. My intimate knowledge of those notorious and vicious murders added an eeriness to every word he uttered through my earbuds. The breaths he huffed between thoughts rustled down the intimate corridors of my ear canals, there in the weak spot where my very own skull opened up and invited him in. Sometimes I had to check that I was still alone.

And other times, with his voice in my ear, it felt as if the recordings were all mine. As if he were talking just to me.

But it wasn't me he was talking to.

One evening, I was listening to an old field recording, one I must have heard a dozen times already: the discovery of Leonard Pinkley's hand, as Henri and Officer Brian Degeyter trekked through the woods:

HJ: I said, come on! We gotta get outta here. I dropped my fuckin' knife somewhere back by the truck. I want to go find it.

BD: Alright. Hold your horses, Judice. This shit's thick out here.

HJ: You can do it, Degeyter. Just pump those little flat feet. [He lowers his voice back to a whisper.] I swear, Brit, if this is what passes for police around here, no wonder Ma's so tired all the time. I'm about ready to just . . .

The recording continued. Degeyter hollered when he found the hand. Henri began documenting the details. He paused for several seconds and seemed to consider his next move. Then he turned the tape off.

But my mind was still stuck on the beginning.

I'd always considered this tape to be consistent with Judice's other official field notes, especially the more obsessive ones that had followed Dane Fuselier's death. He griped about his constant surveillance, and then, upon finding the hand, he systematically detailed the time and place of Degeyter's discovery.

But now, it was obvious to me that this recording had begun in a very different fashion from the others. It was personal. And not in the usual way that Judice would often digress into opinions on the state of the world or the ineptitude of the St. Landry Parish Sheriff's Department. This one *began* as a reflection on his current state of frustration. And then, the word that caught my attention: "Brit."

Brittany Judice, Henri's ex-wife.

This recording wasn't an official log, at least not until Degeyter stumbled upon the severed hand, at which point Henri carefully recorded the details of the discovery and saved the tape for reference. It was stored away with his other patrol logs and found there by investigators, who would cite Judice's multiple attempts to lure Degeyter away from the scene as evidence of his guilt and his knowledge that he might have left evidence behind in the area.

But before the discovery of the hand, this was quite obviously being recorded as a sort of personal note to his ex-wife.

Which started me wondering: Were there more of these personal recordings, ones that he hadn't kept for reference?

Was there an untapped pile of evidence hiding somewhere?

I finally decided to track down the ex–Mrs. Judice.

BRITTANY

HENRI AND BRITTANY had met at the 1996 Fur and Wildlife Festival in Cameron, Louisiana, one of the state's four hundred annual festival events. Brittany Alleman had been talked into competing in the festival's beauty pageant, and Henri had talked his way into being a judge. He'd swapped roles with Mitch, who then filled in for Henri in the nutria-skinning competition. "Just as well," Mitch said of the swap. "That boy couldn't skin a nutria if it had a zipper on it."

Brittany won the coveted crown of Miss Fur and Wildlife, no thanks to Henri. He'd cast his vote for the runner-up, Missy Morvant, a decision that would haunt him for most of his married life. He would later claim to Brittany that he hadn't thought he had a shot with her, so he aimed a little lower. What else was he supposed to say?

After the competition, they met behind the stage. Henri congratulated her, and she snubbed him over his errant vote, which was regrettably not on a secret ballot. But when he smiled an apology and made to go try his luck with a suddenly humbled Missy Morvant, Brittany grabbed his arm and said, "Aren't you gonna at least make it up to me with dinner?"

They made a nice couple, admired by both his friends and hers. They complimented and took the piss out of each other in equal measure. Building up and taking down a notch to maintain a lovable equilibrium. They fit together. Two gears that spun in perfect synchronization. But over time, the gears bit and chewed at each other, ground the cogs down and began to slip just enough to grind even more. Their playful jabs and barbs became a little more venomous. Before long, there was no turning back.

After the separation, Henri rented a trailer at a mobile home park near Krotz Springs, Louisiana, on the other side of the parish from the home that he and Brittany had once shared. One evening, he drunkenly stumbled through their old bedroom door around eight thirty, while Brittany was stepping out of the shower. He claimed to have come home out of habit, exhausted from post-storm cleanup efforts and having forgotten that he lived someplace else now. When his ex-wife wrapped the robe around her body like a frightened stranger, he left with his tail tucked between his legs.

She had the locks changed two days later.

But the mortgage bills and utilities kept coming in the mail and piling up on the kitchen counter, all of them bearing his name. Within a few months, she'd disappeared from St. Landry Parish, eventually landing about three hours north in Shreveport, in the two-story home that had recently belonged to her grandmother.

After Henri died and the nature of who he'd been and what he'd done had finally come to light, something in Brittany broke.

On the morning of Friday, February 13, 2009, she drove her Honda Civic to the First Federal Bank in Shreveport and withdrew $402.03, every penny she had in checking. The teller would later say, "I thought maybe she was sleepwalking, she looked so out of it." It probably didn't help that she was still wearing her robe.

She got back into her car and threw it into drive rather than reverse. She pressed on the gas and drove straight through the bank's double glass doors. A local shop teacher was in the doorway, and Brittany's front bumper pulverized his leg eighteen centimeters up, a full two and a half centimeters higher than a standard Honda Civic bumper, indicating to authorities that the car was in full acceleration at the time. She pinned him against the doorframe for seven seconds, reversed the car about ten feet, then accelerated into him again.

A security guard was able to break her window and drag her out of the vehicle, which continued to idle into the fallen teacher's neck for another twenty seconds, propping him between the car and the brick wall.

He spent two weeks in the ICU and never walked again.

Some said that before his tragic injuries, he bore a passing resemblance to Henri Judice.

Brittany's attorney successfully pleaded not guilty by reason of insanity and had her admitted to the forensic wing of the Central State Psychiatric Hospital in Pineville, Louisiana.

On October 21, 2019, I made the drive up to Pineville to see her for myself.

LA MAISON GRANDE

October 21, 2019

BUILT IN 1849, West State Hospital was the first mental health facility in Louisiana. It initially consisted of a two-story Acadian-style house with twelve rooms. In 1880, Dr. Elias Washington of Shreveport took over the hospital and, bemoaning the overcrowded living quarters, began construction on what would be known thereafter as "La Maison Grande." The Greek revival mansion, which at fifty feet dwarfed the original building and boasted six massive columns along the marble front porch, was built almost entirely by the patients admitted there. Over the following century, five other buildings of progressively diminishing size would be erected by the inhabitants of West State.

By the early twenty-first century, the state-run facility was already scraping the bottom of the budget, and only La Maison Grande was still in operation. The other buildings were either used solely for storage or had been abandoned entirely. Dilapidated shacks with boarded-up windows and empty, shadowy corridors peppered the twenty-acre property.

It was a popular destination for ghost hunters and mediums.

By 2019, the patient population had dwindled to only forty-seven souls, those admitted to the forensics unit, having been deemed mentally unfit to serve out their sentences in prison. Everyone else had been transferred elsewhere. The staff had dropped to seventeen.

As I steered my car up the gravel drive, I noticed several patients toiling in the field, in between a row of ancient oaks and a plot of crooked, splintery crosses, the hundred or so signifying the unmarked graves of former patients. A slender man in nursing scrubs sat in a foldable lawn chair and monitored them. The farmers watched me blankly, dirty potatoes and carrots in hand, as I headed for the big house under the cloudy gray sky. The man in the chair said something into a walkie-talkie.

My shoes padded dully on the front marble step, which was caked with years of grime and dirt. The columns flanking me were splotched with mildew. I rang the intercom, and about three minutes later, the oak door opened with a creak.

A tech in maroon scrubs secured the door behind me with a click. "Who are you?"

"Dr. Vincent Blackburn. I'm a psychiatrist from Breaux Bridge."

He nodded and then a scream from upstairs pulled his attention. He started up the staircase with a tired sigh.

"Is there a medical director I can talk to?" I called after him.

He kept climbing and chuckled. "Not today, Doc. Not most days. Just wait down here. Someone'll be down." And then he was gone.

Two patients ambled silently by with a mop and a sponge.

Five minutes passed and no one came, so I made my way up the stairs.

The second-floor corridor was empty and silent, the overhead fluorescents flickering ominously.

I kept moving up the stairs.

On the third floor, I heard a commotion at the end of the hall. I tiptoed toward the sounds of a woman groaning and struggling.

In the last room on the right, the tech had joined another man of considerable stature, also in maroon scrubs. They were struggling to pin down a woman who couldn't have weighed more than a hundred pounds. The walls were padded and white. The man who had let me in held her bottom half and muttered, "Come on, Rose. Cut this shit out." He finally managed to jab a syringe into her hip and pushed about ten milligrams of clear liquid into her muscle. She winced a bit but didn't stop struggling.

"Excuse me," I interrupted.

The tech with the syringe looked up. "Jesus. What do you want?"

"I'm looking for one of your patients."

"If you couldn't tell, we're a little busy here."

"Brittany Alleman?" I pressed.

The other one looked up. The woman was beginning to settle. "Why do you want to talk to her?"

"That's between us, if you don't mind."

The two men shared a glance. "You from the State?"

I decided it was in my best interest not to answer. "Where is she?"

Rose was calm now. The one with the syringe finally said, "Kitchen. Second floor. East wing, all the way down."

"Thanks," I said, and started to go.

"You've got ten minutes," he insisted.

~

Brittany Alleman's size seemed to diminish the nearer you drew to her, like an optical illusion. I approached cautiously, well aware that, like the now paraplegic shop teacher, I bore a resemblance to her ex-husband.

She was alone in the building's modestly sized kitchen, stirring a simmering pot. If not for the paper scrubs and the bars on the windows, she might have been at home.

"Brittany?" I asked.

She stared down into the pot, stirring and stirring.

"Brittany, I'm Dr. Vincent Blackburn. I'm a psychiatrist, and I'm working on a book. I'd like to talk to you."

The lights flickered, but she didn't seem to notice.

"I'd like to ask you a couple questions... about Henri, if that's okay."

Finally, she looked up. Her eyes studied my features. Then she turned back to the pot and said, "Okay."

I'd expected more resistance. I skipped past my rehearsed explanation about who I was and what I was doing, and I got to the point. "What was Henri like when you were together?"

Her shoulders loosened. I suspect not many people asked about Henri outside of his murderous scandal. I might have imagined it, but it seemed she almost smiled. "He was sweet. Thoughtful. Until he wasn't."

"Until you got divorced?"

"Until we got married."

I chuckled. "My wife might say the same thing about me."

She didn't laugh. "You might want to work on that."

I glanced inside the pot. "That smells good."

"Thanks. Red beans every Monday. No sausage, though."

I surveyed the shabby kitchen and meager supplies. "Too expensive?"

She looked up again, her eyes serious and lucid. "You need a knife to cut it."

Somewhere down the hall, a man screamed something about the government.

"That's Billy. Don't worry about him. So, why are you here?"

She seemed so calm. So direct. So sane. The exact opposite of what I'd expected after talking to the two techs in the isolation room.

"I was just about to ask you the same thing."

"Go read the news."

"I did. And I looked up your file. You were eligible for discharge three years ago. You're here voluntarily. And, no offense to anyone else on the unit, but you're no Billy."

She stirred the pot. "Anyone can be a Billy. It's safer if that happens in here."

The lights flickered again, and down the hall, Billy screamed.

"The guards didn't seem eager for me to talk to you," I said carefully. "Are you being treated okay here?"

Out the window, a man I assumed to be a patient wandered around in a field. Brittany saw him too but didn't seem to care.

"They don't want you to talk me into leaving. Then their fat asses will have to cook for everybody. But they don't have to worry. You're not talking me into anything."

"I hear they might be shutting the place down either way."

Another scream. The two techs rushed past the doorway, glancing inside before chasing down the racket.

"They don't tell us much. But everyone's been getting discharged, so probably."

"Everyone but you."

She shrugged. "I had a roommate named Tonya who was just discharged, thank God. Nasty as cat piss. Always scratching up her arms and picking little chunks of skin out of her face. She got sent here after she left her two-year-old in her car all afternoon while she hung out in some bar in Maurice, trying to get laid. It was July." She turned the heat down on the stove. "She always asked about what I did and where I was from. Used to make fun of me for living in my grandma's house, and laugh at me every time I took my meds. She'd say, 'Me, I'm sleepin' with one eye open tonight, because you're *actual* crazy, Brittany. I'm just fakin' it.'"

A middle-aged woman shuffled into the kitchen, cradling a baby doll in her arms. She stared at us, shushed her baby doll, and left.

"That's Patrice."

"Oh," I said. "What's she here for?"

"No," Brittany corrected. "Patrice is the doll. The old lady is Cheryl. She sticks that nasty thing up under her gown, between her legs, every night and gives birth every morning. You can hear her hollering from downstairs. And I don't know what she did to get sent here, but I can about guess."

"Brittany," I said, "I'm here because I'm looking for something. It might not even exist, but I have to ask. Did Henri ever send you any tapes? Recordings? From 2008, maybe even 2009?"

She just stirred.

"Brittany?"

"That stuff was for me. What do you want with it?"

So there were more.

"I want to know that I'm right about Henri. That you were

right about him. That he was sweet and thoughtful and not the monster everyone said he was."

Two techs struggled past the door, dragging a plastic board with a man restrained to the top. He twisted and writhed and cried on the board, his feet bound to the top end and his head down by the ground.

"There goes Billy," Brittany said.

"Please. Maybe I can pull some strings. Get you admitted someplace decent if you want. I just want to know if you still have those tapes."

Brittany sighed. "Here," she said. "Take a bite. Tell me what you think."

She held a spoonful of the red beans out to me.

I hesitated. Then took a bite.

"Delicious." I could see why they liked having her around.

"They're at my house. In the bedroom at my grandmother's place in Shreveport. There's a key behind the AC unit around back. Knock yourself out."

"Really?"

"I'm never going back there. That isn't my home. It's just a house full of memories I'd rather forget. You want to take some off my hands, have at it."

"Okay. Thank you, Brittany."

She turned her attention back to the pot and added a shower of seasoning. "Anyone ever tell you you look like him?"

I froze. "Um, yeah. Do you agree?"

She considered. "No. But I can see why other people might think so."

HAUNTED HOUSE

IT WAS ALMOST dusk when I pulled up to the wide-open security gate. A neighborhood sign, hidden behind years of overgrown vines, proudly announced the entrance for "Piney Grove." The speculative neighborhood had once been sold to the residents of Shreveport as the new wave of housing and economic development, before the bottom fell out in 2008. Now it sat in disrepair and neglect, a faded memory of another time. I drove through the gate and followed my GPS coordinates past empty McMansion after empty McMansion. Finally, I turned into the driveway I was looking for: Brittany's grandmother's house. Twilight simmered on the horizon, leaving everything around me gray and fading. The wind blew like a long sigh, bringing the tree limbs to life, and a chill trickled down my spine as I left my car.

Brittany's great-grandmother had been Shreveport's premiere dressmaker in the early 1900s, just as the area was enjoying a petroleum windfall. Oil barons, landowners, and other titans of industry all flocked to the matriarch for ballgowns and debutante dresses and pageant costumes. The trade had been passed down to Brittany's grandmother and mother, who both relocated their bustling workshop and home to the budding gated community of Piney Grove. Not long after, a carbon monoxide leak in the house would take the lives of both Brittany's mother and her grandmother. And as I stood before the two-story, five-bedroom amalgamation of medieval, colonial, farmhouse chic, I prayed that the leak had been sufficiently accounted for in the years since.

The brick facade had long since faded, leaving the formerly vibrant Venetian red a dull brown clay. Nearly all of the seventeen floor-to-ceiling windows along the rotunda were either broken, spiderwebbed, or covered entirely with cardboard.

I made my way around the side of the house through the thicket of weeds that made up the front yard. I found the massive AC unit, strangled in a jungle of Virginia creeper and poison ivy. It was almost impossible to distinguish between the two.

I knelt and used my jacket to mat down what foliage I could. Then I reached my bare hand into the toxic vines, feeling around for a key. I reached deeper, my face pressed into the brick, the angry green leaves caressing my neck. The key was gone. Either Brittany had lied to get rid of me or had misremembered where she'd left it a decade ago, or some creature had scampered off with it.

I could almost feel my skin begin to itch. I backed away, defeated, and started for my car, when I noticed a gap in the window above the AC unit, open just a few inches.

I made a quick scan of the empty neighborhood around me, and I climbed on top of the unit.

With a little work, I managed to shimmy the window open enough to stick my head through and see that the room was empty. No bed. No furniture. No pictures on the wall. Just a handful of cardboard boxes, water-stained from the ground up. Before I realized what I was doing, I had climbed my way inside.

The carpet was soaking wet. A brown semicircle stain arched across the room with the open window at its center. The fetor of mold and decay was overwhelming, more putrid than rot had any right to be.

The roof had leaked in the corner of the empty bedroom, sending a weeping streak of brown water down the plain beige wall. It was dark inside and humid. Surely no one had paid the power bill in years. I thought I spied a pillow lying in the corner, split and spilling its stuffing. But I quickly realized it was a dead possum whose belly had ruptured out a horde of maggots, explaining the odor.

Only now did I realize how high up that window was without an AC unit on the inside to climb.

I checked the closet for a cache of tapes, eager to get out of this place. But it was bare.

Moving out of the room, I struggled to see more than two feet in front of me. I flicked on my phone's flashlight and froze in fear.

There, lining the long dark hallway, stood a handful of life-size human figures. Like a line of wedding guests sending off the bride and groom. Beckoning me onward. *Great party!* Some wore tailored suits and velvet dresses. Some were nude, some covered in muslin panels. I stared at the mannequins, forcing my brain to see them for what they were, but that did little to slow my heart. I tiptoed down the center of the hallway so as not to let one of them grab me.

Up above, on the second-floor balcony, the head of a mannequin child was sticking through the bars. My imagination filled in the eyes on the blank face as it glared down at me.

I glanced into the dining room, just off the foyer, where I found a long oak table with twelve chairs. More mannequins sat in the farthest three, in various states of undress. The nearest seat, the head of the table, was empty. A plate of rotten food sat moldy and decomposed on the table before it.

I crept up the stairs in pursuit of the tapes.

I poked my head into the first room on the right and spotted two nude mannequins splayed out on the bed, one mounted on top of the other. Another was watching from the corner. Who had posed them all like this? Brittany? Her grandmother? Each possibility seemed as unlikely as the other, and any alternative explanations only frightened me more. I hastily opened the closet, only to find it empty.

Down the hall, in the second bedroom, I found yet another figure in bed, this one posed under the covers. I stepped into the room.

KWOGHK! A deafening, phlegm-coated cough jolted me nearly out of my skin.

I turned around and realized the figure lying there in the bed was human and alive. Her black, tangled mess of hair and her shotgun blast of picked sores along her face and arms told me immediately who she was: Brittany's old roommate, Tonya. I killed the flashlight.

She turned onto her side with a loud snore and seemed to settle. A burned metal spoon and a plastic empty fifth of Dobra vodka lay on the floor next to a pile of fast-food wrappers and empty chip bags. The house key I'd been looking for sat on the nightstand beside her.

I waited, and Tonya didn't move again. Trying not to disturb her further, I crouched and crawled across the carpet to the closet. With only the dim twilight trickling through the window to guide me, I peered in.

A pile of old laundry lay in a mound on the floor. The articles were dusty and stiff, retaining their curved planes as I peeled them away one at a time.

I wrapped my fingers around what I thought was an old sock, only to find my hand squeezing a dead mouse.

I flung it across the closet and held back a scream laced with every profanity I'd ever heard.

I glanced back to reassure myself that Tonya was still passed out. Then I noticed a shoebox. Under the bed, right below Tonya's pockmarked face.

I crawled over to it, flattening my body as much as humanly possible.

I pulled the lid off and exhaled.

Dozens of tapes.

I slid the shoebox out slowly. I'd nearly gotten it free when the edge caught a stack of CD cases and sent them tumbling with a clacking racket that might as well have been a bomb.

I froze there, just inches from Tonya's dry mouth. Her putrid breath hovered down on me like a lowland mist of mustard gas and canned meat.

"Hmm?" her lethargic voice wondered up above.

I waited there on the floor next to the bed, petrified and impotent, arms outstretched and clutching my precious tapes.

An hour might have passed, maybe seconds.

My arms felt like fire ants had taken over, but logically I knew it was too soon for the poison ivy to have set in. It was all in my head. It was all in my head ...

When I heard her roll back over, I crawled out of the room.

I climbed to my feet and hurried down the hall. Past the bedroom with the fornicating mannequins, onto the landing, over the plastic child stuck between the bars. Down the stairs. I was running now. Across the foyer, past the dinner party at the table. Had their heads always been turned toward me like that?

In the hallway, something tugged on my pants, and I spun around to find I'd hooked my belt loop on an outstretched mannequin hand. He tumbled onto me. This time I did scream.

I could hear the thump upstairs of feet padding across the carpet. Lumbering toward the landing.

I ran back into the room I'd entered through and tossed the box of tapes out the window, then climbed up myself, feet kicking and pedaling against the wall. I tumbled out into the yard, beside the shoebox of tapes that had spilled in the tall grass. I gathered them as fast as I could, ran to my car, and yanked on the handle. The door didn't open. I looked up at the house. A candle's light was flickering in an upstairs bedroom. With trembling hands, I punched the unlock button on the key fob and jumped in.

Throwing the car in reverse, I sped out of the driveway just as the garage door staggered open, revealing no fewer than a dozen mannequins, all in formal wear. There was movement between them. The black rat's nest of Tonya's hair was weaving through. Coming.

I tore ass out of there, forcing myself not to look in the rearview.

WHAT LIARS DO IN THE GRAVE

I RACED HOME from Brittany's house and found an old microcassette recorder I'd used for microbiology lectures way back when. The tapes were unlabeled. Undated. My brain on fire and my skin catching up, I played the first one I grabbed. Henri discussed the upcoming Valentine's holiday. He elaborated on imaginary plans they would've made if they had still been together. Breakfast in bed. A walk along the Toledo Bend shore. Steaks cooked over cast iron. In another world, these two were still living their Lifetime movie.

I picked another tape. Henri's voice absentmindedly described the difference between frogs and toads.

I grabbed more.

I was huddled on the floor of my home office, furiously scratching my neck and my arms and sifting through the tapes, when Elsie walked in. It was just past midnight. She was wearing her threadbare sweatpants and a gray men's XL T-shirt that I lovingly (and obnoxiously) referred to as the potato sack. I used to deflate when I'd see her come to bed in that combo. It sent a solid message: bedtime, and no funny business on the way. But tonight I barely noticed.

She hummed and shushed into the ear of our daughter, who was asleep on her shoulder. Elsie didn't scoff at me or roll her eyes, and I almost wished she would have, so that there could have been some amount of bitterness to push back against, to convince her that what I was doing was important. Instead, she just sighed a weary smile, like you would at a dog pawing helplessly at a bag of treats he can't and shouldn't get into. "Get some rest, okay?" she whispered gently. And with one more soft, worried grin, she carried Ivy back to her room.

I looked at the new artwork taped to the wall. A pair of orange handprints in the shape of a jack-o-lantern hung beside the closed-finger autumn leaves, the spread-finger smiling sun. The one with two red footprints connected at the heel for a Valentine's heart was my favorite. "Ivy & Daddy" was written underneath (by the teacher, of course). I realized that it had been months since I'd taken her to a park to feed the ducks. I decided to make time for an outing first thing in the morning, after heading straight to bed for at least a few hours of sleep.

Just one more tape first.

It began as usual with the familiar click. That sound was Pavlovian to me by that point. I practically salivated. But he hesitated longer than usual. For several seconds, there was nothing but the rumble of an engine, the occasional car whooshing by outside. Then his voice, at a whisper:

Fuckin' bowlines. Pretty tricky little knots. You start with the lapin runnin' a circle, hops out his hole, makes a run around the tree, back down in the hole. Pull tight. Daddy taught me that one when I was little. He knew all them knots. I see it every now and then. [He hums a brief tune, as if from some distant memory.] Man liked his bowlines. He'd come home... get drunk... high. His eyes all dull. Pupils huge. And he would turn into just about the scariest thing I've ever seen. And he'd use that old bowline on Mama. I couldn't do anything. I tried... a bowline... like on those campers.

I'm stalling. Brit, I don't even know how to... I killed him. [deep exhale] Jesus. I killed him. [There's a loud rustling sound on the tape.]

Y'know Dad died in '85. I went to the funeral. And I thanked God I'd never have to see those crazy, dull eyes of his again. But today. In that little house out in the middle of nowhere... I mean, that piece of shit Langlinais. Don't know why I ever trusted... I swear his eyes looked like Dad's. But worse. I swear they was red. Just these big black circles surrounded by red. He busted in, all pale and covered in nothing but dried up mud and hair. Looked like... [He clears his throat.] ... Had blood and shit all round his mouth too. You're gonna think I'm crazy. I don't want you to think I'm crazy, Brit. But I swear. That wasn't Langlinais anymore. It wasn't human anymore. It was a monster. It's just like Uncle Mitch said. There in that dark little room, just a few steps away. I didn't even have time to think, I just drew my Sig. And fired. Like a coward. That's the truth of it. I'm a big fuckin' coward. That's it. Langlinais didn't even—what I'm trying to say is, he didn't have a gun, Brit. He just walked in, and I shot. Fuck...

Wasn't until after that I noticed the rifle propped against the AC next to me. I heard Edward say something from the other room. I don't remember what. I panicked. Slid the rifle over to Langlinais before Edward came out. I'm pretty sure he didn't see. But I don't know. Maybe he knows. Suspects that I'm ...

When Edward came out and we checked him, I guess I was still a little jumped up, 'cause I got my gun in one hand and a big ol' buck knife in my other hand, expecting I don't know what to happen. But when we got up on him, it was just him. Langlinais. Like after all the adrenaline left me and I got a good look, there wasn't no monster anymore. Just this person. I don't know. It's like there's something wrong in here. My brain's playing tricks on me. I swear I'm not ...
[There's another loud rustling and a long pause.]

I stopped the tape.

The room around me seemed darker than it had been when I started listening. Emptier. Yet somehow, I didn't feel nearly as alone as I would have liked.

Henri's haunting description of Langlinais clung to my brain. It seemed my cousin had fully embraced the lore of the Rougarou. Whether he had begun to identify himself with the beast yet is another question, one that would consume me for months. The grizzly nature of his accused crimes to this point certainly supported the theory that his mind was already lost to this delusion, that he already considered himself plagued by the same curse he saw in Langlinais that morning.

I suppose he could have been lying here, leaning into the

Rougarou imagery to justify executing his drug dealer and accomplice. *"The man was a monster, so of course I shot him. I panicked."* It's hard to say with certainty whether he believed any of it.

A 2011 study in *Psychiatric Times* discussed ways of identifying deceit in psychiatric interviews. Forensic psychiatrist Dr. Margaret Mayer proposed a few distinct elements that, when pooled together, indicated untruthfulness:

1. Liars often give overly formal, noncontracted statements. ("I *did not* have sexual relations with that woman"—just as a completely hypothetical example.)
2. Liars employ lower vocal tones and slower cadence in an attempt to underline the gravity of their denial.
3. Liars use distancing language like "that man" or "those events" to separate the liar from the subject of the lie. (See the very one hundred percent hypothetical example in number one.)
4. Liars will not lie about themselves in an unflattering way.

As I listened to the tape, I kept trying to identify any hints that Henri might be lying about his encounter with Langlinais.

And I couldn't find a single one.

His language never becomes formal or uncontracted: *"I'm a big fuckin' coward." "Langlinais didn't even—what I'm trying to say is, he didn't have a gun."*

His tone remains consistent throughout, never deviating from the other recordings I've heard a hundred times.

He refers to Langlinais by name throughout, never distancing himself, never referring to him as "that guy" or "the victim." He never once shies away from his personal connection to the man he admits to shooting.

But more than anything else, I kept coming back to number four.

If you're lying, you don't make yourself look bad.

You don't fabricate embarrassing or incriminating details. You don't call yourself a coward. You build yourself up. Gacy claimed he was giving those boys helpful advice. Bundy needed that ski mask because he was such an avid fan of winter sports. Case study after case study, you'd be hard pressed to find a single serial killer or sociopath who makes a simultaneously untrue *and* defamatory statement about himself. Judice never tried to inflate himself in this recording, even when speaking directly to an ex-wife whom he was eager to win back.

Henri told police that Langlinais had pointed the gun at him, and so he shot. That statement—"At that time, the deceased walked in, and unfortunately I was not really in a position to take cover..."—was full of telltale signs of dishonesty. And of course it was. That lie makes sense. It's a lie that makes him look better. In the eyes of the law, self-defense is certainly preferable to the alternative. But if his dishonesty continues onto this recording, why alter the lie at all? Furthermore, why morph it into a new story that makes him look worse? One that makes him seem frightened and insane, scared of some boogeyman in a spooky house? Slaying an unarmed man?

Henri wasn't lying here.

He believed in the Rougarou.

MITCH

December 1, 2008

THE MONDAY AFTER Thanksgiving, only a few days after the events at Pinkley's house, workaday commuters tuning into Cajun 101.3 on the FM dial were greeted by the familiar sound of Bobby Davenport and Skeet Robinson's *A.M. on the FM Morning Show*.

Mitch Judice was ready for that morning's broadcast. He'd placed an old Panasonic radio/cassette combo beside his truck speakers, recording the program as the vehicle ran idle in the front yard. He planned to save the taped radio show with all the newspaper clippings and VHS recordings he was already compiling, archiving anything that mentioned his nephew, the newly minted local hero.

Over the muffled lo-fi artifact, you can hear Mitch slurping his coffee and clipping his toenails.

Bobby Davenport: Oh, and did you hear about this? The Saint Landry Parish Sheriff's Office has reported that they've found the man responsible for several recent killings, including those missing campers from a couple weeks back and a Wildlife and Fisheries agent back in August. Word is, he'd been keeping some of his victims in the freezer and, um, well, I guess he was eating them.

Skeet Robinson: Yikes!

BD: Yeah, I know. The suspect, Troy Langlinais, was shot and killed at the scene. Apparently, they found this guy buck naked, running around with a big ol' gun.

SR: Sounds like my honeymoon. [A canned audio rim shot badoomp-tssss.]

BD: Officials say the suspect was tracked down and killed by local Wildlife and Fisheries Agent Henry Judas.

Mitch Judice: [mumbling over the radio] *Judas?* Uh-uh, motherfuckers. [The truck door creaks and slams shut.]

SR: Wildlife and Fisheries? This cannibal get caught shooting over his limit?

BD: Hey, I just read the news the way it comes in.

SR: Y'know back in the seventies, our serial killers were at least respectable enough to put on a pair of pants. What in the world is the world coming to, Bobby?

BD: Okay, so it's the nakedness you have a problem with.

SR: [laughing] Yeah, exactly! The nakedness.

BD: Maybe he wasn't expecting company.

SR: That's a good point. I mean all this went down in the middle of the night, right?

BD: Uh-huh.

SR: Okay, yeah. I take it back. Somebody pops into my house at midnight, ain't no telling what they gonna get a load of. That's on them.

BD: Hang on. We have a caller. Is this . . . um, *Mitch?*

[Mitch Judice's voice is now muffled through a phone line on the radio broadcast.]

MJ: Yeah, look, y'all messed up his name.

BD: Mornin', Mitch. Welcome to *A.M. on the FM*.

MJ: Uh-huh, hi. First time in a long time and all that. But y'all messed up his name, though.

BD: Whose name?

MJ: Henri. Y'all called him Judas. It's Jud*ice*. That's my godchild, Henri. He's the one that shot that sicko dead. Prolly saved a hundred more lives, y'ask me.

SR: Hold up, Mitch. You *know* this game warden?

MJ: *Know* him? I'm his goddamn parrain!

BD: O-okay there, Mitch. It's still early. Let's keep the language PG. But that sure is something, what your boy did.

MJ: You're tellin' me. One shot. Pew! I taught him how to shoot, y'know.

SR: Well, I reckon we owe you a debt of gratitude then, aye, Mitch?

MJ: Only if you don't like gettin' eaten by crazy naked bastards runnin' around in the woods.

SR: That's a firm no from me, for the record.

MJ: Yeah, my boy Henri, he really stepped it up. He used to be so shy too. Afraid to rustle anybody's feathers. He was kinda like that 'bout this whole Rougarou thing here. But I tol' him, you gotta shake it up! Blow caution to the wind and get out there! Guess it's a good thing I did.

BD: Sorry, Mitch. Did you say Rougarou?

MJ: Mais, why else you think that Langlinais fella was nekkid as a dog in heat?

BD: Well, this is news to us, Mitch. I didn't realize there was a supernatural element to this story.

MJ: Padna, ain't nothin' more natural than a Rougarou. You wanna talk supernatural, my buddy Cephus got him one of them phones that you can just slide your finger across the screen and it flips through the pictures. Tell me how *that* works, and I'll give you a hundred bucks.

SR: You got me there, Mitch.

BD: So, Mitch. Was Henri aware that Troy Langlinais was a . . . um, Rougarou?

MJ: Hell yeah! Prolly why he shot him. You don't mess around with a Rougarou, no. Lucky for y'all, Henri comes from a long line of Rougarou hunters.

BD: That a fact, Mitch?

MJ: Mais yeah. You seen any swamp monsters lately?

SR: Can't say that we have.

MJ: Yeah, well, you welcome then. Ungrateful sons of . . .

BD: Okay there, Mitch.

SR: Now hol' up, Mitch. Couldn't he have just put out

	thirteen rocks on the doorstep? I hear Rougarous can't count higher than twelve, so they'll just freeze up right there if you do that.
MJ:	Well that's just ridiculous.
SR:	Sorry about that. You're right, Mitch. *That* part is a little ridiculous.
MJ:	Alright, boys. I gotta go make sure my tape's still running. Can I request a song?
BD:	Not really that kind of show, Mitch.
MJ:	Okay, well "Susie Q" by CCR if you change your mind.
BD:	Okay. Thanks for calling in to the show, Mitch. Please feel free to ring us up again. Please. Anytime.

EYE OF
THE STORM

December 7, 2008

A WEEK AFTER Mitch's radio interview, Joey Darden rocked back and forth in his home office and stared at the Sunday morning headline: "YVETTE FUSELIER WINS RUNOFF IN ST. LANDRY SHERIFF'S RACE."

It was all because of that goddamn game warden.

The race had been in Darden's hands heading into late November. Yvette's poll numbers had been steadily plummeting, and Darden's insistence on state officials opening an investigation into her adopted son's activities had drawn fervent support. And then the son of a bitch went Charles Bronson and flipped the whole thing around with a single shot to Langlinais's head, turning himself into some sort of local hero.

Meanwhile, Cole Cormier's body still hadn't been found despite hundreds of work-hours dedicated to the search and a twenty-five-thousand-dollar reward for any information.

Darden stared at Judice's photo on his computer screen, the article attached extolling his bravery, lionizing his ceaseless pursuit of justice. And Darden wondered for the thousandth time: *How does the same man find one victim (who just happens to be his brother), stumble upon an amputated hand, find a third victim with whom he had a personal acquaintance and possible flirtation, and then kill the prime suspect before the supposed perp can be interviewed by police?* It was either coincidence or bullshit, and Joey Darden didn't believe in coincidence.

~

Sitting in her Blazer, Yvette sipped her coffee and flipped through the crime scene photos of Langlinais's corpse. She stared at the macabre images, trying to sear his lifeless face into her memory, hoping that her brain only had room for one. For months now, those snapshots of Dane were all she'd been able to see when she closed her eyes.

His blank stare into nothingness. Lips parted just barely. Blood trickling from the corner of his mouth. All imprinted there on the back of her eyelids. Maybe if she stared at this Langlinais son of a bitch, this lowlife shit heel and the meaty hole in his head, maybe, just maybe she could forget. Maybe this new cadaver could take the place of her son's, and she could get some sleep.

Maybe she could stop worrying about Henri for a minute. About the chasm between them. About his growing reclusiveness out there beyond the edge of society. The price he was now paying for avenging Dane's death. For going too far. For doing what she'd secretly hoped he might.

And that was the hitch, wasn't it? She'd wanted him to do it. The morning after Langlinais's killing, she told the state investigators, "If I'd have found myself face to face with the man that killed Dane, I'd have put a bullet in his head too."

Henri had just gotten there first.

She closed her eyes and prayed that the image on the back of her eyelids now would be Langlinais's, not her dead son's. She waited. And then there it was: the hole in his head, his pale white skin, hazel eyes glazed over, staring up at the ceiling. She sighed, thinking for a moment that maybe it had worked. Then slowly the face there morphed and became a mixture of both men, a strange amalgamation of Langlinais and Dane. Their features melded together. Inseparable. The same recumbent corpse, the same blank stare, the same dead eyes. In their intertwining, they became something altogether different and disgusting. Something less human. And for the briefest of seconds, in that strange, lifeless animal, she thought she saw a flicker of Henri too.

~

In early 2009, a small Louisiana-based production company began work on a short film based on the heroic story of Henri Judice. *Atchafalaya* would later premiere at the New Orleans Film Festival and show at Lafayette's Southern Screen Film Festival a few months after that. It focused primarily on the fictionalized infidelity of the game warden's wife and ignored any of the complicated questions that had begun to arise about the film's protagonist as production went on. It received mixed reviews.

Despite his short-lived celebrity status, few saw Henri. As the runoff headed toward the finish line and her poll numbers suddenly lifted, Yvette had swallowed her pride and asked him to take part in a quick interview with KATC news. But Henri refused to help deliver the knockout punch, accusing her of just wanting to capitalize on Dane's murder for her own election. They wouldn't speak after that.

Wildlife and Fisheries put him on paid leave for a month following Langlinais's death. He spent most of his hours holed up in his mobile home or driving his truck around increasingly desolate, uninhabited back roads. When he finally did return to work, he issued zero citations throughout all of duck season. Later, after his death, most assumed he had been lying low during these months, waiting for the smoke to clear before he killed again. Maybe even plotting his next attack.

But the taped recordings he left for his ex-wife paint a different picture. They reveal a tortured soul, a man broken by his actions. Someone who might have pulled the trigger but who bore a terrible burden as a result. Certainly not the heartless sociopath I'd once written about.

And maybe that's just what he wanted someone to believe when he recorded them. Unfortunately for him, mine were the only ears to hear them and the only heartstrings to be plucked for an entire decade, long after his death. Long after judgment on his legacy had already been cemented.

His voice in the recordings from this period is tired, cracking and rasping against the microphone. He whispers through most of them, cries through a few. He's very convincing. If it's not an act, if he was actually that tormented by his crimes and yet for some reason kept committing them, then I fear his mind was even more lost than I'd once thought.

No matter how hard I tried to remain objective, I couldn't stop myself from wondering what that meant for the rest of my family.

≈

Recording from sometime in January 2009:

[Click] I don't know what to do anymore, Brit. I can't sleep for more than an hour or two. I just lay there and hum to myself, the same old song Ma always sang to me when I couldn't sleep. Don't even know the words. Just the sounds and this feeling that it'll be okay, but now I know it won't. I just—every time I close my eyes, I'm right back there. Killing 'em.[6] It's in every dream I have. It's like this itch on the back of my brain. This thing. The bloody teeth and the yellow claws. And red eyes. The eyes are always red.

I've killed my fair share of God's creation. I'm a hunter. But this was different. It's spreading, and I can't seem to stop it. I'm not saying I want to get used to it, but God, I wish I could sleep.

---

[6] It's difficult to decipher whether Judice is saying an abbreviated form of "them," in reference to all the victims; or "him," in reference to an individual male whose murder seems to have affected him the most.

HAPPY ACCIDENTS

THIS IS HOW Henri Judice got caught:

In 1933, E.A. McIlhenny, president of the Tabasco empire, imported nutria rats to Louisiana from the South American subtropics to bolster the Acadiana fur trade. The overgrown rats (up to twenty pounds, always soaking wet), with blunt noses and orange incisors three inches long, were for some reason in demand. Runaways infested the area with its first wild population. With no natural predators in sight, those lucky few got luckier still and propagated to upward of twenty million within a decade.

The Russian and German fur markets made for good business, and the little pelt donors were allowed to flourish until the turn of the 21st century, when the industry collapsed and the demand disappeared.

Without a price attached to their hides, their only antagonists stopped shooting, and the nutria flourished even more. Folks quickly agreed that the bulbous rodents were nothing more than a nuisance.

They had taken over, wiping out entire crops of sugarcane and ravaging the coastal wetlands. They scurried their way north from the coast, into St. Landry Parish and beyond.

On February 4, 2009, one particular little beast of the wild, a direct descendant of those first escapees from the fur farms, wiggled his wet way into the utility room of the St. Landry Parish Police Department. He used his chisel-like incisors to gnaw through a stretch of wiring that powered the freezers in the forensics unit. The wire poured 240 volts of electricity into the soggy bastard's mouth and fried him on the spot, leaving little more than a pelt on the floor. Unfortunately for the department, the Russian and German fur markets were still in the can.

Thirty-five pounds of cold evidence went rancid, and it fell on Deputy Mike Ronsonnet to sort it all out the next day, when the stench had become evident. Ronsonnet dutifully sifted through the items, discarding the spoilage and filing the salvageable material into a row of portable ice chests, checking each item against the ledger as he went. He made his way through the collection from Leonard Pinkley's house and stopped when he got to a packet of raw ground beef.

This one wasn't on the ledger.

He turned the packet over in his hands. No markings. No prints. The thing had never even been dusted.

Ronsonnet broke into a cold sweat. The Langlinais case had been his assignment. And somehow, this one packet of meat had slipped through the cracks.

He was already skating on thin ice. He'd barely passed the academy's written exams, and he worried that any oversight might mean the end of his budding career. He took it upon himself to dust the thing for prints and add it to the ledger before his superiors caught wind.

After a bit of work, he found a complete print. He was nearly ready to file it away and be done with it when something caught his eye. Curiously, the print didn't seem to match any of the others from the Langlinais case. There were six other samples scattered before him, and not one bore a single print that looked like this new one. Even if Langlinais had grown an eleventh finger, it wouldn't have approximated this print.

And it didn't belong to Pinkley or any of the other victims either.

So whose was it?

Ronsonnet finished sorting the items and hurried back to his desk. He pulled up the online database and sought out a specific set of prints, a set that he wanted to check against this newly discovered sample. He looked again at the little gray swirls on the packet, growing more and more certain of their source. Something had always rubbed him the wrong way about the guy. Every time they crossed paths, he felt it in his gut. There was something off. Something suspicious. He checked over his shoulder to make sure no one was behind him.

And then he typed into the search bar: "Henri Judice."

NEW NORMAL

February 7, 2009

Ee-ee-ee-ee-ee-ee-ee-ee-ee-ee-ee-ee-ee . . .

The smoke detector screamed at Edward Harper, reminding him that the black plume pouring from the pot was in fact still billowing. "You think this is funny?" he hollered over the racket at his daughter, Nicole, who was beside herself with laughter at the kitchen counter. He grabbed the pot, hoping to get it in the sink and drown out some of the smoke, but he burned his fingers on the handle. "Goddamn!" He dropped it back onto the elements with a clang.

Yvette, who had been observing the hysterics with mild amusement, finally stood. She sighed, set her beer down, and grabbed a broom from the laundry room. She poked it up at the alarm, mercifully silencing the screeching. In the newfound quiet that felt like a fresh breath, she cracked open the kitchen window for some ventilation. Then she returned the broom to its hook and sat back down at the counter beside Nicole, smirking at the girl's helpless daddy and shaking her head.

Edward stared at the pot.

The roux was burned, little black specks marring the concoction so temperamental and scalding as to bear the regional nickname "Cajun Napalm."

Yvette took the last sip from her beer. "Told you not to walk away."

"She told you not to walk away," Nicole parroted with a canaille grin.

"Well, if one of you bums could've grabbed me a beer out of the fridge . . ." He pushed the black slurry around. At least it had stopped smoldering.

"Forget about it. It's done," Yvette said. "Just gotta cut your losses and start over." She laid a warm kiss on his cheek as she strode across the kitchen for the fridge. "And this time, don't stop stirring. Not for nothin'."

"Whatever you say."

"That's right." She grinned and grabbed a pair of fresh beers from the fridge. "Don't worry, baby. You'll get the hang of it." She made her way back across the kitchen, giving his ass a covert squeeze as she laid the beer bottle in his hand.

"Thanks." Edward smiled, his pulse quickened by her presence—the tiny rush he still felt when she called him "Edward" or "babe" instead of "Dr. Harper."

"Baby" had been his favorite, though. She had first used it the morning after their third date, as he rolled over to find her smiling face whispering, "Morning, baby." They'd been seeing a lot of each other lately, as much as they could while still keeping things private. Given Yvette's recent reelection and Edward's presence in the spotlight after Pinkley's, they both wanted to avoid any wrong ideas by the public. Sometimes the relationship felt like a dream, seeing her pass through the hospital in uniform, formally crossing paths at some fundraising event. Flashing a quick, knowing smile and moving on. But here, it felt as real as anything. Even now, he felt her hand linger on his, their fingertips interlocking for just a moment around the bottle she'd handed him. He snapped back to the burned pot of would-be gumbo. Mama T's scorched roux.

He prayed Mama T had another jar of gumbo grease in the freezer. If this was the last of her supplies, if on his first attempt he had killed off the end of her line, he'd never forgive himself.

It had been a difficult month since Mama T's passing. The myotonic dystrophy that had taken her daughter had finally caught up with the matriarch. Nicole had taken her grandmother's death in stride, but Edward feared that maybe she just hadn't understood the permanence of it. When might it all come crashing down on her?

He officially resigned from his post as coroner the day after Mama T's funeral. He blamed it on the unpredictable hours, the juggling of which would be impossible without his mother-in-law's help. But records show that he had already spoken with the mayor about his decision back in early December, after the events at Pinkley's.

Together, he and Nicole were finding their new normal. He was always home for dinner now, most of which he cooked himself, with varying degrees of success. Yvette became a part of that new normal as well, coming by to help out at least three times a week, providing the poor girl with some semblance of maternal grace in the face of yet another loss.

Yvette and Edward rarely spoke of Henri or of the events at Pinkley's house. Both were keen to put the whole thing behind them and focus on each other instead. Or maybe their concern for the game warden and their impotence to help ease whatever haunted him kept them silent. She no longer blamed Edward for getting caught up in it all. She knew how Henri could be, the way he could pull you in.

She just wished Henri had pulled her in instead.

Edward found another jar of Mama T's gumbo grease in the back of the freezer. The last one. More precious, he realized, than its weight in gold. Reluctantly, he spooned the goop into the freshly cleaned pot and grabbed the bag of flour off the counter. *Here goes nothing.*

And then he froze.

Yvette watched Nicole watch her daddy, who seemed stuck in place. The poor widower just stood there. Yvette imagined what he must be going through, grappling with the loss of the family's anchor and petrified at the thought of risking the last of her supplies. She had to do something before the little girl felt the gravity of it all. Yvette went to the stove and said as nonchalantly as possible, "Alright, Chef, let me take a stab at it this time."

But Edward didn't stand down. And he didn't look up from what had caught his eye on the counter. He just slid the folded newspaper a few inches toward her. At the bottom of the front page, below the fold, she saw the headline: "MISSING WOMAN FOUND; LIMBS SEVERED."

THE EDGE OF THE ATCHAFALAYA

February 6th, 2009

CHASE PELLERIN[7] SHOULD have been at baseball practice. The season opener against Saint Thomas More was a month out, and Beau Chene High liked their chances this year with Pellerin on the mound. Scouts from UL Lafayette and LSU had already pitched their programs to him.

Skipping so much as a batting practice would have been unthinkable a year ago. He'd never wanted to be anywhere but the diamond. All his friends were on the team anyway, and he'd never bothered much with girlfriends, who seemed like more of a headache than anything else. So how was he supposed to spend his afternoons if not at baseball? Go home and play Xbox or stare at a computer screen like those pale emo gamers? He was a man of the outdoors. A ballplayer. And he was good at it.

But then there was Jackson.

They'd met the previous summer at the house of a mutual friend. Jackson Domingue was four months younger than Chase,

---

7 Pseudonym.

but he seemed to have lived a lifetime in his seventeen years. He never knew his dad, never spent much time hunting or fishing or throwing a ball. He grew up sweeping the floor of his aunt's beauty salon for a few bucks a day and eavesdropping on all the ladies' gossip, usually spoken in that strange Cajun mixture of French and English that no one can seem to write down. A constant feed of idle talk and a string of men who passed through his aunt's doors over the years had given him a pretty decent glimpse of the adult male specimen. He was unimpressed by the options but intrigued by the possibilities.

And Chase was full of possibilities. The star pitcher was sweet, if a little cocky. And sure, he talked about baseball *a lot*, and Jackson didn't give a rat's ass about ERAs or RBIs or OBPs or any other abbreviations. But the boy did look good in his uniform. He'd give him that.

Jackson had scored some weed off his cousin earlier in the week (mostly stems, but beggars can't be choosers), and with very little convincing, had gotten Chase out to the banks of the Atchafalaya River for the afternoon.

Whether there was anything romantic going on is up for debate. Chase would adamantly deny it, his protestations practically preempting any accusations. He would go on to marry his first serious girlfriend only three years later, after a brief and unremarkable stint in the minor leagues. They would have four children together. Jackson, on the other hand, recounted on multiple occasions the tightness of Chase's thighs inside his jeans, the firm curvature of his throwing arm's bicep, the surprising softness of his hands. He spoke with sad affection of the beautiful small-town jock who would never quite "figure himself out" and how for almost a year, it seemed as though he might. After high school, Jackson would move to New Orleans, leaving behind the cultural constraints of rural life.

And medicating away the memories of that night.

The two reclined there on the riverbank, sucking up the last ashes of their shared joint and gazing up at the pink twilight. Within minutes, everything was black. No street lights. No cars. The overcast sky blotted out the heavenly bodies above, insulating this patch of the Earth in its own unremarkable darkness. The mosquitoes swarmed in, their appetites oblivious to the winter chill.

Flushed from their idleness by the ceaseless bloodletters, the boys jumped into Chase's red Jeep Wrangler and began the trek back to civilization. The circle headlights carved a path back through the pitch black.

Jackson watched Chase guide the stick shift into third gear. His eyes meandered down to the driver's thighs. "You oughta wear your uniform to where the pants stop just below the knee," he said. "You know, with the long socks for your calves."

"Shit," Chase spat. He said it like he had a mouthful of chaw, the way he did around teammates. Old habits. "Nobody does that Pippi Longstocking bullshit no more."

"You should. You got nice calves."

"Shut up." Chase smacked Jackson's shoulder.

"You know it's true. Don't deny it."

Chase stiffened suddenly under the flirtation that had apparently crossed some line. He averted his gaze uncomfortably out the window to his left.

Jackson took note and retreated a bit further into his seat, disappointed by all the ground he had yet to cover with this shy, conflicted boy. He turned his eyes back to the darkness ahead of them. "Chase!" he screamed.

Chase whipped his head back to the road. Swerved the Jeep just in time.

Around something. Right there in the middle of the road. Caught in the quick flash of the headlights.

A pale, thin figure.

Chase barely managed to keep the Jeep out of the ditch. He slowed to a stop and looked back, squinting into the thick plume of gravel dust behind them. The brake lights cast a red pall on the haze. A great big crimson cloud of nothingness.

"Shit," Chase exhaled with a relieved laugh. He gathered himself and regained his composure. "You see that?"

"What the hell was that?" Jackson asked. "A deer or something?"

"Motherfucker. I bet somebody hit it but didn't finish it off. Jesus. That thing coulda wrecked my grill."

He shifted into reverse and crept backward, into the deep, glowing scarlet aura.

"What are you gonna do?" Jackson asked.

"I don't know. I don't got a gun. Or else I'd put it out of its . . ."

Slowly, the thing materialized there in the fog.

It was limping toward them. Jackson couldn't tell what it was, but he knew it wasn't a deer.

That's when the dust cleared enough to fully reveal the approaching figure.

A woman.

Completely naked.

Caked in blood and mud.

Both her arms were severed above the elbows. Charred into crusty, black stumps.

She staggered toward the Jeep, barefoot and weeping in fitful, howling sobs that contorted her face into an expressionist's twisted portrait.

Chase stopped the Jeep with a crunch of gravel. Jackson cautiously approached the woman and covered her with his jacket, and they led her to the vehicle. She fought them at first, kicking her legs and flailing what was left of her arms, her cries echoing off the surrounding walls of wilderness. Jackson grabbed hold of her right bicep and noticed the end of her humerus protruding from the charred, crusty tissue where her elbow would have been. Finally, they calmed her enough to get her inside. Jackson peered into the still, black tree line to his right, and then his left, wondering where she'd come from. It all seemed to go on forever.

Chase sped the Jeep toward the interstate.

"At one point, after what seemed like forever, she stopped screaming," Jackson told police. "Like she went into shock. She sat back and started mumbling to herself. I couldn't tell what she was saying at first, and she was breathing so fast, you couldn't hardly make sense of it. I thought she was saying, 'It ain't me.' Like that old Bob Dylan song. So I tried to calm her down. I asked her, 'What's not you? I don't understand.' But Chase leaned over and said real quiet that wasn't what she was saying. She was saying, 'It *ate* me.' Over and over again. 'It ate me. It ate me.'"

Within a few minutes, the woman's mumbling faded. She slumped over in the seat and went quiet. Just panting.

And then the panting stopped.

CUT OFF

HER NAME WAS Allison Ownbey. The twenty-three-year-old redhead from Cleveland, Tennessee, loved the outdoors. She'd spent most of her summers rafting down the rapids of the Ocoee River. Spring and autumn would find her hiking the Appalachian Trail. In winter, she'd bundle up somewhere beside a fire on Lookout Mountain.

In late 2008, she decided to see the rest of the United States. Soak up its culture. Bask in its wilderness. She had recently broken off a three-year engagement and had glimpsed the approaching new year as an opportunity to get away and experience the vastness of life outside of that betrothal. Her parents had been disappointed by the breakup. They'd liked the boy and thought Allison was making a mistake letting him go. They refused to pitch in for the trip, offering parting hugs and kisses and no more. But Allison didn't mind. She wouldn't need much, and she'd been saving up. It seemed she'd had this plan—or one like it—in mind for some time.

Friends from her days at Emory had recommended a stop in Acadiana on her way from New Orleans to Texas hill country. A kayak ride through the eerily beautiful South Louisiana swamps would be right up her alley, they said. But she doubted she'd have time. Maybe if she caught a wild hair she'd stop for a night, but probably she'd save it for someday down the line. There was so much of the world for her to see, a lifetime to soak it all in.

She left home with enough money and clothes to last two weeks. Maybe longer if she got sidetracked, as she tended to do. After she kissed her folks goodbye, they would only hear from her twice more.

A missing person's report was filed, and a website was created by her parents to aid with the search; www.findallisonownbey.com lurks there still, gathering dust on the World Wide Web, unaltered, for over a decade. A time capsule dedicated to the diminishing hope of a desperate family. The "Updates" section reads like a murder mystery in reverse, beginning with the most recent news—her death—and trickling back through the preceding month and a half, the red herrings and the false leads. The family's optimism growing grotesquely with each post.

HELP US FIND ALLISON

Update February 7:
Our dear Allison was found last night by two teenage boys on a backroad in South Louisiana. She is said to have passed away en route to the hospital. Thank you for your help and support.

Update January 23:
It is still unclear whether Allison did in fact come to Galveston. So far, no one we've met with in town recognizes Allison from

photographs. We have not heard back again from Jacob C. since he claimed his reward. We have placed photos in local bars and restaurants. PLEASE contact us with any information. There is still a $2,500 reward for any information.

Update January 18:
A heartfelt THANK YOU to Jacob C. in Galveston, TX, who has called in with brand-new information! Jacob reported having spent the night with someone matching Allison's description on January 15. This could be the lead we've been looking for!

Update January 17:
We are now offering a $20,000 reward for any information that leads to the finding of Allison Ownbey.

Update January 13:
No new updates. Please contact with any info.

Update January 10:
No new updates. We believe she's probably somewhere in Texas. Police in Austin, Houston, and Dallas have been contacted. Hospitals in the areas have as well. We know our sweet girl is still out there. She's a fighter.

Update January 8:
Friends in Houston who Allison was planning to meet up with have not seen her or heard from her. If anyone in TX has any information, please call.

January 6:

Friends and family of Allison Ownbey are asking for help locating her. Allison left home for a cross-country road trip on December 26 and hasn't been heard from for the last five days. Allison is 23 years old, 5'3", around 115 lbs. She has medium-length curly red hair. She left in her blue Subaru the day after Christmas and called home from her first stop in New Orleans on December 27. She called home again on January 1 and told her parents that she was planning to head west for Texas that day. That was our last contact with Allison. Our daughter is a kind, gentle soul and a dedicated friend. Please comment below or call our tip line if you have any information.

"HAPPIEST CITY IN AMERICA"

HAPPINESS HAS ITS limits.

In the weeks following the disappearance of the three campers, firearm sales in the Acadiana region shot up by over eight hundred percent. After Allison Ownbey was found staggering around in her amputated state, purchases rose by another two hundred and fifty percent. This, of course, in an area already renowned for its high rate of gun ownership and gun-related crimes.

For the first decade of the twenty-first century, Louisiana led the nation in homicides. Crime and violence are more prevalent here than virtually anywhere else in the union. But somehow and for some reason, citizens of Acadiana tend to feel insulated from such harsh realities. The Cajuns are a fiery, passionate people, impervious to the cold pragmatism of statistics. Emotion often overrules logic here, and with the smiles and home cooking and door holding and joie de vivre, Acadiana *feels* safe, so who cares what a bunch of statisticians *think*? All those guns and homicides, that's New Orleans. Not us. We're the "Happiest City in America." So when the Cajun Cannibal struck in 2008 and 2009, Acadians found themselves wondering, *How could this happen here?*

Floodlights soon coated nearly every backyard in a stark, harsh illumination reminiscent of a barbed-wired prison yard during a jailbreak. Panhandling all but disappeared for a while. No one would so much as roll down a window for fear of being eaten alive.

A renewed wave of Satanic panic crashed over the small towns. It manifested in hushed tones and whispers. Salacious gossip at dinner parties. Hunting camp tall tales.

"Susie saw a pentagram on a tree in the woods behind our house."

"I heard a bunch of teens sacrificed a calf out in Carencro last week."

"Did you see that guy at the bank with the black nail polish?"

Church attendance climbed while volunteer work at homeless shelters and halfway houses dwindled. Everyone assumed a vagrant had infiltrated their community. Someone from the outside. Someone who resented their bliss. It was the only possible explanation. It couldn't be one of their own.

But just in case, they'd keep a floodlight or two angled toward the neighbor's house. Glance around the church and note who wasn't there. Just in case.

Distrust of local law enforcement naturally followed, and by early February, a few small militias were taking shifts patrolling the area, armed and ready.

THE NIGHT HENRI DIED

(Excerpts originally published in the
International Journal of Forensic Medicine)

THE VARIOUS ACCOUNTS of the night Henri Elton Judice died, including phone records and eyewitness testimonies, provide a fairly consistent timeline of events.

February 9, 2009

3:13 pm: Edward Harper calls Henri, inviting him over to Edward's house, where the doctor and Yvette Fuselier are waiting. "We wanted to talk him down," Harper would later explain to authorities. "We'd heard rumblings around town. People spotting him driving around, all hours of the day and night. Running in and outta the woods all over the parish. We just figured he was putting himself back on the case. Back in the middle of it like before, and we both wanted to tell him to back down and let the authorities handle it before he got himself in deeper shit."

~4:18 pm: Henri Judice walks into Mom 'N' Pop's Stop 'N' Shop. The cashier sees him swallow a pill from an orange pill bottle and pace up and down the back aisle, studying the available rope options. She notes that he seems to be glancing out the window the whole time, looking "completely paranoid." He leaves without buying anything.

~6:15 pm: Henri Judice parks his truck in front of Dr. Edward Harper's house and rings the bell three times in quick succession. Upon entering, Henri seems surprised to find Yvette there. "He was flat pissed," she would later recall, "but we managed to calm him down. Well, *Edward* managed to calm him down. I don't know that I had much part in it. And I told him that, for his own good, he needed to take a break. That the department was on the case, and if he had any leads, we were happy to hear it. But he just started rambling a million miles a minute about how we couldn't see the truth right in front of us. About needing to stop the monster that was doing all of this. Over and over."

"I do remember him saying something about a monster," Edward corroborated in a separate interview. "But I felt like he meant 'what sort of monster could do these things?' That kind of monster. Not an *actual* monster. I don't think he was *that* . . . I don't know. When you look back on it all . . . I just don't know now.

"I didn't realize he was talking about himself at the time. And that's when he starts going off about how he's been seeing this thing everywhere. In his sleep. In the mirror. Behind his house. Behind *my* house. Says it must be trailing him around somehow,—*attaching* itself to him is how he put it. Haunting him. He keeps looking out my windows like he's some spy being followed, like he expects to find it right out there. Says we have to kill it before it kills again. Says he doesn't think he can do it alone. He calls it a curse."

"He said," Yvette remembered, "he said, 'Mama, there's something wrong.' He looked so pitiful when he said that. I started to say, 'Don't worry, baby,' 'cause I didn't know what else to do, and he said, '... with me.' Like, 'There's something wrong with *me*.'" If Yvette betrayed any emotion in her retelling of this, the transcript didn't convey it. She simply added, "Well. He was right, wasn't he?"

~6:30 pm: Henri becomes angry with the two and begins shouting. "I straight up tell him he needs professional help and I think he needs some rest more than anything. And he walks up and looks like he's gonna attack me, or maybe even Yvette. Then he just freezes. He's staring right past me. I turn and see Nicole, my daughter, standing there behind me. He's staring at her, like she spooked him, or maybe jolted him back into the reality of the situation. Made him see himself for what he was becoming. I tell her to go back to her room, and then he starts muttering, 'She's not safe, none of you are safe,' and then he turns and leaves." Henri storms out of Harper's house. "That's the first time I start to really think that maybe he's behind it all. The killings, I mean."

When asked why he'd managed to convince himself of Henri's innocence up to that point, Edward explained, "I'm not an idiot, okay? I'd entertained the possibility that maybe Henri could've killed Dane. Maybe even Pinkley too. But I just couldn't bring myself to believe it. There were... there was something holding me back, I guess. I can't really say what. I suppose I *was* being kind of an idiot. But the way he looked that day, I guess that finally shook some sense into me."

~8:30 pm: Worried about Henri, Yvette finishes her fourth glass of wine as Edward puts Nicole to bed. Yvette decides to spend the night rather than drive home. She retires to Edward's bedroom by nine.

9:19 pm: Edward calls Joey Darden and apologizes for the late hour. He informs him that he wasn't being completely honest in his interview with state investigators after the events at Pinkley's house, the day Henri shot Langlinais. "I think Darden already knew something was up with our story. I tell him, 'So, when Henri said Langlinais came in pointing a gun at him, that was a lie. That gun was already in the living room when we walked in. See, Pinkley had this old Fedders window AC unit, 5100 BTUs. Must've been from the early '90s by the look of it. I only really noticed it because of the loud rattling sound it was making when we walked in. I know those old units. They don't rattle like that, and when they do, you got problems. So it definitely caught my attention. Then I noticed a rifle propped up against it, accounting for the racket."

It wasn't until the unit had shut off and the rattling had stopped that Edward would notice the sound of the deep freeze in the bathroom. Officers' reports from later, after Langlinais was dead, reveal that they were able to hear the deep freeze, even as the AC unit ran, because by that point, the gun was no longer leaning against it. "Langlinais didn't have it when he walked in. He couldn't have. It would've been across the room from him, next to Henri. Langlinais wasn't pointing anything at anybody. Henri planted it on him after he'd already shot him.

"I don't even know why I lied in the first place. It seemed so obvious that it was Langlinais. That he was the killer. I guess I just didn't want to get Henri in hot water. But obviously, I know better now. Then, Darden asks if I've seen Henri, and I tell him about that evening at my house. Turns out Darden's got a whole mob out looking for him. I ask him what happened, and he says they found something. Some overzealous cop sniffed out Henri's prints on some stuff in Langlinais's freezer. He's convinced about a dozen cops and a handful of other do-gooders to help him arrest Henri for the murders. All of them: Fuselier. Pinkley. Langlinais. Reed. The Cormier boys. Breaux. Even Barrilleaux.

"Now, I'd made damn sure to keep Henri away from the freezer while I searched through it, so that alone tells you he was up to something if his prints were inside. So this cop started digging more. Digging through Langlinais's phone records. From his landline. Finds out Langlinais made a phone call about an hour before Yvette got word on Dane being shot. They think he was calling someone to let 'em know Dane was there at the trailer. I ask who he called, but of course I already know. Henri. Son of a bitch." Shaken by the revelation, Edward agrees to call Darden if he hears from Henri. He hangs up and gets into bed. He considers waking Yvette to give her the news but doesn't. "I couldn't bring myself to tell her yet. I didn't know how."

~10:00 pm: Henri tapes his final recording, which he would leave in his truck. "I have to put an end to it. All of it. This curse. This rot. This infection. This ... this won't be over 'til whatever it is dies. If it has to take me with it, well, what does it matter anyway? How else are you supposed to get rid of a killer?"

10:48 pm: Edward and Yvette are sleeping in the primary bedroom with the television on in the background. Edward awakens to the abrupt sound of silence, as the noise of the television cuts out.

The house is pitch black for a second or two before he hears the generator outside crank up. The light of his alarm clock glows again in the darkness, flashing twelve midnight. "I'm a little foggy from sleep and all, but I remember thinking it's strange that the power cut out, 'cause the weather outside is pretty clear. I sit up in bed and wait, because I know how loud that damn generator is on at Nicole's end of the house, and I know she'll be running into my room any minute, and we're gonna have to find a way to make room in that bed for her. I wait for a good three or four minutes there, doing jack shit, while she . . ."

Edward finally gets out of bed. "Since she never comes in, I go to make sure she isn't scared. I figure maybe the sound didn't even wake her up, though I have a hard time believing that. I think something inside me knew. I could feel it. Something was wrong. I must've known, 'cause I remember checking the windows and the doors, making sure they're not all busted in. It's calm outside, the only noise is that damn generator rumbling. So I head to Nicole's room. Open her door just a crack and peek in to see if she's awake. The cold air hits me the second I stick my head through the door, like I'm passing into this other realm. That's around the point when I realize her window's open. I turn, and her bed's empty. Sheets on the floor. Everything else in the room's completely undisturbed. She's the only thing missing."

Edward shouts Nicole's name, waking Yvette in the primary bedroom. By the time she gets dressed, Edward is already sprinting into the backyard with a flashlight. She runs out front, in case Nicole is out at the street. She begins calling out for her when she notices Henri's truck. Yvette runs back inside, grabs her gun, and then heads for Henri's Dodge, which is parked two houses down the block. When she looks inside, the truck is empty. She decides to follow Edward's voice, calling out for Nicole, and heads into the woods after him. "A few seconds later, I heard another man's voice deeper into the woods, shouting something that sounded like her name. But—I don't know—angrier in the way he said it. Furious." When asked if this second voice could have belonged to Henri, Yvette answered, "It was him."

10:59 pm: Edward calls Joey Darden and alerts him that Henri has broken into his home and kidnapped his daughter. Joey Darden rallies his troops and heads for the woods behind Edward's house.

~11:15 pm: Yvette and Edward claw their way through the dense forest, calling for Nicole. At least twice more, they hear another voice, which by this point, they are sure belongs to Henri. They begin to follow in the direction of his shouts. Yvette draws her gun. "The ground started getting pretty soft out there," she recalled. "We musta been about a quarter mile into the thick of it by that point. And I could feel it sloping down, like we were heading into some pretty swampy shit. We hadn't heard Henri's voice for a while. I figured we'd either lost him or he'd found Nicole and was bringing her back home safe, and that's why he stopped hollering." Edward, armed with the new information from Joey Darden, took Henri's silence with decidedly less optimism. "We don't hear his voice for a while, and I'm imagining the worst now. 'Cause now I know what he is. What he's capable of."

The two find their feet (Edward's bare and freezing) sinking into soft, ankle-deep mud. With the trail seemingly cold, Edward considers turning back for the house to rendezvous with Darden. "But then we hear it up ahead. A little girl's scream. *My* little girl. So I just start trudging into the mud." Yvette follows him into the waist-high water.

About a hundred yards into the dark swamp, the two make out what appears to be the edge of a structure. As they wade closer, a dilapidated houseboat reveals itself to them. At a slight tilt, sunken half-way into the swamp, it seems to have been abandoned months, if not years, before. Edward starts to shout Nicole's name, but Yvette stops him, both to ease his panic and to preserve any element of surprise they might still need. She has him shut the flashlight off as well. "It was bright enough without the flashlight. There weren't any clouds overhead, and the full moon was lighting the swamp up pretty good. So I told him to keep quiet. If somebody has her in there, we don't want them knowing we're coming. And also we don't want to scare her if she's okay in there, if Henri found her and she's okay. The way he looked at me when I said that."

Edward recalled, "She says something about what if Nicole is okay in there with Henri. Like she still doesn't understand what's happening. And I realize I have to tell her. I tell her about Henri's prints in the freezer. How Henri killed Langlinais unarmed. I tell her about Langlinais's phone records. How he called Henri to tell him Dane was there. How Henri's been lying to all of us from the start. All of it. I tell her that I think Henri's responsible for the death of her son. I look her straight in the eye and tell her that her boy is a monster."

-11:51 pm: Yvette and Edward approach the houseboat. The deck of the portside bow is sunken at least a foot below the water's surface. Carefully, they grab a corner post on the submerged side and draw themselves out of the water, onto the slippery porch. The sliding screen door is open. Yvette holds her gun at the ready. Edward stated, "It's silent in there at first, but then we start hearing some rustling. So we know someone's inside." Yvette leads the way in, Edward right behind.

"We couldn't see much," she said. "But you could feel your feet crumbling the floor beneath you, it was so rotten. The smell of it, and the decay. Everything was so brittle, the surfaces and the grime and filth inside, every nook and cranny of it. The whole thing felt dead. Not dead in the way a house or a building or a table or a chair has never been alive. Dead in the way an animal or a person is dead. Corrupted."

They step carefully toward the bedroom in the back, which lies adjacent to the rear exit. Suddenly, they hear dogs barking in the distance. The search party is closing in. Joey Darden hollers something indecipherable over a bull horn. Yvette and Edward notice that the rustling at the rear of the houseboat is growing louder, their element of surprise rapidly slipping away. Edward nearly trips over something as they rush toward the bedroom door.

"I stub my toe into something soft and look down and see him. I don't know it's him yet. We don't find out until later that it's the Cormier boy. The last missing camper. He's stripped naked. Lying there dead on the floor. Big nasty wound on his left forearm. Neck snapped at this god-awful angle. Then we hear a shushing sound from the bedroom. Yvette angles into the bedroom first, aiming. And the commotion in there gets louder, a bunch of splashing around.

She shouts, 'Freeze!' And by the time I get in there behind

her, I see Nicole there in the closet, sitting in a foot of water, an old burlap bag over her head. She's flailing against a bunch of ropes that he's trying to tie her up in. She's terrified, getting all tangled up in them. And then I see Henri there next to her, holding a gun to his head. And he looks at me and then Yvette. And then, that was it."

11:58 pm: Henri Elton Judice shoots himself in the head and drops dead in the closet.

CLOSURE

IT WAS OVER. The regional string of killings ended with Henri's death. And so did the local panic.

The Cajun Cannibal was gone.

In time, folks in town trickled back into the great outdoors. They started hiking and boating and fishing and hunting again. The ones outside town, those along the city limit peripheries, turned off their floodlights. Some even went back to leaving their doors unlocked. They put their guns back in the closet when they slept at night.

Things went back to normal.

Joey Darden had ultimately been the one to put the pieces together, linking the deaths of Barrilleaux, Dane, Pinkley, and the campers all to Henri. Darden concluded that Henri had roped the dim-witted Langlinais and Pinkley in as scapegoats, convincing them to come along for his abductions (and get their prints all over the crime scenes in the process), even going so far as to store the evidence at Pinkley's house.

Henri was the monster, and he had gone to Pinkley's that night with Edward to keep his unreliable accomplice quiet. For good. He wanted Edward close, but not too close. (He tried multiple times to send the doctor back to the truck so that he could kill Langlinais alone.) It was dumb luck that Edward happened to be in the bathroom when Langlinais finally arrived. Dumb luck that he didn't see the idiot was unarmed, that Henri had planted the rifle at his side. Everything else was part of Henri's plan.

Case closed.

Darden would win the next three elections handily.

Yvette waited just long enough for the case to officially conclude before selling her house and moving—to where, no one seemed to know.

Edward didn't even wait that long. He withdrew Nicole from school, citing "medical leave." Within three weeks of Henri's death, he'd closed his practice and left South Louisiana.

Among my own family, the fall and winter of 2008–2009 might as well have passed in the uneventful blink of an eye. It was as if they'd all slipped into a shared coma and woken in March, oblivious to what one of their own had been doing while they were out. There was no funeral for Henri. No visitation or burial. No grave. His body, along with his memory, seemingly just disappeared. My mother and her sisters, who had rarely spoken to or of their brothers back in Arnaudville for decades, now seemed convinced that no such brothers had ever existed. Henri's father had been enough of a stain on his own, they thought. Now, with his chip off the old block a confirmed killer, it was decidedly better to chop the entire block off and move on. Mitch, Henri's parrain and the last living Judice to remain in rural Arnaudville, was an unfortunate casualty of this amputation. Collateral damage. Guilty by association.

My grandmother, who was still living at the time, was kept

mostly in the dark about it all by her daughters. She only knew that Elton's boy had fallen on hard times and gotten himself into some trouble. Anything beyond that was deemed unnecessary. Out of disgust, she'd been avoiding the papers and the evening news for years. "It's not like it used to be," she'd grouse. "Everybody's out to hurt each other now. Not like when I was a girl." She'd apparently forgotten about the Holocaust and Jim Crow and her neighbor who walked with a limp because of his dad—which was probably for the better.

Everyone did their best to forget a whole host of unpleasantness, and like my grandmother, they were fairly successful. They were good soldiers. Citizens of Lafayette, the "Happiest City in America."

And now I was going to pull the rug out from under them, the same rug they had swept all the ugly under. Henri wasn't a monster. He wasn't evil. He was a human being, debilitated by psychosis. All of the sensational slug lines, the horror movie tropes, the ghost stories and panic and condemnation, I would take the air out of it all. I would reveal the sad complexity of Henri Judice.

Or so I thought.

HENRI: PORTRAIT OF A PSYCHOTIC

January 1, 2020

THE RETURN TO my Acadian roots lacked the homecoming romanticism I might have initially sold myself. We knew virtually no one in the area. My extended family maintained a hospitable but still unfamiliar distance. We wore the extra space in our bigger home thoroughly, wandering sometimes aimlessly through every square inch as if a random nook or cranny might inspire us with something to do.

Elsie received a grant to document what the national news had begun calling "the crisis of climate refugees," those disappearing Indigenous communities along the receding Gulf Coast, displaced by rising waters, rerouted waterways, and disappearing wetlands. It seemed "civilization" wasn't done with them yet.

In her spare time, she filled my inbox with "How to Get a Literary Agent" links. She even reached out to an old friend from Loyola who worked at a publishing company in New York.

We got Ivy situated in her new daycare. Twice, we took her to Girard Park to feed the ornery, mutant-looking Muscovy ducks, whose bumpy red wattles around their beaks and eyes had Ivy convinced that their brains had begun to leak out of their faces. She adored their chicks, however, with their downy yellow fuzz and unblemished beaks. Soon, genetics would catch up to them as well and plague their faces with the same leprous lumps of flesh as it had their parents.

I sat in my home office on New Year's Day, relieved to be putting the final touches on my book, *Henri: Portrait of a Psychotic*. Finally, I would dispel the black-and-white police-sketch picture of my cousin as a cold-blooded killer and paint him with a more honest and empathetic brush, one that would finally let the world understand his real struggles. His real illness. The real curse of psychosis and wendigo and Rougarous.

Soon, I would put the project behind me. Soon, I could reprioritize and refocus. Very, very soon, I'd once again know sleep.

I read through the introduction. There, I had at one point mentioned Reddit message boards, cited as evidence of a niche but passionate community of Cajun Cannibal enthusiasts. In the interest of authenticity, I opened my web browser to pull some specific Reddit threads. I found the ones that had caught my eye over a year ago. No updates since that time for most.

But one stood out. It was new, only a few weeks old. "Cajun Cannibal in Texarkana!" I rolled my eyes. I'd seen posts like this before. Bonita Springs. Galveston. Schwab City. People go missing after a camping trip or a hike, and naturally someone on the internet is bound to concoct some thin connection to the Cajun Cannibal.

But unlike those missing persons cases, there was something about this particular post that drew me in: This time, there was a body. I clicked to open it in full.

Adrian Mangrave (22) was found dead last Thursday in the woods just outside the city limits here in Texarkana. The police haven't given much details, but KTBS got hold of a photo of his body. They wouldn't air it, but somebody at the station posted it to Facebook. Just try looking at this and tell me it wasn't the same guy who killed all those folks in Louisiana a few years back. This has Cajun Cannibal written all over it.

The poster was most likely referencing the torn bits of flesh hanging from the victim's upper arm and shoulder. It was gruesome, of course. Familiar even, in its gore. But Henri Judice, the Cajun Cannibal, didn't have a monopoly on violence. I went to close the tab, but something else caught my eye. A small gash on the victim's neck, about three or four inches long. Probably a few weeks old. Poorly healed. A stratified rim of black and then ruby red surrounding it. Just like the one on Dane's shoulder. And Langlinais's torso. And Barrilleaux's neck. And Cole Cormier's arm.

Same mark. Same ragged edges. Same bizarre discoloration. Same pale, naked skin surrounding it.

The poster, inconceivably, was right. She had to be. This attack had Cajun Cannibal written all over it.

I stared with a combination of dismay and dread at the other window on my computer. The book, which I'd considered almost finished, wasn't done at all.

Someone was still out there.

PART III

BUILDING UP INSIDE OF ME

I DON'T KNOW WHY, BUT I KEEP THINKING . . .

September 2016

Through Baton Rouge and north into the twisting, climbing back roads of Tunica, the swampy flatlands of southern Louisiana give way to rocky outcroppings and forested creeks that feel like another world. You leave the traffic behind just outside the state capital. Now, only the occasional car passes. And soon, you realize it's been twenty minutes since you've seen another soul on the road.

Angola State Prison materializes out of the wilderness, a hexagonal guard tower first, then an access gate flanked by barbed-wire-lined walls, looking like a checkpoint for the world's most heavily fortified border patrol crossing. Once through, you crunch along a gravel road that winds through empty fields of neatly shorn grass and alongside a series of peaceful ponds, toward death row.

The place itself is intimidation incarnate. The concrete building houses four corridors, each radiating like spokes from the central hub where the guard station sits. A great big X on a map. A dozen inmate cells line one side of each corridor. A death row cell spans around eight feet by ten feet, the square footage of its occupant's entire world. Three of the four cell walls are made of solid concrete; the other, dull metal bars. A small window hovers high across the corridor from the bars, tauntingly out of reach, providing the only hint of natural light one might glimpse in the long tunnel. Fans along the corridors volley the humid air back and forth. There's no air conditioning there, and the summer temperatures routinely climb into the triple digits outside. In 2018, a few inmates would successfully sue and force the prison to divert some of the air conditioning from the guard quarters in the event of, and only in the event of, the heat index approaching ninety degrees.

Each inmate is permitted one hour per day out of his cell, which he usually spends showering or walking the length of his corridor. Maybe some days he'll step "outside" into what might pass for a dog kennel most other places, but with no shade and little room to roam, it's hardly ever worth it. The other twenty-three hours he bides in solitude, deprived of any human interaction.

On the second week of my rotation, I visited my first patient again, the one who had mistaken me for the Cajun Cannibal.

He entered the exam room under guard escort, shackles rattling against one another. He sat across the table with the same glazed-over emptiness in his eyes.

I started with the usual line of questioning: "How are you sleeping?"

"Fine."

"Have you had any changes in your mood over the last week?"

"No."

"Any thoughts of self-harm or suicide?"

"No."

He seemed more cooperative today. Or maybe just more docile. Either way, I couldn't help feeling relieved.

"Do you know who I am?" I asked.

"The doctor."

"That's right. I'm your doctor." Still, he didn't look me in the eye. "In the last week have you heard any voices?"

"Yes."

"Are you hearing voices other than mine right now?"

Pause. "Yes."

"Inside your head or outside your head like you hear my voice?"

"Outside." His eyes flicked to the empty corner of the room.

"In the last week have you seen anything or anyone that might not have been there?"

He hesitated. "Yes."

"Can you describe it?"

"Him."

"Okay. Can you describe him?"

"Mean."

"What did the mean man look like?"

"Not a man."

"Sorry. You said 'him,' so I just assumed."

He didn't reply. He just stared through my chest, at the thick metal door behind me. In psychiatry, they tell you to never position yourself between a patient and the door. It makes them feel uncomfortable, unsafe. Here in prison, the rule was reversed.

"So, was it a boy you saw or a . . . ?"

"He looks like he always did." His patience with my questions was wearing thin.

"You've seen him before?"

"I seen him my whole life. Big. Mean eyes. Redness. Black mouth. Hate. Seen him my whole life just about. This one's fake. Imposter. He used to be real. Not like this fake phony."

"It's someone you know?"

"No."

He stopped talking after that. The guard walked him out and brought the other inmates in, one by one.

I knocked on my attending's office door later that afternoon, deep in the treatment center wing of the prison. "Well if it isn't the Cajun Cannibal," he cackled from his lair of Jazz Fest posters and Widespread Panic bootlegs. Psychiatrists tend to be the bohemians of the medical community, and this one took the stereotype to heart. I sat down with my notes and began rounding on the inmates I'd seen. I suggested that the first inmate's dose of antipsychotics should be increased. He was on a regimen that was half the strength of the maximum recommended level, and clearly he was still floridly psychotic.

"Can't do it, my man," my attending said.

"I don't understand."

"First, do no harm." He shrugged. "Hippocratic oath. They still make y'all recite that shit, right?"

"Yeah." Though I didn't see what that had to do with anything.

He sipped from his shot of cayenne and ginger juice cleanser and winced. "Look. You're right, Vincent. The dude's psychotic. He's sick. Very sick. Can't even tell you what's real and what isn't. And he's also awaiting execution."

"Okay . . . ?"

"You're smart. You know the rules. What could legally stop a man on death row from being put to death?"

I considered carefully. "Lack of capacity."

"Bingo. Lack of capacity. If that man in there doesn't have capacity to understand his situation or why he's being executed, if he can't tell right from wrong, or real from fake, or a shrink from the goddamn boogeyman, he can't be put to death. Suddenly, it would be *inhumane*." He grinned bitterly under the Ray-Bans propped atop his head. "If we increase his medicine, and he gets better, they get to kill him. Those voices he hears and those monsters he keeps imagining in his cell are the only things keeping him alive. Ignorance is bliss. And delusions are a fucking guardian angel." I clearly wasn't the first fellow he'd tried to convince. "First, do no harm, Vincent."

October 2016

Angola State Prison was getting to me. I began sleeping less, getting in three or four hours per night of fitful, uneasy slumber. I sent at least three separate middle-of-the-night emails to my department heads about the conditions of the facility. I called my representatives in Congress weekly to complain about Angola and then about everything else. I strategized a march to raise awareness for prison reform, but I neglected to submit any of the proper paperwork or convince anyone to join the crusade. By the end of my three-month rotation, some of my clinic patients had begun voicing concerns to my chief fellow regarding my "intensity" during our visits. I'd cut them off mid-sentence, my words pouring out like water from a busted hydrant. I'd mess up prescriptions, conflating similar-sounding medications or inflating doses by mistake. Soon, I was forced to take a semester off and meet weekly with a psychiatrist for therapy and medication management. If the stress of the place, for only a few hours a week, had impacted me so severely, what could it do to one of its residents? An inmate who knows he'll never leave?

I think a lot about Angola and specifically about that inmate these days. As I try to get to the truth and rid myself and the world of whatever delusions we might have concerning Henri Judice, I wonder if I'm doing the right thing.

I think about that inmate when I can't get Rougarous out of my head. I wonder what exactly he thought he'd been seeing his whole life. What he believed used to be real but wasn't anymore.

I think about him often.

I spent three months at Angola sitting with that man and his psychosis. Two days a week. I never nudged his medications up a single milligram.

First, do no harm.

And when I picture him, probably still sitting in that concrete closet of a cell, baking in the heat, staring at a square foot or two of sky that he'll never touch, tormented by some demon he's seen and will continue to see his whole life, I wonder what kind of harm we thought we weren't doing.

PART OF THE STORY

January 20, 2020

> Hi. My name is Vincent Blackburn. You already know that from my profile, don't you? I just wanted to reach out. I'm a forensic psychiatrist. In your old stomping grounds, as a matter of fact. I was just hoping we might be able to chat. My number is 337-***-**** if you ever get a moment to talk.

I STARED AT the message draft on my phone and at the blinking cursor.

At the message recipient: Edward Harper, MD.

At the "Send" button waiting below. It almost seemed to be growing. Pulsing. I took a deep breath and hit it.

Yvette Fuselier had proven impossible to find. Edward, on the other hand, was only difficult. A google search of "Dr. Edward Harper Louisiana" had yielded no leads beyond some old articles referencing the events of 2008–2009. The investigation. Henri's suicide. An outdated Healthgrades profile citing Harper's old clinic location. This is usually where I would stop.

But on this night in late January, I had pressed on and

signed into Doximity, a national networking site for health-care providers. It had somehow never occurred to me to try there, probably because I was always satisfied with the standard

google dead end, content to use it as an excuse to turn back to safer, less personal waters. But now, propelled by my new conviction that the real killer was still at large, I'd decided to type "Edward Harper" in the Doximity search bar. There he was, buried in the results below a physical therapist in Tulsa, Oklahoma, and a neurosurgeon in South Barrington, Illinois. Edward Harper, MD/Internal Medicine, Elkridge, Maryland. His profile picture was just a blank circle with "EH" in the middle. No photo. Minimal background info. But it was him. I knew it.

After hitting "Send" and committing myself to the endeavor, I sat and stared at the screen.

Waiting.

Maybe five minutes. Maybe twenty-five.

I checked the time. It was late. Or early, depending on the timing of your insomnia.

Ivy was asleep in my arms. Croup had taken hold of her airways and forced anything more than the slightest breath into a pitiful barking cough that would wake her up every fifteen minutes. Elsie and I took shifts staying awake with her, cradling and shushing her throughout the night, snot-smeared shoulders and bloodshot eyes to show for the effort.

I started cutting my dose of medication in half, so as to keep up with the late hours. I'd been on Latuda ever since my episode in fellowship. After moving to Breaux Bridge, I had convinced my new GP to continue prescribing it for me. He hesitated at first. "I don't usually prescribe antipsychotics, Vincent. Shouldn't you see a specialist for this?"

"I *am* the specialist for this, Doug. Besides, it's not for psychosis. Just to keep my moods in check. Just keep an eye on my glucose and lipids every year, and we'll be good."

Finally, he agreed. The mood stabilizer had always done a decent job of keeping me on an even keel. But it was also sedating and would reliably hold me to a consistent and healthy eight hours of sleep each night, which suddenly felt like a handicap on my abilities as a caregiver. Parents don't get a consistent and healthy sleep schedule.

The half dose would keep my moods steady enough while allowing for a bit more nocturnal flexibility. And if it allowed me a few extra hours each night to dig through evidence or hunt down contacts, so be it.

I kept telling myself that I knew what I was doing. But I knew what I was doing.

Rather than ask for a lower dose, I got a pill cutter and started splitting what I had, reasoning that I shouldn't waste the medicine in the cupboard. In truth, I didn't want to admit to my doctor what I was up to. Moreover, I didn't want Elsie spotting the lower dose when she reached for her toothpaste.

By night three, I was getting by without the between-shift naps, using my already roused brain to dig deeper into the Cajun Cannibal mystery. And soon, I started to feel a familiar rush, the same discombobulated surge of neural electricity that had taken hold of me back in my Angola days. By night five, I barely missed the sleep I wasn't getting.

The Doximity instant messenger window popped up without warning.

EH: Can I help you?

There he was.

Is this how it feels to be rescued from a deserted island after months and years alone in search of hope? Another soul who might understand, a ship materializing silently on the horizon where just a moment ago there was nothing?

Can I help you? How do you answer that?'

Finally, my thumb tapped out: I was wondering if you might be willing to talk with me about what happened in 2008. And 2009.

I waited for two full minutes.

My phone's battery was at five percent.

EH: I don't think so. Sorry.
VB: Okay. Totally understandable.

Down to four percent. While I sat and tried to think of a way to persuade him to say more, he sent:

EH: So long.

Before he could sign off, I caught my thumbs typing out: The killer is still out there. Henri was innocent.

Sent.

I waited a minute. It felt like thirty. Down to two percent.

And then, with no further comment, the window read: "EH has left the chat."

My phone died.

I tried to put Ivy down in her crib, but she whimpered the second I tipped her toward horizontal, so instead I carried her downstairs and plugged my phone into the charger in the kitchen. Her head was heavy on my shoulder. I had to admit that it fit perfectly there.

I made for the coffeepot, not that it mattered. Fifty milligrams of Ambien couldn't have put my mind to sleep by that point. I scooped heap upon heap of grounds into the basket and sent the machine brewing with a sputter of steam.

Then, my revived phone rang. I rushed over to find an area code I didn't recognize on the caller ID. I brought the phone to my ear, but the charger's cord was too short to allow me to stand erect, so I bent at the waist, trying to keep Ivy's head nestled into the nape of my neck. "Hello?" I whispered, so as not to wake her.

"What the hell makes you think he was innocent?"

ZEBRAS

"Edward?" His voice didn't sound like I'd remembered from the police interviews. I felt like I'd grown to know the man over the years. The mild-mannered fish-out-of-water greenhorn. Uncomfortable with his place in everything, afraid to step on any toes. Charming. Tentative. Passive. But the abruptness of his intonation now was, how can I put it? Imposing, maybe.

He repeated, "What makes you think he was innocent?"

I took a deep breath. "Edward. The real killer is out there. In Texarkana right now. I think he might have been in Corpus Christi last year. Bonita Springs, Florida, a few before that." I tried my best to explain the Reddit posts, the photo I'd seen, how much it resembled the crime scene photos from a decade ago. The words spilled out of my mouth, abandoning any hint of punctuation or pausing for breath.

"Oh," he said. Over the phone it was difficult to tell if his sigh was one of relief or disappointment. "Well, okay. Thanks for reaching out, Vincent."

"Wait," I hissed. "I'm not crazy."

"You're the shrink."

"Edward, please."

"Sorry. It's just a little thin. I don't see what a few maybe similar-looking gashes have to do with Henri being innocent."

I tried another approach. "I've been looking for Yvette. Maybe she'll be able to shed some light on this. Do you have any idea where she might be?"

He inhaled and exhaled into the receiver. "On a farm somewhere would be my guess. But that's just a guess."

Well, that narrowed down my search to one half of the geographical United States. I stared at the counter, losing hope, still convinced I was right. At the stack of mail. Junk. Bills. Credit card offers. Ivy's lab work from a few days before. I stared at the labs as something in my brain clicked. "What about porphyrins?" I demanded.

"Porphyrins?" he repeated. "What about them?"

I speed-walked into my office as quickly as I could without waking Ivy, plugged my phone into a new charger, and put it on speaker. I tore through a stack of old transcripts and notes. "Early on, with Barrilleaux's hospital notes, you remarked on his elevated porphyrin levels."

"Uh-huh?"

"And then in your autopsy report on Dane, same thing. Elevated porphyrins. Your report on Langlinais, porphyrins."

"You're trying to insinuate that there's some connection between the labs and the victims?"

"*I'm* not insinuating anything. You never mentioned in the notes why you were even checking their levels."

"Precaution."

"Precaution?"

He sighed. "April Theriot. College kid who washed up on the edge of the Basin earlier that year."

"Right. You brought her file to Henri when you started to suspect a connection. Blowing up the anvil—"

He continued as if I hadn't interrupted. "Her death was chalked up to a probable boating accident, what with the chunk of her leg missing and it being the gator-infested waters of the Atchafalaya. I don't really remember the details. She'd been floating around out there for days, though, so it was hard to tell with all the swelling. She was a St. Martin Parish case, so I wasn't involved in the autopsy. But I recognized the name. She had come into clinic a few weeks earlier complaining of abdominal pain, eye redness, some confusion for about a month. So I ordered some labs, which included a workup for porphyria."

"And she had it?"

"No. Not really. Porphyrin levels were high, but the other values didn't fit. Anyway, I never reviewed the labs with her. She went missing before her follow-up visit. But it was fresh enough in my mind when Barrilleaux came in that I guess I checked. Again, just precaution."

"What if she was a victim too? What if there's something about the killer or how he kills these people that raises their porphyrin levels."

"All I'm hearing are a lot of 'what-ifs.' And I certainly can't think of anything that could do that. Can you?"

"No," I admitted. "But you told Henri that you thought there was a connection between Barrilleaux and Dane. That they'd been attacked by the same killer. Maybe you were right about the porphyrins."

"Where'd you go to med school, Vincent?"

"Indiana."

"They ever talk about horses and zebras when you're diagnosing?"

I didn't answer.

"You're out on a ranch and you hear hoofbeats approaching. Don't go looking for zebras. You'll miss the horses stampeding right at you.

"Here's what we know, Vincent. What we *been* knowing: That guy High Pocket saw Henri's Wildlife and Fisheries truck messing around by that duck blind right before they found Barrilleaux. Langlinais called Henri over to his camper right before Dane was killed. Henri's prints were on the gun that killed Dane. Then, Henri shot Langlinais, unarmed, in the head to keep him quiet. I was there. He had his prints all over the stuff in Langlinais's freezer. Henri broke into my house. He kidnapped my little girl and—" His voice wavered.

I calmed my voice, trying to slip the words through his defenses.

"Edward, this can't just be a coincidence. Let me at least send you the photos from these Reddit posts, and you can see for yourself."

"You keep saying Reddit like I know what that is."

"You don't..." I'd neglected to take into account our age gap. "Reddit. It's a... news aggregator. User-generated discussion boards. Memes." I felt like an idiot.

"Sounds like a bunch of people in their basements with too much time on their hands and a laptop."

"Nicole's never shown you anything on Reddit?"

A pause on the other end of the line.

"Hello?"

"Listen, Dr. Blackburn. It's obvious you don't have all of

the story, so let me provide some clarity. My daughter passed away not long after that animal blew his brains out all over her Sesame Street pajamas. I buried her next to her mother and grandmother out there, along with the rest of my reservations and doubts about who and what Henri Judice was. Quit digging around for zebras when the horse is right in front of you and has been for eleven years."

"But what if you're wrong? What if he's still out there?"

The line went dead.

SPINNING PLATES

THERE WAS TOO much to do. Too much evidence to comb through. Too much to figure out on my own. Yvette was nowhere to be found. And Edward was blocking all my calls. I stuffed his Doximity inbox with all the Reddit posts I'd found. I checked back occasionally to see if he had responded. Nothing.

Even after Ivy recuperated, I continued along with my half dose of Latuda. The extra few hours of wakefulness each night were too valuable to forfeit. I began to feel that old itch in my ribs, like my very core was rattling inside, ready to burst out.

At work, I scanned routinely through my patients' lab results, monitoring for the usual shifts in glucose and lipids and vitamin D, but my eyes glossed over it all. None of it was interesting. None of it had anything to do with murder victims or mysterious cannibals. It was all so dull.

At night, I dug deeper into the message boards, contacting the regulars, seeking out any leads. Was the real killer still at large? Did the odd lab results in some of his victims have any actual significance? Leonard Pinkley, Angelle Reed, and Tim Cormier all had normal porphyrin levels on autopsy;

Allison Ownbey's, Cole Cormier's, and Henri's had never been checked.

I even began to entertain the wilder conspiracies. Government cover-ups and corruption. Organized crime and gambling money paying off witnesses. Maybe Henri hadn't died. Maybe he was still out there hunting. Nothing was off the table. The accepted facts couldn't be trusted. Anything was possible.

I needed more hours.

So I started skipping doses, just once or twice per week. Those nights, I could get by on an hour or two of sleep. The rest of the time, I took my half tablets and flushed the unswallowed halves down the toilet so that Elsie wouldn't find them.

I felt invigorated. Driven. And if Edward wouldn't assist me, if I couldn't find Yvette, I'd find the answers on my own.

Elsie noticed the bags under my eyes and the shift in the tone of my voice. She suggested I take a week off work. I resisted at first, but eventually I gave in and rescheduled my patients for the week. Then that week turned into three. I spent the bulk of my time off sequestered in my home office, pretending to rest. Skipping two or three doses per week. Then four.

I was on to something. I knew it. Just as surely as I knew that only I had the ability to uncover this truth. And there was something in me that could also feel a resistance outside, a force hell-bent on stopping me.

I'd answer my office phone to find no one on the other line, and I'd wonder who was tapping my calls. I'd convince myself that the same black Suburban parked outside my office had been parked outside my house the night before. I'd swear that the tap water at home tasted different. The certainty was so strong as to lead me to the main water valve outside in the middle of the night to see if someone had opened it recently. (They hadn't... Or maybe they'd just covered their tracks.) The paranoia only propelled me more. It told me I was getting close.

February 14, 2020

On Friday evening, as I hunched over my yellow legal pad, Elsie knocked lightly on my office door and entered. I tried my best to blink back the fog of sleeplessness and make eye contact of an appropriate intensity.

"Hey. You reach out to my friend at the literary agency yet?" she asked.

"It's not quite ready."

She bit her lip and nodded in silence. I turned my gaze away, back to my notes.

"You know what," she said matter-of-factly. "I ran into Phil today at the grocery store."

"Phil?"

"Yeah. LeFevre. I didn't realize he was practicing in Lafayette now."

"Uh-huh, I think I heard something about that." Phil and I had done our psychiatry residency together back in New Orleans. He was a year ahead of me and had always been a good friend, especially during my forced hiatus, but we'd mostly lost touch after I moved to Acadiana.

"Anyway," she continued, "I mentioned that it would be good for the two of you to meet up."

"Mm-hmm," I hummed, still focused on my notes.

"He said you could stop by his office tomorrow."

I finally looked up. "What?"

"Yeah. He said he sometimes goes in on Saturdays anyway, and he'd be happy to chat with you."

"Elsie, what are you saying? What did you . . ."

"I just mentioned that you were under a lot of stress lately. Maybe . . . I don't know. Maybe he can help."

"Is this a big topic of conversation in the deli section of Rouses now? How crazy your husband is?"

"I didn't say you were crazy."

"You want me to meet with a psychiatrist!"

"With a friend. And so what? I hear you complain all the time about getting rid of the 'stigma around mental health.' Now seeing a psychiatrist is something to be ashamed of?"

"That's not what I mean. When people need it—"

"You need it, Cent." And the conviction in her tone stopped any argument I might have offered. She lowered her voice, removed any trace of anger or accusation. All that was left was concern. And love. "You never come to bed. You barely make sense half the time you're talking. Look at your hand right now. It's shaking."

I moved my hands into my lap, under the desk.

"I love you. I just want you to be okay."

I lowered my eyes back to my notes, but I couldn't manage to read any of the words laid out before me. "What time?" I mumbled.

"Noon," she answered, unable to conceal the relief in her voice. "He said he'd have lunch if you wanted some."

"Okay."

She walked over and planted a long, warm kiss on my forehead.

"Happy Valentine's Day, baby," she said, laying a piece of

pink construction paper on top of the legal pad. A pair of toddler handprints in red, overlapped at the fingertips to form a heart. Ivy's hands were bigger than I remembered.

I looked up at Elsie. Kissed her lips. "I love you."

And then she left.

I pinned the heart up on my bulletin board and cast my eyes back to the legal pad. My ever-growing list of tasks. I added yet another to the bottom.

- ~~Contact Edward Harper~~
- Get a lawyer
- Track down autopsy report and death certificate; may need J. Darden's help
- Provide information to Senator Cassidy
- Find Yvette Fuselier
- Pressure sheriff to reopen investigation
- See Phil

OFFICE HOURS

February 15, 2020

JOEY DARDEN'S LEFT hand wrote in an effortful staccato of jerks as the marker slipped and squeaked across the whiteboard on his lap—his pink weekend polo looked as crisp and uncasual as a starched white button-up. He flipped the whiteboard over.

Why you want autopsy report? it read in almost childlike handwriting.

This had been his primary means of communication since the stroke he'd suffered three months prior. The deformation had hindered me as well. One of my intentions for this visit had been to ask a few questions and get a read on Darden, feel him out, study his reaction and his tone of voice. That was impossible now.

My leg bounced incessantly while the neurons inside my skull sizzled and strategized over how much information to offer voluntarily and how much to withhold. My eyes darted from wall to wall, looking for context, trying to build a picture of the man before me, my temporary adversary. A framed family photo on the desk. An enshrined "hole-in-one" golf ball on the shelf.

A game ball from the 2010 Superbowl, signed by Drew Brees, in a glass case.

Darden sipped his morning cup of coffee and stared at me, trying to find the real answer on my face before my lips could lie. His wife peeked in from the other side of the ajar doorway, probably wondering why some stranger had paid an unannounced weekend visit.

I took a deep breath, hoping to convey as much normalcy as possible, but I could feel my chest vibrating. "There just seems to be a lot of red tape over at the Coroner's Office. I can hardly get anyone on the phone. They don't seem eager to provide information to non-family. Like me." I emphasized this last part. There was no way I wanted him associating my bloodline with Henri's. His expression was stone. "I thought maybe you could help, seeing as how you were sheriff at the time."

His mouth twisted into a lopsided grin, and he tapped the marker against the board to reiterate his question, which I still hadn't answered.

"I just need the necessary documentation for my official record," I said. He seemed to need a little more convincing. "I want to make sure the world knows how you finally caught him. The Cajun Cannibal."

After a moment of unflinching inspection, he wiped the whiteboard. Then he sent the marker once again to scribbling and squeaking.

My eyes resumed their search. On the bookshelf behind him, framing his head, titles popped out at me: *How to Win Friends and Influence People*, *Code Talker*, *In Cold Blood* . . .

He flipped the board over.

I check with Coroner's Office Monday. Closed now. He started to stand, his eyes ushering me toward the door.

"No. It needs to be now," I blurted, refusing to budge. Who knew what would happen to me by Monday? Darden paused and then lowered himself back into his chair, scrutinizing my insistence with either nervousness or a cold suspicion—under the circumstances, it was impossible to tell which. "Today, if possible. Please," I continued, trying to stifle my vigor. "I'm just... I'm almost done. I don't know if I can wait another two days. I'm sure you understand."

Convinced that I wouldn't leave voluntarily without his help, he nodded cautiously and scribbled again on the board: *OK, I make call.*

"Thank you so much," I nodded and then did my best to add a little sauce to the gratitude. "You really have a beautiful home, Sheriff."

He nodded. The marker squeaked again.

To my left, a Blue Dog painting, no doubt a George Rodrigue original. I had recently read that despite being called a blue "dog," the cute creature was actually Rodrigue's rendering of the Rougarou. I couldn't look away from his haunting yellow eyes.

Darden flipped the whiteboard to me.

Thx. Invested in securities at right time. ☺

The vague explanation, punctuated with a smiley face, felt cynical, especially when juxtaposed to his own tortured contortion of a grin. I tried to guess how much of the furniture and artwork and memorabilia in the room had been bought through sound investing. How much had been paid for with casino profits. Given freely as a preemptive thank-you for greased wheels and blind eyes.

He scribbled again.

I began to wonder what was in my coffee and how much I'd drunk out of nervous habit despite swearing to myself that I wouldn't have a sip. Joey Darden. Just how unenthusiastic was he to see me today? What would he do to keep the corpse of Henri Judice buried in the past?

He flipped the board back to me.

Call me if u find anything new

The twisted grin writhed along his jaw, and his eyes squinted a bit. Was that a taunt? A threat?

I nodded and thanked him again. I grabbed his limp right hand and shook it. Maybe it was his post-stroke weakness, but his hand seemed immediately eager to slip out of my grip.

Memory is a strange thing. I find myself doubting what I saw in those days more and more. I'm still not entirely sure what was real. But that day, as I got in my car and pulled away, I would have testified under oath that in the rearview I saw Joey Darden clocking my license plate and mumbling it into a phone.

≈

When I arrived at the Coroner's Office at eleven, the door was unlocked. A young woman in yoga pants and a sweatshirt was behind the desk. She let me review the autopsy report, her eyes analyzing me warily before darting over to the police officer on foot patrol outside the glass doors. He'd passed by twice already, which seemed too frequent for chance. Had Darden sent him? Why?

He glanced inside and kept walking.

I turned back to the file in my hand. It was all too easy. She had been so cold and inhospitable yesterday. Or had that been someone else? Her hair was different now, but maybe it was just her casual weekend attire throwing me off. She now had a lanyard and badge bearing the name "Brittany." Was that a sign? A warning?

"Thank you," I said, and emphasized her name, *"Brittany."* She didn't respond, just kept smiling. Her eyes bounced once more to the officer. What was she so afraid of?

The report was thin. I guess I was expecting a five-inch stack of dog-eared and coffee-stained notes and files, poured through and obsessed over throughout the last decade. But the manilla folder looked fresh out of the pack.

Had no one cared to look at it? Or had someone cared too much, enough to replace it with a new one? My ability to untangle the truth in front of me was growing thinner. I suddenly noticed myself mumbling incoherently. I clamped my lips shut and looked up to see Brittany holding on to her nervous smile.

She scanned my ID into the computer's logbook and went into the back to run a copy of the report. With the coast clear, I turned her computer monitor toward me and studied the logbook. There was only one other entry on file for the autopsy report. Someone had obtained a copy nine years prior. Back in 2011.

Someone named "C. C. House." In the address column, simply "Melville, Louisiana." My mind reeled. Who the hell was C. C. House? And where the hell was Melville?

I searched for an ID attached to the entry, but there was none. Hearing the footsteps of the returning attendant, I turned the monitor back around and graciously accepted my copy of the autopsy report.

In my car, I pulled up the internet browser on my phone and frantically typed "cc house melville, la" into the search bar. Nothing. No listings for anyone named C. C. House. Just a bunch of realtor links for purchasing and renting in Melville, Louisiana. I searched for Melville in the maps app. It was a small town on the outskirts of St. Landry Parish. A thirty-six-minute drive from where I was.

If there's one absolute truth about small-town Louisiana, it's that everybody knows everybody else's business. Surely someone in Melville had heard of this C. C. House.

I glanced at my watch. I was due to meet with Phil in less than half an hour. Just the night before, I had agreed that seeing my old friend and colleague was probably for the best. I had found myself in a brief window of insightful self-reflection, but now, whether I could sense it or not, that window had slammed shut. I knew he would only try to stop me from uncovering the truth. He wouldn't understand. How could he?

I started my car and proceeded along the route to Melville. As I merged onto I-49, a tickle of paranoia whispered across my brain, a vague suspicion that I was being followed. I eyed a navy Ford Escape in my rearview as it disappeared behind an eighteen-wheeler. I stepped on the gas and set my eyes on the road ahead.

C. C. HOUSE

MELVILLE'S TOWN HALL was closed for the weekend. So were the post office and the health unit. The library had locked up at noon. The streets were empty, the sidewalks abandoned. It was starting to seem that finding C. C. House would be harder than I had imagined.

What I needed was a sign.

I stood near the corner of 1st and LA 105, staring at a retired school bus parked in the grass to my left. Its yellow exterior had been partially painted over in patches of green and purple, and the back five or six rows had been sawed off from the windows up, converting the thing into some sort of Frankenstein's monster truck.

A gentle nudge against my leg nearly launched me into the stratosphere. I looked down, struggling to calm my now racing heart, and found an orange and gray cat stopped in his tracks. He seemed annoyed that my leg had gotten in the way of his usual route. He stalked around me and resumed his path toward a white vinyl-sided building next to the bus. If not for the ramp outside and the neon Bud Light sign in the window, I might have pegged it for someone's home. He stalled by the door and glanced back at me, practically beckoning me over. His lips curled into what looked like a smile. Then, he darted behind a dumpster.

It was the best lead I could find.

I walked up the ramp and stepped inside what seemed to be a lounge. Neither the bartender nor any of the three barflies had ever heard of a C. C. House. Each of them scrutinized me with a look of grave concern. What did they know that I didn't?

I thanked them and started for the door, when the man closest to the jukebox mumbled to the bartender, "Gettin' sorta hungry 'round here, Pat." Without hesitation, Pat grabbed the phone and called in an order of muffuletta sandwiches, and my stomach grumbled. Was this my sign? Maybe the barfly had sensed my hunger. Maybe this would lead me to C. C. House. I no longer believed in coincidence.

I asked the bartender where he had called the order in to.

"Hardware store," he answered dryly. It seemed the city boy had worn out his welcome and would get nothing but sarcasm from the riffraff.

"Sure. Thanks a lot," I muttered, and left.

I was speed-walking along LA 105, still praying for a sign, when I passed a small white brick building with a window display that read "Cannatella's Grocery and Hardware. Jumbo Shrimp $5.95/lb."

I practically ran inside.

The woman behind the counter had never heard of C. C. House. She called out to her thickly bespectacled cohort, who seemed more interested in "why the got damn barcodes been gettin' smaller and smaller" on the inventory, and who hadn't heard of House either. "I'm sorry, babe," she said to me. "Are you okay, hon? Can I call somebody for you?"

Who was she planning on calling? The police? Joey Darden? "No. I'm fine," I insisted.

"Okay, hon. Can I get you somethin' ta eat then?"

"Runnin' a sale on caulk," the one in the glasses added.

"Maybe a good meal will set things right," the woman suggested, pointing up at the dry erase board menu.

My stomach grumbled again. "What did the bartender order?" I demanded.

"The what?"

"The bartender. He called earlier. I want what he had, and I don't want anything else, you understand?"

"He got a muffaletta."

"Then I want a muffaletta too."

I watched her make it behind the deli counter. The woman seemed unaccustomed to an audience, but I wasn't taking any chances. Soon, I sat down and tucked into the sandwich, which was the size of seven dinner plates stacked one on top of the other. About halfway in, I felt as if the skin around my abdomen would split a seam.

The woman approached me cautiously and offered to wrap the leftovers. She seemed eager to see me go for some reason.

I carried my doggy bag outside, initially intending to continue down the street, to my left. But I realized that I should probably double back toward my car and stow my leftovers before pressing on, so I turned right instead.

After a few paces, I saw him again: the orange and gray cat. He looked right into my eyes before bounding off behind the hardware store.

I'd followed his lead this far. And it seemed everyone else in Melville was determined to stop me from finding C. C. House. I chased after my little friend, into the fenced-in junkyard behind the store.

The ground was littered with stacks of signs and old bits of cypress. Scraps of plywood used for boarding windows during hurricanes. An antique Esso sign. Political ads from the '80s. As I crunched through the gravel in search of my new feline spirit guide, something caught my eye. Stacked in between signs, hand-painted in red, one word was visible:

HOUSE

I dropped to my knees and pulled away the plywood and old sheet metal, the heavy signs crashing in a heap. And then, there it was, a wooden sign, red letters peeking through years of dirt and grime:

THE CAJUN CANNIBAL'S HOUSE OF HORRORS
C. C. House.

The other half of my muffuletta fell to the ground.

I had been looking for a *who* when I should've been looking for a *what*.

The address was scrawled out in a tiny font along the bottom of the sign. My sign.

I knew now that the universe was on my side. If the cat hadn't led me to the bar, if my stomach hadn't grumbled, if they hadn't ordered lunch from a hardware store, if I hadn't gotten the biggest sandwich on Earth and needed to return the leftovers to my car, if I hadn't found the cat again, none of this would have happened. I'd wanted a sign and here it was. I would solve the mystery of the Cajun Cannibal. Fate would be my guide.

I jumped in my car and plugged in the address. The House of Horrors was only a ten-minute drive away. I stepped on the gas and sped off.

～

I pulled over in the tall grass and killed the ignition.

A slightly cleaner replica of the wooden sign I'd seen at the store stood before me. "The Cajun Cannibal's House of Horrors."

Beyond the sign, looking ready to be swallowed up by the wilderness behind it, sat a small home. No cars in the driveway. No signs of life. A chill ran up my spine.

I climbed the block of steps. The house itself had shifted and tilted away, leaving a roughly three-and-a-half-inch gap between itself and the slab of concrete I stood on.

A laminated, handwritten note on the door read, "Enter If You Dare!" in bloodred lettering. Below was another note: "Adult $10, Child $7, Under 2 Free."

I knocked and waited.

Nothing.

I turned the knob, and the door creaked open.

It was dark inside. The odor of mold and old Lysol assaulted my senses. I groped along the wall for a light switch and flipped it.

The lights clicked on with a buzz.

And there, standing in the middle of the room, was Henri Judice.

I stumbled back, knocking over a stack of boxes behind me. I glanced back. The overhead fluorescents cast a glare over his creased, glossy face. A frozen, uncanny expression.

The fog of confusion dissipated as the infamous game warden revealed his two-dimensional state—a life-size cardboard cutout.

The rest of the room was a cross between a DIY museum and a hoarder's wet dream, cluttered with artifacts and junk, only a narrow path winding its way through it all. Exhibits scattered on the wood grain walls displayed magazine articles, newspaper clippings, family photos of Henri and grainy Xeroxed photos of his victims in life, as well as starkly spotlit crime scene photos of those same poor souls in death.

It was like walking through a manifestation of my research, my own obsession made incarnate. An old TV/VHS combo sat at the end of the path. I turned it on and pushed "Play." A home movie sprang to life—two young boys clad only in tighty-whities and spraying each other with a garden hose. I only recognized the older boy as Henri based on his resemblance to my own squinty-eyed smile and hysterical laugh from childhood. It was like watching an alternate reality version of myself. The younger boy, I reasoned, must be his brother, Cedric, sometime not long before his passing.

Beyond the TV there was a doorframe draped in cypress moss like a beaded curtain. I moved in and flipped on the lights.

In here, all the bulbs were red, draining every other color out of the room. This alcove was a shrine, not to a man, but to a beast. Painted on the wall in an unskilled and cartoonish rendering was the Rougarou. Surrounding it were framed book pages, blurry polaroid photos, and internet printouts.

I leaned in to read a couple of articles.

Arnaudville, LA

Stacy Breaton called 911 on January 4, 2009, when she heard what she believed to be someone breaking into her kitchen in the middle of the night. When she peeked into the kitchen, it was determined to be not a person, but a large bipedal animal that had somehow gotten into her home. She described it as around six feet tall, with pale skin that was covered in dark brown/black hair. It had opposable thumbs and sharp claws on all of its fingers.

[Here, there was a paid ad for a free identity search engine.]

She screamed, and the creature fled. The next morning, she found her pet terrier dismembered outside in the flower bed. Police found a single footprint beside the flower bed, bearing a resemblance to the footprint of a large man, with the heel elevated off the ground.

The article beside it was from www.therougaroutruth.com. It read as follows:

Sighting #5:

In January 2009, Mark Cranfield was driving home along—yep, you guessed it—Bayou Gerimond Road,[8] when he noticed someone hunched over in the ditch on the side of the road. The site was near a rumored Native American burial ground (you can't make this stuff up). Mark slowed down, thinking maybe someone was sick and needed help. When his headlights landed on the scene, the "man" stood up and turned to face him. Cranfield described the beast as a cross between a man and a bear, covered in matted black hair sparse enough that its pale white skin could be seen underneath. Blood covered the creature's face from the nose (or snout) down to his neck.

---

8 Bayou Gerimond Road is frequently cited online as a location of Rougarou encounters, like a local Bermuda Triangle.

[Here, an amateurish artist's rendering of Cranfield's description is inserted. Then, an ad for a free credit report.]

Cranfield drove off quickly. When he returned to the spot the following morning, he found a half-eaten deer carcass lying in the ditch. He called local . . . [The page cuts off.]

I snapped a few pictures with my phone and backed into the main room. Glancing around, I noticed another door in the corner. I imagined that this would have led to the bedroom before the home had been converted into the House of Horrors. I nudged it open a bit and peeked through the crack. The interior looked like fairly normal living quarters, at least from what I could glimpse. No shrines or memorabilia. Wood-paneled walls. Waterfowl and bass mounted and scattered about in frozen poses of action. Deer heads regally boasting racks of antlers and staring ahead with black, lifeless eyes. A single twin bed with a purple and gold crocheted blanket. A small flat-screen TV. A cold gun barrel, suddenly touching my nose.

"Who the fuck's there?" came a voice from the other side of the door.

"My—" Gulp. There was nothing wet in my mouth to swallow. "I was just hoping to take a tour."

"We closed."

The gun didn't move, and out of respect for that fact, neither did I.

"I said we closed," and then the clack of a shotgun pump reiterated the point. The barrel dug harder into the cartilage of my nose.

"Can we just talk?"

"We talkin'," the disembodied voice growled. "And now we done talkin'."

The door opened wider. The gun dug deeper into my nose, forcing me back. The gunman stepped into the light. Paused.

"Holy Bocephus. You look just like him."

For my part, it was like seeing a ghost. A memory from long ago. He'd hardly aged at all. Maybe a few finer lines. A little more gray up top. But it was unmistakable.

"Mitch?" I managed.

Mitch Judice looked me up and down, eyes wide, like he too had seen a ghost.

"I'm . . ." I started.

"I know who you are. Dr. Blackburn, I presume." He scoffed and lowered the gun. "Well come on, Theresa's boy. We got some talkin' to do, you and me."

ROMAN POLICIER

I FOLLOWED HIM through the museum to another door labeled "OFFICE: No unauthorized personal." He pushed the door open to a tiny kitchen, directing me toward the rickety card table next to the stove. I sat down in the kind of brown metal folding chair you'd find littering a school assembly. He retrieved a bag of coffee grounds from the freezer and added a single fresh scoop to the damp cake still sitting in the hopper from yesterday before running the water over that to re-up the pot.

"I read ya articles," Mitch spat.

"My articles?"

"Yeah, Joe College. Ya medicine articles. *International Doctor Digest*, or whatever the fuck y'all call it."

"Oh. What'd you think?" I asked.

He scoffed. "I think you got it about as right as all that bullshit out there." He thumbed back at the museum behind him.

"So you don't really believe Henri was the Cajun Cannibal?" I asked.

He shrugged with a show of indifference. But behind it, I could sense his pain. "Give the people what they want." He handed me a cup of coffee.

"Well, I'm working on a follow-up. A book."

"What the hell else you think you got to add to that pile of trash you already wrote?"

"I don't think he did it. Not anymore."

His eyes narrowed skeptically.

"Um, for one, there's the tapes." I told him about Henri's confession to Brittany after the Langlinais shooting, the one that had first sowed the seeds of suspicion in my mind.

"Mm-hmm. So. You think Henri was innocent. And you think he was innocent because of how he sounded on a few tapes." He shook his head. "Don't see the St. Landry Parish Sheriff's Department bending over their backsides to open up a new investigation because Henri *sounded* kinda innocent."

"I know," I confessed. "The evidence is stacked against us. And I'll admit, I don't know how to explain some of it away. Take, for example, the night Dane died. There's no getting around the fact that Langlinais called Henri when Dane showed up at his camper. Probably to tell him he was there. That looks bad. Or Henri's prints in that freezer. I don't know what to make of that."

"You talkin' 'bout the freezer at Pinkley's house, right? The one Dr. Edward said Henri didn't go diggin' in, but it had Henri's fingerprints inside, so they just assume he musta been messin' around over there before that day? That freezer? Shit, I can tell you what happened with that freezer."

"You can?"

He went to a gray Rubbermaid storage container in the corner, ripped the lid off it, rifled around in it for a few seconds, and produced a folder. He flipped through until he found the page he needed. "Hell, Mr. Smartypants. It was in ya own goddamn article or whatever. The police reports too. Right here.

That doctor told police, 'So with the gloves on, I grab hold of the lid and lift up on it. *It sticks a good bit* at first, but I put a little more weight into it . . .' Half an hour later, the cops come in and open it just fine. No stick. Boom. There you go."

I wasn't getting it. His smile telegraphed just how much he relished being a step ahead of me.

"Do me a favor, Theresa's boy. Go put the coffee up for me. Right over there."

He pointed to his own deep freeze, where he had just retrieved the bag a few minutes before. Confused, I stood and brought the bag of coffee grounds that way and pulled on the handle. It was stuck. I pulled harder and harder until it gave way with a *fffffwup*.

My freezer at home does this too. You open it and let the cold air out. When you close it and let it re-cool, the temperature change creates a vacuum inside. If you try to open it again within a few minutes, it sticks.

Mitch reclined in his seat, nodding with a cocky grin. "Okay," I said. "So what's the point?"

"The point is, Henri didn't touch that freezer until the day they got there. He opened up that freezer just a coupla minutes before the doc. Prolly when Doc was runnin' out to the truck. That's why the thing stuck. And that's why his fingerprint was inside. Not because he was in cahoots with that Langlinais nutjob."

"Maybe. But still," I argued, "it doesn't make him look too innocent if he dug around in there and then lied about it. Just sounds like he was trying to hide something. Maybe something that made him look guilty."

"Or made me look guilty."

I eyed him.

"Henri came over here, a few weeks before he went to Pinkley's house. Was talkin' about how he lost my knife. Had my name on it. It was on one of them tapes, I think."

"Yeah, I remember."

"He gave me back that knife two days after the whole Langlinais mess. He didn't tell me, but I know what happened. Whoever was really killing all them people found my knife out there in the woods, prolly following Henri around. He brought it home and threw it in that freezer. When Henri finds it, he takes it out so no one starts thinkin' I had somethin' to do with it."

I recalled the recording of Henri and Officer Degeyter finding Pinkley's severed hand, the moment toward the end when Henri paused, as if he'd either heard someone following them or was calculating his next move. I was starting to believe that the former was true. The real killer had been right there.

Something clicked.

Something that had puzzled me before but that I had just chalked up to unreliable testimony. I dug into my own stack of notes, a mirror image across the kitchen table from Mitch.

I found what I needed. "In Edward's testimony, he said they parked at Pinkley's house, and Henri, quote, *grabbed his gun* before they got out. The police reports said that later, just before Yvette arrived at the scene, officers confiscated two things from Henri: *his gun and his buck knife*. So Henri walks to Pinkley's house with just his gun. And by the time police get there, he's got a gun *and* a knife."

A broad smile took over his face. Mine too. We were onto something.

"Mitch, did you tell anyone about this?"

His smile faded. "Shit. I tried. No one much interested in what I had to say." He opened another folder to a slew of pictures and news clippings, items he had been collecting for years. Everything he felt pointed toward his nephew's innocence. At least a quarter of it was about Sheriff Joey Darden, about the brand-new casino that was underway in Opelousas, thanks to the gaming contracts Darden had helped secure.

"It's obvious, ain't it?" he said. "Henri wasn't just wrongly convicted. The boy was framed."

"Framed?"

"You betta b'lieve it, hoss." He sipped his coffee. "And was more, he didn't shoot hisself out there either. I looked at the autopsy report."

"I just got my hands on it."

"Uh-huh. Well, read up. Wasn't even no gun resin-do on his head. Shit. E'rbody knows suicides got gun resin-do."

"He was lying in a couple feet of water. Coroner said it himself. He was too wet for any residue."

"Padna, you believe that and I got some mountain-front property in Ville Platte to sell you."

I could feel myself getting swept up in the theorizing. "Mitch. How do we even know for sure that Henri died that night?"

Mitch just shook his head. "He's dead, Theresa's boy."

"No. Yeah. But I mean, suppose Darden managed to, I don't know—"

"He's dead, alright?" he snapped. "Say hi to him y'self, you don't believe me." He motioned over my shoulder to the corner. I turned to see a small wooden box on the cabinet. "All those high-falutin' crematerias wanted to charge me an arm an' a leg just to burn him up. Just 'cause they thought he was a murderer, they figured they could jack up the price. Nuh-uh, padna. Brought him to the vet down in New Iberia. Friend of mine. Owed me a favor." He sipped his coffee.

"Oh. Mitch, I'm sorry..."

"I figure it was prolly one of Darden's goons who killed him."

"But Yvette was there. She saw it happen."

"Hell. Maybe she was in on it too."

"Wait. You think Yvette let Darden shoot her adopted son, frame him for murder, so that he could ruin her reputation, take her job, run her out of town, all to build a new casino in St. Landry Parish?"

He chuckled. "You know how much money those casinos pull in for the state? Shit, the federal gov'ment? Besides, no figurin' the mind of the fair sex. I've seen me plenty of Columbos. You just gotta eliminate suspects until you got your man."

"Okay, yeah. I mean it's worth looking into," I said, open to all possibilities at that point. I could feel my heart rate quicken, my breaths trembling. My whole being was ignited by Mitch's dedication to the case, the puzzle pieces falling into place. Still, I knew even in that moment that real life doesn't play by the rules of a murder mystery. You aren't presented with a list of potential suspects and a guarantee that one will be left guilty at the end. I tried to ignore the very real possibility—hell, the near certainty—that if Henri Judice hadn't killed all those people, the real killer was someone I'd never heard of.

"But listen, Doc. You wanna know who *really* killed all them people?"

I leaned in.

"Or I should say *what* killed 'em." He winked and lowered his voice into a grave, dramatic register. *"Rougarou."* He leaned back in his chair with a creak and folded his arms. Case closed.

"Right." I know the man had a ruby-tinted shrine to the legendary swamp monster just outside his bedroom, but actually hearing the word "Rougarou" said aloud and unironically had me rethinking the entire visit.

"Think about it," Mitch continued. "You and me both know it wasn't Henri. Sure as shit wasn't Langlinais because the killings kept happening after he died. They still goin' on. Shit, just look at North Mississippi! Gotta be half a dozen missin' people between Booneville and Tunica alone. So whoever was doin' the killin' ain't dead. Darden might be a son-of-a-bitch, but he didn't kill nobody. He's a suit. And I'll admit me and Yvette never saw eye for an eye, but I know one thing: That woman loved her boys. She woulda killed herself before she woulda hurt a fly on their walls."

"And Edward?" I was a bit surprised to find myself suggesting it.

He smiled. "Yeah. I thought about that fancy- pants doctor for a minute too. But no. I ruled him out a long time ago."

"How?"

"I saw him on the news. Wearing a tie I bet cost more than my whole closet. And you know what he did when they showed him out there outside of Pinkley's house?"

"What?"

"He walked *around* a puddle. You hear me? *Around* it. Pshh. Ain't no serial killer cannibal runnin' around in the woods choppin' people up, who can't even step in a puddle. No, it was a Rougarou. You betcha bare ass on it, padna."

~

I could feel the car behind me on the trip home, even when I couldn't necessarily see it. I'd felt a whisper of paranoia while making my way up to Melville, but now that hunch had grown into a certainty.

The car wasn't *there* exactly. The old back roads were empty, as they should have been. But they somehow felt too desolate. The long stretches between Palmetto and Port Barre were eerie in their silence. If the occasional car did appear in my rearview, I'd feel my heart stomping on the ceiling of my stomach downstairs. I could barely keep my eyes on the road ahead until the vehicle turned and the path behind me once again felt too barren.

Was it always the same car?

I took a long, circuitous route home just to be sure. I stopped at a Home Depot just off the interstate and browsed around the indoor plumbing inventory, my eyes darting up and down the aisles. Only professionals mess with plumbing, I reasoned. I'd be able to spot anyone who didn't have a "contractor vibe" about him.

A bearded man appeared, seemingly out of nowhere. No plumber's uniform. No name tag. No telltale peeking butt crack, though that occupational hazard may just be an outdated stereotype. From about fifteen paces out, he snuck a glance my way, and I froze. I kept watch of him out the corner of my eye as I sidestepped away, farther down the aisle.

He looked again, more intentionally this time.

Then again.

Predatory. Like he would pounce right there. He moved my way.

I took another step in retreat. I was ready to bolt out of the building when I bumped into a shopping cart that I'd been unintentionally approaching. It was made to look like a race car. A little boy, no more than three, was sitting behind the phony wheel. He looked up at me, totally unfazed, and said, "Our toilet is leaking and I got pee pee on the floor." I stared at him, trying to decipher his strange code, when his dad, the bearded man, grabbed the cart and wheeled him away. He shot one last glare back at me: the creep hiding in a Home Depot, sneaking up on small children.

I got back home after another two hours of evasive driving.

I rushed through the kitchen, where Elsie was scrubbing through the pile of dishes I was supposed to have cleaned the night before.

"Cent?" she said, looking up from the stack in the sink.

"Hey, yeah, just a second!" I called over my shoulder as I ran into the next room.

I sped through the living room, where Ivy was playing with a set of stacking blocks, and into my office. I slammed the double French doors behind me and peered through the blinds, scanning the street. The road was empty. There was usually more traffic at this time of night. I wondered if someone might be blocking the entrance to our neighborhood.

I turned and saw the office door handles jiggle, then heard a knock. Elsie's voice called out from the other side, "Cent, you okay?"

"Yeah, yeah. All good!" I turned back to the road.

"How did it go with Phil today?"

I turned to the French doors and pictured her waiting on the other side.

"Cent?"

"Yeah. All good. All good, I'm just getting a few things together in here, and I'll be out for dinner in a sec."

I was about to provide more nonsensical explanations, when the doorbell rang.

≈

I couldn't move. Couldn't speak. Couldn't tell her to get Ivy and run. My eyes darted back out the window. A blue Ford Escape was parked at our mailbox.

I was certain I'd seen that same vehicle that morning. And again in Opelousas. And Carencro.

The bell rang again. I heard Elsie huff, "No, no. I'll get it. Please, I insist."

I wanted to shout out a warning, but I couldn't come up with the words to explain my fear. I knew they would only make me sound crazy.

And I wasn't crazy.

I poked my head out of my office doors, but I couldn't see the foyer.

Ivy was still playing on the living room floor. Right there in the open.

I sprinted for my daughter and snagged her off the floor, praying I could make it to the garage. I wasn't even sure if my keys were in my pocket, but there was no time to check. I bolted across the foyer and into the kitchen.

"Cent!" I heard Elsie shout. But it wasn't the panicked, blood-curdling cry for help I was expecting. She sounded insistent. And embarrassed.

I ground myself to a halt and took a breath. Petrified, I craned my head out of the kitchen, only to find her there, holding the front door open.

"You have a guest," Elsie said.

A stranger stood there, but the face was familiar. I'd seen it over my years of research.

Unmoving. Unflinching. Older. Grayer.

I moved to her. Stared into her eyes.

"Yvette?" I finally said.

She gazed back into mine. There was a pain behind her stare. Her hand reached out to touch my face.

She took a step forward, and her eyes grew wide. She lost her balance and staggered into my arms.

THE WANDERING WOMB

c. 400 BCE–2009 CE

THE PHYSICIANS OF ancient Greece, who, it should be noted, were all men, had found themselves flummoxed. What to make of the varying and unwieldy temperaments of the fairer sex? How to explain their swinging moods and delicate sensibilities? Their fainting spells? Their anxieties? Their fatigue? Furthermore, how to explain that they themselves, robust and virile men, suffered from none of these ailments?

The uterus of course.

The womb, they argued, was a free-floating, fickle entity, hovering this way and that inside the body, an "animal within an animal." One Greek physician (male) described the organ as "altogether erratic. It delights also in fragrant smells...and it has an aversion to fetid smells." So you're a sluggish lady of Greece whose unreliable uterus has strayed too far from home and found itself up somewhere in your rib cage? The cure is simple. Have a physician (male) place some sweet smelling flowers and perfumes in your undercarriage to lure your womb back down. And for good measure, prop some rancid waste and excrement by your nose to nudge the troublesome organ back down where it belongs.

For centuries, "female hysteria," the accepted repercussion of this wandering womb, would be used as a medical explanation for a whole host of symptoms. Of course, as science progressed, the stuff with flowers and perfumes just seemed silly. Soon, the most appropriate treatment for "hysteria" became full removal of the uterus—a total hysterectomy.

There. Problem solved.

In his 1603 text *Suffocation of the Mother*, English physician Edward Jorden (male) sought a more scientific explanation for what had previously been viewed as supernatural territory. He proposed that the throngs of wicked women accused of witchcraft were simply suffering from this notorious and broadly defined medical condition. Rather than burn them at the stake, maybe try treating them with compassion and sympathy. And then cut out their uteruses.

Progress.

Still, I have to admire Jorden. At least he was trying. Trying to temper an unenlightened panic, to make sense of a horror story with what passed for science at the time. One can empathize. He reminds me of all the things we thought we knew. Of all the things we think we know now.

Over time, diagnoses of wandering uteruses dwindled. The experts realized that those bloody wombs were happy where they were for the most part. But that didn't stop the widespread use of "hysterical" as a synonym for "a crazy, emotional woman."

And it was this term that often found its way, occasionally in the papers and on radio, but much more commonly in idle talk and gossip, to so many retellings of the night Yvette Fuselier watched her adopted son shoot himself in the head. "She was hysterical afterward," they'd say, without a single thought about what the label meant, where it came from, or what she'd really been through.

February 15, 2020

Yvette Fuselier sat at my kitchen table, staring into the dinner bowl in front of her.

Elsie, having recognized Yvette from the photos in my office, had invited her to rest inside and regain her strength with some supper. The color slowly returned to her face after a few bites of the picadillo Elsie had prepared. We ate in silence, out of respect for her recovery, even as thousands of questions raced through my mind. As I contemplated everything I wanted to tell the former sheriff and everything I wanted to avoid telling my wife, Yvette turned her eyes over to Ivy, who was catapulting spoonfuls of picadillo onto the floor.

"How old is she?" she asked.

Elsie answered, "She's a very precocious eighteen months."

Ivy sent her spoon ricocheting off her highchair. She cackled at her trick, which in turn drew a small chuckle from Yvette.

"It's like looking into an alternate universe," Yvette muttered. "Sorry 'bout all the drama at your door. It's been a long day. Traveling. Didn't eat much. I just didn't expect you to... You look a lot like him." She tore her eyes away from me back toward Ivy.

"Hard to escape those Judice genes," I shrugged.

"Harder for some than others." Elsie aimed a quick side-eye my way, then turned back to Yvette. "They are hard-headed, aren't they?" She winked. "We have a spare room if you'd like to stay the night with us, Ms. Fuselier."

It took her a second to register the name as her own. "Oh. Yeah. Sorry, I mostly go by Harper these days. And thank you, but the hotel's fine."

Harper?

"Where are you visiting from?" Elsie continued.

"Elkridge, Maryland. I moved up there a few years back with my husband."

"Your husband? Wait. Edward?" I blurted.

She didn't answer, but she didn't need to. The look she turned my way was all the confirmation I needed. They were married. Edward had been lying to me all along.

"Maryland, huh?" Elsie continued. "Is your husband from there?"

"Mm-hmm. We moved up there and got hitched...oh Lord...about ten years ago. Actually, shoot, married exactly ten years as of yesterday, now that I think about it." There was a touch of melancholy in her voice as she realized the occasion had passed.

"Valentine's Day." Elsie smiled. "Very romantic."

"Pshh." Yvette swatted and cackled. "*Romantic.* It was supposed to be the Sunday before, but the Saints were in the Super Bowl that day. So I got bumped a week."

Elsie chuckled. "What kind of work do you do up there?"

"Home security mostly," Yvette said. "Nothing very interesting. I just answer the phones."

"So, you and Edward..." I couldn't help mumbling.

Elsie turned. "Cent, do you know Edward?" They both stared me down. Elsie did her best to stay nonchalant, but I could see her gears turning as she tried to piece together how much I'd been keeping from her.

"Um. No, I don't" was all I could manage. "I mean know *of* him. But I don't recall ever—"

Mercifully, Ivy started wailing. Had Yvette not arrived at our door that evening, our delirious toddler would have been bathed and in bed by now. I started for her, but Elsie called me off. "Please, El. Let me. It's my turn," I said, hoping to collect my thoughts and figure out my next move.

"Oh, it was your turn two weeks ago. I got it. You stay." The glare she shot practically shoved me back into my seat, leaving me to lie in the grave that I'd dug. Elsie grabbed the bleary-eyed Ivy and carried her off.

The room was quiet without the two of them. Yvette stared at her now empty bowl. I felt my voice waver a bit, struggling to find an appropriate volume in the newfound silence as I asked if she wanted seconds.

"Why you lying to me, Vincent?" she demanded in a tone far removed from the cordial one she'd used up to that point.

"I'm . . . not," I managed.

She aimed her eyes up from her bowl and into mine. A new demeanor. Steely. Sheriff Fuselier was still in there after all.

"Don't lie to me, boy. We're family."

All I could manage was a nervous chuckle.

"I don't wanna play games, Vincent. I'm tired. I'm old. And you need to get back to your wife and daughter. So I'll keep it simple. Where is he?"

"Who . . . Henri?"

She slapped her palm down on the table. "*Nnnope*. Cut the bullshit. *Edward*. Where. Is. Edward?"

"How . . . How should I know?"

"Because you talked to him. Three weeks ago. I traced the number to your cell. He took off first thing next morning, and he's been gone since. Left a note that he was going visit family, but I called and they ain't seen him. That was three weeks ago. I'll ask you again, Vincent. Where is Edward?"

"I swear to you, Ms. Fuselier—Harper, I have no idea. He hasn't answered any of my calls."

She nodded slowly, reeling in the anger that she had unwillingly let escape. "Okay then. So, what did y'all talk about?

～

We moved into my office, hoping to keep Elsie from overhearing my latest misadventures. I offered Yvette a seat, but she seemed more comfortable pacing and passing her eyes over the various documents and case files I had amassed.

While she stalked around the room, I told her about my theory, which, after my conversation with Mitch, had morphed into my certainty that Henri was innocent.

"And you think Edward believed that shit?" She scowled.

"No, actually. He sounded pretty dismissive."

"So where the hell did he go? His phone's straight to voicemail. Won't show his location . . ." A small quiver in her voice betrayed her fear at what the truth might be.

"I did mention to him that I found a few postings online about a string of similar killings out in Texarkana. Based on similar scarring on the shoulders of the victims, I thought the killer might be the same."

She studied me carefully. "You don't really think Henri was innocent, do you? I mean, beyond the whole trying-to-clear-your-family-name stuff, you don't actually *believe* it?" It was an accusation, not a question.

"I'm afraid I do. Yeah."

A long silence followed.

"Ms. Yvette, what happened to Nicole? Edward mentioned that she passed not long after . . . Did she ever give an account as to what happened that night?"

"No."

"Perhaps she mentioned something—anything—about her kidnapper. She had a bag over her head. Anything she could've said might help Henri's case—"

Yvette cut me off like she wasn't even listening. "She'd been fighting the dystrophy off for a while. Her mama had it too. Girl was strong. She was doing good for a little bit. But there was no coming back from that night. The stress of it was just too much. She died in 2010, about a year and a half after Henri busted into her room and dragged her into the woods and shoved her in a closet and blew his brains out. That's why Edward can't sleep at night. It's why he's out there right now."

She turned and looked me dead in the eye.

"He shot my boy, Vincent. You know it and I know it. Troy Langlinais called him the minute Dane pulled up. Henri drove over there and put five bullets in my son's body. And then he sat there with my boy on the floor, sat there watching him bleed out for fifty fucking minutes before he even called me. Let him get cold. And hard. Felt like a mannequin by the time I got there. Henri robbed me of even getting a chance to hold my baby one last time." Her voice was trembling with rage. Lost in her own memories of that night.

But her memories were right. I hadn't really thought much about the timeline until then, but she was right.

"Fifty minutes..." I repeated dumbly.

Nearly an hour had elapsed between Langlinais's phone call to Henri and Henri's phone call to Yvette.

I heard the floorboards creak down the hallway. Probably Elsie, standing guard.

"Fifty minutes..."

I produced a map of St. Landry Parish and folded it twice to section out the northeastern corner. I laid it on my desk. I had already scrawled, among other notations, one X in the northeast corner for Troy Langlinais's trailer, the crime scene. And just three miles west of that, another X for Henri's trailer. Where he lived after the divorce. Where he lived the night Dane died.

Three miles apart. Less even.

I studied the time stamps from my notes. "Okay, so hang on," I said, as much to myself as to Yvette. "Henri gets a call from Langlinais at 8:32 PM, letting him know that Dane's there. Henri barrels over from his trailer to Langlinais's, all of a five-minute drive. He kills Dane, lets Langlinais take off. And then he doesn't call you until 9:20? Why?"

"Because he was rotten, Vincent. That's what I'm telling you."

"But just—devil's advocate," I continued, "is it possible that Dane wasn't shot until later? Around 9:20?"

"No way," she insisted. "No signs of restraint. No evidence of a prolonged altercation. And anyway, my boy was strong. That burnout Langlinais couldn't have overpowered him for more than a minute, even with Henri's help. And Dane sure as hell wasn't going there to chat Langlinais up. Had more sense than that. Hell, he left his truck running. No, he wasn't in there for more than a minute. I'm sure of it."

She was right. About all of it. Every single word. "So either it's like you said: Henri shoots him and stares at his body for fifty minutes before he calls you, or..."

"Or what?"

"I'm not sure. I just can't make sense of that missing fifty minutes. Fifty minutes is a long fucking time. I've had some stubborn patients who sit there for fifty minutes and barely say a word. Fifty minutes is a long time to sit silently in a room with someone who's alive, much less someone who's..." I finally noticed the tears fighting their way to the surface of her eyes.

"What if he wasn't home when Langlinais called?" suggested a voice from behind me. It was Elsie. How long had she been standing there? "What if it took him fifty minutes to drive there?"

"Maybe. But then where was he?" I asked.

"Who knows? He was a Judice," she shot back and gave me that same glare from dinner. That mixture of disappointment and worry. Like she knew she was already on her way to losing me. She quickly brushed it aside. "Sorry to barge in. Cent, why isn't my house key working?"

I'd forgotten to tell her. "Oh. I, uh, had the locks changed while you were out yesterday."

She blinked. "You had the locks changed."

"Yeah." I tried to keep my tone as nonchalant as possible. "They say you should do that every five years. You know, just in case."

"Who says that?" Elsie asked.

"You know." I forced a casual chuckle. "Probably big

locksmith lobbyists or something. Maybe it's a racket, but you really can't be too careful."

"Do they also recommend you put dead bolts on all the bedroom doors?"

I could feel Yvette scrutinizing me. "I just thought it might be a good safety precaution."

"A one-year-old locking herself in her room isn't much of a precaution."

I gulped and forced an unconvincing chuckle at Yvette, then turned back to Elsie. "Okay, I'll call the guy back and have him take them out tomorrow."

"Tomorrow's Sunday, Cent. Locksmiths don't work on Sundays."

"Okay, then first thing—" My voice cut out.

Elsie waited for the rest, but the gears in my head were engaged in another job. I rushed to my file cabinet and dug out a spiral-bound notebook.

I tore through it until I found my notes from several months prior, when I had poured through Brittany's old testimony.

In my chicken-scratch scribbling, I was able to find the section I needed. I practically shouted to both Yvette and Elsie, "Listen to this. Brittany told investigators about an encounter with Henri one night after their divorce. He had let himself into their old home, drunk, acting like he still lived there."

Elsie nodded. "She pulled her robe around herself and asked him to leave."

"Yeah. How'd you remember?"

"The whole thing sounded... scary. For her." She'd been folding her arms tightly against herself but now let them fall to her sides.

"Right. Well, she estimated that it had to have been around eight thirty PM. She couldn't remember what day it was, but she was clear about two things.

"Number one: It all happened within the week following Tropical Storm Edouard's arrival, because Henri was complaining about being tired from all the post-storm cleanup.

"And number two: She had the locks changed two days later. I never understood why it took two days. I mean your drunk ex-husband finds his way into your old bedroom while you're naked, scaring you half to death, and you don't change the locks for two days? No, you change the locks ASAP. You change them the very next morning. Unless you can't because the next morning is Sunday and the locksmith is at fucking church!"

They both stared at me.

But I knew I wasn't crazy. "Don't you see? This means that their run-in must have happened on a Saturday. More specifically, at around eight thirty on the Saturday following Edouard's landfall. That's Saturday, August 9, 2008. That's—"

"The night Dane died," Yvette finished.

"Exactly." I stepped toward her. "Yvette, when Henri got the call from Troy Langlinais at 8:32, he was on the other side of the parish."

I unfolded the rest of the map. Revealing the west side of the parish.

There, a red circle that marked Brittany's house.

"Yvette, how long do you think it takes to drive from there to there?" I slid my finger from Brittany's circle to Langlinais's "X."

She bit her top lip and finally answered, in almost a whisper, "About fifty minutes."

Then she found the chair behind her and lowered herself down.

"There's our missing fifty minutes," I said. "Henri didn't sit there and wait to call you. He called you the moment he found his brother. By the time Henri got there, Dane was already dead."

~

Yvette took us up on our offer to stay the night. I first offered her the studio, but it was filled with Elsie's photography equipment, so Elsie and I made up the couch for her in my office.

After our realization, Yvette shut down. She barely spoke another word.

For whatever reason, she still hadn't explicitly agreed with me that Henri was innocent. I figured that maybe it was all just too big of a shock to her system. Too cataclysmic. Too fast. But I knew she was starting to feel the pull of the truth.

Thankfully, Elsie was already asleep by the time I climbed into bed.

I tried to calm my brain enough for sleep as well, but I knew it was a fool's errand. Too many questions still lingered: Who was the real killer? And where was Edward? Would we find him in time? I got out of bed a little after midnight, unable to snuff out my neurons. I went for an aimless drive and ended up on the living room couch, watching reruns of *Coach*.

I awoke around five AM, surprised to have dozed off at all.

I grabbed Ivy, who had also just woken, and walked over to the office.

Yvette was gone.

The blankets were neatly folded on the couch, the pillows arranged precisely as Elsie always set them. The usual mess on my desk was now orderly. I could tell she had spent the entire night looking through the files.

I glanced back at Ivy, her soft morning coos serenading my restless brain. She was playing with her dinosaur toys. Battling clumsily, bashing their gaping jaws into one another and thrashing at one another with their claws. The *T-Rex* mauled the *Triceratops*, who then impaled the *Parasaurolophus*. The *Parasaurolophus* turned and stole a clutch of imaginary eggs from the *T-Rex*'s nest. The *T-Rex* attacked in kind, and so on. I'm sure she'd played with them like that before. It all just seemed too vicious suddenly.

Still, I watched from the couch as something began to clarify within me. Perhaps it wasn't horses or zebras. Perhaps it was something else entirely. I didn't interrupt or interfere. And by the time Ivy had moved onto stacking a set of magnetic blocks, I was certain that I knew who the Cajun Cannibal was.

BELIEVE YOU ME

I TOOK A deep breath. I knew I would need it. There was so much in my head, so many loose ends finally connecting to one another. So many mysteries suddenly making sense. I had to get it all out. Had to put it in someone else's ears.

"Okay," I said to Elsie, "so I've been racking my brain trying to figure out who could have killed all these people, right? Langlinais was dead for the last two killings. Cole Cormier was out of the country for the first two. Turns out Henri was across the parish for Dane's. So, what one person could have done all of this? And this morning it finally dawned on me: The killer wasn't one person.

"It was *several* people. A plague.

"Dane was acting strange after the storm. Never home. He had a nasty gash on his shoulder. His porphyrins were elevated. *He was infected.* It made him . . . it made him something different. *He's* the one who attacked Barrilleaux. Left him for dead, only to be found in a duck blind with some strange infection and elevated porphyrins. The Wildlife and Fisheries truck High Pocket spotted out there by the duck blind belonged to Dane, not Henri. By the time they finally contacted Liu Wen, they were so sure it was Henri, they never even asked her what the game warden who stopped her looked like.

"And the propofol in Dane's system wasn't because Henri was drugging him. Dane was trying to sedate himself, buying it off Langlinais to try and stop himself from killing again. So Dane goes back to Langlinais, looking for more. Langlinais calls Henri, his usual customer, to tell him his game warden brother's back. He sees how strange Dane's acting, and he's probably starting to have second thoughts about having sold to him. That's why Henri knew what was in Dane's system on the tox screen. Langlinais tells him what's going on and tells him to come get his brother away from him. Before Henri can get there, Dane attacks, gouging out a chunk of Langlinais's chest. And then Langlinais shoots him.

"Now Langlinais is infected.

"Henri never mentions the call because he doesn't want to admit that he's still in touch with his dealer, still using, still has a bottle of propofol and other drugs at his house. And the phone records aren't found until it's too late for him to explain. So Langlinais escapes to his cousin Pinkley's house. Starts acting crazy. After a few night hunts with Pinkley out by Mom 'N' Pop's Stop 'N' Shop, Langlinais turns on his cousin and kills him. Abducts the campers. Kills two of them. None of them have elevated porphyrins because he kills them on the spot. You only get an infection if you're alive, right? Right.

"But Cole Cormier gets away. Alive. And infected.

"Now, after Langlinais dies, Cole's out there in the woods. Acting strange. Attacks Allison Ownbey on the side of the road. Starts eating her. Bit by bit. He doesn't have a freezer to keep her in, so he has to keep her alive in between feedings. He starts cauterizing the amputation sites, her limbs that he cut off for food. But Henri's hot on his trail. Cole sees him around the corner a few too many times. He tracks Henri down to Edward's house one evening, sneaks his way inside, but instead of Henri in there, he finds a fresh victim in Nicole. Henri hunts Cole down onto the houseboat and snaps his neck. He wasn't guilty. And he wasn't crazy. He was the only one who could see the truth!

"But maybe that's not the end. Maybe there was some other victim along the way. From Cole or Langlinais. Maybe from Dane. Maybe from before. Someone who got away and moved along to Bonita Springs or Corpus Christi or wherever.

"And now that same person is out there, killing again."

I noticed that my hands were gripping the armrests of my chair.

I sat back and waited for a response.

Elsie nodded slowly. Not a hint of excitement registered on her face. "Come with me," she said.

"Elsie, I figured it out! I've finally got it!"

"Please," she insisted.

I rose slowly and followed her back into our room. And into the bathroom. "I need to call a reporter," I said. "Or the sheriff. Definitely Senator Cassidy. With any luck we can have the case declared ongoing and..."

She stood by the toilet, eyes cast down into the bowl. I walked over to see what she was looking at.

In my morning fog, I must have missed it. There, bloated at the bottom of the bowl, were my two unflushed half pills of Latuda.

"Did you meet with Phil yesterday?" she said.

I didn't respond. By her tone alone I could tell she already knew the answer. I stared into the toilet bowl without so much as a blink.

She turned and left. And, according to what she tells me now, I called out after her, my voice full of conviction, "This doesn't mean I'm wrong."

~

Phil came over right away at Elsie's behest. She very delicately explained to me that she only wanted to "get another opinion" on my theory, and then she left me alone in my office.

Phil sat down across the desk from me and shot the shit as if we were back in residency pulling an all-nighter in the ER together. As if no time had passed. As if nothing had happened. Then he sighed and smiled. "So listen, Vince. Elsie and Ivy are going to spend some time in New Orleans with her mom. So you can get some rest here."

I blinked hard. "See, Phil, it never made sense that one person could have done it. Cole Cormier was backpacking in Europe during the first killing. Langlinais was dead for the last two . . ."

I could see Elsie cross the doorway carrying a suitcase out to the car.

Phil spoke softly, "How was the move for you guys, Vince? I mean Amy and I are settling in okay in Lafayette, but I do miss a few things about the old stomping grounds. Don't you?"

As Elsie headed toward the garage, I could hear the muffled sounds of her sniffling.

"The infection thing makes sense, though," I said. "Don't you think? I read about a villager in New Guinea in the nineteenth century who suffered from some type of porphyria. He had skin discoloration and extreme bouts of psychosis. Even cut off his own foot. He began eating other villagers. Cannibalism was the only thing that eased his symptoms. Like a blood transfusion."[9]

Phil shrugged agreeably. "Lots of things are possible, I guess. You can drive yourself"—he stopped himself from saying "crazy"—"up the wall thinking about all the possibilities. I guess sometimes you just need to take a step back and regroup."

"You remember mad cow disease?" I asked.

"Sure, it's . . ." he started.

"Prions. Exactly. Degenerative brain disease in cattle, caused by prion proteins in the central nervous system. Remember, they thought at first that it just existed in cows."

"I remember, Vincent," he said.

"But then, in the early '90s, someone ate tainted cow meat and started having psychiatric and behavioral changes. Eventually died from it. It caused a whole host of—"

"Yeah," he cut me off. "I remember. It was a variant of Creutzfeldt-Jakob disease."

"Right. See? They called it something else to make it less scary. But no matter what the name, it's the same thing. Mad cow. I think . . . what I'm trying to . . ."

Elsie carried Ivy into the office, but only a few steps past the threshold. Her feet wouldn't take her any further into my realm.

"What I'm saying is," I continued, staring at Phil, "this isn't all that different."

"We're all set," she interrupted, struggling to keep the words emotionless.

My own righteousness wouldn't allow for any sadness. The

---

9 "Porphyria; Cannibal's Curse?" Wyckoff Smith, 2018.

only acceptable emotion was betrayal. She didn't understand. She had never understood. "Okay," I said coldly.

She waited a second or two for me to stand and give Ivy a kiss, but I didn't. I just lowered my eyes back to my yellow legal pad. The corners of the top few sheets had begun to curl.

"Okay, 'bye," she said. "We love you."

"Love you too," I mumbled. And then she was gone.

Phil didn't say a word.

I tapped my finger on the top sheet of the legal pad, the to-do list. "I should call the sheriff. He'll want to know. And the DA. But I've got to work around Darden. For all I know . . ."

Phil let out a long exhale and slid a pill across the table to me. A bottle of water beside it. "Let's just throttle back a little. Okay, bud?"

I noticed he had taken my keys off the desk.

I stared at the pill and then at him. He wasn't going to move from that chair until I agreed. Reluctantly, I took the pill and swallowed it.

He eyed my jaw with that same skeptical stare I had aimed at so many uncooperative patients in the past. I opened my mouth to prove I hadn't cheeked the pill.

"That's good, buddy. Thank you. I'm gonna make some calls in the other room. You just sit tight. Holler if you need."

I nodded and he left the room. I could hear his voice through the door; he suddenly sounded much less casual. I began to wonder whom he might be on the phone with. One of the partners in his clinic moonlighted at Vermilion Hospital. Probably there now. Waiting.

I started scrambling. Who knows what he had given me? Who knows how long I had before I was incapacitated? I searched around my uncharacteristically clean and orderly office for clues. That's what I actually called them in my head: *clues*. I might as well have had a deerstalker hat and a pipe. There was nothing there. I had infected Yvette with my theory only hours before, and she had left nothing behind to show for it. I clutched my trusty legal pad and found myself pacing. Then I noticed that under the curling top sheet of the pad, there was a page missing, the ragged edge revealing where it had been torn out. I hadn't done that. Yvette was the last person in here. Maybe she hadn't left anything behind but had left the memory of the thing.

I could just faintly make out the indentation of a few lines in the paper.

Honestly, I probably could have made it out right then and there, but that wasn't compelling enough. I grabbed one of Ivy's crayons and went to work shading very lightly over the pad. Watching it unfold like a decoded message stirred something inside me. Validation.

Slowly but surely, Yvette's heavy handwriting began to reveal itself. A few key words materialized:

Porphyrin

Reddit

And finally: *Booneville, MS*.

I pulled up the latest "medical mysteries" Reddit forum. Under a section keyworded as "porphyria," I found a new post detailing stomach pains accompanying some mystery illness. It read, "Anybody else's gums bleeding?" The poster, a user named "MistersippiGregorySmith," also mentioned eye redness and some mild confusion. He claimed to live in Booneville, Mississippi.

At that moment, a rumbling sound drew my attention out the window to the road. A familiar pickup truck pulled up in front of my house. Out jumped Mitch Judice, turning around a full 360 degrees and then back again, checking the house numbers around him. What the hell was he doing here? I checked my phone log, and sure enough, I had sent him a text begging him to come over, about two hours earlier. I barely even remembered composing the message.

I could still hear Phil's voice on the other side of the office door. It sounded as if he was either on the phone with EMS or the police. He mentioned something about "no sirens."

As quietly as possible, I climbed out the window and stumbled across the yard to Mitch's truck. My legs felt like rubber, either from adrenaline or something exogenous. I had expected some resistance from him as I hissed, "Get me out of here!" but he just slapped the hood with an enthusiastic "Hot damn!" and jumped in the truck.

He floored the gas, and we sped away. I could have sworn I heard engines revving and a fleet of cop cars giving chase, but when I looked in the mirror, the road was empty.

"Where to, mister?" Mitch cackled.

His voice wobbled around inside my head with a long metallic echo. Whatever Phil had given me was setting in. I could hardly lift my head up from the seat. I turned and managed to get out two words before drifting off to sleep: "Booneville, Mississippi."

447 MILES

Sleep and wake melted together. Consciousness became a continuum along which I slid in wide vacillations.

My eyes fluttered open. The dream inside my head poured out of them and coated the world around me in a thick layer of phantasmagoric sheen. An infinite tree line rolled alongside me, blurring into a single body. The gray branches reached ahead and behind to shake hands with the future and the past. My eyes closed.

And opened.

A crow hovered overhead, leading us, drawing the hood of our truck forward along the road like a tugboat towing a vessel down a canal. The crow swerved right, and I felt the truck lean in anticipation, readying itself to veer off the highway in pursuit. I closed my eyes, bracing for a crash that didn't come. My eyes stayed shut.

They opened.

An invisible rain drizzled outside, the last gasps of a storm. The trickling sound the only evidence it left behind. The sunlight was blinding. Mitch drove beside me, two hands on the wheel and a third clutching his penis, stuffing it into a plastic Gatorade bottle. His ears saw me watching, and his mouth chuckled, "Eyes off the prize, Doc." I pressed my eyelids together so tightly that their molecules converged and entangled with one another. They wouldn't open. Nothing in my brain's power could separate them. I was surrounded by total blackness and emptiness.

And then, even the emptiness disappeared.

INTO THE WILD

The first thing to return was sound. Muffled voices murmured nearby but remained separate from my existence, as if I'd been gestating in a womb. The voices argued, a man's and a woman's.

My head ached but seemed more stable inside, my synapses calmer. What had before felt like a Fourth of July fireworks finale now felt more like the smothered thumps of mortar blasts over some distant horizon. I could only hope that I was retreating from that horizon rather than advancing on it. The newfound quiet in my skull felt cavernous, like the empty silence hanging in the air after a hurricane has blown through, when you finally step outside to assess the damage. The blackness around me melted into a dull pink light pressing on my eyelids.

I blinked my eyes open and squinted against the waning sunlight beaming onto my face. I was still in the front seat of Mitch's truck, pulled over on the side of the road somewhere. Wilderness towered all around me. The trees were bare and gray, looking like old death. There were no signs of civilization anywhere save three giant crosses sticking out of the barren ground like toothpicks, marking the spot either for a would-be or a has-been church.

The arguing voices, while still muffled, became more definite in space. They certainly existed, and they seemed to be coming from behind the truck. My first thought was that we had been caught. The cops had tracked me down. I stumbled out of the truck, one wobbly leg ready to go and rescue Mitch, the other leg taking a step toward the woods for an escape. When I peered behind the truck, I realized that my instinct had been correct. We'd been found by a cop. Just not the one I was expecting.

Yvette Fuselier stood at the hood of her Escape in mid-argument with Mitch.

"Well, now hol' up, Miss Yvette," he hollered. "Y'ask me, *you* the one that followed *us* out here."

"Jesus Christ." She rolled her eyes.

"Well, for fuck's sake, whose car is behind whose truck? You s'pose I followed you out here in reverse or somethin'?"

She turned to me, simultaneously enraged to see my face and relieved to speak to someone other than Mitch. "I spotted this idiot's truck rumbling through town. How'd you find me?"

I explained the notepad and the Reddit message boards. MistersippiGregorySmith in Booneville.

"That's right, bootiful Booneville!" Mitch unfolded a new, crisp map of the county on the open tailgate of his truck, beside a blue tarp that barely contained a cache of survival gear beneath. "Look, I'll show you why we here. There and there is where they found them two kids, respectfully." He scribbled two Xs.

"What two kids?" Yvette and I asked in unison.

"C'mon, y'all. Keep up. New post on truemonsters dot N-E-T. Found it after you text messaged me this mornin'. Figured that's what you was so excited about tellin' me. Couple a kids up here went missin' last week. They found one of 'em two days ago. All eaten up. E'rbody calling it a bear attack, but we know better, huh?" He winked at me.

"What the hell's he talking about, Vincent?" Yvette asked.

"He means the infection. *People* being infected." I put extra emphasis on the word "people."

"If by people, you mean Rougarous," he muttered, but thankfully, she didn't seem to hear.

I quickly took the lead. "We're talking about pathology here. Medical mysteries." I explained my theory that there were multiple killers, that like rabies or mad cow disease, something was spreading, changing people's behavior. Something contagious. I told them everything.

When I finished, Yvette just stared at me. "So you're trying to say Dane, my boy, was a killer. Am I getting that about right, Vincent?"

"I'm saying he was a victim. Just like the others. He just passed it along."

"Shit." Mitch rubbed the nape of his neck in profound amazement. "So it was a whole *bunch* of Rougarous."

"A whole bunch of people, yes," I clarified before Yvette could pounce on his theory.

Mitch smiled at me. "Right, *people*. I'm one hundred percent in agreeance. Bunch of people. They all start out that way, right? Next thing you know, they tearin' out a boy's throat and rippin' some gal limb from limb and eatin' the heart right outta some dude's chest. *People* doin' all that." He nodded and pouted his lips in faux sincerity.

Yvette turned on him with a suspicious glare. "You sure do seem to know a lot about these attacks, Mitch."

"Just enough to get the job done." He grinned.

"And we're supposed to trust you out here because you're what—some kind of an expert?" she demanded.

"If there's one thing I know—and there ain't, by the way; I know a whole bunch of stuff, me—but if there *was* one thing, it'd be huntin'." He continued with his map. "Look here. Them two kids..." He drew a single small circle. "Here's where they went missing from." Then he circled his pen around a larger circumference, incorporating the marks, "So we gotta presume it's stalkin' somewhere out in these woods. And here's where you wanna be." He stabbed his chapped sausage finger a few miles into the woods from the highway. Walden Lake. "Lake attracts animals. Prey. And where there's prey, there's predators."

"Vincent." Yvette sighed. "Booneville's a few miles back. Surely somebody's seen Edward."

"Ah, so the good doctor's missing, huh?" Mitch asked.

"Yeah, he disappeared about three weeks ago," I said.

"Interesting timing..." Mitch said.

"What are you implying, Mitch?" Yvette growled.

Rather than answer, he tilted his head to one side, noting her anger with a perverse interest. "Wait, are y'all two...?" He twisted his first two fingers around each other. When he saw her grit her teeth at the question, he guffawed. "Go 'head on, Miss Yvette. Getchu that doctor money!"

She tried her best to ignore his presence. "Conventional wisdom says we ask around in that town. He left in his white Volkswagen Atlas. If anybody's seen..."

"Germans..." Mitch spat on the ground.

"Mitch, give it a rest for a second," I said.

Mitch shrugged. "Alls I know is, sounds like our two interests are intersected. And if you took the time to give up your search in town to tail me all the way out here to the middle of fuckin' nowhere, how much luck was you really havin'?"

No response.

He continued, "You wanna go hand out flyers? Staple some 'lost doctor' posters onto telephone poles? Maybe you think the wise old sheriff in town'll have all the answers. Though I bet even you don't believe in fairy tales like that no more." He began to unload supplies from the back of his truck.

Yvette was recoiling, so I tried my best to reel her back in. "Yvette, I don't know where we'll find Edward. But what I do know is that the attacks back home all happened in the woods. And it sounds like the kids that went missing up here all went missing from these woods. So, if we want to get to the bottom of it, this seems like the place to start."

Her eyes were full of resistance and suspicion. They locked on Mitch, who had removed his buck knife from its leather sheath, for inspection. The same knife Henri had borrowed so long ago. The sunlight glinted off the blade and onto her face.

"Fine," she said, and she made for her car to grab a heavy coat and a Glock 19, keeping a peripheral glance on Mitch the whole time.

Mitch heaved an overstuffed pack onto his back and smiled at her. "You do look as pretty as ever, Miss Yvette. That's the God's honest truth."

Perhaps the hurricane hadn't passed after all. Perhaps I was just in the eye.

UNSOLID GROUND

WE HIKED UPHILL most of the way. The trees began to silhouette themselves against the sky as the katydids and crickets tuned up. Mitch leaned in and whispered to me, "Gettin' ta just about spooky time, Henri. Let's put a little vinegar in our piss." He reached into his ice chest without missing a step and tossed me a beer.

That was the first time he called me by his late nephew's name.

It wouldn't be the last.

Yvette heard the can crack open. "Are you fucking kidding me, Mitch Judice? I didn't realize we were trying to pass a good time out here."

"Can't spell 'search party' without P-A-R-T-Y," he bellowed.

Old Mitch was like a pack mule under all that gear. I can say with near certainty that he'd never seen the inside of a gym. He had the kind of old-man strength forged in sugarcane fields and crawfish ponds and manual steering columns, the kind of strength that never chiseled a man's physique superficially but worked itself into his bones, the kind that even decades of hard living and easy taking can't strip away.

Yvette kept a measured distance behind us, but not for lack of endurance. Mitch and I were huffing and puffing while her breaths billowed out smooth and steady. Her footsteps fell with hardly a sound.

After about an hour of trekking, we arrived at Walden Lake, roughly twelve square miles and surrounded on all sides by dense, deep woods.

"Alright, now what we wanna do is make camp out here in the open," Mitch said, surveying the lake.

"You're thinking of sleeping out here?" Yvette said.

"Well, Miss Yvette, I ain't tryin' to stay up all night for no hanky-panky, if that's what you mean. Least not with the boy around." He winked at her. I was the "boy," apparently. "Okay, so we want to get us some visibility on all sides . . ."

"Expert hunter, my ass," Yvette muttered in spite of herself.

"Say what?" Mitch shot back.

She sighed. "Look. If you're stupid enough to let the battle come to you—and I'm guessing you are—that's where you wanna be, at least." She pointed out a miniature peninsula penetrating about a hundred feet into the lake. "You got water on three sides. Sole opening into the woods. One way in. One way out. The perfect hunting ground."

"Or killing field," I added.

She shrugged. "Suit yourself."

"Now lookie there, where would we be without you, Miss Yvette?" Mitch said with a wry smile and headed toward the peninsula. Yvette just shook her head and huffed off, heading toward the woods in search of at least a little distance from Mitch.

I followed Mitch onto the soft earth of the peninsula, where we set our things down. Mitch nodded with approval. "Let's hope that old son of a bitch can't swim good. Gather some firewood, and I'll set up the tent."

"Won't a fire attract attention?" I asked Mitch.

"Mm-hmm," is all he said back. He started loading rounds into a .30-06 rifle.

"Got one of those for me?" I asked, only half joking.

"No, no, Old Bessie's one of a kind," he said with an adoring pat on the gun's dull, rust-pocked barrel. He reached over and lifted up the 12-gauge pump-action shotgun. "Know how to use one of these, Theresa's boy?"

"I used to hunt," I answered. I left out the part that what I used to hunt were snakes and it was with my pellet gun. He handed me the shotgun, decidedly heavier than my old Daisy.

"Mm-hmm." He tossed me an old, dirty Crown Royal sack. I pulled out a few shotgun shells. Homemade. I'd seen the shotshell reloading press in his kitchen the day before. I slipped three into the loading port. He piped up, "It's a four and one, Rambo."

"Right," I said and pumped a shell into the chamber before sliding two more into the port. "You always make your own shells?"

"When occasion calls," he answered coyly. Noticing my inquisitiveness about the vague answer, he grinned. "Only one way to hunt a Rougarou." I caught the faintest gleam of sunlight flickering off the custom round he loaded into his rifle. Pure silver.

~

"You needa piss?" he asked before stuffing a wad of dip in his mouth.

The three of us had trekked about two hundred yards into the thick woods that extended out before our camp, finding a small clearing among the trees.

He didn't even wait for my response. "A'ight, go from that tree"—he pointed—"to that one over there. Gimme a good steady stream between 'em."

"Me?" I asked.

"Well, I ain't about to ask Miss Yvette to drop trou in front of us and start spraying all over the place like a goddamn skunk." He nodded a courteous smile at her to cement this great gesture of chivalry.

"Why don't you do it?" I asked.

"Oh, I got that other end covered." He reached into his cargo pocket and pulled out a Gatorade bottle from the drive, full of his old lukewarm piss. So I hadn't dreamed that. He unscrewed the cap.

"Oookay," Yvette blurted, hands up. "I've seen enough."

Mitch turned to her, his piss sloshing almost out of the bottle as he did so. "Whatchu got in your craw?"

"What. The fuck. Are you doing?" she demanded.

"Well, shit, Yvette. How pre-tell do you plan on catching a Rougarou?"

Yvette's eyebrows jumped halfway up her forehead, and she turned to me. I interjected, "Let's just use the word 'suspect' for now. Okay, Mitch?"

He shrugged, "Well you can call a crawfish a crayfish, but it don't change the flavor. Just makes you sound like a idiot."

Yvette pinched the bridge of her nose. "Guys, I'm tired. Can we please stop pretending this is an episode of *Scooby-Doo*?"

I tried to keep the peace. "We probably just need to avoid getting caught up in the semantics."

"Vincent, please don't tell me you think you're going to catch a Rougarou out here."

Mitch admitted, "I mean, I know it's a little far north from where they usually is. But you gotta suspect ya disbelief a little bit on that."

"Vincent, you can't be serious."

"I'm just trying to entertain all—"

"Lookie here. You gonna need a little piss if you wanna catch a Rougarou. Sorry. That's just the way it is."

"I'm out of here."

"It ain't that complicated . . ."

"Vincent, I'll be in town, if you come to your senses."

"Please wait."

"We leave us a little trail, and some Rougarou sniffs it . . ."

"Suspect," I reminded him.

Mitch continued undeterred—emboldened actually: ". . . some Rougarou! Some big, hairy, nutsack-draggin' swamp monster sniffs it, and bam! We got him. What? You think he's gonna just waltz up to us with his own free accord? *Without* any piss? Hell to the no!"

I knew there was a lot going on, but I couldn't help wondering where Mitch had heard the phrase "hell to the no" and when he had started using it unironically.

"This is insane." Yvette threw her arms up and then looked me in the eye. "Vincent, for all you know, this guy here is the killer, and he's leading you up here for the slaughter."

"Ha!" Mitch barked, a little defensively.

She grinned at him, sensing a tender spot beneath his armor, and poked. "Mm-hmm. Maybe he thinks you're getting too close to the answers. Sure. I've seen it a million times."

"Gimme a break," Mitch swatted.

She pressed on, "Makes about as much sense as anything else

I've heard today. He was around for the killings back in 2008. He sure as shit thinks he knows a lot about what's going on up here. Hell, he said it himself: He knows hunting."

"You don't really believe that," I said, trying hard not to make it sound like a question and trying even harder not to let my eyes wander over and analyze Mitch for any signs of guilt.

"I might have actually considered it once or twice. But no, I don't think that the guy holding a bottle of his own pee is that clever. And I don't intend to stick around and humor him anymore than I already have." She turned her eyes from his face to mine. "And I really don't think you should either, Vincent. You don't know what you're doing, son. Out here. With him. You need some rest, and honestly, you need some help, and this man right here sure as hell ain't it." She shook her head and headed back into the woods behind us.

"Hey, Miss Yvette!" Mitch called out, stopping her in her tracks. "'Fore ya go, can you settle a bet between the doctor here and me?"

She rolled her eyes. "Sure, Mitch."

He stepped toward her, a wild smile in his eye. "So, we was talkin' yesterday. And doc here thinks my boy Henri shot his self in the head out on that houseboat."

Her eyes narrowed.

"But I say nuh-uh. Not *my* Henri. Not in a million . . ." Another step. ". . . billion years." His smile intensified, squeezing all joy out, leaving room only for boiling, bitter spite. "Seein's how you and Edward was the only ones out there, and seein's how Edward is probably in about seven or eight pieces right about now—or hell, maybe he's the Rougarou we out here huntin'—I thought maybe you could tell us who won our little bet."

She didn't answer.

She just glared at him. The light was dimming, but I could see the glossiness of tears in her eyes. "Goodbye, Vincent," she finally muttered.

By her tone alone, I realized that Mitch was right. Henri hadn't died by his own hand.

I remembered something Yvette had said long ago, after Henri shot Langlinais: "If I'd have found myself face to face with the man that killed Dane, I'd have put a bullet in his head too." That's exactly what she'd thought she was doing out on that houseboat. I finally began to realize why Yvette and Edward had been so resistant to my insistence that Henri was innocent, why they refused to even consider the possibility.

For them, it really did change everything.

"Yvette, is it true?"

She stared at me. Took a deep breath and released a shaky exhale.

She left, and I watched the forest swallow her up into its darkness, wondering if I should let her go. If I should follow. Who was less trustworthy at this point: her or Mitch?

"Oh shit, I almost took a sip." Mitch chuckled. He lowered the bottle of urine from near his lips, shook his head, and started drizzling the contents out. He turned back to me. "C'mon, Theresa's boy. We ain't got all day."

"You knew?" I asked him. "She shot him. And you knew?"

"I know my boy. That's all I know. Now c'mon. You wanna catch this Rougarou? Start squirtin'."

I dawdled over to the tree, unzipped and got started. At a certain point, you just steer into the skid. "Move those feet!" he yelled from behind me. I jumped to it, shuffling in a staggered two-step. "Atta boy," he yelped. About five feet from my finish line, my shoe caught a tree root and I went down hard.

Wild laughter drew my attention away from the wet spot on my pants. I looked over to see Mitch on his hands and knees, howling. Between gasps, he cried, "Son of a . . . bitch . . . I shoulda been filming . . . send that shit into Danny Tanner . . . Henri, you shoulda seen yoself . . ."

That was the second time.

I gathered myself and zipped. Mitch had recovered from his fit and was picking up a folded piece of construction paper, which had apparently fallen from my pocket. He unfolded it, revealing Ivy's Valentine's heart. I didn't remember grabbing it before I left, but here it was.

He handed it to me. "Cute, doc. You plannin' on proposin' to me out here or somethin'?"

Mitch moved toward an old oak at the end of my piss-trail and cracked open a Pelican case he'd brought along. He looked so small and solitary against the vastness of the forest before him.

So insignificant out there alone.

I looked down at the card in my hand. A sudden urge rushed over me. I needed to speak to Elsie. And to Ivy. I needed them to hear my voice. I needed to feel like a part of them again. I reached into my pocket.

Empty.

I'd left my phone back in Breaux Bridge.

I turned to find Mitch backing away from a small electronic device he'd affixed to the oak. He was mumbling something to himself, his eyes stuck on the ground at the foot of the tree. There was nothing there worth studying that I could see.

"What's that?" I asked, pointing at the device.

He looked up at me, bewildered, like I'd just awoken him from a dream. "Whatchu want?" He said it like I was a stranger stopping him on the street. Like we hadn't just spent the last seven hours together. Like I hadn't watched him pour his own piss out of a Gatorade bottle.

"Mitch. The thing on the tree there, what is it?"

He squinted at me, hard.

I pointed forcefully, hoping to ground him back into reality. "*That thing,* Mitch. Right there."

Finally, he turned and spotted the device. "Right. Oh yeah. Mais, that's just a...um. A...um. Called a...trail camera." The life seemed to settle back into his face. "Motion activated. Yeah. Use 'em for deer usually. Somethin' comes by, this sucka flashes a little light and takes him a picture." He slapped me on the back and effectively erased from his mind whatever spell of incoherence he'd just suffered.

I tried to forget it too.

"Gonna see if we can't get us a Rougarou Glamour Shot." He stepped back and waved his hand in front of the camera, eliciting a little flash.

We set up two more cameras on our way back, at about one hundred yards and fifty yards from camp. At each site, Mitch drizzled his piss along the ground and assured me we would catch our monster. I was beginning to have my doubts.

It was twilight when we finished. I was surveying the darkening woods around me, willing my eyes to acclimate more quickly, when I bumped into his back. He had frozen there, staring at the ground.

I matched his gaze to a patch of mud before him, at a single footprint indented into the earth. Imperfect but clear enough, it was just the top half of a foot, five toes lining the print.

"See that? No heel print. Just like a man walking up on the balls of his feet. The way a dog walks. Just like the one they found at that Stacy Breaton's house out in Arnaudville. Just like it." He snapped a picture with an old digital camera.

"Could be a bear, right?" I'd seen a few bear prints before, early in my research.

"Naw, padna. This is it. We gonna see us a Rougarou tonight."

CAMPFIRE TALES

Mitch grilled venison steaks over the fire. "By the way," he said, chewing on a chunk of gristle, "you can call me Uncle Mitch if you want. I *am* ya uncle after all."

"Oh. That's... okay," I said. "I mean, I appreciate that. It's just hard to start calling someone uncle in your thirties."

"Suit y'self." He grabbed an old Panasonic cassette-deck boombox and pressed "Play." Buckwheat Zydeco was halfway into "Tee Nah Nah" when the tape started. He reached into the ice chest and called back, "Ay, Henri. How 'bout a reload?"

That was the third time.

After he tossed me a beer, Mitch threw another log on the fire, sending a flare of sparks twisting up into the night above us.

I scanned the still darkness surrounding us on all sides. "Don't you think we oughta kill the fire now?" I suggested.

He laughed. "Hell no! What, you wanna be insuspicuous? Sneak up on him? Tap him on the shoulder? No way, José. Here's what you don't do with a Rougarou: You don't sneak up on him. That's for damn sure."

"So how do you plan to catch one?"

"You don't." He sipped his beer and smiled. "You let him

catch you." He cranked the volume up on the radio. Buckwheat's wailing vocals blared out of the speakers, and Mitch hollered along into the night, in something approximating a melody, about being in love with a married woman . . ." His voice echoed off the tree line, and I reached to make sure the Remington was still at my side. I had to admit he was right. If there's one thing we knew about whatever we were after, it's that it preyed on campers.

So here we were. Campers.

"Whatchu think he looks like?" Mitch asked.

"Who?"

"The Rougarou. Whatchu think that son of a bitch looks like?"

"I don't know. I've got some theories."

"Uh-huh," he prompted.

"Well, based on Edward's progress notes and Henri's recordings after he killed Langlinais, I think we can expect a few things from someone who's been infected."

His eyes lit up.

I continued, "So they'll have pale skin. Almost translucent. And bloodshot eyes. Everywhere that would usually be white would be deep, deep red. Their pupils would dilate so big that you wouldn't be able to tell if they'd been blue or brown or green. It would just be one big black circle in that sea of bloodred. Most of this seems to clear up after death. There also seems to be some bleeding from the gums. Maybe even some patchiness to their hair patterns. And rapid breaths, almost like a dog panting. If those tracks we saw tonight were actually from someone who was infected, I don't know, maybe they walk up on the balls of their feet. Kind of like a . . ."

"A wolf?" He beamed. "Whooooo, hot damn. I bet they get 'em some big ol' claws and some nasty fangs for teeth too."

"I don't know." I shrugged. I realized I was growing more and more reluctant to find out.

We whittled through the Coors Light one by one before he pulled out a flask the size of a Bible.

"Maybe we should take it easy, stay alert," I said.

"Just playin' the part, Doc. Nothin' to see here, Mr. Rougarou! Just a uncle and his nephew passin' a good time!" He took a long swig and handed it over. "Warm y'self up."

I took it. "You know alcohol only makes you colder, right? It pulls warmth away from your core."

He just stared at me like I was speaking German.

I took a swig of the jet fuel inside. Lord knows what he'd siphoned into there. Probably homemade. I felt the burn of it scratch its way down my throat and into my chest, where I immediately felt its warmth. "You colder, Mr. Science?" He winked.

An Art Neville ballad crooned from the speakers now, interrupted intermittently by an occasional "Mm-hmm" from the DJ. Mitch had apparently recorded a weekend Zydeco Stomp broadcast from the public radio station in Lafayette. Probably didn't trust local radio outside of Acadiana.

He took another swig. "How old's ya li'l one?"

Something howled in the distance. I grabbed the shotgun.

"Relax, Doc. Just a coyote."

Somehow, I actually found that reassuring. I laid the gun back down, but not far from my side. "Uh, she's . . . um, Ivy's a year and a half."

"That's a good age. I know they say that about every age. But yeah, that one's a good one."

"She keeps us busy."

He nodded at the fire. "Bet she's a cutie. Got them good

genes, huh?" He smacked my arm and sat back, contemplating whether to ask his next question. "So. How's ya mom 'n' them? Back in Lafayette."

I wondered if he even knew that my folks had moved away all those years ago. "They're good. Miss you."

He chortled. "Sure." He took a swig. "Look, it's been damn near forty years since Henri's daddy died. And I don't miss that son of a bitch an inch. Dollars to dogshit, ya mama feels the same about me. I don't blame her. Although, I did help bring you into this world, young man. Don't forget that."

It's true. All those years ago in the bathtub out in St. Martinville. "Yeah, thanks for that, by the way." I lifted my shirt to show him the protrusion of my outie belly button, the mark he and his surgical skills had left on me.

"Got damn!" he guffawed. "Looks like a extra little pecker pokin' outcha belly! I just hope the rest of you outgrew that nub! Didn't start out with much as I recollect."

"I *was* about one minute old."

"Gotcha. Grow-er, not a show-er." His laughter died down in a cough. "Hey, how's Marie? She still givin' e'rbody hell and runnin' the show? Y'know, we never got much along, her and me."

My Aunt Marie, the eldest daughter, served as the family's unofficial CEO. If anyone outside the Judice clan ever asked about Mitch, Aunt Marie would offer up a polite but terse smile and say, "Oh, you know that old lone wolf. He just doesn't like to roll his wheels." And that would be that.

"Yeah, she misses you too. You oughta come into town some time and visit," I said, knowing full well he wouldn't. "They'd be excited to see you."

"Yeah, maybe. I don't know. I'm pretty busy, me." He took a

longer, more determined swig from the flask. He coughed hard on it this time.

"You okay?"

"Aw yeah. Been a while. Whooo. Hadn't had a drink in . . ." He started flipping through his fingers. "Eight years. Them doctors tried to shut ol' Mitch down. But hey, I'm wit a doctor now, so . . ." He shrugged. I tried not to react as he handed me the flask.

"Yeah," I said. I took a swig and wondered if I should hand it back. Afraid of inciting a fight over his drinking, I did.

There was another howl from the woods. Louder this time.

Mitch ignored it. He stoked the fire absentmindedly. "So, how's Brit been?" he slurred.

Brittany Judice.

Henri's wife.

I didn't answer, hoping he'd catch his mistake. But he didn't. "Um. You mean *Elsie*?"

He looked up at me with that same befuddled stare from before.

I couldn't keep playing along. "Mitch. I'm not Henri. You know that, right?"

He blinked hard for a second or two, then snapped his gaze away. He tossed his poker into the fire with a scoff. "I know."

"It's just you've called me Henri a few times tonight and . . ."

"Fuck's the matter with you?" He tightened up. "I know who the fuck you are. Ya name's . . . uh . . ."

After a second, I said, "Vincent."

"*Vincent*. I know. Whatchu think—I'm stupid? I know you. Yeah, I know you. You're the asshole that wrote all that bullshit about how your cousin was guilty and how he was just some crazy son of a bitch."

"Mitch, I didn't mean . . ."

"We all know whatchu meant. But lemme ask you this: You lose sleep over it? Huh? Parading him out there like a monster, getting all them eyeballs on some fucked-up version of the truth? Did it eat away at you? Did it tear up your insides and make you smash every mirror in the house? No. I bet it didn't. Cause you too good for all that, huh? All y'all fuckin' snotty Lafayette assholes witchya PhDs and ya big fuck-you attitudes... y'know we ain't the... the..." He fumbled in his anger.

"Mitch, I'm sorry."

"Ain't nothin' to be sorry about." He stared at the fire and mumbled to himself, "Get a couple doctors in the family, and all of a sudden y'all can't even wipe y'all own asses. So ya fuckin' bankrupt the rest of us for every little portal or stent or whatever you put in so you can hire somebody to wipe it for—" He cut himself off, biting his lip and simmering there in the cold.

I stared at the fire for a while, thinking about Mitch's Cajun Cannibal House of Horrors and how much he must have hated himself the longer he went on with the freak show. How much he must have despised every dollar it gave him. Every bill it paid.

No one spoke for a few minutes.

"I wish I'd known him," I finally blurted. "Henri, I mean. I wish I had known him."

Mitch chewed on his lip and kept his eyes on the fire. "You woulda liked him."

"Yeah."

"He probably wouldn'ta thought too much of you, though. He hated doctors."

I laughed. "Can't say I blame him."

We sat there a minute. Then I said, "He was a good man. Certainly not the monster everybody else thinks he was."

Mitch took a sip.

I continued, "That night that Yvette..." I could hardly believe it but I knew it was true. "That night she shot him, he probably saved Nicole's life, going after Cole Cormier. He knew what Cole was. He knew the kind of monster he'd turned into. And he chased him down anyway. He hunted him down to that houseboat and snapped his neck, all to save a little girl he barely even knew."

"Uh-huh. That's my boy" was all he said in return.

"Mitch, how did you know Henri didn't shoot himself? I mean besides the vague autopsy report. You were so certain earlier with Yvette."

"'Cause we was supposed to go huntin' together the next day. We had made plans."

"Hunting?"

"Yeah. He wouldn'ta made plans and done...that. He woulda called me first. He woulda..." His voice cracked.

"What were y'all going hunting for?" As far as I knew, all the usual game were out of season when Henri died. "Mitch, what were y'all planning on hunting?"

He didn't answer. He didn't have to. Maybe he was embarrassed. We both began to realize what this trip was really about, why he had agreed to come out here, what we were really getting out of it. The ghost of Henri was as palpable there as the smoke pouring out of the fire.

We sat there and listened to the fire crackle.

Suddenly, a cacophony of howls echoed throughout the woods.

Mitch killed the radio.

Their frenzied yips and barks echoed deep in the forest, like a hundred little record scratches piling one on top of the other. Growing nearer.

We stared at the tree line in front of us. The darkness revealed nothing.

"Coyotes hunting?" I asked.

Mitch slowly shook his head. "Naw. They sound scared."

Then a dim flash.

Mitch's first trail camera. About two hundred yards into the woods.

The panicked yelps grew louder in the darkness.

Wilder. Closer.

Another flash. The second trail camera. One hundred yards out.

Mitch picked up Old Bessie. I realized that at some point I had grabbed the shotgun again. I fingered the safety, but in the darkness I couldn't make out the orange indicator to tell which way was on or off.

The final trail camera flashed. Only fifty yards out.

I gritted my teeth to keep them from chattering.

I blinked hard, willing my eyes to see something. Anything.

Suddenly, the tree line exploded with motion. A frantic pack of fur and paws beating the earth for their lives. The chorus of howls heading straight for us.

They veered off to our left, away along the bank of the water.

Then stillness. A terrible quiet.

A loud, solitary yelp rose from the woods before us. Like a child's scream. My hands were shaking. The screech pitched up and down, from glass-shattering shriek to guttural moan. At its highest pitch, it suddenly cut short, as if the needle had been ripped off the record.

I exhaled. "What were they running from . . ."

A flash.

The trail camera fifty yards out.

Another.

And another.

"Goddamn son of a bitch," Mitch muttered.

Steady beats, strobing every second.

He climbed to his feet with a groan.

"What?"

"Camera's busted."

"You sure something's not right in front of it, setting it off?"

"Naw. They fuck up like this sometimes. Gotta go reset it," he said with a step forward.

"Are you insane?" I jumped up.

"Maybe," he said. "But I ain't gonna hide here and piss my panties. C'mon."

"What? I'm not going out there." My adrenaline was surging.

"Whatchu scared of, Theresa's boy?" he said, grinning at me. *"People?"*

I paused. Weighing the metrics of my masculinity.

"Giddyup." He smacked my back, and started walking toward the tree line. "Keep ya eyes on a swivel!"

I fell in behind him despite my inclination to hide in the tent. I hesitated at the tree line, considered turning back, but seeing Mitch disappear into the dense, dark woods, I followed.

Away from the fire, the February chill bit at my flesh through every gap in my jacket. Wire-thin branches and thorns and tangled brush scratched against our faces and clothes as we pressed on, as if trying to hold us back. The path hadn't felt this difficult the first time. Every stick that crunched underfoot sounded like a cymbal crash. My eyes darted all around, waiting for the unseen danger to strike. Mitch stopped suddenly. My gaze elsewhere, I ran smack into him, nearly knocking him over. "How 'bout you wait here, couillon. Watch my back," he commanded through gritted teeth. I nodded apprehensively.

Ten yards ahead lay the clearing where we had set the camera that was malfunctioning. The light strobed steadily on the opposite end. Mitch lifted his rifle and crept off to the right, along the tree line. I found a large oak and pressed my back against it, relieved to stay behind in the cover of the forest. I watched Mitch pass around a tree and disappear into the darkness.

I waited for him to emerge.

And waited.

What felt like ten minutes passed. Surely it had only been one.

I craned my neck away from the tree to get a better look. But still, no Mitch.

I risked a cautious step to my left in hopes of gaining an unobstructed view.

And then another step. And another.

The strobing light made it impossible for my eyes to spot anything in the blinding brightness or adjust to the darkness that fell between flashes.

Then I smelled it. Something foul and rotten. Like decay.

A noise to my left. A deep, guttural groan.

Then silence.

Again. A low, grunt. I turned my head slowly to the left, at the edge of the clearing, trying to place the sound. My fingers clamped down on the stock of the shotgun.

Finally, I caught a hint of movement there. Just a moment glimpsed within the strobe of the camera.

A figure was hunched over, about ten yards from me.

It looked like a ghost out there in the stark light of the camera's flash.

I searched the other edge for Mitch, but the flashes were too blinding for me to see anything in that direction.

Back to the creature. It seemed closer somehow, though it hadn't moved an inch. It huddled its pale, gray frame over something in the grass, something slick and wet. I could hear the sound of its ravenous gnawing, chewing and tearing away at muscle and tendon. I knew the mass pinned beneath it was a body.

The creature's movements came to me in still-frame images, caught in the one second intervals of the pulsing light. In the blackness between flashes, my eyes were useless.

Flash. It was buried face first in the carcass.

Flash. Its head had jerked away, ripping off a chunk of flesh.

Flash. Back down for another bite. Scraping with its hands.

Flash ... Flash ... Flash ... I didn't make a sound. I didn't so much as breathe. But suddenly, with another flash, it was looking up at me. Right at me. Blood soaking its pale, beastly face.

Flash. It was standing on two legs now, in a crouch, still staring me down. Eyes glowing in the camera's light. Sparse patches of filthy black hair matted against its mottled gray naked skin.

Flash. It had lowered itself again.

Flash. It was closer now, charging toward me.

I lifted the gun, aiming into the darkness, toward the direction of its pounding feet.

Flash. Closer still. In that instant, all I could see was its mouth. Snarling, bearing its bloody fangs. I squeezed, but the trigger didn't move. The safety was still on.

I fumbled in the dark with the safety, finally pushing the button in with a click. I aimed again.

Flash. But the beast was gone. Disappeared into the tree line to my left. Or into thin air.

Then the post-flash blackness held. The pulses of light ceased. My heart was kicking against my rib cage. The breaths I'd been holding in were bursting out of my lungs in fits. I struggled to acclimate my eyes to the dark, peering all around me for some sign of the creature.

But nothing.

The trees and brush that had provided some cover now seemed to be closing in on me. I felt claustrophobic, vulnerable. Still clinging to the shotgun, I stepped out into the clearing, my eyes trained on the darkness of the woods.

Still nothing.

I found myself drawn to my left, where the beast had just been. Morbid fascination pulled me. Closer and closer. Nearly there, when my foot caught the root of a tree and down I went. The shotgun sailed out of my hands as I braced for the fall.

I felt myself land on soft earth, my hands sinking into thick, sticky mud and tangles of moss.

But the pungent copper odor filled my nostrils and churned my guts.

I lifted my hands out of what I was still praying was mud and moss and detritus. But the warm blood and entrails coating them shimmered in the moonlight.

I looked down, my eyes fully adjusted now, to see the fresh carcass of a coyote, its back flayed and oozing blood.

I froze, simultaneously awed and repulsed. The carnage was devastating.

A flashlight popped on from above, throwing a beam down into my eyes, blinding me.

"There you are." Mitch's voice was quiet, severe. No hint of humor at all. "After all these years. I gotchu, you son of a bitch."

"Mitch, it's okay. It's just me."

"You changed back quick, huh?" His consonants were garbled, and I realized he was holding the flashlight in his teeth. His hands were gripped firmly around Old Bessie, aiming her right at my face.

"Mitch. Whoa. Easy."

"Uh-uh. Don't you move."

I didn't. "Mitch, I'm not the Rougarou."

"Then whatchu doin' there, huh?" He flicked the flashlight's beam quickly from my bloody hands to the carcass.

"No, Mitch. Listen, I—" My eyes darted back at the tree line, waiting for the creature to return. I wasn't sure who to be more afraid of.

"Eleven years I been waitin'."

"No, Mitch. *Uncle* Mitch. Listen. I came here with you."

"I'm alone out here, padna."

I heard him click the safety off.

"No! Uncle Mitch, please. *Please.* You drove me out here. I live in Breaux Bridge. Remember? Me and my wife, Elsie. My daughter, Ivy. She's eighteen months old. My mom is Theresa. Sweet T! Your baby sister. You said you might come visit the family soon." The words were pouring out. I couldn't spot his face past the flashlight to see if it was working, if any of it was sinking in. "I'm Henri's cousin! We're family. Me and you. We're family! Please. You brought me out here. We're not alone out here! There's . . . something!" The tree line beside us was still.

The gun barrel was trembling.

His voice came out thin, shaking. "I'm here alone."

"No," I pleaded. "You're not, Uncle Mitch. Please."

He held the barrel on me, the battle within himself—with himself—tearing his poor, booze- and grief-addled mind apart.

I could hear the tremor in his breaths. In-in-in-in-in. Out-out-out-out-out. Each tortured exhalation billowed clouds of steam along the beam of light emitting from between his teeth. He bit down on the flashlight.

Finally, the gun began to lower.

A growl from the left. I looked over to the outer rim. The brush trembled with the motion of the beast.

Mitch swung the flashlight and leveled Old Bessie at the spot of movement. Without hesitation, he fired. The rifle rounds exploded in my ears.

Three shots. And the dull thud of a heavy body hitting the ground.

We walked over to where the body lay. Mitch shone the flashlight on his victim.

We saw the creature now for what it was.

"Black bear," Mitch muttered.

It was thin. Probably starving. Balding with mange. What little hair clung to its sickly gray body in rotting, matted tangles.

"Just . . . a bear," he repeated.

He collapsed to his knees, laying his hands on the dead bear. His quivering whimpers broke into loud drunken sobs. A wave of disappointment and anguish washed over him. He'd built his life around this pursuit, when the pursuit was all he had. Without it, all that was left was emptiness and the threat of having to come out of the wilderness and fill that void with something else.

I let him weep, and I released a long exhale at the full moon floating over our little clearing. "It's okay, Uncle Mitch. It's okay."

THE MORNING AFTER

(As found in the online Google Doc entitled "Research")

February 17, 2020

THIS MARGE CHARACTER keeps staring at me from behind her desk. She's doing it right now. At least I think she is. It's hard to tell on account of her lazy eye. She's either staring at me or the vending machine, but the only thing left in the vending machine is a packet of Pop-Tarts and a Hostess Honey Bun, and it's two in the afternoon. So she's probably staring at me.

I'm assuming her name is Marge, because there's a cross-stitched sign behind her proclaiming that "Marge Is in Charge!" So, either she's Marge or she's filling in for Marge. But she certainly seems to think she's in charge of this computer, so I'm probably right. It took five minutes of pleading and twenty dollars cash to convince her to let me use the office PC so that I could find the address I need and then put as much down in this Google Doc as I can in whatever time I have left.

But I'm getting off point already.

The reason I'm writing right now in this fly-infested car rental office, is that I'm scared.

Shit.

Marge just asked if I was okay. Maybe she knew I was writing about her.

I'll change the subject, just in case.

I woke up this morning—which means I must have dozed off at some point during the night—alone in Mitch's tent. I found him outside, whistling over a fire, pushing around a couple of sausage patties in a skillet. And when he saw me, he made a comment about how "the Rougarou tore that poor coyote up pretty good last night."

I didn't know what to say. I tried to remind him that it was a bear. We had the carcass to prove it.

He scoffed at the idea. Said there was no way that scrawny, mangey thing he had put out of its misery could have caught that coyote. Or killed those kids. Nope, he said. Something else did it and got scared off by his camera flashes. The bear was just scavenging.

But Mitch was convinced we were close. Said he could feel it. Said, "He'll be back, that son-of-a-bitch Rougarou. We'll see him tonight."

That's when I knew he would never let go. But what scared me most was that I considered staying with him.

It scared me enough that I had him drive me here, to the Corinth, Mississippi, branch of Hertz.

Here at Hertz, Marge is apparently also in charge of television programming, and she's an ardent fan of the twenty-four-hour news cycle. When she isn't looking at me, she's reading her *People* Magazine and listening to the cable news pundits on the television she's got propped up in the corner of the room.

Most of what they've been discussing for the last hour or so has been some new virus slowly making its way across the globe. I don't think they're talking about the one I've been obsessing over, the one I've nicknamed the RG virus. Not sure how seriously to take any of it, really. In fact, someone just said that "this virus poses, quote, 'a very low risk' to Americans..." Sounds like Italy is getting the worst of it. So it's definitely not the RG virus and therefore not my concern.

Anyway, Marge hasn't looked up from her *People*.

But all the epidemic hubbub, which is maybe nothing, does have me thinking. Specifically, thinking about those Reddit posts. And that's what led me to this computer in the first place.

There's probably a missing person's report on me by now back home. You must be worried sick.

I did try calling you, Elsie, if you're reading this. I swear. Marge let me use the phone for another ten dollars. It went straight to voicemail, and then I ran out of money. I know it's not the point right now, but you should really empty out your voicemail box. You might miss an important message one day.

I know that's not funny.

I'm sorry, honey.

The one thing in-charge-Marge hasn't billed me for, but probably only because there's some kind of law against it, is the county yellow pages. I've got it right here. Looking at three different listings for Gregory Smith in Booneville. Mistersippi-GregorySmith from Reddit. Bleeding gums. Abdominal pain. I found him. Or at least I found three of him.

Oh. And guess what. Turns out MapQuest still exists. Yeah. Turn-by-turn printouts and everything. Like I'm back in high school. Maybe I don't need my smartphone so badly after all.

As soon as this rental car gets here, I'll check out the addresses. Ask around. I'm so close.

And then I'll come home, Elsie. I swear.

But if anything happens

If

If anything does happen, I just want you and Ivy to know that I love you both more than anything. And I'm sorry.

THE LEAF

Everything happens so fast after that. Marge swipes my credit card, hands me the rental keys, and asks that I please log off the computer now.

It takes me twenty-five minutes to get to the first Gregory Smith's address, in a small neighborhood in the center of Booneville. Overlooking two acres of lawn, the two-story home sits a comfortable distance from its neighbors, without the need for a fence. A long driveway borders the foot of the front lawn's slope, leading to a closed garage. There's a small soccer goal on one end of the yard, the ball resting not far away. A white bench swing hangs from the columnated front porch beside a pair of rocking chairs. I look for an omen or a sign of anything nefarious: a locked-up woodshed, a bloody footprint tracking around the garage, blackout curtains on the windows, an orange and gray cat to lead me somewhere. But there's nothing.

I ring the bell and hear the first seven notes of "Für Elise" chime inside. I check the other two addresses I've scribbled on a Post-it Note. The next one is about ten minutes away. The third is on the edge of town, bordering the woods.

If I hurry, I'll still have time to make it to both today.

And then I can go home.

The door opens only enough to clank against the chain lock. A pair of pleasant green eyes widens on the other side. "Yes?" she says.

"Hello, ma'am," I begin my rehearsed routine. "My name is Dr. Vincent Blackburn. Is there a Gregory Smith who lives here?"

She hesitates. "Um. Can I ask what this is about?" Her voice is hospitable, just the slightest twinge of a Southern drawl.

I glance down at the other addresses. I can be at number two by three o'clock if I don't drag this out too long, if I can keep any rambling chitchat in check. "Yes, ma'am. I'm just looking for a certain Gregory Smith to talk about some medical problems he's been having. I'm not even sure of his address."

"Like a... house call?" She studies me with a befuddled expression.

"Something like that, I guess. I'm sorry to bother you, ma'am."

"No, no bother. Doctor... ?"

"Blackburn."

"Right. Dr. Blackburn. Do you have an ID of some kind or—I don't know—a medical badge on you? It's just you can't be too careful these days."

"Of course." I show her my state medical license and my driver's license for the photo. She studies both carefully while a young woman pushes a jogging stroller down the otherwise empty road behind me.

"Louisiana?"

"I'm just passing through really. So, is there a Gregory Smith who lives here?"

She hesitates, understandably suspicious of the strange man on her doorstep. "Well, my husband goes by Greg usually. But I don't . . . I'm sorry. This is all just a little strange." She giggles to diffuse the awkwardness.

"I know. Trust me, I know."

"I'm sorry. I'm not very helpful."

"No, it's okay. I appreciate your time."

She glances through the crack in the door at my license once more, which I've lowered but kept in view. She sighs, and part of her guard chips away. "I don't know. I don't mean to be impolite. I mean you seem nice enough, Doctor. Are you thirsty? Can I send you off with a glass of lemonade or somethin' for your trouble?"

"No, ma'am. Thank you. You've been plenty of help, really." I take another look at the Post-it, at the third address. Before retreating from the porch, I show it to her. "Do you know by any chance if the woods along this last address connect to the ones off Highway 130? By those three big crosses out on the side of the road?"

She studies the address and tsks on her teeth. "Can't say." She studies my face again. Finally, with only a hint of residual reticence, her hand reaches up and unlocks the chain. "Come on in. I've got a map somewhere around here."

"No, that's okay," I start to protest as she opens the door.

"It's no problem, really. Like I said, you seem nice enough." She ushers me in and tugs down on the waistline of her Lululemon hoodie, pulling it lower over her black yoga pants. The act of modesty is enough to make me feel like a predator under her gaze, a perverted monster who could pounce at any second. I shrink my posture down a bit and make an effort to keep my eyes up, avoiding even the semblance of a wayward glance. She looks to be around my age, maybe a bit younger. Her face is still hanging onto the last remnants of baby fat, but a mild weariness in her kind eyes provides a decent preview of what middle age will hold when the lines set in. Her hair is pulled back into a bushy ponytail, the ends damaged from years of dyeing and straightening. "Kitchen's right through here, Doctor."

I follow her through the wainscoted foyer and the impeccably decorated living room. I imagine they call it a sitting room.

She ushers me into the kitchen, a Restoration Hardware ad ripped from the pages of the latest quarterly issue. Viking appliances. Subway tile backsplash. A separate faucet above the stove, for filling pots.

She has me sit at the table in the breakfast nook as she digs through drawers, looking for a map. "You sure I can't get you some lemonade? How 'bout some coffee?"

"No, thank you."

The second hand on my watch is cacophonous in the quiet kitchen.

"So, Louisiana, huh?" she says, rummaging through the drawers. "Kinda a long way from home, aren't you?"

"Yes, ma'am. I guess so." Glance at my watch.

She shuts the drawer, peeved at the missing map. "Hmm." She glances around the room. "I'm sorry. I don't know where that dang thing went."

"Really, it's okay." I start to stand but stall as she pulls up a seat opposite me, clutching a cup of coffee.

"More in the pot if you want a cup." She smiles.

"No, really, I'm fine." I've already wasted ten minutes here. "Well, thanks anyway..." I start. And then I notice her wrist.

Her sleeve falls back a bit as she lifts the mug to her lips, revealing a purple and green bruise on her arm. Yellowing at the edges, where someone's fingers have grabbed her. I've seen dozens like it before.

I stare a little too long. She notices and pulls the sleeve back down with an effortful smile.

I settle back into my seat and pocket the other addresses. For the first time since arriving, I'm not thinking about them. "You know, I didn't get your name."

"Oh, right." She sets her coffee down. "Lily. Greg's wife." She wiggles her ring finger for proof. Her identification.

"Lily. Let me ask you . . . Your husband, Greg, has he been feeling sick lately? Like the person I mentioned earlier?"

She sighs like a kid caught in a white lie. "Well, maybe a little. It's just that he didn't say anything about postin' online."

I glance around to reassure myself that the rest of the house is empty. No lights or televisions or any other distractions are on outside of the kitchen. "Lily, where's Greg?"

She seems reluctant to admit the truth of her husband's dire situation or where he might have gone. "Maybe *I* can try to answer some of your questions."

"Okay. Tell me, Lily, has Greg been actin' strange?" I leave the "g" off my verb without slipping too far into an accent, mimicking her Southern twang just enough to endear myself but not enough to suggest mockery. Opening the door to her trust.

I'm just like you. Tell me what happened.

She proceeds cautiously. "I guess a little. I mean, he was worried, of course, when neither of the doctors could help him feel better. Angry. Y'know, about the lack of answers. But that makes sense, right? I mean I was worried too."

"Of course. Did that bruise on your wrist happen before or after he got sick?"

She pulls both sleeves down past her fingertips.

I keep my voice calm, nonjudgmental. Casual. I sigh,

"Marriages are hard. You say things. You *do* things. Sometimes you hurt each other with words, and sometimes..." I shrug and let the unfinished thought hang there for the taking. In her silence I can tell she finishes it on her own, makes the sentiment her own, as her eyes avoid mine and drop down to the table. I lean in. "Hell, my wife and I have barely spoken in the past month."

I'm just like you. Tell me what happened.

"I should be home right now, in fact. With her. I'm *supposed* to be home with her, and here I am running around Mississippi trying to find answers. We do all these things we regret. You love each other, and you trust each other. And the last thing you want to do is hurt each other. It can just be so hard, right? Knowing when to ask for help. When to admit there's a problem."

I suddenly realize that in my confession, I've stopped studying her. Her eyes have grown glossy. I home in again. "Lily, you can trust me. I want to help. Are you okay? When's the last time you saw him?"

A glimmer of a tear puddles and quivers in her reddening eyes. She forces a closed mouth smile, fighting against reality, trying to maintain the act that everything with Greg is fine. That she's fine. "He's been through a lot."

"Of course," I reply, my heart pounding. "You both have. Tell me, why did he go to the doctor in the first place?"

She wipes the tear with her sleeve. "He was having some stomach pains for about a week. Feeling kind of faint. That's about all he told me. He's not big on complainin'." She shakes her head. "This one time a few years back, he came home after a night out and said his finger kinda hurt. He just put some ice on it and went to bed. Next day, he woke up and his hand was purple. Finger all twisted off to the side. He'd broken the damn thing *and* dislocated it! I told him to go to the ER, but he just grabbed it and jerked it back into place. Showed up thirty minutes late to the office and stayed an extra thirty minutes to make up for it. That's the way he's always been."

"Did the doctor prescribe him anything? When he went in for stomach pains, I mean. Did he see a specialist or anything?"

"No. Just the one doctor at the walk-in clinic. He ran some lab work. Told him to take some Tylenol and call if things got worse."

"Oh . . . And he never referred Greg to anyone else?"

"No sir."

"Okay. So did things get worse?"

Lily purses her lips and shakes her head. "It's just so hard to tell with that man. He's like my daddy. You just never know what's going on with them. When I met Greg—this was back after high school; seems like forever—my mom kinda warned me. Not like warned me off of him. Just saying, 'You'll have your work cut out for you with that one.' She knew. She'd been through it with my daddy. I probably just rolled my eyes at her. What did she know, right?"

I chuckle along in agreement.

"It's funny how you marry someone like your daddy. I don't mean that it's gross, because it isn't. I love my daddy. It'd make sense I'd want to marry someone like him, right?"

"Sure. I guess that makes sense."

"I just mean that it's funny because you inherit all these little . . . I don't know . . . quirks. What d'ya call 'em? Piccadi—Picca—"

"Peccadillos?"

"Yeah. Those little things. They make you just like your parents, and then you get the chance to water that down and find somebody different. Somebody who might add something new to the mix when you have babies or whatever. But you pick someone just like your daddy, and we all keep everything the same. It all just gets passed along."

She chokes up on the last couple of sentences. I wonder if she knows how far gone Greg is. How much does she realize? How much has she witnessed? Her tears fight their way through the dam as it all starts to crack.

She knows where he is. I just have to get it out of her.

I move to the counter to grab a tissue for her, but my hand stalls as I'm reaching.

Glancing out the kitchen window and into the backyard, past the patio set and the ceramic grill, beyond the swing set and the ivy-covered trellis, at the far end of the yard, my eyes land on a tarp covering what appears to be a large car or SUV. Peeking through from underneath are the front tires and a white bumper. The plates pulled off. The tarp conceals the specifics of its shape, but I'm almost certain there's a VW Atlas underneath.

Mitch's voice echoes in my head. *"Germans..."*

My heart drops into my stomach.

Edward drives an Atlas.

Lily says something that I don't hear. I barely notice her voice. The house seems too quiet all of a sudden.

I turn back and smile politely, wondering if she caught my stunned gaze. If she did, she doesn't let on. I hand her the tissue, and as her sobs die down, I return to my chair across from her, unable to keep my eyes from darting around for any sign that Greg is here with us.

She sniffles and continues, "But I don't know. Maybe all men are the same. That's been my experience."

I nod and smile, practically oblivious to what she's saying, but aware that her tone of voice called for a pleasant confirmation.

Somewhere in the house a gentle alarm coos. Synthetic harp strings plucked from some operating system. Lily's head perks up a bit at the sound. "Oh. He'll be home soon."

My throat clenches, but I manage to choke out, "Who?"

She doesn't answer. Her eyes drop back down to the crumpled tissue in her hands.

"Lily. You said Greg only saw the one doctor in town."

"Yes, sir." Her voice is more detached now. I can feel her slipping away.

"I thought you had said earlier that he was upset about how *neither* doctor could help."

"Did I?" She smiles thinly.

I try to swallow, but the spit feels like sand in my throat. "Did some other doctor come by the house to check on him? Maybe someone else from out of town? Like me?"

She shrugs. "I must've just misspoken. You sure I can't get you some coffee?"

My guts turn cold. I can feel the sweat beading on my back. My heart hammering against my ribs. "Um. You wouldn't happen to have a phone I could borrow?"

She giggles in the way a ventriloquist's dummy might, an approximation of some familiar emotion. "Well, see, with everything going on, Greg forgot to pay the phone bill. And I never really dealt with it before. So . . ." She shrugs. "I'm sorry."

Until now I hadn't really thought much of our seating arrangement, of the fact that she had positioned herself between me and the front door. I stare at the foyer behind her. It feels so far away. Then I look into her empty, smiling eyes. "Where's Greg, Lily?" My voice is shaking.

She taps her fingers on the tabletop. Her stomach growls.

"He's here," she says, holding her vacant smile. "Just in that room."

Her eyes bounce to the laundry room behind me.

The room is empty. Not a living soul inside. But through the open doorway, I can hear the hum of a deep freeze.

"Want me to fetch him for you?"

I blink and try to remember how to speak. I notice the nails on her tapping fingers. Coarse and dirty. Filthy, in fact. Black residue buried under the edges. Like she's been scraping and clawing through something unspeakable. "Um. No. That's okay."

I suddenly realize how bloodshot her eyes are. Perhaps it's from the tears, but it seems more than that now, as if they've hemorrhaged and bled themselves into an unholy shade of red.

Black, dilated pupils swimming in those bloody pools.

I stand.

So does she.

She suddenly seems bigger, though she obviously couldn't have grown an inch. I notice that she's up on the balls of her feet, as if ready to pounce. Like a predator. Was she standing like that before?

"I should probably get going now."

"Really, it's no trouble. He's right through there." She steps closer, backing me toward the laundry room. Toward the freezer. Toward the SUV out back. "You house-call doctors sure do ask a lot of questions. Does your wife know where you are, Dr. Blackburn?"

All I can picture is Elsie. In her sweatpants and potato-sack shirt. Hair a mess. Shushing Ivy in the middle of the night. My daughter's face smeared in snot from whatever latest cold she'd acquired. A pile of slimy Kleenex drying into a crust on the nightstand. I want to be back home with them so badly.

I back into the laundry room, toward the back door. The deep freeze buzzes beside me.

Lily looms in the doorway to the kitchen, glaring at me with those black on red eyes.

Adrenaline courses through my body; reality bends to its will. Nothing is in focus. She grins, and I can see her tongue sliding along the jagged edges of her pink, blood-tinted teeth.

Her bare toes are dirty. I finally notice the trail of filth tracking away from her black feet across the kitchen tiles.

Her skin is pale. Translucent. The veins visible underneath, like blue bolts of lightning striking across her ivory face.

Her quick, panting breaths seem at odds with her slow, stalking approach.

I realize only now that the home smells just the tiniest bit sour, like spoiled meat.

I reach behind me, blindly grabbing the handle, but the back door doesn't budge.

She takes another step forward, stalking into the laundry room.

I might pass out. My lungs have stopped working somehow. I can almost feel the oxygen in my brain dissipating. I know I need to breathe. Why won't I breathe?

I throw myself against the door, shattering one small windowpane. The handle still won't turn.

Lily grins again and takes another step, just feet away. She puts a filthy finger to her lips, and she shushes me like I'm her tantruming baby. Her bony, clawing digits reach out for me.

And then, the alarm sounds again. Gently plucked arpeggios.

Lily freezes. Her hand hovers in the air. Her eyes blink. She gazes through the wall to my left. Suddenly, it's as if I'm not even there.

The strings slowly ascend in volume.

She steps back into the kitchen. And then she disappears around the corner.

I can't tell how much time passes.

My eyes are glued to the spot where Lily once stood, waiting for her to spring out again. I chance a quick glance at the dead bolt behind me. Locked. A sigh escapes my lips, and I give it a turn. The door opens with a gentle click, and I tumble down the steps into the backyard, my eyes never peeling away from the house. I stumble into the patio set, knocking the grill over. Struggling to my feet, I hobble around the side of the house to the front yard. It feels like running on pool noodles.

I turn the corner, my top half nearly toppling over, desperate to outrun whatever my legs can muster.

Someone's knocking at the door.

I nearly bolt past her and into my rental car when I hear her call out, "Vincent!"

I turn and find Yvette there, rushing down the porch steps toward me.

How did she find me? When did she get here?

It doesn't matter. My words pour out. I tell her about Greg. And Lily. The monstrosity inside. Like my torso outpacing my feet, my mouth won't wait for my brain to catch up.

"Shit," she mutters. "Listen, Vincent. You need to calm down before this gets any more out of hand than it already is. I called the police, and they're on their way. They won't hurt you, I promise. Just cooperate with them, and don't go anywhere until

I get this smoothed out. I need you to wait right here while I go speak with Mrs. Smith. Lily, is it?"

"No! You can't go in there."

"Vincent, I know you're struggling right now. You're sick, Vincent. I know. But the police will be here soon, and we'll get you some help. First, I need to talk to Lily and hopefully clean up whatever kind of mess you're in. But I need you to wait here. Do you understand me?"

"She killed Edward! His car. The freezer. I'm not crazy!" Tears burn the edges of my eyes.

Yvette's jaw clenches. She gathers all the patience she can. "Okay. Sure. Just let me go talk to her. Make sure she's not too shaken up."

She heads around the side of the house toward the back door.

I can hear her call out, "Mrs. Smith?" as she heads inside.

A minute passes. Probably less. Her voice occasionally calls for Lily inside. But there's no reply.

I creep back around to the backyard, no longer hearing Yvette's voice.

I pace back and forth. Toward the door and away. Waiting. Wondering if I should help. Or run. Doubting myself. Questioning everything. The stench of spoiled meat lingers in my nostrils. But I wonder now whether the scent is any different from my own kitchen a few hours after I've fried a pan full of bacon. After the once enticing aroma has lingered too long and grown stale. I should've gone home. Seconds feel like hours. I stare at the tarp and the SUV, and I'm no longer sure. Is it a VW? Does that even mean anything? What had I really seen inside that house? I pace past the ceramic grill, cracked on the ground, surrounded by a pile of ashes. A glint of light catches my eye.

I crouch down to inspect it. Wipe away the soot. A gold wedding band. Clinging to a charred briquette. When I pick it up, I realize it's not a briquette at all, but a blackened finger. The ring slides off. An inscription inside: 2/14/10.

Valentine's Day. Ten years ago.

"Yvette!" I scream as I run up the back steps and into the house. The only sound inside is the steady hum of the deep freeze.

I rush through the laundry room and into the kitchen. Empty. I whisper Yvette's name as I press on. My mind slips away from the present moment, from the terrifying circumstances around me, and latches onto a memory that isn't even my own. A night eleven years ago...

"Yvette?" No answer.

...A sunken houseboat. Out on the edge of St. Landry Parish...

I move into the hallway. Empty. "Yvette?"

...The moon hovering in a cloudless sky. Yvette finding Henri huddled in a closet. Her gun drawn...

I step into the living room.

I see Yvette first. Her back to me.

"Mrs. Smith?" she says in a calm, steady voice.

Then Lily, standing motionless, on the other end of the room, facing a large bay window that looks out onto the front lawn.

"Mrs. Smith, I realize my friend Dr. Blackburn probably scared you." She takes a step closer to Lily. "He's having a tough time right now, but I don't want you to worry. I've got things under control, and we're going to make sure he's okay."

...Henri slumped in the closet. A hole in his head. The heat radiating off the barrel of Yvette's pistol...

And in that moment, I hesitate, afraid of what might happen if I tell Yvette the truth. Afraid of what she might do.

She's inches away from Lily. Within striking distance. "Lily? Is everything okay?"

I have to stop her. *"Yvette,"* I hiss. "Stop. She—"

Yvette wheels around to me. "Vincent, I told you to wait outside!"

"No, Yvette. She killed Edward. It's the truth. You have to—"

"Listen. You've already gotten yourself into a whole mess of trouble. Now if you don't . . ." Her voice cuts out when she spots the ring sitting in my palm.

A police siren whines in the distance.

Yvette stares at the wedding band in disbelief.

The glare she turns back on Lily is as cold and contemptuous as any I've ever seen. The sirens grow louder and seem to spur her on, forcing her to act quickly.

She reaches into her jacket and unholsters her pistol.

Lily just stands there in her hoodie, soiled hands on the glass, gazing out the window. Oblivious.

Yvette barks, "Hands up, Mrs. Smith!"

Lily doesn't flinch.

Yvette tenses and takes another step forward, pressing the pistol into the back of Lily's skull.

"Vincent, go outside. Now."

But my feet are frozen.

"I said go outside, goddamn it!"

The muscles in her forearm flex, and her shoulders tighten, bracing for the recoil.

My eyes drop to Lily's hands, expecting them to shoot up and swipe at the gun.

But no one moves.

The sirens are deafening.

Right outside the house.

Yvette grabs Lily's shoulder and turns her like you would rotate a statue. The gun barrel is inches from her mouth.

Yvette pulls the hammer back with a click.

Lily offers no resistance. Her vacant stare lands somewhere on the wall. Her eyes are still bloodshot, her skin still a ghostly shade of pale, but as long as she stares at the wall instead of me, she doesn't seem quite so monstrous anymore.

Yvette looks at Lily. Their faces inches apart. Searching for some meaning in those bloodshot eyes.

Finally, Yvette gives up. She lowers the gun. Drops it to the floor. She backs away and raises her hands above her head in anticipation.

The front door bursts open. Two uniformed officers train their weapons on us.

"Hands up!" they shout. I do as I'm told.

"Are you okay, Mrs. Smith?" They rush to comfort Lily, keeping their weapons aimed in our general direction. "Is there anyone else in the home?"

Lily mumbles an inaudible response. The only word I pick up is *soon*.

I blurt out, "She's the one who killed those campers..."

"Am I talking to you?" the deputy shouts. He drops a hand on her shoulder. "Mrs. Smith, did these people hurt you? Speak to me."

She mutters after him on repeat, like some doped-up parrot: "Speak to me... speak to me... speak to me..." She turns back to the window, staring through her own reflection. I know she's only repeating whatever meaningless words she just heard, her brain operating in a sort of stripped-down backup mode. But in this moment, I nearly convince myself that she's calling on some monster within, some demon she wants to summon back to the surface.

"Speak to me ... speak to me ... speak to me ..."

But the demon doesn't return.

The deputies cuff me and Yvette.

"My name is Yvette Harper. I was sheriff out in Louisiana a few years back. Officer, please. I'm the one that called you..."

"Shut up!" he barks while his partner whispers soothingly to Lily.

"Lily? Lily, it's Caleb Patton. Annie's dad. Remember me? We are going to get this sorted out..." His voice fades as an officer shoves us out of the house.

They read us our rights and stuff us into the back seat of a squad car for trespassing.

Soon a school bus rumbles up the street.

"Yvette, I'm so sorry," I say. "About everything."

Her gaze stays fixed on the front window of the house.

We can see Lily inside. An officer wraps a blanket around her.

"How'd you find me?" I ask.

"You used your credit card at the rental place," she mutters. "Pinged your wife. She called me up, all worried. I went and found your search history on that computer."

The school bus hisses to a stop in front of us.

"You gave Elsie your number?"

She nods.

"So, what happens now?"

She doesn't answer.

The bus doors squeak open and let out a single child. A boy.

Around seven or eight. He surveys all the commotion and starts for the front door of Lily's house.

A deputy stops him. "Can't go in there just yet, buddy."

The deputy leads the boy to another squad car and ushers him into the back seat.

An ungodly howl bellows from inside the house. Tortured. Inhuman.

Our eyes dart back to the window. The drapes flutter. A uniformed body whizzes by in a blur. Screams from the deputies.

A loud crash. Like a glass table being shattered. And another.

Voices cut in over the cruiser's radio. "Officer down, officer down! Jesus Christ—"

For a chilling string of moments, the house is silent.

A figure appears in the doorway.

The thing that used to be Lily.

A dark slick of blood like tar runs from her mouth and nose down to her chest.

Her empty black eyes reflect back our cruiser's flashing reds and blues. They find us there in the back seat.

She stalks down the porch steps, up on the balls of her feet. Hunched over. As if being dragged along, a deranged puppet on strings.

I blink hard.

"Yvette?"

Yvette, numb and frozen, turns away from Lily. She stares straight ahead out the window, where, just past the house, she's spotted Edward's Atlas, partially covered in the backyard.

I pull at the cuffs, the metal digging into my wrists. I scramble back, away from the approaching Lily. My back presses into the opposite door.

I fumble for the handle and tug at it.

"The door won't open," I cry out.

"Not from the inside." Yvette sighs.

The thing moves closer.

Right outside the cruiser, her pale, wiry forearm reaches forward, nails stained black with viscera. She rips the door open.

Her hyperventilating shriek pierces the air.

CRACK!

Her head explodes onto the open door. The spongey bundle of circuits and everything that's gone wrong in there trickles onto the pavement.

Her body slumps against the car and falls to the ground with a dull thud.

A bloody officer comes limping down the porch steps, pistol in hand.

Lily's son in the other police cruiser pounds his fists on the window, wailing and confused and terrified as the officers stagger to the body of his mother.

Yvette turns to him with an impassive gaze.

A moment later, she wipes her eye with the back of her hand and breaks her stare away. She leans back in her seat, eyes fixed on the ceiling. Mumbling a tune that I can't begin to place. Then I recognize a few of the words. Another language. From another time.

> "Fèy yo gade mwen nan branch mwem
> yon move tan pase li voye'm jete . . ."

There's a moan of thunder in the distance. I shut my eyes and collapse back into the seat as the rain begins to thump against the roof of the squad car. At some point, I pass out.

EPILOGUE

May 2022

I SPENT THREE weeks in a psychiatric inpatient unit in Texas. Phil managed to find a facility across state lines so that I wouldn't end up sharing a room with one of my patients. I spent my second sleepless day there trying desperately to contact the CDC to warn them about my "RG virus" and the elevated porphyrin levels and the altered mental status and the severe behavioral changes it caused. But they had their hands full with other things in early 2020.

Before long, my phone privileges were revoked. I spent the time between group therapy sessions rereading the daily issues of the *Houston Chronicle* and trying to sleep.

Five days in, as I flipped through the *Chronicle*, I found an article on the Booneville serial killer. Authorities had found the remains of a missing boy in her freezer. Right under her husband. And what was left of a doctor from Maryland. The hand in the freezer that belonged to Greg had tissue and blood samples under the fingernails that matched DNA from Edward and the campers. Two Booneville police officers died from the wounds they'd received in Lily's house. I wrote to thank the one who saved us, but he didn't write back.

Most experts agree on the following sequence of events: Greg attacked and killed Edward when he knocked on the door inquiring about the Reddit post. Around that time, Greg began searching the woods and found the campers, whom he killed and partially consumed. Lily tried to intervene at some point, and Greg attacked her, leaving the bruises on her arm (and, by my theory, infecting her). Lily, now fearing for the safety of her son, killed Greg and hid him in the deep freeze with his victims.

Lily's son would be placed in foster care. The miracle, apparent only to me, was that she had managed to keep the effects of the infection at bay for approximately ten days while caring for him and fighting off her symptoms as much as humanly possible. According to reports, there were no signs of abuse or attack evident on the child. One can only assume that he wasn't infected. Not by the RG virus anyway.

Elsie came to visit me on the eighth day of my hospitalization. I'd have to wait another two and a half weeks to see Ivy, once Elsie was convinced enough that I was serious about getting better. She could see that desperation in my eyes. Doctors have a reputation for making the worst patients, but not this one. I swallowed every pill, contributed to every group, meditated in every class, and ate every bite of shitty hospital food off my tray. I forgot about Booneville and infections and whatever it was I saw out there. I wanted to get out, and I wanted to make sure I never found myself in there again.

I cut my hours back at the clinic and started spending more time at home. I sought weekly therapy sessions and biweekly marriage counseling. As a recommended source of closure from my therapist, Elsie helped me finish my book. I completed the last few chapters and immediately converted the home office into a playroom for Ivy. I've got nowhere to hide now. It's better that way. Occasionally, Elsie's phone will ring, and on checking the caller ID, she'll step outside and chat for an hour or so. I know who it is. And I know the check-ins are as much for Yvette as they are for Elsie. Two women bound not by blood, but by choice and by circumstance to the Judices. Twice a month, Elsie attends a support group for families struggling with mental health issues. Like Al-Anon for mood disorders. That's how she spends her Thursdays now. Thursdays used to be nights out with her friends. I'm positive now of what I've always suspected: I don't deserve her.

Every few months, I get a text or an email from Mitch. Invariably, it's a link to some Rougarou-dedicated website—almost always laid out on a black background with Comic Sans font; otherwise, in Courier. I always text or email back with a quick thanks and a "how ya been" follow up. I almost never click the link. When I do, I rarely read past the first sentence. But every now and then, the story is compelling enough to stir up that old itch. That's when I close the window. I avoid the itch now. I know I'll just scratch until it bleeds.

Last month, in between waves of Covid variants, we took a trip to New Orleans to visit Elsie's family and spend some time bouncing around our old haunts from back in the day. Most of the usuals were still open; a few had relocated or shut down altogether. Our three days there were at once nostalgic and eerily unfamiliar, like a strange dream in the altered hallways of your childhood home.

Without a single exception, the old friends we visited in town couldn't help but mention the recent rise in crime in New

Orleans. Homicides were up by sixty-seven percent since we'd left, carjackings by one hundred and sixty percent. Most blamed the shift on Covid. The lockdowns had decimated the city's economy, which depended so heavily on the food and entertainment industry. As usual, the hurt trickled down to the most desperate residents. Their desperation had hit a breaking point, and the end result was always going to be violence. Now, in a city that had thrived on a "front-porch" culture for centuries, people were suddenly locking themselves up in their houses, further hampering the vital service industry and fanning the flames of the city's desperation. It all gets passed along.

On Thursday, we braved the city and took Ivy to the Audubon Zoo. The May heat had forced most of the animals to disappointing distances. The lion napped in the shade of the most remote corner. The orangutan lounged lethargically in its hammock. Ivy's cheeks reddened, and her sweaty hair matted against her forehead. We sought reprive in the air-conditioned display of Spots, the albino alligator.

I took a few pictures, and as I pocketed my phone, my eyes finally glimpsed the creature that had been haunting me all these years. The Rougarou, in all its ridiculous glory. It formed the centerpiece of an exhibit directly across the room from Spots. The bargain brand Muppet with felt fur and exposed seams posed lifelessly on two legs, its cartoonishly big, yellow eyes glowing in the dark. Sharp fangs protruded inexplicably from its fuzzy snout in every direction. One four-clawed paw reached out in malice. The other clutched a long walking stick, which the creature had apparently jabbed into a bear trap on the ground, springing the trap in a display of its unexpected cunning. Children's shoes and human bones littered the ground before it.

Cast in overly dramatic crimson light and soundscaped with canned recordings of spooky swamp ambience, the absurdity of the display was thick in the air.

Ivy's attention was drawn that way, either by the sensationalized scene or by my own obvious fascination. She stared wide-eyed at the monster and insisted I read the plaque nearby. I recognized her awed gaze, the way she leaned forward toward the thing, lured to it as if caught in a tractor beam.

She came by it honestly.

I cleared my throat and did my best to undersell it. The last thing we need is another family member obsessed with the legend. I was relieved to find her attention wavering only a few sentences in. Before I could even get to the part about it possessing the "body of a human and head of a wolf," she was back fawning over Spots the Alligator. I let my voice taper off.

Elsie sidled up behind me and wrapped her arms around my neck. She whispered in my ear, "Is it everything you hoped?"

I bought a coffee mug with its likeness at the gift shop. It currently sits on my desk, holding my pens.

When we returned home, I sorted through the stack of mail that had piled up in our mailbox. Among the bills and junk mail, one envelope stood out. It was handwritten in an elegant, old-fashioned kind of cursive. In place of a return address, there was just a single name: "Harper." I opened it and read the letter inside.

> I'm not sure why I'm writing you. I'm not sure of much anymore. I'm trying to be okay with that. I can't really say for certain what happened out there in Mississippi, what we saw. What you and Edward were so desperate to figure out.

I do think maybe you were right about some things—about Dane and the others, about the sickness. About Henri.

Your wife tells me you started looking around for publishers for your story. I don't know what I expect you to do with this, but it doesn't stop me from feeling like I have to say it.

I adopted Henri when he was eleven. I'm sure you know that. I'm sure you read it and cross-referenced it with another source and so on. What you probably don't know, because of course it wasn't in the adoption paperwork or any of the official statements that you collected, was that I had love for that boy since the first day he came to our house. That's the problem with all those stacks of records. They make you think you got the truth in your hands. They're all so official. But they can't even scratch the surface, can they? How can you fit a mother's love into a police transcript? I had love for that boy from the start. Dane brought him over after school one day, and I could tell by the way he looked at me that he'd never set foot in a Black woman's home before that afternoon. I knew about his folks. You hear things. I knew a lot of the school board in those days, and his daddy had been fighting to get him transferred to another school for over a year. Wanted him some place "safer." Which we all knew meant "whiter" to them. Always yelling about sending him some place safer and then letting him come home to an empty house every afternoon, guns and drugs scattered all over the place.

He broke my heart, that boy. He used to have this way of almost caving into himself if you looked at him too hard. He'd get real quiet, and you'd swear he had shrunk a few inches and a couple dozen pounds all of a sudden. Like he was trying to get all tiny and invisible.

I loved that boy. And every time I contemplated whether it was dangerous to bring a broken child like that, from a family like that, into my own home, it was that love that won out. Every time.

For eleven years I thought that he had betrayed my love, defiled it. I thought he had murdered my baby, and I hated what had happened to him in the end, but I understood it as what had to happen.

And then you came calling.

Now I don't understand anything.

I'm thinking of leaving Maryland. Should've left two years ago when all this lockdown stuff started, I guess. But I don't know. Where else would I go? I still miss Edward and still love him, but the strange thing is that over these last couple of years without him, I haven't felt much emptier than I felt before. That might sound cruel, but I think I'm just realizing how empty I've been all this time. I guess people sometimes come together after they both lose something and expect the other person to fill that void. But not a thing in the universe can fill the hole in my heart. It's shaped just like Dane and there's nothing that will ever fit inside it. You try to lean on someone to help you move on, and you just end up passing that pain along to each other. And maybe you get rid of some of the sadness over time, but you just replace it with disappointment that it wasn't more. I drive around this city that isn't my home and go to work at a job that isn't my career and give people a name that isn't my own, and it all starts to pile up in my head how much I've really lost.

Go ahead and write your book. Hell, maybe you'll make me a character in it. I think Henri deserves it. And Edward too. But what do I know? I spent so long trying to convince myself of what Henri did and didn't deserve, I've gone back and forth on it so many times, I just can't say anymore.

Just don't convince yourself that your book will be the truth. Because you can't find the truth in a bunch of old files and reports and statements to police. Lord knows.

But if everyone accepted one version of a lie for so long, it wouldn't hurt to give them a different version to chew on for a while. And then, maybe some of them will end up with something close to what really happened. But no one will really be able to say, and I guess that's okay.

At the end of the day, there'll always be people calling him a monster. Maybe some will call me that too. But that's just a word. It explains about as much as all those records you have on your hands. Less even. If monsters exist or if they're all in our heads, it doesn't really make much difference. Not if the pain we feel is the same either way.

ACKNOWLEDGMENTS

WE'D LIKE TO raise a warm beer to crazy uncles, crawfish boils, and tall tales around hunting camps. To the Zydeco Stomp on Saturday morning and drive-thru daiquiri shops in the afternoon. To Acadiana, our home and inspiration, merci.

Our biggest thanks goes out to our wonderful agent Anne-Lise Spitzer. Your tenacity and sage advice was invaluable in shepherding us through the strange and unfamiliar world of publishing. You and the incomparable Kim Lombardini move mountains.

To our solid gold editor Jess Verdi, thank you for being the ideal collaborator and making sure we rookies felt heard and understood throughout the process. We couldn't have asked for a more supportive and collaborative team than you, Thaisheemarie Fantauzzi Pérez, Rebecca Nelson, Dulce Botello, Mikaela Bender, Stephanie Manova, Megan Matti, Doug White, Matt Martz, Heather VenHuizen and the rest of the Crooked Lane team. Thanks to the sales team at Penguin Random House for giving our monster a home.

The two of us have been blessed with the most supportive group of friends we could have ever hoped for over the last two decades and change. Thank you to Hab Barton, Mark Schexnaildre, and Curry Smith not only for lending us bastardized versions of your names for different characters in this book, but also for remaining a consistent set of soundboards over the years, as we continue to blast you with bad ideas and pitches for whatever projects excite us. And a huge thanks to Brian C. Miller Richard and Kenneth Renaldo Reynolds who championed the project in so many ways throughout its Rougarou-like transformation.

Without Sherryl Woods, this project would have never made it out of the cover letter stage. Your curiosity and cheerleading was pivotal. To our copy editor, Jill Pellarin, thanks for catching all of our dumb mistakes and wading through Uncle Mitch's dialogue in stride. To Master Sgt Harriet Reynolds (Ret. Army), thank you for lending your time and expertise to help breathe life into our Sheriff. Thanks to the Atlanta Writers Club for supporting and platforming a community full of hungry writers.

We set out to write a book about heritability and family at its core, and we know as well as anyone that we are nothing if not the products of families that nurtured our curiosity and happiness above all else. Thank you to Bob, Molly, Mary-Margaret, and Jake Lavin for tolerating a smartass know-it-all who knows he knows very little besides how to be a smartass. And thanks, of course, to Meghan Lavin. When people ask how a full-time physician and father of three little things has time to co-write a novel, the answer is that he has the best, most understanding wife imaginable.

Thanks to Neal and Donna Burke, and Darci Meyerhofer for allowing *Jaws* to be played on a twenty-four hour loop on the only television in the house growing up. Thanks to Cecilia Leal for being an engaged ledge-talker-off-er and a continual inspiration of what a healthy curiosity looks like.

And finally, a sincere and drunken thanks to Barrel Proof in New Orleans and your $3 old fashioned happy hours from 4-6 every weekday. We couldn't have written a word without you.

ABOUT THE AUTHORS

N. L. Lavin is a full-time child and adolescent psychiatrist, a part-time writer, and a husband and father in whatever time he has left. He was born and raised in Lafayette, Louisiana, where he once again resides with his family.

Hunter Burke earned a BFA in Performing Arts from the University of Louisiana at Lafayette. His acting credits include roles in the Oscar-winning film *The Big Short*, the Netflix show *Sweet Magnolias*, and the Amazon series *Bosch*. Originally from Broussard, Louisiana, he now lives in Los Angeles, California. Follow Hunter on Twitter/X and Instagram: @iamhunterburke

For more fantastic fiction, author events,
exclusive excerpts, competitions, limited editions and more

VISIT OUR WEBSITE
titanbooks.com

LIKE US ON FACEBOOK
facebook.com/titanbooks

FOLLOW US ON TWITTER AND INSTAGRAM
@TitanBooks

EMAIL US
readerfeedback@titanemail.com